THE ORRIS PROJECT

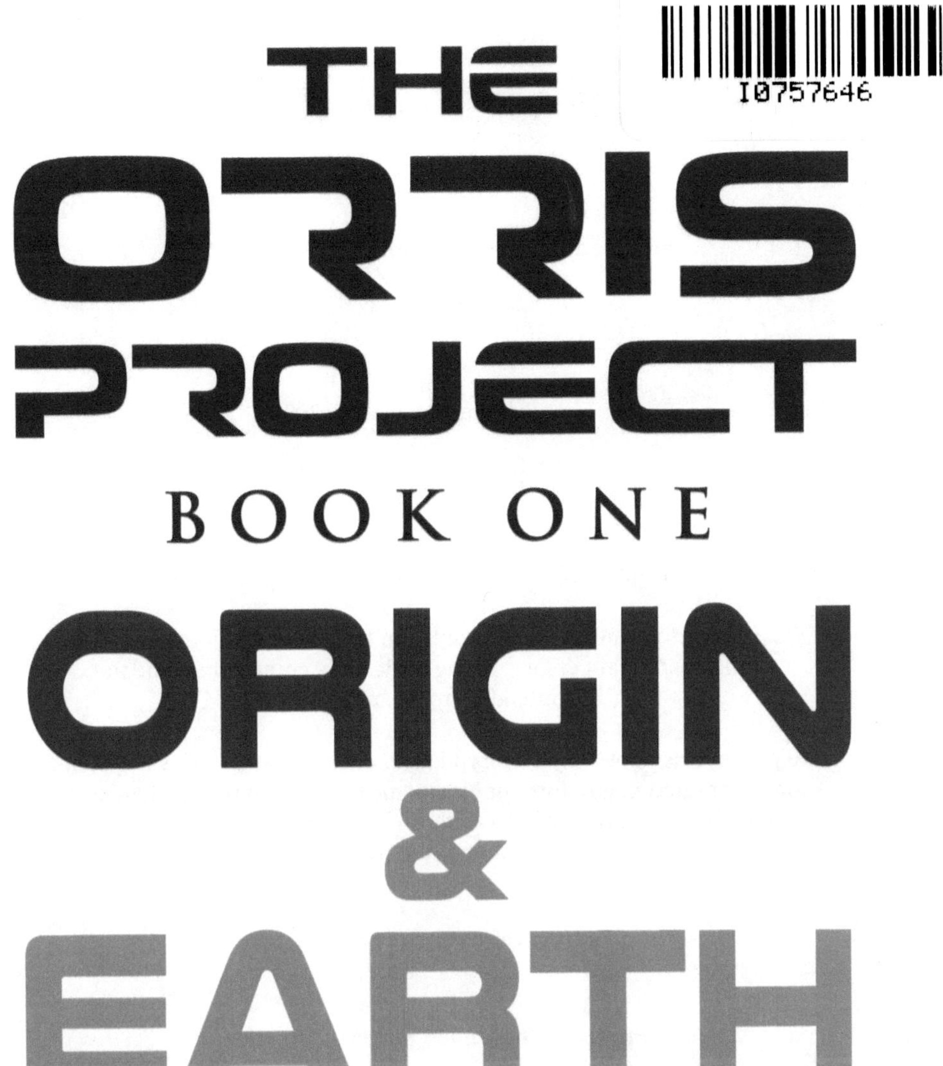

BOOK ONE

ORIGIN & EARTH

DAVID SALISBURY

Published by Dinesta Central Publishing, LLC

Slingerlands, NY

First Printing December, 2021

10 8 6 4 2 1 3 5 7 9

ISBN-13 978-1-957222-00-4

Printed in the United States of America

Cover Art: Emily Salisbury

To Rob Salisbury, my little brother. The endless banter all throughout our childhood and well into our adult lives inspired this book, and all that follow.

Contents

Chapter 1

Arrival

1

The Envoy walked in moonlight. His heavy boots scuffed the dark red surface of the barren desert for the thirteenth night since he crashed there. The huge silver disk above him shone so brightly that he could see everything as though it were dusk or dawn. Dust, sand, and rubble made up the floor of his current stage, and except for the occasional rock or, less commonly, boulder, nothing else. Nothing lived on the stony tract around the Envoy, but a light breeze spun up devils of dust and sand across the landscape. Droplets of sweat stood on his forehead, and every icy gust reminded him he was losing precious water.

It was midnight, or around midnight. The horizon to the east and west was an abrupt line between burnt orange land and starry black sky. He maintained his gait, trudging eastward, but questioned his course. *Maybe I stop for a minute, maybe I think about this.* His new home was a lifeless rock orbiting a new star, and the air was acrid and painfully low in oxygen. He winced when he inhaled and felt a sharp bolt of pain cut through him from deep in his core. He was dying. He needed water, and he needed food.

Soon, tomorrow. The dark brown canvas bag strapped to his back weighed on him. He could not remember a time it felt heavier.

To the north, the view did not differ from the east. *But it might be cooler*, he thought. *The days might be shorter.* He had observed the celestial activity with scrutiny since the moment he landed and expected the northern hemisphere to be edging into winter. *It's worth a shot.* Changing course presented little risk, so he hiked his bag up on his back, turned north, and walked away from the ever-changing faces of the moon.

The enormous white fixture in the night sky was new to the Envoy. It was so bright that if he started walking while the moon was up and before the sun went down, his body would cast two shadows: a sharp-edged crisp shadow from the sun and a dim, less defined one from the moonlight. The only other features in the sky during such an event were two pins of light, one pale blue, the other a deep orange. Planets. The closer of the two, the pale blue, was already awash in water, but it did not qualify for his mission. It was much too small. Its mass could not sustain a core that would block the solar wind for long, and he needed time more than anything else.

It was his fifth mission, his last. The first four planets had nothing like the bright white satellite. No such large moon filled the night sky of the others except Vesir, but that was a small, irregularly shaped body that orbited Distria, his first mission planet. Otherwise, all the skies were a cold black except for thousands, sometimes tens of thousands of stars.

Walking at night was far preferable to day. The daytime landscape would shift and shimmer in his squinting view. The heat of the day was too much to bear. Direct sunlight on his skin stung and left visible redness and inflammation wherever it touched.

Most of the other worlds he visited had been much further along when he arrived, except for one. He arrived on the planet Telraed the same way he arrived on the fifth planet and was grateful. It helped him to prepare his mind, body, and resources for the fifth, his last. The first stage on Telraed had been a living hell. It had been the most painful, torturous time of his life. The experience, though, had trained him to prepare for the worst. His fifth planet was Earth, but he did not know that yet. He landed on Earth barely after it was born. It had only just begun cooling from a molten blob, freewheeling around the infant sun; its cataclysmic meeting with Theia only a half billion years before his arrival.

The Envoy was searching for a cave, a semi-permanent shelter that could protect his fragile body from the elements for millions of years. He had no guidance with this task. There was no formula for telling which place would work and which would not, but he had no other choice. His ultimate goal was to wait for the intelligent life that would likely evolve, and he would need a safe place to put himself while those countless years passed.

He walked north for two more hours and looked for shelter. About three hundred yards ahead, there was a large, round boulder, and he aimed for it. The massive rock had to have been fifteen feet high and would provide the desperately needed shade. Over his shoulder, he peered at the eastern horizon. It was getting brighter by the minute as the planet's star ascended.

2

The Envoy slept for four hours. The sun had made its way to the western part of the sky and was at its hottest. His throat was drying out, and a stitch had formed in his side. The combination lifted him to consciousness, and the moment he awoke, he drew in a deep, hard breath that carried with it a significant amount of dust. It triggered a spastic coughing fit that did not stop him from launching out of the hole that would have been his tomb if he did not move. He dug his sleeping holes down only eighteen inches when there was cover, nothing like the graves he would dig when he had nothing to shield him from the sun.

When he emerged from his hole, the sun's light immediately stung his forehead and cheeks. The bright white glare off the land stabbed him in the eyes, forcing them instinctively to snap shut. A second later, he could feel the searing heat on the backs of his hands and neck. There was one word in his mind, and it was screaming: *COVER!* It was not the first time this had happened. The problem was simple; he had overslept. He would normally have prepared by making a thick shroud from his supplies to provide a temporary but effective shelter as he evaded the sunlight while traversing the boulder. There was no time for that. He briefly opened his eyes only long enough to locate and grab his bag with one hand and his dark blue, nearly black blanket with the other. He reeled and ran doubled over so his back would take the bulk of the fire from the sky until he reached the other side of the boulder. Rounding the corner, he gasped when he saw the wide strip of shadow there. He had *really* overslept. He dove into the darkness to get out of the bath of radiation emitted by the young sun.

It turned out to be a mistake. In his urgency, he had forgotten that the ground, sand and bits of fragmented rock in the precious shade, had been baking recently in the very sunlight he was trying to escape. The stinging pain tore through the palms of his hands and the side of his face, and soon after, his chest, gut, and legs. At once, he rolled onto his back and pulled himself into a desperate fetal position, trying to tuck every part of him deeper and deeper into a ball and away from the madness. After a few minutes, he could not bear the pain another moment. Being careful to maintain his position, he settled on his side in the spot that had already had most of its thermal energy removed by his badly burned back.

He laid there with his eyes clasped shut and his face buried in his crossed arms for over an hour. When he lifted his head, the greater part of the heat had subsided.

He had to drink. The constant straining and squinting to bring anything at all into focus had given him a headache. He was hesitant to go to his pack for any of the consumables contained within, but he would not die there with a bag full of life-sustaining supplies, either. He always tried to wait until just before sunrise to drink; the water was always coolest then, but he was feeling the pangs of organ failure. Pain twisted through his guts. He was lightheaded, and his vision was as bad as he could remember it ever being.

The water was warm and unpleasant. It did not slake his thirst at all, but rather aggravated it. He daydreamed about what it would be like to drink ice-cold water and the pleasure it brought with it. His logical brain knew that drinking the unpleasant water was beneficial to his health, but at that moment, his stomach hurt, and he was afraid that he might vomit the precious substance up. Eyes closed, he placed a hand over his mouth, clenched his jaw shut, and swelled his tongue to the back of his throat, waiting for the nausea to pass. *Keep it down. You have to keep it down. You can't waste any of it.* It took an unnerving amount of time before he felt comfortable removing his hand. He had consumed about half the bottle and stowed the rest for later that night. His water supply was getting dangerously low. He coughed hard. The air was exquisitely dry. He imagined the only moisture in the air was that which came from his breath and the vapor from his sweat.

Water was not his only need in that moment. When the nausea passed, the screaming hunger resumed. His food was limited, and he had eaten only twice in fourteen days, but it was time again. He had dried meat, each piece about the size of his thumb. He tore open the plastic packaging of one and picked it apart, eating slowly to avoid losing it to another round of nausea.

With the morsel of food consumed, he closed his eyes and leaned back against the rock face, hoping he could achieve a state of half consciousness that would allow for the time to pass more quickly. It took almost an hour, but his mind flitted between true wakefulness and the beginnings of shallow sleep. It was in that state that he imagined Orris, the vast machine-world in interstellar space that was the single most massive, daring, and unbelievable project undertaken by living beings in universal history. The images in his mind were the product of his imagination.

Orris had only been a hollow ring of framed material orbiting his home planet when he left so many ages before.

In his mind's eye, a brilliant network of pulses and flashes of light sparked along its complex network of artificial gravity cylinders, nuclear power plants, and anti-matter storage tanks. It was a structure as long as an inner solar system was wide, collecting resources and preparing for its ambitious effort to escape the collapse with its precious cargo.

3

When he awoke, the Envoy was pleased to see that the small shadows on the ground cast by stones and small rocky outcrops had stretched. He sighed, and a smile touched the corners of his mouth. He was not lightheaded, and his vision was sharper. The pain in his gut was still there, but it was more of a hunger pain than a pleading, dying, desperate pain.

To the north, the horizon appeared a deep indigo, and it was hard to make out the line where soil met sky. As his gaze moved back to the ground in front of him, an alarm rose in his mind. His more sensitive peripheral vision had picked up an irregularity at the otherwise smooth joining of earth and sky. When he looked back up, he did not see it. He stared. It was there, not due north, but close. A touch to the east, the Envoy saw a peak. *Target acquired,* he thought.

He did not stop walking for almost three hours. The air had so dried out his eyes that they were again beginning to blur and sting. *Rest, at least for a few minutes.* The pain in his legs and especially his calves was quickly developing from an irritant to agony. He stopped and dropped his gear to the Earth beside his left boot. The respite from the weight of his bag was welcome, and he laid down on his back. Eyes finally closed, the relief was immediate. He knew the comfort was temporary, and that if there was going to be any genuine, lasting relief that he would need to get up and move. At almost the same time, the wind rose and stole his breath with its acrid dryness. He sat up and pulled the collar of his shirt out far enough to plunge his face into the large opening. He breathed deeply of the damp air there created by his sweat. The odor was sour, but the physical relief in his nasal cavity and throat more than made up for it. *Get up.* He drew one last deep breath from his shirt and stood. *Move.*

On the first night after his arrival, he had studied the star positions relative to the planet and found that he could make out a mostly fixed "north star." This was important because the night had gotten to its darkest, and it had been hours since he could see the peak. Although it was not a perfect replacement for visual confirmation, he knew that using the mostly north star would keep his travel within a few degrees of his intended target. He fixed his gaze on the star, leaned toward it, and resumed his effort.

It would have been possible to walk for another two full hours, he imagined, but only one hour later, he saw a shape in the distance. Thirty yards and a little to the left of his path, he saw a long thin stretch of pure black. No dull orange or red hue, no blurriness. Pure, sharp black. He knew at once that it could only be one thing. *A void,* he thought, *nothing near it to cast a shadow*. He took a few steps toward the void and stopped to survey the eastern horizon. The horizon had not just blurred, it had developed the beginnings of a genuine glow. The sun was coming.

As he approached the void, his heart beat faster. He was afraid that he would either see solid ground six inches down, providing no cover, or that he would not see the bottom at all. Instead, when the opening in the ground drew near, he found he could see the bottom and it was three feet down. It was perfect. He set his bag on the ground near the edge and sat, legs dangling into the hole. Stretching his right leg, he pressed on the sunken Earth with one toe, being sure to brace himself with his hands in the event it gave way. It was solid. Tentatively, he slid off the edge and put his full weight on the depression floor. After considerable experimentation, shifting his weight and walking back and forth, he convinced himself it was the gift he had hoped it was. He crouched down and felt along the walls with one hand. The whole depression was about fifteen feet long and only three feet wide at its widest. The western wall was vertical but sloped toward him in a few places. After about three feet on his return trip tracing the eastern wall, his hand slipped into another void; a void within the void. Excited, he moved faster and discovered that the hole was about ten feet long. He smiled, pulled his bag in, laid down, and slid backward into the opening. Gripping one of the shoulder straps on his bag, he shimmied up to where the hollow started. In the crook of rocks and sand, he gently wedged his bag. His head, at least, had an earthen grave in which to sleep. The sunlight would invade the space, but he expected it would be much later in the day, and when it did, he had only to roll to the other side for shade. He rotated himself, shifted his legs, and crossed his arms behind his head. The last thought that went through his mind was that it would be a peaceful rest. After only eighteen seconds, as his rapid breathing was still slowing, he fell into a deep and dreamless sleep.

4

Two hours of sleep was all he managed before being called back from unconsciousness by a scream. His body jerked in place. *What is going on?* Whooshing and screeching, chattering and clattering. It took three seconds for the Envoy to remember where he was and do the mental detective work to figure out what was happening all around him; he had been in a deep sleep. There was light, starting at his waist and going all the way down past his feet, but it was not steady. It pulsed brighter and dimmer in irregular intervals. He laid still in his shelter and listened. The whooshing was wind, the screeches were gales whistling off rock faces, likely the edges of the void in which he was taking cover. The chattering was sand being blown into the void, the clattering small stones and flaked rock clicking off the depression walls. A windstorm. It was the first of his arrival. He pulled his shirt up over his face again as a shield from the dust pushing in and out of his space. *This is maddening.* As he mentally moaned his frustration with the noise and its seemingly expert ability to prevent sleep, he acknowledged that the shirt trick made it much easier to breathe. He hoped the storm would calm quickly so he could get back to sleep.

At first, it did the opposite. It grew louder, the pressure changes more rapid and violent, so much so that he slid his arms through the straps of his bag for fear of losing it. He heard an unfamiliar sound, a deep sound that barely cut through the howling. *Thunder*, he thought. It was thunder; his suspicion was confirmed after ten minutes, when the storm cell had closed in on his position. It brought with it a phenomenon of brief but intensely bright flashes of light. So bright that the Envoy registered them with his eyes closed, face under his shirt and pressed into the soft canvas of his bag while half buried under the ground. The stone floor beneath him vibrated with each crash. He counted the flashes, reaching seventeen when the freight train passed over his position. The deep, sharp sound started softly but increased in volume evenly until it was deafening. When it grew so loud that he thought it would burst his eardrums, the pressure dropped, and he felt his body slide across the depression floor. *No!* Instinctively, he swung his legs up in front of him and thrust them out. The soles of his boots connected with the opposite wall, and he shoved his upper body back into the hollow in the void. His shoulder blades crashed into the uneven stone wall, pinning himself in the gap. The locomotive above him also stole his air. He braced himself but could not breathe. After only two seconds, it went from one extreme to the other. A battering ram of wind crashed into the void and pushed the last of his reserved breath out of his lungs. His mind skipped a step, and he realized he was teetering on the edge of passing out from oxygen deprivation. There was little oxygen in the atmosphere, and his body's ability to cope with that was paper thin to begin with. He gasped, choked, and after a few seconds of frantically working his diaphragm, he was breathing again. His heart was beating at a thousand beats per minute. It pounded so hard that he genuinely worried it would explode in his chest. The wind continued to wail, and the gales continued to scream, but his heart rate slowed, his breathing slowed, and his frantic mind calmed. He had been through worse and was lucky to have found this exceptional cover when he did. Exposed, it could have ended badly, and permanently.

Twenty minutes passed, and the wind calmed. Another twenty minutes and there was barely a breeze. Ten minutes after that, he was deeply asleep once again.

5

The Envoy walked in dark starlight. He walked in dim light; he walked in bright light. He walked and walked, the light strictly dictated by the position and phase of the moon. He walked for five nights until the entirety of what was once the tip of a peak in the distance had revealed itself completely. It looked like a giant had smashed a fist into the Earth and the ground gave way, splintering up one enormous, jagged shard that pointed to the western sky. It was more like a thick, sharp needle that had thrust itself out of the smooth plain than a tectonic mountain. The needle did not point up into the sky but leaned heavily to the west. He thought he could even walk up its eastern face.

The needle towered above him, and he could see a significant crown of rubble surrounding its base. An impact had birthed the strange, massive outcropping. *East or west?* He shrugged, and started walking east.

As his eastern travel became more north than east, he could see that near the base of the needle, the ground gave way to darkness. The crown of rubble had completely departed. *Please, let this be what I think it is,* the Envoy thought. As he closed the distance, he observed an opening where the flat plain should have met the giant stone slab. When he reached the cut, he paused and grinned. The needle continued its slope down beneath the surface into the black interior of the planet. The entrance to what he hoped was a cavern or a system of caves below was so large that he estimated walking down through it standing upright would be easy. He looked around for a roundish rock and found a fist-sized chunk that would serve his purpose. There was no wind, not even a breeze, and the air was deadly silent. With his left hand, he bowled the rock out onto the needle. It veered off to the right and began its tumbling descent down the slope and into the darkness. *One-one-thousand, two-one-thousand,* he counted in his mind. After five seconds, he could hear no more clicking or clacking. *This is good,* he thought, *this cavern is deep, and just because the sound stopped doesn't mean...*

Thunk, hissssss

He froze. *Was that water? Or did I imagine it?* He shivered deeply and his entire body filled with a new optimism; pure joy, pure, heart-pounding excitement. He tried not to think about the genuine possibility of death often, but a quiet, nagging voice reminding him of it never left his thoughts for long. At that moment, it *was* gone. The thought of drinking until his stomach hurt was no longer a daydream; it was a realistic goal. With a few steps, he could fully hydrate himself for the first time since leaving Telraed.

The Envoy took his first step onto the needle. He was smiling but knew that his descent would be difficult and dangerous. The slope was not an easy one to traverse. After only five steps, he noticed his eyes were dead level with the surface of the Earth. He thought he could see the first blurred edge of light on the horizon and thanked all the stars it was not raining on the planet yet. *You can still slip on sand, though, don't forget about sand.* If he slipped, he might be able to stop himself, but it would only be through tremendous physical effort, and he would still come out of it injured. If he could not stop himself, it would not matter.

Suffering the fate of the rolling rock would kill him. If it did not kill him, it would injure him badly enough that he might opt for the kill pill resting silently in his right shoulder pocket. The pill was a merciful way to go. Dr. Ben Estes had explained the pill to all of the envoys. *Place it under your tongue, lie back. In two minutes, you will slip into a deep sleep, and in another two you will slip away.*

Twice during his descent, his left foot, which he led with, slipped out from under him. He allowed the weight of his body to drop to the needle floor so he could brace himself with his right hand, elbow, and hip. He was crab-walking to make travel on the slope possible. The descent was tiring and tedious. After only ten minutes, very specific muscles had become warm and tired, and very specific joints were fatigued and ached. When he felt the first touch of genuine pain, which came as a spark in the calf muscle of his right leg, he sat down. With only a minute's rest, he rolled to his left and abused the other side of his body. He continued on that way, flipping from his left side to right and back again, for another thirty minutes. When he felt his foot slip off the needle entirely, he stopped. *This is where the rock stopped rolling and started falling.* His eyes were useless. There was no light. He pushed himself up the slope to gain a little distance from what he thought was the edge and laid flat on his back.

6

It was silent in the needle shaft. It was not sound that awoke the Envoy, but light. The image on the lids of his eyes shifted from black to dark pink, and it was enough to stir him to consciousness. When he opened his eyes, he smiled, seeing the cavern brightly illuminated. The needle ended in a neat line about four feet beneath where he sat, as he suspected.

The sun had not yet aligned with the shaft, but a significant amount of the cavern's mouth was bathed in direct sunlight. It reflected down to where the Envoy rested, and he had a much better understanding of his situation. The roof of the cavern started about eighteen or twenty feet above the needle floor but must have dropped gradually to about ten. The needle itself was a plain, gray, slate-like flat rock, but the roof appeared a dirty yellow-white foam. The Envoy was knowledgeable in many scientific disciplines, a prerequisite for getting into the Migration Division, but he was no geologist. White rock, gray rock. That was about the best he could do in that field of study.

The slope ended and gave way to a black patch of space that extended as far as he could see. Judging by the ceiling, which continued at a constant descent, it was about fifty feet before it all faded into black. There was no telling how deep the hole was, but he was becoming comfortable with the idea that it would be his home for an extraordinary number of years. From his perspective, it looked to be an enormous, protected cavity.

He sat up and turned toward the mouth of the cave. He stared at the clean line where the edge of the direct sunlight ended on the needle floor, far in the distance. The line was moving toward him slowly, but it was only getting faster, and it would be upon him sooner than he would have liked. He thought it would be a brief episode. The mouth of the cave was narrow, so his full-illumination event would be short-lived. His concern about the direct light was minor. The surface was hot to begin with, and there was nowhere to hide. Beneath the cavern roof the air was cooler, the rock was almost cold, and the exposure would be brief. He estimated a full day on the young planet was about ten hours, and he had exposure to only one degree of the sky. That meant he would have about a minute of bright, direct light. Probably eighty precious seconds. He had to prepare himself to use them to assess the drop and its contents. If he could not strategize his plan in those seconds, he would have to wait another full day before he could try again; the hypothetical water below called to him.

He laid down on his left side and rotated his entire body around, so he was lying on his stomach, facing the drop. The soles of his boots faced the impending sunlight. With both hands gripping the ledge, he pulled himself forward so his chin and throat cleared the sharp rock. The light was racing down the needle floor. Everything around him was getting brighter. He rested his chest on the rock to free his arms, laced his fingers and made a visor out of his hands, which he clamped to his forehead and temples.

The light and heat washed over him in an instant, and he marveled at how rapidly the space below him flooded with light. It was not so bright that it was unpleasant, but the image was crystal clear, except in the distance. It was enormous. It was so large it may have been another world on its own. The cave floor was the same rusty red color as all the other places on the planet. There were many black pools, but immediately to his left was a large, crooked lake. It twisted its way deep into the darkness, beyond what he could see. Ahead of him the features faded to black, but to his left the floor of the cavern stretched so far, he had a hard time estimating how far it went. Rocks and rubble dotted the solid dry surface, and many larger rock features emerged from both the dry and wet alike.

Tick-tock, you're running out of time! The light was bending. He was staring and squandering his limited strategizing time. He had only seconds before the fading light would plunge all the majesty back into darkness. To his left, he had already cataloged a sheer drop to the Earth, about a hundred feet below. He swung his head to the right and, almost on cue, the light faded. Before he lost all his vision, he could see a feature that gave him hope. Through either wind-blown material or perhaps a collapse of the roof or wall, a steep sand and rock ramp descended into the refuge below, against the southern wall. If he tried to climb down the slope, he would fall to his death. There was no question about that. It was painfully steep and appeared to be nothing but loose material that would cascade to the bottom if disturbed. *But that might also be the answer.* For the next ten minutes, the Envoy sat and did thought experiments with the ramp-pile. Once he formed a plan, he gathered his pack, strapped it to his back and crab walked south to the near wall.

7

The Envoy awoke hours later and could see the first touches of daylight blotting out the stars. He retrieved a length of black cord from his bag and tied one end to the bag's strap and the other about his left arm, just above the elbow. He could not afford to lose his pack and was afraid that during his descent it could tumble to the floor of his new home, damaging its contents. He placed his right hand against his chest to find the pear-shaped pouch under the fabric of his shirt, suspended by a fine chain of titanium. The pouch contained the Sterilex, the only thing that made it possible to survive and accomplish missions spanning gargantuan amounts of time. Once he confirmed its presence on his person, he pulled it out from under his shirt and swung it around behind him, so it rested between his shoulder blades. Once it was safely in position, he turned his focus to his next task.

Sliding down to the edge on his belly, he peered over the needle ledge to see if he could make out the top of the ramp-pile. It was dim, but he could see it, and it was only about three feet below where the surface of the needle stopped. More light would have been helpful while attempting his descent, but the thought of falling in the darkness comforted him. Death would be easier if he could not see it coming.

Still face down, he spun around feet first and allowed his legs to fall off the edge. Once they were dangling, he reached back and gripped the ledge with both hands. Using his palms as a fulcrum, he stiffened and straightened his body until he was upright, standing on thin air and held up by his locked arms. Leaning his upper body slightly forward, he lowered himself down into the abyss.

The Envoy was neither tall nor short, but the tips of his toes touched loose sand before his chest had even reached the needle ledge. Complying with his strategy, he straightened his feet down into stiff points like the tips of two spears. He continued to lower himself and the material gave way, parting and dribbling down the ramp. Besides his own breathing, the sound of sand-rain and the small clicks of rock bouncing off rock were the only things that breached the silence of the place. Once suspended from the tips of his rapidly tiring fingers, his anxiety level exploded as he realized the ramp-pile had barely increased in resistance as he lowered himself into it. It meant he would fall; he did not have the energy to pull himself back up. With his eyes closed, he tried to play out the scenario in his mind. If the bulk he fell into loosened and slid down the slope, he would go with it and there would be nothing he could do to save himself. He would die either from the impact or the mass would envelop him, burying him alive. If that did not happen, he might have a chance, but none of it was up to him anymore. His life was firmly in the possession of the ramp-pile.

Stiff as a board. Stiff as a board. Stiff as a board. He let go.

8

The Envoy's entire body plunged into the mass of sand. Before letting go, he had taken a deep breath and locked it into his lungs. He ended up submerged only to his shoulders, but the act caused a layer of material to slough off the surface and tumble down the grade. The rumbling went on for another few seconds and sounded like thunder.

Over the course of the next four hours, the Envoy applied his plan for survival. He intentionally caused the avalanches, either with his hands or his feet, his only tools. While being careful to stay pressed against the needle's face, he kicked, shoved, and slammed his heels into the aggregate. These measures caused chain reactions that brought thousands of pounds of material deeper into the cave with each effort. When he had manipulated the pile down to about twenty feet above the floor of the refuge, he acknowledged that the slope had softened to a forty-five degree decline. That, in concert with how close he was to the ground, convinced him to slide down the rest of the ramp-pile on his backside.

When he hit the solid rock floor, he rolled over onto it, away from the pile. He breathed deeply. The air, although poor in quality, was not only the thickest he had breathed since his arrival, it was damp. It was so pleasant to lie there and breathe the dense, damp air that he smiled, a rarity since arriving on Earth. He was in a state of exhaustion so deep that after lying still, sleep took him almost instantly.

9

When the Envoy opened his eyes, it was as though he had not. It was lamp black in the refuge. Sprites and flashes of phantom light jumped and raced through his field of vision, but he knew that this was only his unstimulated eyes creating mischief. He had no bearings, but that did not discourage him; he was too excited to sit idle. On his hands and knees, he went out exploring with his fingertips, crawling like a baby. After only the first few feet, his hand ran into loose debris, the pile. He turned around and set off deeper into the cave.

After ten minutes of probing and feeling, he reached his goal. His right hand slid forward and splashed unseen ripples into the life-giving liquid. He scrambled ahead and lay his whole upper torso in the pool, submerging his face. Stopping himself after only a few sips, he drank from the pool. His body craved the water, but he would have to recondition himself to drink large quantities without vomiting.

Light glowed on the ceiling about fifteen minutes after he discovered the pool, and the cavern revealed itself once again. The dim light was adequate for the Envoy, as his pupils were at full dilation. The first thing he noticed was that he had crawled past twelve pools before reaching the one he found in the dark. He laughed. After replacing his satchel and slinging his pack over his shoulder, he walked straight and fast toward the lake.

Twenty yards from the edge of the lake, a series of events interrupted the echoing sounds made by his boots, stopping him dead in his tracks. The first was a whip-crack sound so loud he could feel it in his gums, made worse by the echoing properties of the cavern. The pressure in the cave increased; he could feel the breath pushed out of his lungs. A quaking shook the floor so violently that he lost the ability to support himself and his body slammed to the ground. The lake before him was churning, the peaks and valleys of the waves trading places and breaking. It only lasted for five seconds, and once the floor movement had calmed, thunder crept in, getting louder and louder until it was a steady, continuous rumble. He kneeled there anxiously, listening to the thunder for thirty seconds before deciding to ignore it. The discomfort from damp clothes, desperate thirst, and a pounding hunger made itself known once again. His entire body itched, and he was looking at a calm, clean, deep body of water. He dropped his pack and satchel, stripped off his damp clothing, and laid it all out to dry. He made the rest of the journey to the lake, where he waded in waist deep before diving and swimming closer to its center. When he was close to the midpoint, he stopped and stretched out to see if he could feel the bottom with his toes. No. He took a deep breath and plunged himself beneath the surface, swimming down hard with his arms, trying to feel the bottom. About three feet down, toes still not touching, he heard a muted *thunk* sound, immediately followed by two more in rapid succession. He swam back up to the surface, and as he emerged, tried to wrap his mind around what was happening in the cavern.

The first thing he was aware of was the sound. Clicking and clacking and rain and thunder, all multiplied by a million. It was a hot, loud roar. The interior of the cavern was a beehive of motion; rocks, small boulders, sand, and dust were crashing into the cave from the needle opening at unbelievable velocities. It was utter chaos. About fifty feet in front of him, a bright white plume of sparks exploded from the floor at a sharp angle toward the interior of the cave. It put the Envoy in a shallow trance, broken only when a small piece of rock hit the water about eighteen inches from his face. Finally recognizing the danger, he drew another deep breath and thrust himself back down into the lake as deep as he could go, which was only about three feet before his endurance failed. When he reached this depth, a spark of pain touched his forehead, above his right eyebrow. Almost as soon as he recognized that he had been hit, the turmoil above faded. It was only a second later when his lungs screamed at him; he kicked once and floated back to the surface. A fog of dust and silence received him.

10

The Envoy crawled out of the lake, exhausted from the unexpected effort to avoid being hurt by the anomaly. Dark red blood dripped onto the light red rock bed, tracing his path. He pressed his palm to the wound, counting to one hundred to give it time to clot. In place of where he left his bag, there was only a scratched and scuffed section of rock. Hand still pressed firmly to his forehead, he stood and walked deeper into the cave.

He found the bag after only three minutes of searching. Standing above his pack, naked and dripping, he estimated it was about twenty yards deeper into the cave than he had left it, but his satchel was nowhere in sight. *I'll find it,* he thought, telling himself not to worry, even though losing the satchel was a certain death sentence. After scanning for only a few seconds, he spotted it nestled against a chunk of rock, which he surmised was a newcomer to the cave.

Although he had been confident the items in the satchel would be unscathed, he smiled nonetheless after inspecting them and finding all parts intact. He repacked the satchel, hung it about his neck, and returned to his bag. Two neat holes, an entrance and an exit were in the canvas and there were two cracked water bottles, but no damage otherwise. Once it was repacked and slung over his left shoulder, he picked up his still-damp clothes and walked deeper into the cavern.

After only ten minutes, he came upon what he was looking for. A rock outcropping about twice as tall as he was and about three times as long. It stood only ten feet from a water pool that was small but two feet deep at its center. He made this his camp for the rest of his time here until going under the influence of Sterilex. There were small outcroppings and several boulders near the feature, and he laid all his clothing out on them to dry more completely. He took all ten intact bottles from his bag and filled them at the pool.

He moved back to the outcropping and sat with his back against the massive rock and again emptied his bag onto the ground. He found the purse containing the small needle and thread kit that was part of his inventory. As he stitched up the holes in the canvas bag, the whole cavern became sharply brighter. The sun was passing over the opening, which meant he had little light left. With a day on the young Earth being only ten hours, he guessed there was only enough light to see by for two-and-a-half or three. He badly wanted to move on to his next chapter on the planet. *Tomorrow*, he thought, *I have to go tomorrow. I'm not spending any more time here.* He pulled out a bottle of water and drank half of it. He waited for the nausea, but it did not come, so he finished it. Without hesitation, he consumed a second bottle. His ribs hurt from the sheer volume of water pressed into his shrunken stomach. *No matter,* he had to urinate before he could go under, and he would make sure that happened. With a third bottle in hand, he watched the last of his vision wash out. The sprites and phantoms came back. Ignoring them, he began stretching his tired muscles, tendons, and ligaments in a long and elaborate ritual, necessary before going under. He started with his toes and feet, ankles, and on up through his legs, buttocks, and into his torso, shoulders, arms, hands, fingers. He finished with a series of neck-rolls, then massaged his temples, ears, nose and finally worked his way through his jaw muscles.

Although the hunger sensation was strong, he wanted to move on, and eating that soon before going under was forbidden. He drank the third bottle of water and laid on his side, but sleep never came.

11

Once there was enough light to move about, the Envoy stood up and brought his bag over to the pool. All ten bottles were empty again, so filling them was a lengthy process. He shoved the full bottles into his bag and walked around, gathering his clothing and dressing as he went.

The qualifications for the next location were simple. It had to be a permanent shelter, fully protected from the elements and any anomalous events that could kill him. After surveying three different options, he settled on the one most likely to suit his purpose. There was a depression in the south wall, about eight feet off the ground. It was large enough for him to lie down and stretch out, with plenty of room left over for his supplies. He stacked several rocks atop one another to make a series of three steps, threw his pack and the satchel up into the cavity, walked up his mock-staircase, and pulled himself up and in. The surfaces of the carve-out were mostly rounded, but he was happy to find a flat, if not concave geometry to the small floor. The ceiling was not high enough for him to stand upright, but it was close, and it stretched back at least twelve feet into the rock wall. *At least I can sit up without hitting my head.*

A nervousness had grown in his chest. Before he left Telraed, he had his light brown hair cut, but it had since grown considerably and was wet with sweat and hanging in his eyes. He sat down and surveyed the landscape outside of his new apartment. He nodded, happy with it. There could be a considerable flood in the cavern, and he would be untouched. If any debris fell from the ceiling, his surroundings would protect him. The Envoy was not naïve; he understood there were an enormous number of things that could kill him while he was under, no matter where he camped, but there was no other option. The only thing he could do was make the smartest decision possible.

He wondered if his nerves were a result of concern for his wellbeing while under, or because he had to do it again at all. He hated it. Anyone that had ever gone through the experience felt the same way. It was horrible, though inarguably amazing that it worked as well as it did. *This isn't even going to be the worst one,* he thought. *The worst one will be the next one.* He shivered hard.

Preparing for the Sterilex stint involved some work, so he got started. He would need the direct sunlight to read the placard for the dosing procedure, so timing was important. If he missed it, he would have to wait for the next day. He retrieved the blanket from his pack, unfolded it, and spread it out. Next, he pulled out a black bag with a large opening that loosely cinched down and a jar about the size of his fist from his pack. He unscrewed the top of the jar. It was a salve, a paste that he would rub on his skin to prevent moisture loss. "It should also prevent critters from smelling you while you're under," Arthur Sterritt had said, billions of years before. He started with his feet and rubbed it all over everything, undressing and redressing as the process required. He finished by rubbing it in his hair, making his best effort to reach his scalp. It was unclear whether the stuff wore out over time or if it was only a mild version, but he never had to remove it after waking up. He propped the small black bag on top of his head as though it were a hat while he continued to prepare. The satchel had wound up close to the edge of the cavity. He grabbed it and laid out all of its contents: the placard, the glass bottle containing the Sterilex, the two glass rods and the blade he used for shorter stints, on the floor of the east side of his apartment. In that position, he could use the bright western sunlight to his advantage.

He rehearsed the actions in his mind many times over the next hour. He tried to remember the placard prescriptions; Arthur had made them memorize it cold during his training, but memories fade. He remembered *"R1" this, and "G7" that, "Q3" and years, and thousands of years, millions, more. As soon as I can see the impression in the light, it will all come back to me.* He sat with his legs crossed and with the placard in between the forefinger and thumb of his right hand. Rubbing the face of the print side with the pad of his thumb, he could feel the scratches of the imprinted text. He was in position, and he waited for the light.

The illumination event was not subtle. It was fast, bright, and painfully brief. *Showtime,* he thought. With the placard about ten inches from his eyes, he rolled and shifted it in the light until the stamped text stood out sharp and clear. He located the duration column and found the 300M and 600M entries, one above the other. *Closer to 300,* he thought, and read the code: R2-G1. Below it was the prescription for six hundred million years: R2-G2. He opened the bottle of Sterilex, picked up (R2), the larger glass rod, and dipped it into the liquid in the bottle. Once the depth reached the <u>1</u> hashmark on the rod, he pushed past it slightly into the world of G2, but only a little… not even close to the <u>2</u> hashmark. He withdrew the rod, waited for it to drip one time, then smeared the liquid left on the glass on the underside of his tongue. He winced, as he always did when taking the drug. It tasted bitter, and sour, and awful, but…

The clock was ticking. He replaced the bottle cap on the Sterilex, placed (R2), the larger glass rod, in its place next to (R1), the smaller rod, in their pouch. With the thick felt rolled back up in the satchel and cinched, he tossed it on top of his pack. He quickly shuffled over to the ledge of the apartment and urinated down into the cavern one last time. With that done, he laid down on the edge of the blanket and pulled the black bag over his head. Grabbing the edges of the blanket above his head and down by his knees, he rolled himself up in it the way a butcher would roll up a cut of meat. He was in position. The only thing he had left to do was wait for the misery. One minute later, his consciousness was dancing in and out. His breathing and heart rate were slowing. The dreams started, and what was left of his consciousness argued with itself, as always. It was starting.

12

The dreams were bright, fast, violent, painful, and exquisitely pleasant. Visions of Osa, Distria, Telraed, and Katya, the disaster planet, flashed and faded in his mind at numbing speeds. He panicked and responded to a growing feeling of sickness within him.

SOMETHING'S WRONG!

> *no, it isn't, it's the same.*

He stood on the patio of the launch facility where the Migration Division was having a farewell gathering for the departing Envoy and his family. He was hugging his sister, who was sobbing with her ten-month-old son on her hip. His nephew that he would never see grow up.

IT'S NOT WORKING THIS TIME!

> *it is, you need to relax.*

He stepped out into a lush green field on Distria, his first mission planet. The air was fresh and exquisitely rich in oxygen, his attitude consumed with optimism and energy.

I WON'T WAKE UP THIS TIME!

> *you will, relax.*

He turned just in time to see the length of pipe come down on his head and Jacko's conflicted expression as he brained the Envoy.

THIS IS KILLING ME!

no it isn't, relax.

He stood in his third-grade class with a billion butterflies churning in his stomach as he received a kiss on the cheek from his crush, Margot.

I CAN'T BREATHE!

you don't need to breathe right now.

A spray of blood splashed across the bulletproof window on the control room door as his wife took her own life right in front of him. She understood the Lance was about to start, and she could not stop it.

MY HEART! IT'S GOING TO EXPLODE!

no, it won't.

He shared a firm handshake with Enos Domitor, President of Temur, the most powerful country on Telraed.

I DIDN'T TAKE ENOUGH!

yes, you did.

He was back on Osa, standing on his balcony, staring up at the sky, looking for Orris among the stars. He could not see it yet but looked anyway and took great comfort and joy in knowing that they were up there, building it.

I TOOK TOO MUCH!

you took the exact amount required.

He was in space, but without his transport. There was a small red star in the distance. As the star got brighter and bigger, he noticed it was not a star, but a planet. It was planet 5, and it was shades of red and orange. He was moving toward it at a break-neck speed. It filled his field of view before he pierced the atmosphere like a bullet, sending a shock wave across the whole of the northern hemisphere. A moment later, he careened into the ground, blasting millions of tons of material up into the sky. Some of the material even escaped the atmosphere and went into temporary orbit around the planet. He had *become* one of the projectiles; not an orbiting one but cruising through the sky at white hot speeds. Descending, he saw a sharp, pointed feature in the distance. He slowed and fell and passed over the point and down into the Earth through a crack in the surface. He entered a dim cavern and plunged into an underground lake, about eighteen inches in front of his own face.

Chapter 2

Osa

1

"I can't believe you're serious about this," Brenia said. She brushed her hair out of her eyes. "This is insane. What happened to Orris?" She glared at her younger brother, tears pooling in her eyes.

Garrett looked back at her with tears of his own forming. "I'm still processing it myself," he said. His eyes dropped from hers.

They stood in the kitchen of their parent's house, where they grew up. Both of them visited often, as Brenia lived only a few doors down and Garrett returned regularly for food and conversation with his parents, who shared many of the same interests as he did.

"Processing?" She was getting loud. "You just told me you said yes, Garrett! What the hell do you mean you're 'processing?' You get asked the stupidest, most insane question in your entire life, and instead of laughing at them and walking away, you say yes?" He looked up at her but did not speak. "What in all the worlds would make you say yes to that, Garrett? What would make you throw away everything you've worked for your entire life? Me? Mom and Dad? All of your friends? Everyone you've ever known? Orris? You'll never set foot on Orris! I thought that meant everything to you!"

Garrett looked at his sister with wet eyes, but he did not cry, and his voice did not hitch. He spoke softly but confidently. "It did. It still does. But until today, I believed the best I could hope for was to be a division head. And in the best of cases, be on board when it left Osa's orbit for the first time, as a feeble old man." His sister started sobbing. "When they approached me today, I thought they were going to serve me with my rejection. Instead, they talked about the migration. Then they asked me if I would consider training as an envoy. I was stunned. I stood there like an idiot, my mind spinning. Once it sunk in and I regained my senses, I couldn't say no. Saying 'no' never even occurred to me. It's the opportunity of a trillion lifetimes."

Her sobbing turned into bawling. She tried to speak during the episode, but he could not understand her. As she calmed down, she rushed toward him and clamped her arms around his waist. Her wet, swollen face pressed into the hollow of his chest. Garrett wrapped his arms around her shoulders and her mass of long brown hair. She was still talking, but it was a harsh whisper, and he could barely understand her. "You'll die."

"We all die, Breni. The only thing that matters is what we do with the time that we have here. I have the opportunity to explore other worlds and possibly even save, or at least preserve, entire civilizations of people."

She stepped back from him and pulled a tissue out of its dispenser, blew her nose, and tossed it in the waste bin. "When would you leave?" she asked. Her voice had calmed a little, but still strained, and an octave higher than it would normally be.

"Not until next year. There is an aggressive training program that starts next week. It will go on until a week before the launch, then we'll have some time off, to do whatever we need to before we leave." Garrett scratched his head through his short, light brown hair. He knew the news would be harder on his sister than their parents. The plans were first announced four years prior, and his parents had urged him to take the exam and submit his DNA for consideration. The Migration Division of the Orris Project was the most difficult division to get into, as it was extremely complex and dangerous. He had agreed to apply but had done so because his goal was to get a job on Orris itself. There was a rumor that applicants to the Migration Division who did well, but did not qualify, would be fast-tracked into roles in other divisions of the project.

Brenia walked back to her brother and put her arms around his waist again, and her head back on his chest, apparently choosing that position to continue the conversation. *She doesn't want to look at me*, Garrett thought. "How can you even survive long enough to do anything on these missions? Aren't these other planets billions of miles away?"

He chuckled lightly. "No, Breni, much farther. They assign the first planet to us, and for me, that is Distria. It's one of the closest, but it is still thirty-nine parsecs from Osa. That's about seven hundred and fifty trillion miles."

She said nothing at first, but then in a defeated voice, "Those numbers mean nothing to me. They're too big. My real question is how long will it take you to get there?"

Garrett knew how she would react when he answered her, so he took a deep breath first, and let it out slowly. "About a hundred and fifty years." He awaited her reaction, but the door to the kitchen that led out to the front porch interrupted them, swinging open. A thin, middle-aged man with still mostly black hair and the beginnings of wrinkles creeping into the corners of his eyes walked through the door. It was their father, and unfortunately for him, Brenia's focus shifted.

"Did you know about this?" she shouted at him. Their father bore a look of surprise.

"I… what? What are you talking about?" The two men could hear all the air rush out of Brenia's lungs. She stared at the space between them for three seconds, then shook her head, turned, and walked out of the room. "What the hell was that all about, Gar? What don't I know about?" Garrett walked over to the refrigerator and pulled out two bottles of beer. He opened both and held one out to his father. Alan Rhodes took the bottle from his son tentatively. "What's going on, Garrett?"

Garrett took a long swig from his bottle and said, "The recruiters approached me today."

His father's face lit up. "Well, it had to have been good news, Gar! What did they say?"

His son laughed in a way that either said *you are really wrong* or *you are really right.* "They want me to train as an envoy," Garrett said. Alan's knees weakened. As he fell, he side-stepped, pulled out a kitchen chair in one fluid motion, and sat down hard.

"Envoy? I don't understand." His father's look of puzzlement increased until it was closer to a look of disgust. "What, what group?"

"One," Garrett said.

2

It was Alan's turn to lose his breath. He was familiar with the Migration Division's plans. At first, he muttered to himself, *envoy, group one?* He looked back up at his son, and in a small voice, almost a whisper, asked, "What position?"

"One."

Alan's expression did not change, but the whole of his weight shifted over onto his elbow and the heavy wooden kitchen table. His eyes stared off into nothing at all. Less than one hundredth of one percent of the planet's population of twelve billion were qualified to apply for a job working on the Orris Project. Of that pool of about a million people, the recruitment team estimated an elite subset of seven or eight hundred qualified to apply for the Migration Division. The division only needed a total working team of about ninety people. Of the ninety, they would select the twenty-seven most capable as envoys. Garrett was the first one chosen. Alan was trying to embrace the fact that this meant his son was the most qualified person in the world for the most difficult job ever proposed. That was a large pill to swallow. He had always been proud of his boy, both as a child and as the man he had grown into, but a lot of fathers were proud of their children. *This is on another level,* Alan thought. He was not even sure what to say. Fortunately, Garrett rescued him. "I know it's a shock. I was shocked, too."

"I can't believe it," Alan said, sitting back up and rubbing his head. "I mean, I *can* believe it, but what are the odds? You understand the gravity of them selecting you *first, right?"*

"I do," Garrett said, and shuffled his feet. Alan did not notice.

"Gar, I have… I have a thousand questions!" Alan said, laughing nervously. "But, but also I… I can't even begin to explain the emotions. I'm so proud of you, Gar, really. I'm so excited for you, but I'm also devastated. Heartbroken. I think this is the only side of it that Breni is going through. It's awful."

"I didn't tell Breni. She was obviously distraught, and I don't think she would have cared anyway, but OPM is going to send counselors to talk to the family."

Alan nodded. OPM was Orris Project Management, the top level of the project and the group who coordinated everything project-related. Alan leaned forward but did not get up and did not look up at his son. "It'll be like you're dead. We'll never get to talk to you again once you leave, right?" Alan asked, wringing his hands together.

"No, once I leave, I'll only be awake long enough to orbit Osa once. Then I'll go to sleep for the duration of the trip. When I wake up…" he paused.

"We'll all be dead," Alan finished. "From old age." He sat back in his chair. "And you, you will wake up as though no time has passed? I can't wrap my mind around that. You'll be the same age as you were when you left?"

Garrett shook his head. "They will go into a lot of detail about Sterilex and how it works in the first week of our training, so I don't have many answers now. My general understanding, though, is that no time will have passed for me." He finished his beer and placed the bottle in the recycling bin. Alan rested his forehead on his left palm.

"That's… amazing. Truly it is. And this guy, this Arthur Sterritt guy, is alive? Alive and well?" Arthur Sterritt was the inventor of Sterilex. After doing many small, controlled experiments with promising results on animals, he had volunteered to be the first human trial and put himself under using Sterilex for one hundred and fifty years.

"Yeah, he's alive. He's on the board. He's actually the board liaison for the Migration Division. I'm going to meet him next week," Garrett said.

Alan nodded again and stood up. "We have to tell your mother."

3

Brenia Kane laid on the couch in the living room of her parents' house, waiting for her mother to get home. She had stopped crying, and she realized she was more angry than sad. She had walked the three blocks from the house she shared with her husband, Rodney, to tell her family *her* news, before her brother had ruined everything with his. It only made her anger worse that she understood so little about what Garrett had signed up for. Three years earlier, soon after the President had introduced the Orris project, OPM had announced a program that involved people permanently leaving the planet. She had paid little attention to the details, had cared little about any of it. It was not a topic talked about at the salon where she worked as a stylist. It was *always* a topic of conversation when she visited with her family, though. Her father was a nuclear engineer for Coremat, a private mining company. Her mother was an astrophysicist who worked for the government, specifically the Department of Defense, and then there was her brother, the prodigy since he could walk and say his first words. He was at the top of his class in everything, always. He had even skipped two grades in school, so he graduated the same year she did, although he was two years her junior. He was fit and slim, exercising regularly, and she had slowly and consistently been gaining weight in the years since they had finished school. She was the idiot in the family. The stupid hairdresser. She grew up not understanding ninety percent of dinner table conversations, even though her little brother would often be interested and engaged in the topics her parents were discussing. Her mother would often drop in a question to her like, "How was your day, Breni? Learn anything interesting in school?" The questions always embarrassed her. Her mother may as well have been saying, "We know you're too stupid to understand any of this, Breni. Is there anything you want to bore us with, so you don't feel left out?" She was smart enough to see that.

When she heard her mother's voice added to that of her brother's and father's in the kitchen, she stood. Unconsciously leaving her right hand on her belly, she walked around the corner to join them.

4

"…so, it wasn't what we expected at all," Cynthia Rhodes was saying as her daughter walked into the room and over to a chair at the kitchen table. "Oh, Breni! I didn't know you were here!"

Brenia took a seat at the wooden table where they had all shared countless meals. "Did they tell you yet?" Brenia asked. She looked at her brother, who would not meet her gaze.

"Tell me what?" Cynthia, a tall woman who wore her dyed blonde hair in short curls, looked from her husband to her son and back to her husband. "Alan?"

"Why don't we all have a seat? I made tea," Alan said, and placed the teapot on the kitchen table along with four teacups. They sat down, and Garrett spent the next ten minutes laying out the details of his encounter with the recruiters. Although Cynthia Rhodes was a government-employed astrophysicist, she did not work within the Orris Project and was only privy to scant details regarding it.

"That's a lot to process, Garrett," Cynthia said. "Are you sure this is something you want to do? I know your father and I encouraged you to apply for the Migration Division, but I think we all had a much different idea of where that application would lead. Didn't you?" Garrett understood this was his mother's way of saying she did not want him to go.

"I did. As I told Dad and Breni, I was shocked when they asked me. I didn't even understand *what* they were asking me at first. But then the pieces fell into place, and I understood the opportunity I had available to me. I understood it would be the only time in my life that I would get an opportunity like it. I couldn't say no." He noticed the expression change on his mother's face and could hear Brenia sob again. "I know that sounds cold." He paused and looked at his sister, but she had her face buried in the neck of the bulky gray sweatshirt she was wearing, not able to acknowledge him. "Someone has to do this job. Twenty-seven people, actually. Twenty-seven people have to leave their families behind. I know I'm not making any of you feel better about this. I guess that's what the counselor is for, but I see this endeavor as being bigger than any one person, or even any one family. To achieve this would be…" Garrett searched for the word. When he could not find a better one, he settled for, "amazing."

Cynthia was staring at her teacup, rocking her head up and down slightly, as though in tentative agreement. She surprised both Alan and Garrett with the next question. "You will send large groups of these civilizations to Orris, or at least, that's what I understand. My question is, what will happen to you? When you finish with your missions, if you survive, where will you grow old? Where will you die?" The color drained from Garrett's face. He had not yet considered that there would be an end to the mission. "Hadn't thought about it? The way I see it, you have a few options: You could live out the rest of your life on the last planet you visit, provided it isn't destroyed because of your interference. You could join the migrants on their voyage and die on the ship, or you could just kill yourself." She fixed her blue eyes on her son, her face deadly serious. Garrett opened his mouth, not knowing what he would say, when Brenia spoke up.

"Or you could stay here with us. Mom, Dad, me, and Rodney… and the baby." All three of them looked at her with surprise. She had a small smile growing in the corners of her mouth. Her mother jumped up to hug her.

"Oh! Breni!"

Garrett stood to share a congratulatory hug with his sister. When they embraced, she whispered into his ear, "Don't leave me. Don't leave us. I don't think I could bear it."

Garrett, not wanting to make promises he could not keep but also not wanting to cause his sister any further distress, replied, "I have a lot of thinking to do." She squeezed him tightly before letting him go. As she embraced his father, Garrett looked up at his mother, who was staring at him with no emotion.

5

Garrett lay in bed in his small, one-bedroom apartment that night, shrouded in darkness. Sleep eluded him while he thought about what his life would look like were he to go through with the missions before him. Was his mother right about the three options for his end of life? Was there not a fourth or even a fifth option? *Die on the ship*, she said. She was right. The people who left for Orris would never reach it. In most cases, their offspring would not even reach the great intergalactic machine. It could be three or four generations, depending on the timing and how far Orris had traveled before they left. But how would dying on the ship be good for him? Why would he spend his last years in cramped quarters breathing recycled air just to die twenty percent or even *ten* percent of the way through the total journey? *So that they could lay my bones to rest on Orris.* Maybe. Or should they put him in the soil of the last planet he visited? No more Sterilex stints. He could enjoy his elder years quietly and comfortably on his final mission planet.

But that was not what he wanted. None of that. All his objectives accomplished, he wanted to make it back to Orris. He wanted to walk on the deck. He wanted to review the progress and learn the strategies and goals for escaping the eventual collapse. More than anything, he wanted to find out what had happened to the other envoys, what successes they had or, more pessimistically, what failures. He wanted to know how many mission planets sent populations to Orris. He wanted to know if the different populations assimilated completely or if there remained factions of unique peoples. The most satisfying way he could grow old, the most appropriate way he could die, would be on Orris, among the results of all his and his counterparts' efforts. That would be the beautiful end to an amazing life, lived completely.

6

Garrett walked into the OPM building the next morning at 10:08 to report for his 10:30 appointment with the Migration Division recruitment board. Printed on the glass doors was:

ORRIS PROJECT MANAGEMENT

CENTRAL OFFICES—Dinesta, Rep. of Korrah

His nerves concerned him. He did not want to sound like he had hesitations in the meeting. He walked into the large reception area, which appeared to consume the entire front half of the first floor and possibly the second and third floors. The exterior wall facing the street was all glass, and natural light filled the large space, constructed almost entirely of dark gray stone and bright chromed steel. The ceiling was thirty feet from the floor. At the reception desk was a smiling woman in her mid-to-late forties with dark blonde hair that fell to her shoulders and a name tag that read "Cecilia" pinned to the lapel of her jacket.

"Good morning. How can I help you?" Cecilia asked. Her smile was sweet and did not look forced. She seemed to be in a genuinely good mood, and that helped put Garrett at ease.

"Hi, I have a 10:30 appointment with the Migration Division." Garrett placed the folder with the information packet and a variety of forms the recruitment team had given him when he verbally accepted their offer on the reception countertop.

"Okay, do you know who specifically the appointment was with?" Cecilia asked, while typing something into her computer, not looking at Garrett.

"Yes, the recruitment board," he said. She stopped typing and looked up at him over her reading glasses. "Oh, that's a high-profile meeting. What was your name?" Cecilia did not turn back to her computer.

"Garrett Rhodes, that's r-h-o-d-e-s." She turned back to the computer, but only hit two keys on the keyboard.

"Garrett Rhodes, 10:30 with the MD recruitment board. Got it right here," she said and stood, pointing behind him. "Have a seat right over there in one of those chairs, Mr. Rhodes. I'll call you back up in a few minutes and I'll need your I.D. card. We'll also do a quick biometric scan so we can skip the rest of the security protocols."

"Thank you, Cecilia." Her smile widened at the sound of her name, and she sat back down. Garrett walked over to the bank of four stuffed blue chairs occupied by no one and sat down. There was a large digital clock over Cecilia's head that read 10:16, and he wondered how long it would take to get from the reception area to the actual meeting place. To his relief, he heard her voice only moments later.

"Mr. Rhodes?" He stood and walked back up to the reception desk, offering his I.D. card once he arrived. She took it.

"Thank you," she said, and keyed some information into the computer. "Mr. Rhodes, do we have your permission to run a biometric scan of your person to verify your identity? If yes, place either thumb on the black pad here." She pointed with one red painted nail to a cutout in the polished stone countertop with what looked like a simple black plastic square about two inches by two inches in the slight depression.

He placed his left thumb on the pad, thinking there was no way it was that easy to get into the building. When his thumb contacted the pad, a tiny red light in the upper right corner flashed quickly. He looked at it and it changed to a steady green.

"Thank you, Mr. Rhodes. The thumbprint is for permission only. Please stand up straight and still and look at the blue dot of light over my left shoulder until I tell you to stop," she gestured with her pen over her shoulder without looking.

That was it. The actual test was about to begin. He could see nothing but the steady blue dot of light set in the blackened granite backdrop behind her and about twelve inches beneath the raised metal letters reading "Orris Project Management." Though subtle, he knew he was being scanned and measured in multiple ways to verify his identity, facial recognition being only a part of the extensive procedure. After only ten seconds, the blue light blinked out and Cecilia said, "Thank you, Mr. Rhodes."

He chuckled. "That's it? No retina scan?" He was smiling and tried to come across as lighthearted.

She smiled back and said, "We scanned your retinas when you placed your thumb on the pad." Garrett was at first surprised but thought of the light starting red then turning green. "We take security seriously here, Mr. Rhodes."

"Yes," he said. "I would expect nothing less."

She handed him his I.D. card and a paper security clearance ticket with his credentials, building floor, meeting room number, and appointment time in large print. "Please take the elevator, place your thumb on the pad next to the 'up' arrow, and it will take you to the twenty-first floor. Your meeting room number is 2106. There will be someone outside the room to receive you."

"Thank you so much, Cecilia, you've been a tremendous help." Garrett watched as a little color rose in her cheeks and he turned to walk to the elevators. She surprised him when she called out after him, surprising because of the informality.

"Garrett?" she called. He stopped and turned toward her. "I'm going to know your name for a long time, aren't I? Probably for the rest of my life." She looked at him with what he perceived as a slight anxiety.

"Maybe," was all he replied, with a soft, small smile, and turned back to the elevators.

7

When the elevator doors closed, he looked anxiously at his watch. 10:24. *Too close. Should have left earlier,* he thought. Relieved, he found the elevator moved quickly and did not stop at any other floors. *Another security measure,* he surmised. Once the carriage stopped and the doors parted, it surprised him to find the entire board standing there, dressed in formal business attire. Before the doors even finished their opening procedure, the group of men and women applauded. Color did not just rise on his cheeks, his entire face surged into a full, embarrassed blush, which caused the group before him to laugh. Finally, Dr. Christine Paige, the one who had offered him the position in the first place, stepped into the elevator and took his left hand, drawing him out.

"We can't tell you how excited we all are that you accepted this role, Mr. Rhodes," Dr. Paige said. She led him out into the elevator bay so the door could close behind him.

A short, overweight man with a balding head and a dark gray suit was next to speak. "This is amazing. So many years of work. And now we can finally put a face with the strategies and mission plans. I'm so happy to meet you, Mr. Rhodes. My name is Arthur." Arthur had a much stronger grip than Garrett had expected, but he returned the firm handshake in kind.

"My apologies for the informal reception, Mr. Rhodes. We should all move to the conference room," Dr. Paige said. She held her arms out from her sides in a herding gesture to the rest of the group. Garrett followed behind the herd, walking next to Dr. Paige, a small woman in her sixties with blonde hair pulled back in a clip. She spoke to him as they walked, in a low voice so the others wouldn't hear her. "Are you nervous, Garrett?" He looked at her with his brow raised high as if to say, *Of course!* "Don't be. These people are a wreck of nerves right now. I'm sure it will be different with future envoys, but right now, these folks don't even know what to do with themselves. I told them I was coming to greet you and they all followed me."

When they reached the conference room, Garrett expected a large table, yards long, with fifty or sixty leather chairs. What he discovered when he walked into the room was a smallish round table with exactly eight modest, cloth-cushioned chairs around it, matching the number of attendees for the meeting. The room itself resembled more of an office than a large conference room. It had only four windows and a litter of random furniture besides the meeting table. He stood before it, waiting for each of the board members to select their seats. A tall, white-haired man in his late fifties or early sixties said, "Grab a seat anywhere, Mr. Rhodes." Garrett approached the closest of the chairs, pulled it out, and waited for the others to sit before sitting himself. Dr. Paige flanked him on his left, and the man who had self-identified as "Arthur" to his right, but once seated, it was a white-haired man who started the meeting in an upbeat and exuberant tone.

"Well, Mr. Rhodes, we can't tell you how happy we all are to have this meeting with you. *I* can't explain how happy *I am* to have had our top candidate accept the role. We knew we could fill the roles, at least in the first group, but we didn't know how many of our top candidates would accept. So, I want to thank you personally. As you can imagine, there are a lot of nerves and anxiety that go along with a project this complex, and you accepting is a huge win for us." Garrett's face once again flushed to a bright red.

"Alex?" Dr. Paige interrupted. "Maybe you should tell Garrett who you are?" White-hair only looked at Dr. Paige for a second, then slapped his forehead comically.

"Of course! Mr. Rhodes, I apologize. I know you met Dr. Paige and Dr. Abbot yesterday, but you have no way of knowing who I am." Alex white-hair laughed at himself for a moment. "I'm Alex Murray, chairman of the Migration Division." Garrett's stomach seemed to drop a few inches. He knew he would meet high-profile people at the meeting, but this did not diminish the impact of the actual encounter. What had that man accomplished in his life to land a job as important and complex as *leading* the Migration Division? He could not imagine.

"So, let's do all the introductions quickly," Dr. Murray continued, with every bit of the exuberance he had started with. "Everyone already knows you, but let me do the honor of introducing you anyway. Ladies and gentlemen, sitting before you here is Garrett Rhodes. Garrett was our number one candidate for the role of envoy. His academic background is exemplary on its own, but he is the only candidate, the *only one*, to score perfectly on his application exam. I can tell all of you, honestly, I could not have pulled that off. Four hundred questions, all extremely advanced." Dr. Murray looked from person to person at the table. "The only other qualifier was the DNA test, and his came back squeaky clean. Mr. Rhodes, you were made for this job." That sparked a fresh round of applause, as though

Garrett had controlled and shaped his own DNA. "Christine?" Dr. Murray sat down, and Dr. Paige stood.

"Dr. Christine Paige. Garrett and I met yesterday. I am both a recruiter and the head of Psychology for the Migration Division." She smiled and sat. Dr. Murray gestured to the man sitting next to her. A short man with a dark complexion and curly, jet-black hair stood.

"Dr. Benjamin Estes, Survival Theory." Estes sat quickly. *Survival Theory?* Garrett thought about what that might mean, with little success. Dr. Murray continued his gesturing, and a thin, youthful woman with red hair that was pulled back tightly against her skull stood up.

"Dr. Lauren Astor, Acquisitions." She, too, sat quickly and stared down at her hands. Garrett thought about what *acquisitions* might mean, and he thought he had an idea. She glanced back up at Garrett and blushed heavily when she discovered he was still looking at her. Dr. Murray skipped himself, as expected, and continued around the table. The next victim was a youngish man with light brown hair combed straight back and a sharp jawline. He stood up all the way and had a small smile on his face.

"Hello again, Mr. Rhodes. I'm Dr. Jack Abbott." He looked out at the rest of the meeting attendees. "Garrett and I also met yesterday. I am a recruiter along with Dr. Paige, and I am the Director of Engineering and Technology for the Migration Division." Dr. Abbot sat. *Big job,* Garrett thought. Dr. Murray smiled, and gestured to the next board member, a large woman with long dark hair and a beautiful smile, probably in her mid-thirties.

"Dr. Olive Francis, Communications. It's very nice to meet you, Mr. Rhodes." She sat and looked across the table to Dr. Astor, who still gazed at her hands.

Dr. Murray nodded and said, "And last but certainly not least, our executive liaison." Alex gestured to Arthur, who stood smiling.

"Arthur Sterritt. Orris board member, Migration Division liaison, head of Sterilex administration." Garrett's stomach fell through all twenty-one floors and landed flat on the ground below them. He had pictured *the* Arthur Sterritt much differently. It never occurred to him that when the man introduced himself as "Arthur" that it would be the famed inventor. Arthur sat, and Garrett stared at the man. Uneasy, Arthur spoke, "Did I say something that upset you?"

"Were you truly born in 3,677?" Garrett immediately regretted asking the question, feeling childish in the formal setting, but Arthur laughed.

"Yeah, I know it's hard to believe," Arthur said. The smile dissolved from his face. "Going under isn't easy, though, Garrett. It is possible, it does work, and it works damn well, but it's a tough experience. And I can only imagine how much harder it might be if you do a lot more than a couple hundred years. But I promise you will know everything I know before you take it for the first time. I promise that I'll prepare you to the best of my ability."

Dr. Murray chimed in. "Well, come on Arthur, don't scare the guy off!" he was smiling. "He just accepted! No take-backs, right, Mr. Rhodes?" His smile was large and fixed, but Garrett sensed concern in the question.

"No, sir. I understood from the beginning that using Sterilex could be…" Garrett searched for the right word, "Taxing."

"Okay, well, that's good. I'm glad we're all on the same page. Now, each of us has a brief presentation to go through, and then we'd like to open for questions. Does that sound good to you?" Dr. Murray asked. Garrett smiled. "Excellent. Jack? Do you want to get us started?"

8

More than an hour passed before the last of the five specialists finished their presentations. The only ones that had not spoken besides Garrett himself were Dr. Murray and Arthur Sterritt. "Thank you very much, Olive," Dr. Murray said. "Well, that leaves me and Mr. Sterritt. Art, do you have anything you want to present?"

"I will coach Mr. Rhodes and the other envoys in a private setting. There is really no reason to go into detail about the substance with people that will never have to experience it. It would be," Arthur paused, searching for the correct phrasing, "a bit cruel? Just unnecessary, I think." Dr. Murray looked like he had the wind knocked out of him.

"Okay, Ar…"

"I'd like to be present," Dr. Paige said. "If this procedure is taxing, as Mr. Rhodes put it, I think I should be present as the head of Psychology." Dr. Murray raised his eyebrows and looked at Sterritt.

"Of course, Christine," Arthur said. "You are welcome to attend. I would like to keep the head count at these meetings as low as possible, though."

Dr. Paige smiled and nodded. "Of course," she said.

"I guess it's my turn," Dr. Murray exclaimed. "I don't have a specialty, as you understand, Mr. Rhodes. I'm in charge of this whole damned monster we call the Migration Division. As you may have also noticed, I'm trying to wash out the formality here. This division is very professional and is also a very formal business environment. But not for you, Garrett, and not for your colleagues. What we are asking you and yours in kind to do is phenomenal. The anxieties and stresses will be extraordinary. So, I want you to know that when you walk into this building, there are no codes, no rituals, no expected formalities of any kind. You have no reason to be nervous when you walk through the doors downstairs. I'm not Dr. Murray, I'm Alex, or Al, if you want. I don't care, and no one else does either. If you have a question about anything, you can ask anyone, and we'll get that question answered. I encourage you to go with first names here, all around, and that's not limited to the Migration Division. If you run into the Secretary of the whole damned Orris Project, he expects you to call him 'Dan.' I know, he told me this morning. The point is, Garrett, we don't want you to spend any energy trying to be the perfect 'puzzle piece' here. This place is yours; we all work for you." Everyone at the table nodded. "You can see this isn't some nonsense I'm making up on the spot. Everyone here already knows. The envoys are the customer. Now, can you tell me you understand what I've just explained to you? Tell me you really believe it?"

Garrett understood. He also knew the right way to answer the question. "Yes, Al, I get it."

The largest smile since the meeting had begun spread across Dr. Murray's face. "Excellent! Now, do you have any questions for us?"

"Yes, I have a thousand questions," Garrett said. "But I don't know what any of them are yet."

Chapter 3

Oceans

1

Part two of the horrible Sterilex experience: your mind woke up before any of your senses. The Envoy awoke trapped in a dark, silent room. He could feel nothing, he could move nothing, no smell, no taste, nothing but his thoughts. He believed his heart had started beating again and that he had started breathing again only because if he had not, he would not be awake. He knew he was not dreaming only because dreams had content. To make things worse, he had no sense of time passing at all. Two distinct comforts lifted his spirits. The first was that it was not his first time, and he knew it would not last long. After ten to thirty minutes passed, his senses would return. The second was the most obvious: he woke up. He was alive. His mind wandered toward the "buried alive" scenario, but he scolded himself for even thinking about it. There was no reason to worry. There was nothing he could do about it until he could move and take the pill. Instead, he imagined breathing. He imagined his chest rising and falling. He imagined the thudding of his heart beating, echoing in his ear canals, an exercise he had used in the past, to help coax him out of his coma. It had always worked, eventually. He counted the breaths he was creating in his mind to see how high he could get before the real thing arrhythmically conflicted with the patterns in his thoughts.

Somewhere between 230 and 240, the feeling in his chest came back, and he had been counting much too fast. His breathing was there, but it was slow. He could hear nothing, but he could feel his chest rising and falling, and the rhythmic *bump-bump, bump-bump* of his heart, also slow.

The next sensation to return was wonderful; it was his sense of smell, and what he smelled was rain. It meant not only was there a lot of water on the planet, but that he would not suffocate. It would be impossible to smell rain without being exposed to the open air. The feeling in his arms, legs, and face returned, and he could feel his salivary glands working overtime, producing a warm slick of saliva. He could taste again, but the taste in his mouth was bitter and metallic, horrible compared to the delightful smell of the rain. It was another several minutes later that he heard a far-off crash of thunder, and then he heard one that was much closer, and the rain itself. It was violent, but he could feel everything, and he was not wet. *Lucky on top of lucky.* The Envoy was still lying on his left side, in the same position he had been moments after taking the dose of "time traveling" elixir. Four hundred million years was long enough on one side, and so he tried to roll himself onto his back. He was successful, but the pain that accompanied the movement was intense.

He laid there, still buried in his blanket with his hood pulled over his face, in global pain, breathing and waiting for it to subside. Complete feeling was coming back to every facet of his body, and with it, the pain that accompanied his adjustment to being alive again. Every single tooth hurt. His eye sockets were two balls of fire, his joints and bones were throbbing, his skin itched everywhere, and his stomach was churning and nauseated. Before he could even think about his vision returning, he found that it had. Lightning struck so bright it penetrated the two layers of blanket and hood, not to mention his eyelids, which lit up bright pink with an immediate baby blue after-image. It was only a second after the flash that the thunder crashed, and he could not just hear it, he felt the vibration in the rock. The rain intensified.

He focused on his breathing and on the sound of the rain and tried to push his pain and general torment to the back of his mind. *I need water. This won't get much better until I get some water.* He began unrolling himself out of the blanket. After one complete turn, and with one to go, he hit his pain threshold, and passed out.

2

He woke up six minutes later, and even though little time had passed, the rain had slowed considerably. There was no noticeable change to the pain, but he still had to get out of his sheathing. He started his unwrapping procedure again, much more slowly and carefully. After an hour, he felt the blanket fall away from his arm. He was on his back again and could hear a loud "tick, tick" sound on his head sock. Rain. He reached up with his right hand and removed the hood. The simple action was exhausting, and he relaxed all the muscles in his right arm and allowed it to fall. It slapped down on the flat, wet rock and sent a new bolt of pain screaming into his brain. *Stupid, stupid, stupid,* he scolded himself. The bulk of the pain in his arm subsided after several seconds, and he remembered he had at least a foot of ledge before the drop off. The Envoy slowly, carefully, slid his body toward the ledge. After only twelve inches, he could feel the droplets crashing into his face. He smiled. Flat on his back, drips and drops hit his lips and tongue as his mouth was open to receive the delicious water. He laid there like that for three hours, slowly hydrating. He was falling asleep again and carefully rolled onto his right side, relaxing his entire body. His pain subsided, but the exhaustion remained. With rain still pelting the skin on his left cheek and temple, he placed a hand over his ear to prevent it from filling with water and fell asleep.

3

A cool breeze awoke the Envoy. The rain had stopped, and the clouds broke. Sunlight streamed in from overhead and heated the saturated floor of earth outside but did not touch his face, as the apartment he had chosen blocked the direct light.

Today's goal: sit up and drink as much of a bottle of water as I can, he thought. It seemed like an attainable goal. His movements were pain-free; the problem was his lack of energy. Every move he made exhausted him, and he would have to wait to recover before making another small move. After four attempts, he understood he would not be sitting up that afternoon. Instead, he crept over to his bag, pushed the satchel off it, and spent the next hour untying the throat. Once open enough to get his hand in, he reached for one of the water bottles made from that amazing Dory-10 plastic that he had taken with him from Osa. His bag, water bottles, purse, satchel and even his clothing and his boots used Dory-10 for every stitch. They had taken the same material and spun it into thread, which they wove into the items. It was not as comfortable as natural materials, and he only wore the clothing when things like cotton were not available. He dragged the bottle out of his pack and although he spilled a lot, he swallowed about half of it. His situation differed greatly from when he first arrived on Earth. He knew water was plentiful and did not care that he wasted some, but he needed the water that he had put in his system to do its magic. With his eyes closed, in the same position, he attempted to sleep without success. He breathed, and he daydreamed of bodies of water on the surface. He did not know exactly what to expect, but the driving rain made him optimistic.

4

The Envoy woke up and noted the bright red sunlight spilling into the apartment. *Either sunrise or sunset,* he thought. *Could I have slept all night?* Without thinking about it, he lifted himself up to a sitting position, leaning on one outstretched arm. Only a moment passed before he realized that the simple action was something he could only have dreamed of doing mere hours earlier. Not wanting to overexert himself, he looked over at his pack and noted the empty water bottle on the ground next to it. He reached into the bag and withdrew another bottle, easily twisted off the cap and drank from it. Once the bottle was empty, he belched and started a rigorous stretching routine. He imagined he would get to a point where his energy failed or the pain came back and he would have to stop, but he finished the routine easily.

The light in the apartment had shifted from a bright red to a brighter yellow. *Sunrise. I can't believe I slept all night.* He slid his backside over to the ledge and swung his legs over it so he could sit more comfortably. The landscape amazed him. It was a *cave* when he went under. He realized the roof, the entire roof, had collapsed across the expanse of the cave. This sparked another thought as he remembered the makeshift staircase he had built to ascend the eight-foot rise to the apartment ledge. He looked straight down to find his feet only inches from the sand and dirt below. *Well, that's convenient,* he thought. He wanted to slide off the ledge and take a try at standing upright at his full height. With his satchel around his neck and his bag was on his back, he slid off the ledge and onto his feet. His legs collapsed beneath him, and after some quick thinking, he rolled down the slight decline instead of slapping face first into it. He sat up. *Well, I have my supplies, but I just gave up my shelter. Nice job, idiot.* His concern was minimal because he knew getting back up into the apartment would be possible if he needed to, but the sun was not baking him. It felt good on his skin, which still itched badly. He heard a rumble and scanned the part of the horizon he could see. There was a dark band of clouds to the west over the nee… *The needle is gone!* It was. After a moment of consideration, he believed it probably had not fallen but gradually sunk back down to the earth over countless years.

He drank another bottle of water without moving from his crash site and tried to stand again. He could do it, but saw stars once he was fully up, so he sat down again. *Eat,* he told himself. He ate.

5

The Envoy slept where he had landed the day before, under the stars. He wanted to give the little food he had eaten time to digest and distribute its nutrition before he tried to stand again. The sun was pushing the night away to the east, and the air was cool. The breeze felt good on his itchy skin. He sat up and looked around. A clear sunrise had been coming in the east, but there were a lot of clouds above him, and it was still too dark to tell if they were rain clouds. He ate another piece of jerky. There would be a lot of walking in his future, and he knew his ribs were becoming visible. He was starving in the truest sense of the word. Following his instructions, the prep team on Telraed dried the meat, dressed it in a heavily salted oil, and sealed each piece individually in a thick Dory-10 packet while under a powerful vacuum. He could not imagine what it would be like trying to eat it if it had not been; it would probably be dust. After he finished his micro meal, he drank another bottle of water.

In the east, the sky was much brighter, but above him was still black. *Rain, maybe, hopefully*. He tried standing again. There were no stars, but his legs felt watery. He risked a step forward, then another. He stopped, stood tall with his head back, and breathed deeply. Oxygen was still a problem. As if his posture were some ritual pledge to the god of rain, the sky opened up and bathed his entire body. He laughed with delight. Standing in the downpour, he stripped off all his clothes and used hands full of wet sand to scrub his body down in the rain to clean himself. Next, he worked on his clothing, letting the articles saturate, wringing them out, and then repeating for good measure. Once he finished his cleaning, he kneeled in the dirt and found a piece of flat rock that had a sharp point as a feature. Holding the rock up in the rain, he also scrubbed it clean as well as he could with his hands and more sand. Still holding it before him, he let the droplets of rain crash into the surface and run off in his best effort to rinse it clean. Satisfied, he tilted the rock point down and to the top of his empty water bottle. He had four empty bottles, but he had left one of them back in the apartment hole, so he filled the three he had with him. It was slow work, but necessary.

He stood and dressed, still in the rain. It soaked all his clothes through, and it felt wonderful. His skin no longer itched. He hung the waterlogged satchel around his neck and placed the waterlogged bag on his back. He walked the seven steps it took to reach the apartment hole, reached in, and retrieved the empty water bottle. One step back, looking at the hole, he nodded. "Thank you." A rare spoken word from the Envoy while on the planet with a population of one.

6

After climbing out of what was once a cavern and then a shallow valley, he stared at the ground and watched the rivulets of rainwater trickle across the earth. The Envoy established his heading. It was not a foolproof method for finding larger bodies of water, but it was much better than guessing blindly. He walked and watched as trickles merged into tiny streams, tiny streams merged into small streams, and so on. He walked until the dark daylight faded into the true dark of night. It was still raining and although it was becoming uncomfortable, he reminded himself of the times he would have killed for a little rain. In the fading light, he looked all around him for cover and found none. He walked until he could no longer see.

7

It was not possible to sleep well while being rained on. It did eventually stop, just as he saw the first signs of daylight emerging in the east. He was so exhausted he rolled away from the light to get an hour of good sleep while the sun came up. It worked, but he had a new problem. It was cool, almost cold, and it had rained all night. The fog was so thick that although he could see his hand stretched out at arm's length, he could not see much farther than that. He located the stream he had been following and continued to follow it, but it spilled into a marsh of concentrated puddles after only ten minutes of walking. *What do I do?* He thought, *there's nothing I can do but wait until this fog breaks, otherwise I could walk off a cliff.* He laughed at the thought of taking two more steps and free-falling to his death. He stood where he was and sung a song from his time as a young man back on Osa. The sound was funny in the marsh; it sounded strange to his ears, or his voice could have changed after being under for hundreds of millions of years. He forgot about it before even finishing the song when he felt a breeze and saw the fog shifting, and something dark close to where he stood. The first word he thought of when he could make out the dark object was "mound," but it was bigger than that. It was more of a significant hill sloping up away from the marsh, which he could see stretched north.

The Envoy walked up the hill, hoping to get the best vantage point he could. He could see far enough that he no longer worried about walking off a sheer cliff, and it had the potential to be progress. The higher he climbed, the thinner the remaining fog got. He could see farther, maybe a hundred yards, and the hill maintained its steady slope up. *This could be perfect,* he thought. *I might find both from up here.* He could see the blue of the sky. At that elevation, the fog had thinned to a weak haze. After a minute more, the fog disappeared, and he could see the summit of the hill. He looked around, amazed at the blanket of white in every direction. It was swirling and churning with the recent addition of the breeze. The sun was getting higher in the sky, and he knew it would only be a matter of twenty minutes or a half hour before it broke completely. He sat, ate, drank, and enjoyed the serenity before it was time to get back to work.

The Envoy watched as deep veins grew in the fog's mass. The veins built up into pockets and then there were only thin streamers of gray/white vapor left. After a cursory glance at the revealed landscape, he gave his vision its best chance at succeeding and climbed to the top of the hill.

Standing tall on the summit with a rudimentary visor made from his hands, he scanned three hundred and sixty degrees of landscape and horizon. No oceans, no mountains. He repeated his scanning procedure three more times, looking for subtleties. On the mountain front, he came up with nothing. The highest point he could observe from the hill was the hill itself. The lack of mountains did not matter at that point. He needed the mountain for prolonged shelter, and he would not need prolonged shelter until he could find the ocean. He saw nothing that gave him hope, so he walked down the hill to the east, the same direction he had been traveling.

8

The Envoy walked for fifty-seven days. Though he had fleeting thoughts while he walked, he mostly found himself in a thoughtless trance. He walked all day, and for as much of the night as he had light for, depending on the behavior of the moon. He estimated each day on the planet was about twelve hours, so it was slowing down. The moon, Earth's once beautiful smooth white skylight, had been pocked and damaged from what appeared to be thousands of impacts and was further away than it had been when he arrived. His thick beard itched terribly. He scratched at his face and especially his neck constantly as he walked. Of the fifty-seven days, it rained for forty-three; he collapsed unconscious nineteen times, drank one hundred and ninety bottles of water, and ate fully half of the food that he had left.

A little after noon on the fifty-seventh day, he thought he could see water. The more he walked, the more he was sure it was an ocean. Thirty minutes later, he was stripping off his gear and his clothes and charging into the rolling waves. It was one of the nice days, no clouds, and the sun was bright and strong. He swam in the surf for a few minutes, the water rushing over his skin and through his beard felt heavenly, and then floated on his back, smiling. Eventually, he drifted closer and closer to shore, and once he felt his heels touch the rocky bottom, he stood and walked back to the beach.

He walked up to where he had dropped his bag, retrieving his clothes as he went. Bag in hand, he walked back down to the beach and stood, waiting for the ocean breeze to dry him off enough so he could dress. While he waited, the Envoy retrieved a bottle of water and drank about half of it before deciding he was dry enough. Clothed and warm, he sat next to his small stow of possessions on the hardpan of the beach, enjoying the natural melody of the waves. He smiled. His next task was the first actual work he had to do in a long while. It was the first task on the mission plan for a new, young planet. Everything until that point had been surviving. That task would wait until the next day. He wanted to enjoy his time on the beach and rest up, as his next journey would begin the next day. The sun was setting behind him, and the surf was a beautiful sight. He stood and walked up the beach to give himself a buffer between himself and the crashing waves. About thirty yards up the beach, he made his camp, which in the warm weather was his blanket rolled into a pillow, and nothing else. He laid flat on his back and stared at the sky. The light blue dimmed into orange and red, and then a deep blue and purple as the stars faded in. As it was happening, he drifted into sleep, exhausted.

9

Cold. Cold and wet. His legs were cold and wet. The Envoy awoke to find the ocean had climbed all the way up the beach. He stood up in the moonlight and picked up his bag, satchel, and the half-full bottle of water he had been drinking. With the satchel safely around his neck, he stowed the bottle in his pack and slung it over his shoulder. He watched the waves crashing in and walked backwards as they approached and reached his feet. He walked that way for only two minutes before tiring of it and turning to walk away from the surf. To his complete amazement, it chased him almost a mile across the surface of the Earth before it paused and then receded. He stood in the cold white light offered by the moon and watched as the ocean left him behind, with only damp ground as evidence it had ever been there. At that moment, he did not understand why the Earth's tidal phenomenon existed in the extremes it did, and then he noticed his crystal-clear midnight shadow, and understood perfectly. He looked up at the moon.

"It's you, isn't it?" It felt good to speak, to engage, even though the moon would not answer him. "You are responsible for this. Do you know how much harder this will make the next part of my mission?" The Envoy was smiling. It was like being mad at an innocent child. Although he could recognize the added work to his already strenuous task, it was equally amazing that such a phenomenon existed at all. He laid down on the ground where he stood, wanting to view the tidal termination point in the full daylight.

10

The Envoy could not believe he missed it. He concluded that he must have seen the ocean before reaching the termination line, and been so distracted that he did not notice the abrupt and permanent color change. The ground went from a sunbaked white to a heavier, dark beige over the course of only fifteen yards. This line extended away from him, north and south, for as far as he could see.

Geared up, he strode back toward the receding ocean. Fifteen minutes was all it took, and the surf was again only thirty yards away. He did not want to take the chance of the sun drying out and killing the first dosing he made, so he once again stripped down to nothing and opened his bag. He pulled the purse out, the small bag-within-a-bag, and opened it. Inside was a rectangular Dory-10 packet with a snap clasping a flap at the top to the main body. He pulled the snap apart and inspected the contents. The molded packet held twenty-five small vials: ten missing, fifteen remaining. The dosing prescription was five vials per planet, but the most any envoy would ever need would be twenty if every planet after their first was a newborn. Always over-engineering and inserting redundancy was the Orris Project. The Envoy had no need for them on the first three planets, and had used ten, double the prescription, on Telraed.

He removed one of the last fifteen vials, re-snapped the packet, and put it away. He held the vial up to the daylight to inspect its contents. There was nothing in the vial but salt, except it was special. The labs added cyanobacteria in suspended animation to the slurry before allowing the crystals to form. Cyanobacteria, the beautiful little gem that multiplied and multiplied and pumped the atmosphere full of oxygen. He took a deep breath to remind himself how unsatisfying the current air was. It was likely that the planet had already established life in one corner or another, but by seeding the ocean with the bacteria locked in the salts he would help the planets biology move toward oxygen dependence.

Vial sealed and in hand, he walked to the ocean and waded out, only diving in when he was about to be pulverized by an enormous wave. The Envoy swam out until his remaining energy level was concerning. His muscles burned, and the fatigue was alarming. He stopped and treaded in place. Slowly spinning, he located the shore and noted that he was drifting south. His belongings were to the right of his current position. He again treaded in a spin until his back was to the shore. Holding the vial in front of his face and placing both thumbnails together and centered, he snapped it, resulting in a spiderweb of cracks and weak stress lines in the material. Gripping each end, he folded it back and forth until a split appeared on one side of the bend. He shook the contents into the ocean water and then flicked the container further into the sea. He took a deep breath, arched his back, and floated back to the shore.

When he arrived at his bag, the surf was only four or five feet from touching it. Setting it up on end made it easier to spot, since so much of the land looked exactly the same. He hoisted his bag up on his shoulder and began his escape from the tide. When he reached the terminator, he ate, relaxed, thought about his next move, and eventually slept. The ocean had left him again, but he knew it would be back when it was dark and preferred sleeping on dry land.

11

Sleep was deep and restful. He woke up refreshed but anxious, knowing his next decision would be critical. North or South? He could not see mountains in either direction, but he had to choose, and he had to stay on the coast to make at least four more salt deposits. The planet had a tilt, which meant seasons, and the potential of freezing and snow to the north, as he was already north of the equator. South meant a lower likelihood of mountains and potentially more geologic activity over the next billions of years, his long run. He thought about it while he walked back to the coast.

Left, right, left, right. The Envoy spent the next seventeen minutes slowly concluding that although the northern route might be more painful, it was also the route he was more likely to survive. *North, then.* His gait bent to the left.

When he reached the coast, he again performed his planetary-life-dosing ritual, located his possessions, and walked due-north, letting the encroaching sea push him westward. As he walked north and slid west, always scanning the horizon, he felt a pang of depression, which his subconscious immediately addressed. The correction came in the voice of Dr. Christine Paige, dead for billions of years by that point. *There are many things that are more dangerous than my mind, don't let my mind become more dangerous than those things.* It was a chant they rehearsed at the beginning and end of every meeting they had with her. She had intended to brand it into the brains of the envoys.

The sun was approaching the western horizon, and the sky was shifting from its daytime blue to its oranges and reds. He had left the coast entirely, searching for the tidal terminator so he could sleep without fear of being rudely awakened by waves crashing down on him. After a few minutes of walking/climbing up a small hill, he found the high water mark. It was closer than he expected, even at the increased elevation. Although the light was dimming, there was no mistaking it, so he climbed to the top, dropped his gear, and made camp for the night. When he laid down, the cool breezes and the general good health he was in made falling asleep easy. He slept deeply and fast. In what seemed like fifteen minutes after losing consciousness, he was awake, witnessing the sunrise, completely baffled.

The Envoy was on an island. Although he understood what was happening, he still had a hard time believing it. He appeared to be on a tiny island and way out to sea. The coast was visible, but it was far enough that he never even considered trying to swim the distance. It was over a half mile. To the north, he saw multiple more rounded peaks popping out of the ocean surface, making an archipelago. Much further to the north, he saw darkness on the horizon, which he expected was another storm; a storm that he would be more than happy to have miss him entirely. He had been enjoying the rain-free days. The archipelago could reduce the amount of walking he would have to do if he could island-hop during low tide. In that moment, it was an annoyance, but there was nothing he could do until the tide receded. *Well, except for this,* he thought, and went to his bag for another vial. *At least I don't have to get wet for this one.* He snapped the container full of special salt and flicked the whole of it as far as he could in the direction the breeze was traveling.

When the tide pulled back, he gathered his supplies and walked off the western edge of the island, which was just a hill again, onto the wet ground and resumed his northerly trek.

12

After walking for two days, he could see that the storm clouds in the far north were not clouds at all, but exactly the thing he was looking for: mountains. It took him seven more days to reach them. During that time, he used the islands to sleep on four more times. He deposited the salts eight more times, having made two dives on the fifth day, which was abnormally warm.

The beach gave way to a slope on the seventh day. Before starting his climb, he filled his bottles with ocean water. The young ocean was still fresh, which surprised him every time he jumped into it. Only twenty paces up the slope, the terminator line was apparent. The Envoy stopped, knowing he was leaving the ocean but would visit an ancient version of it when he awoke. He did not speak to the ocean as he had the apartment that aided him, but he smiled at it. Before continuing, he took the packet with its two remaining vials out of his bag. He took the entire packet and bent it back and forth, feeling the remaining vials bend and pop in his hands. He worked them repeatedly until he was sure they were both cracked and open. Before he cast the packet into the ocean, he noticed a bit of the salt leaking to the earth below, and he nodded. It was a triple redundancy and unnecessary to do at all; but he wanted to be rid of the packet. One less thing to carry around. With a smooth motion and a sharp flick of the wrist, he threw the packet like a frisbee, and it plunked into the crashing waves ten feet below.

The Envoy began the physically taxing process of climbing. His daily travel distances diminished by much more than half for two reasons. Climbing was exhausting, and the higher elevation reduced the already poor oxygen concentration. He passed out twice, collapsing where he stood. He suffered no injuries from the events but thought better of letting it continue to happen. Another fall could mean a broken arm or a split skull. He took it slow and took frequent breaks. He had experienced a comfort, or a sense of accomplishment, as he ascended, seeing the ocean get further and further away.

Still traveling north, he reached a vertical rock face that he could not navigate. He turned west, as an easterly direction would have eventually deposited him violently back into the ocean. Four times after that, he reached areas of the landscape that were too steep to climb, and he descended, still always moving forward, never backtracking. Twice he had slipped on loose sand or gravel, badly enough that he lost his footing and made an abrupt visit to the earth below. He had sustained no serious abrasions from the falls, but he had badly bruised his right hip on the first occurrence.

He was at the base of his latest diversion and staring up at a long, smooth incline. It was steep, but he believed he could traverse the grade. The most interesting thing was that he could see nothing above the slope but sky. He wanted to know what the view would be like at the top. He had thrown the last of the salts into the ocean eleven days before that. It had rained eight times, which kept his water bottles filled. His food was dwindling, but not yet alarmingly so. He imagined he had a few weeks left, but his ribs were approaching skeletal, and his gut was concave, a condition he had not experienced since his beginnings on Telraed.

Judging by the position of the sun, he expected he had another two or three hours before dark, so he started the climb. Slow but persistent, he got two-thirds of the way up before the sun dipped below the horizon. The thought of sleeping on the grade and rolling over in his sleep scared him, so he continued the climb in the fading sunlight. When he reached the top, it was dark. The moon was not visible, so he was traveling by starlight, which amounted to no light. He felt his way up the grade for the last twenty minutes of the climb. When his hand finally escaped the slope and reached a flat spot, he scrambled up onto it and collapsed. Exhausted, sleep was almost immediate.

13

The Envoy woke six hours later, feeling almost as exhausted as he had when he fell asleep. *No oxygen up here,* he thought. *This is terrible.* He laid still for another five minutes, breathing deeply, trying to pull as much of the scarce free oxygen into his blood as possible.

He sat up and looked around. To his right, a steep slope that looked as though it might stretch down a mile to the flat plains below. To his left was a flat, dusty beige surface, and nothing higher. He was on a plateau. It measured twenty yards across where he sat but widened considerably further north, and once he stood and regained his complete sense of direction, he saw that it stretched northeast, not due north. There were few features on top of the near-level surface of rock, rubble, dust, and sand, but in a handful of places, there were larger rock outcroppings. He walked and smiled when he saw a round opening in the ground after only ten minutes. Upon closer inspection, he could see that it was a sheer drop into darkness, probably a drainage point, but the good news was that there was a cave system in the mountain. The Envoy needed to find an entrance he could use and then find a relatively safe place to stash himself while he made the long run; the one that would hopefully end with a planet rich in free oxygen and with an established and growing body of not just animal life, but intelligent life. *It's a lot to ask for when you're throwing a dart in the dark,* he thought.

There were dark rain clouds approaching from the southwest, and he thought they would reach him before the day was out. *That might not be a terrible thing,* he thought. Running water made sleep difficult but offered a lot of valuable information if you were looking for cave entrances beneath your feet. The rain would not come for hours, though, and he had every intention of finding the entrance without its assistance.

He continued to explore the plateau for the next three hours and found two more "vents," as he thought of them. Circular openings in the ground that offered only a fatal entrance into the cave system below. The vastness of the plateau encouraged him. He still could not make out a defined end point, but it was narrowing after having achieved a maximum width of two hundred yards.

The light had dimmed considerably, and large droplets of rain pelted the back of his head and neck. He drew the blanket from his bag and draped it over himself to at least rid himself of the discomfort of the impact. It rained hard for several minutes and pools formed on the plateau. The water moved in every direction. Relief washed over him, being in a prime place for lightning strikes, when no thunder accompanied the rain. Head down, he walked, watching the water swirl and slide and tumble across the surface. He spotted a small stream of water establishing itself, with hundreds of tiny tributaries running northwest, toward the closest edge of the plateau. He imagined it would get bigger and bigger and gain a bit of speed before launching itself off the cliff. Following it with his eyes, he saw he was right. Moving on, he found three more of the small streams running off the edges, and then he saw one that flowed rapidly toward the interior of the large plateau. It had all the tributaries of the past four streams but was not making a bolt for any of the edges. It ran toward a large outcropping, maybe eleven feet tall and about twice as wide, with sharp, jagged edges and much taller on the right than the left. He was still twenty yards away, but it looked more and more like the stream smacked right into the rock and disappeared. As he approached it, he slowed and watch his footfalls carefully, not wanting to go where the water was going, at least not yet. When he was upon it, he smiled, filled with tentative joy. It was another "vent," and it was larger than the others, but he had no way of surveying the entrance point as it was then accepting large volumes of water.

The Envoy stood there staring at the crashing end point of the stream and thought about his current situation. There would be an hour before the sun went down. The sky to the far east was bright, but to the west it was a dark, leaden color. No end in sight for the rain. His water bottles were mostly full, but he took out the empties and filled them anyway, for something to do. The one thing he would not do was leave the position. The plateau was not enormous, but it was big enough that he did not want to risk losing his place. With his bottles full, he optimistically began preparing for the long run. He drank three bottles of water in a row; an excellent prescription for an upset stomach. The stretching routine normally took forty minutes, but he took his time and spent an hour working through it. While he did not think there would be much sleep in his immediate future, the outcropping had a flat place about two feet square on the lower edge, only a foot off the ground. The next course rose into the air at a smooth angle. He sat on the small flat platform and leaned back on the roughly forty-five-degree up-slope. He placed his pack on his lap and draped the blanket over his head and down to his toes. Sleep drifted in and out for two hours. When the rain stopped, he pulled the blanket off his face, shifted his position, and slept for the rest of the night.

14

The Envoy awoke as day was breaking, and the still steel-colored clouds in the sky were thinning in places. Standing up and walking around to the foot of the outcropping, he wanted to look down into the chasm, but the light was not strong enough. He could only see darkness and the ghosts of shapes. Another fifteen minutes would pass before the edges of the opening revealed themselves. As they did, he skirted the edge, pressing down with one tentative foot to find any weak spots, but no material broke off. Except for the long flat edge created by the outcropping itself, the hole was an oval about twice as wide as he was tall. The area around the entrance was getting brighter, but the depths remained the color of tar.

He sat on the edge, with his legs dangling in the opening, and thought to look at the Sterilex placard while he had the light to do so. Although it was still not bright, he could read the metal card, and he did not bother looking through the numbers. The last prescription, the longest stint read:

3B: R2-G10

The problem with the formula was that he had used it on Telraed in a similar situation and had undershot by over three hundred million years. The short stints to make up for that were torture, and he had no intention of going through that again. Knowing that each grade on the larger rod worked out to about three hundred million years, he had every intention of making his own "G11" prescription. He vaguely remembered Arthur Sterritt telling them that the Sterilex would "not" or would "never" be the problem regarding their survival, and there was never a warning about taking too much.

He replaced the placard back in the satchel and stared down into the hole. It appeared the outcropping continued down into the depths, and he could see many other features. It was not smooth rock but appeared to be a mostly vertical shaft that dropped straight through to the center of the landmass. As the sun trekked through the sky and the hole got brighter and brighter, it became clear that climbing down would not be easy, but it would be possible. There were hundreds of hand and footholds. He elected to put the satchel in his bag, hoping the bag would do a better job protecting it, cinched the throat tightly, and knotted it for good measure. With his bag on his back, he stepped down into the hole.

15

After descending thirty feet, the Envoy found a solid ledge to stand on with both feet. He stood there, leaning against his bag and pinching it between him and the rock face. Pointed toward what he expected was the cavern or whatever the cavity in the plateau was, he shut his eyes tightly and covered them with his hands for good measure. In his mind, he counted to one hundred to establish the best low light vision he could. When he opened his eyes, he saw the wall of rock four feet in front of him much more clearly. *Down further still,* he thought, and continued climbing down. After fifty more feet, he reached the floor. Brief glances upward blinded him again in the low light environment, but he could go no further down. He repeated his light sensitivity ritual and was heartbroken to find he was staring at the same rock wall. It had chased him all the way to the bottom. Although it was not perfectly circular, the vent amounted to a tall, straight shaft down, with no apparent destination. He searched the uneven floor, thinking there must be some outlet, otherwise the space would be full of water. He was right. The shaft totaled four feet wide by seven feet long, and in the bottom corner to his left was an opening close to the floor. He laid down and pushed his head through the passage, which he was unsure would be big enough for his ribcage.

He was looking not into a huge cavern but a trough that got wider as it got higher. It had been much narrower in its infancy, but running water had carved it out over the ages. It extended further back than he could see and was over a hundred feet tall where he could make out the ceiling. There were four shafts of light, the vents delivering a weak glow to the interior. The sloped walls were far from smooth, covered in irregularities and pockets, ledges, and small outcroppings.

He backed up, took off his bag, and pushed it through the opening. After spending a minute to work up the courage, he laid down on his back, reached both hands through the hole, and grabbed the inside wall of the trough. He rocked his head to the side, but his skull, ear and face still scraped the topside of the opening as he pushed with his dug-in heels. The whole of the opening hugged his chest and armpits, and he breathed slowly and deeply while he could. *No matter what happens, don't panic.* He let the majority of the air escape his lungs and pushed with his feet and pulled his arms. The pressure on his ribcage increased after sliding only a few inches, and the pain started. He kicked and pulled harder, and a pang of panic flashed through his mind when he attempted to inhale and the pain doubled. *Relax, exhale, and push. Exhale* all the way *this time.* The calmer, reasoned voice in his head prevailed over the impending panic and he pushed more of the air from his lungs, pushed with his feet and pulled with his arms. He felt the opening slide to the base of his ribcage and stop. The Earth was crushing him. He could not inhale, for feal of cracking a rib, and he was stuck. The Envoy closed his eyes hard and clenched his teeth. *Dig deep, there has to be air left in your lungs, push it out!* The pain was agonizing but he forced the last bit of breath he could muster out of himself, kicked, pulled, and writhed back and forth until finally, the ribs on his right side freed themselves from the grip of the opening, followed immediately be the left. He laid half in and half out of the trough for ten minutes, enjoying each breath. His concern for his hips making it through proved fruitless; he had lost so much weight that they slid through easily when he was moving again.

The first conclusion he came to upon taking his first few steps in the trough was that it had to go deeper, or there had to be an outlet to the outside. He was once again walking on damp, uneven rock. The water had not pooled here at all. The second conclusion was that the roof had an expiration date and would collapse long before he woke up. It was a fact that brought a great deal of disappointment to the Envoy, and he began thinking the exploration had been all for nothing. He would have to climb back out, descend the northern edge of the plateau, and continue north. *If I can climb out,* he thought, *if I want to torture myself again.* There were ledges and shelves cut throughout the walls to his left and right, and he explored while the light was available and planned to sleep down there for the night.

Halfway up a ledge that looked like it extended over fifty yards into the trough at a ten-degree angle, he was at a point where he could lift himself onto the next step. It was like climbing a huge flight of stairs. He did the same thing two more times and found that he had reached the halfway point of the total climb. The shafts of light illuminating the trough were bending and narrowing, and he noticed it was already getting darker. He also noticed a new shaft, not even a shaft really, but a pin of light coming in at a much sharper angle, brighter than the others. It was possibly due to the fact that he was still staring at the intense beam of light, or the fact that the general lighting in the trough was failing, but he never saw the gap. He started walking, and his third footfall landed on clear, open air. A moment into the fall, he grasped at the shadows in front of him, connecting with the other side of the gap only enough so his face crashed into his arm and not the rock itself. He could not establish a grip and fell straight down into the black. *This is it...* was the thought going through his mind when he landed in the muck. First his feet, then his buttocks, then his back. To his amazement, other than his forehead and nose and the arm they smacked into, he did not feel any intense pain. He had even managed not to hit his head on the sludgy ground he was lying in. *How many times can one man get this lucky?* He pressed his hand into his landing pad and rubbed the contents between his fingers. Not sand, finer. *Silt,* he thought. It was wet, but there was no standing water. The mountain had excellent drainage. He sat up in the darkness and looked above. He could still see the pin and watched it fade and blink out. The darkness was complete.

It would be eight hours at least, but probably ten before he could hope for any light, and he suspected when that time came, it would not be much. He abandoned his vision for the time being and mapped the area by touch. He slowly and carefully navigated around on his hands and knees, touching the floor and the walls. The room was disturbingly small. He knew there were no drop-off points, ledges, or any other dangers of the sort, and also that the muck was only on one half of the floor. He stood up slowly and retraced his crawling assessment of the entire space. It was round and six paces in diameter. He went around again, paying close attention to the condition of the surrounding walls. They were all sheer. The only material in the place was the silt. No small or large rocks to build a set of stairs. No cracks in the walls, no ledges or steps, nothing to grip with either hand or foot. He was trapped.

I'm going to die here. As he tried to think of escape strategies, the thought kept repeating itself. He closed his eyes, not that it made any difference visually but for the comfort of it. He told himself to think. *There has to be a way out of this*. And there was. There were two, actually. "The pill or the still," his fellow envoy, Tom Holly, had always been fond of saying in the meetings they had with Dr. Ben Estes, the survival theorist. Tom alone thought it was clever and said it often. When in a dire situation, "the pill" would kill you, and "the still" was a reference to the fact that one did not move while under the influence of Sterilex.

"The pill or the still, Tom. I think I've finally reached that point," the Envoy spoke only to thin air. One way or the other, he did not have to decide right then, so he laid down to sleep, waiting to get a good look in the morning, when there was light.

16

When the light finally came, it was miserably dim. Even though he understood that the source was dim to begin with, it did not ease his frustration. His pupils were at maximum dilation, yet he could make out little but dark shadows among slightly darker shadows. There was one sharply black vertical line on what he suspected was the west wall, had he not entirely lost his bearings. *That's where the water goes*, he thought, *and since I'm not a quarter of an inch thick, I can't perform the same trick.*

"Why would anyone take the pill?" It surprised him to find he was speaking out loud. *If the option is pill or still, why wouldn't you just risk 'the still?'* He thought about it for a few minutes. *Cowards. It's the only answer, at least in a situation like this.* He took his bag off his back and walked to the rockier side of the small room. There was no way he would go under while lying under the same gap he had dropped through.

The light was getting to its brightest point, but it was still inadequate. The only saving grace was that the administering rod was glass, and very reflective. As long as he didn't wait, he could put himself under with an accurate dose. *A big dose*, he thought. There was only one positive to going under for a long time: the large dose of Sterilex took you out quickly. The dreams were fast, and then you were gone. There was no panic. Waking up was hell.

The Envoy rolled out his blanket and opened the salve and his satchel, the contents of which had survived the fall. He also tossed a full bottle of water onto the blanket. *I know I'll need it as soon as I wake up. Why not make it easy?* He walked over to the far side of the hole and urinated into the silt. Once he was back, he applied the salve to his body and prepared the administration devices. Head bag on, he dipped the rod into the Sterilex up to the "five" hash and applied it to his tongue. He quickly did it again, this time to the "six" hashmark. G11 achieved. It was time to start the long run.

17

He was in his cocoon, awaiting the inevitable nightmare. His breathing was slowing noticeably. Before he slept, he could hear a soft sound that at first sounded like radio static but got louder and louder and he recognized it as solid rocket fire. He could see stars and...

SOMETHING'S WRONG!

no, there isn't, you're fine.

He was orbiting Sochee, the people of Osa's nickname for their sun. Sochee was growing, and he could see Osa in the distance, a blue dot. Sochee grew and swelled and burned

Osa to ash, and then further burned the ash into nothing at all. Sochee came, and Sochee took it all. Sochee took every fiber of what once was Osa, his home. And then Sochee died. All that remained was a tiny white dwarf, an eternity away from the Envoy's hole.

Chapter 4

Sterritt & Paige

1

"It kills you, technically." Arthur Sterritt was speaking to a group of eleven envoys, the nine from Group 1 and the first and second position from Group 2 who had also agreed to be alternates. Sterritt's office was poorly lit with the shades drawn and the only artificial light resting on his desk. Arthur had arranged folding chairs in a circle with no table centered between them, like they were attending group therapy. Dr. Christine Paige sat opposite Sterritt. "I don't say that to scare you. I say that because I want to be honest with you. It kills every cell in your body, it kills the bacteria between your teeth and in your gut, it kills the fungus in your hair follicles." The group stirred. Flanking Garrett were Thomas Holly on his right and Kyle Gellar on his left, positions three and eight, respectively. Two days before, at the Migration Division's general orientation, they were told their position numbers would only determine launch order. The positions were descending, putting Garrett last to launch in Group 1. "But yet, I sit here before you, clearly alive, or at least I hope that's clear." A small ruffle of laughter.

"Sterilex does a lot more than *just* kill you," Sterritt continued. "It is a powerful preservative, and it has a shelf life. That is to say, it decays. The duration of time that you will be 'under' is directly tied to how much you administer. Within a handful of minutes after the last of the Sterilex decays, the cells will respire again and resume their function as though nothing had happened. The same cannot be said for your body as a whole.

"The first thing to react to being alive again is your medulla oblongata, which will immediately begin sending pulses to your heart. The heart will pump mostly deoxygenated blood through your system. A moment later, it will activate your pulmonary system and your diaphragm will begin its rhythm, rapidly at first, then slowing. You won't know any of this. Even though consciousness returns a few moments after that, you won't have any of your senses. You will be a prisoner in your own mind. You will breathe, but you won't know it, you won't feel it, and you certainly won't hear it. Hearing is one of the last senses to return," he said. The group fidgeted and stirred when Dr. Paige interrupted.

"How long, Mr. Sterritt? How long does it take to come back?"

Arthur's expression was blank at first and then he looked at the floor in front of him, calculating. "I was down for one hundred and fifty-three years and seven months. I can only estimate the duration of the experience, but if I had to guess, I would put it at ten minutes, between the time that my mind woke up and the time I regained my vision." Arthur had been addressing her directly but began looking around at the envoys in the group again. "Which is the last sense to return, understand."

Dr. Paige seemed surprised. "Oh! So, it's not that bad, then. Ten minutes. I imagine any of these men could handle ten minutes of discomfort. It doesn't sound so horrible after all."

"Every part is horrible," Arthur said, again addressing Dr. Paige. "Christine, I was under for a hundred and fifty years. These men could be under for millions or *billions* of years at a time. I want to offer them any comfort I can, but I can only estimate and make educated guesses based on my research, and I will not lie to them."

It was Dr. Paige's turn to stir and fidget. "I certainly was not suggesting that, Mr. Sterritt. I guess the next question is, what can they expect at much longer durations under the influence of Sterilex? What estimations could you make for a million- or a *billion-year* stint?" she asked, looking hopeful, but her ankles were crossed under her chair and her hands were clasped on her lap.

"Well, I could never say for sure, but one thing I can say is that it is definitely not a linear correlation. I believe there is an upper limit, and I believe that upper limit to be between thirty and forty minutes, even for a three- or four-billion-year stint. But being gone for that long presents challenges much more dire than what it would be like to wake up," he chuckled. "Waking time would be the least of your concerns at that point, I think."

Garrett reacted and was speaking before taking the time to consider if his question was appropriate. "But that's an actual possibility for us, Arthur. For every one of us here. Unless we're the luckiest men in the universe, we're all going to do a billion-plus year stint and maybe more than once. So, what are you saying? Why are you laughing? Do you think it will kill us permanently if we take that much? What are you saying?" Garrett was speaking louder than usual. Among persistent agreement from the other envoys, Arthur was shaking his head.

"No, no, no. Not with the Sterilex. I have no reason to believe that the Sterilex will cause any permanent damage. It's the environment. I don't know how anyone in a frail body could survive that long without being swallowed up by the planet on which they reside. It seems like everyone piled onto the idea of Sterilex being a magic potion that could keep people alive forever, but it isn't! There's no magic here!" Arthur was getting loud and pointed at Joe Burkman. "You could have a rock fall on your head, dead! Forever dead!" Randy Vila, "You could get trapped in a landslide, dead!" Jonroe Daniels, "You could freeze to death, yeah! That would still kill you! Dead!" Ken Chase, "The very floor you lay on could collapse, and you'd fall to your death, dead!" his focus turned back to Garrett, "And you Mr. Rhodes? One thing, two things? Thousands of things could kill you while you're under. Ten thousand. You're all just bugs. The crap in the bottle that I give you will keep you alive only if you don't get squashed! You all *have to* understand that!" Arthur had stood and was pacing around the room. Next, he seemed to talk to himself. "I hate this. I hate it. I told them I didn't want to have any part in this. This is a stupid idea, and it's going to get people killed." He took a few more steps and stopped with his back to the group. "That's all for today. I will see you all at ten tomorrow morning." He walked out of the room.

"Well then," Dr. Paige said, "I think it's clear to all of you that Mr. Sterritt is under some stress regarding the totality of this project. Let's all take a long break for lunch and we can meet in my office at one o'clock for the first psych roundtable. Okay? See you all then." She stood, and everyone followed suit, shuffling out of the room.

2

There was a large cafeteria in the back of the building on the first floor. The ceiling was as high as the reception area and huge glass panels lined the back wall, letting the natural light flood the space. Garrett got in a long line to get a sandwich when one of the other envoys, rock-on-head-guy Joe Burkman, walked up to him.

"Hey, Garrett, right?" Garrett nodded and extended his hand. Joe, an average-looking man from his height to his weight to his side-parted light brown hair and dull hazel eyes, shook it. "Joe Burkman. Hey, there's hot food down at the end there, if you want something better than a sandwich." He pointed toward the glass windows in the back corner of the large cafeteria.

"Yeah, that sounds great." Garrett split from the line he was in, and the two walked to the back corner of the room. "I'm surprised there's no line. That means the sandwiches are fantastic, or this food is garbage, which do you think?"

Joe laughed. "No, it means that the sandwiches are cheap and the good food is not. But it doesn't matter to us." It was a point of discomfort for Garrett, knowing that the division paid for everything. Envoys had no salary. They had a badge. Besides the badge, the division made one-time, tax-free payments to each of the envoy's direct blood relatives. Garrett checked, and even though his nephew was still in gestation, he also qualified for the payment, as they calculated it the day after launch. He would be ten months old. It was not a paltry sum; his nephew would be a wealthy baby boy.

The two selected their meals and turned to find a table. "Do you want to find the other guys or sit?" Joe asked.

Garrett saw an empty table by the windows with two chairs and nodded toward it. "I'm hungry, let's just sit over there." They sat, and Garrett scanned the close tables for any familiar faces. He saw none.

They had barely begun eating when Joe started a conversation. "I know that we're not supposed to talk about the selection order, but you're the only one I can talk to about it. You're the only one that beat me," Joe said, and looked excited. Garrett rolled his eyes, but Joe continued. "Seriously though, I'm not a person who likes to toot his own horn, but I didn't think anyone would beat me. Do you know how you got the top spot?"

Garrett shifted in his seat. "How did you do on the application exam?" he asked. It was the only genuine answer he could give without feeling like he was criticizing his counterpart.

"I got 99% right! That's what I mean, I only got four questions wrong on a four hundred question exam! Tom Holly was right behind me and he got eleven wrong. I know, he told me. So, it wasn't even close! How did you do? You must have done even better than I did!" Joe's animation was making Garrett even more uncomfortable with the topic.

"I'll tell you I got fewer than four wrong. But I'll never tell you the real number." Garrett felt the ambiguity would…

"Get the hell out of here. You aced it," Joe said. He was not asking. "You aced an extremely complex, four hundred question exam. You just… killed it."

Garrett looked down at his plate, not wanting to lie to his colleague. His embarrassment escalated when he saw Joe bowing to him. "I am not worthy to be in the presence of such a great man!" He spoke at a volume louder than Garrett was comfortable with; Garrett flushed red and wadded up his napkin and threw it at Joe.

"Come on, man, keep it down. It's not information I want to spread."

Joe looked confused. "What? Why? You're a genius, you didn't punch a baby!" Joe smiled at his own joke, not understanding Garrett's concern.

"If that gets around, everyone will look to me for every answer, like I'm some all-knowing being, a God. I can assure you I am not, and I want no part of that."

"Sorry, pal, and I say this as a friend. Even though the division told us to ignore the positions, they're public. Everyone already knows you're number one, and you really solidified that when you spoke up in the meeting today with Sterritt. You are the king of the envoys, and I am your number two, your pathetic sidekick."

Garrett laughed. "Pathetic sidekick? Joe, you're probably one of the smartest people on the planet," Garrett said with genuine sincerity.

"Next to you, pal? I'm your everyday citizen. No one special."

Garrett laughed hard. It took him a few minutes to calm down before he could speak again. "Seriously though, Joe, taking this job is difficult for a huge number of reasons. It's nice to talk to someone who has gone through all the things I have."

"I agree completely," Joe said, nodding.

"Can I ask you then? What do you think you'll do after the fifth?" Garrett asked. Joe's recent sense of humor melted away. It was his turn to stare down at his plate. He took several seconds before he spoke.

"Honestly? Well, Gar, the honest answer is that I don't think I'll get that far," Joe said, looking up at Garrett with a stern expression. "If you take the number of things we are trying to accomplish and measure the absolute time it will take to accomplish them, with all the things that could go wrong? I don't see any of us ever needing to answer that question." Garrett did not reply at first, only took a deep breath and sat back in his chair. Joe continued, "It's fair to say that we're all going to take on young planets, right? If not three then two, anyway. The luckiest among us might get away with one, but, really, that's unlikely. It's the young planets that are going to kill us Gar, all of us, I think." Joe sat back, awaiting a reply.

Garrett leaned forward. "I agree with everything you said, except for one thing. We have to plan for the end of the fifth. We have to, Joe. It's the mental driver that will keep us going. If you think you will be killed every time you come up against a new obstacle, you won't last past the first planet," Garrett said. Joe laughed, which confused him.

"It sounds like we started the psych roundtable without the others," he said. Garrett also laughed and looked at his watch. Still forty-five minutes before they were due in Dr. Paige's office, but they had finished their lunch.

Garrett stood up. "Let's see if we can find the others. We have some time to kill."

Joe stood up too, picking up his lunch tray at the same time. "Sounds good to me."

3

A minute after dumping their trays in the trash, they saw a table with five of the remaining nine envoys sitting and talking.

"Can we join?" Joe asked.

"What do we got here? It's the superstars!" It was Tom Holly, position three. Tom was two years older than Garrett. He was a tall man, physically fit, and kept his thinning blonde hair cut close to his skull.

"You were right next to me, so take it easy, will you, Tom?" Joe said. The table laughed, and the two newcomers sat down.

Stanley Richman, a small-framed academic with glasses, was the first to speak almost before they were in their seats. "Hey Garrett, we're all dying to know what you got on your application exam, being number one and all..." Before Garrett needed to answer, Joe bailed him out.

"I just spent the last thirty minutes trying to get it out of him. If you think you can then great, but I couldn't crack that egg." Garrett was grateful, and felt the applicable response was to smile.

"Really?" Stan said. "You won't tell us? Damn. Okay, what was the hardest question you had then? You'll answer that, won't you?" he looked hopeful with that question. Garrett did not see a problem complying with the request.

"Sure. Both of the geology questions," Garrett said. The table erupted in laughter. They considered geology one of the easiest disciplines. When the laughter settled down, another member of the table chimed in. It was Eric Thomas, position seven.

"Seriously, though. There had to be one question that was impossible for you to answer," Eric said. Everyone was staring at Garrett, which was exactly what he did not want, but he understood that it would be his role, whether he liked it or not.

"I'm deadly serious. There were only two questions that had to do with geology, and I puzzled over them forever," Garrett said. The group was looking back and forth at each other in amazement. Although only twenty-four years old, Eric scratched his prematurely balding head of once-red hair and followed up.

"Geology is so easy. How could that be the one thing you had a problem with and not the quantum mechanics?" he asked. All eyes on Garrett again.

"I can't do this job without knowing the mechanics cold. Does everyone agree with that?" A table full of heads nodded. "Okay, now, when a rock the size of a truck falls on me and kills me, would knowing what type of rock it is and exactly how that rock formed save my life?" Blank stares and mouths agape. "See? I don't care about rocks, so I never paid attention. And that is why they were the hardest questions. And your name is…?" Garrett asked the balding man. Eric came back to life and shook his head.

"Sorry. Eric Thomas, position seven." At that, Garrett smacked the table and stood up.

"Please guys, don't announce your position numbers. They mean nothing. Eric, are your tasks going to be easier than mine or Joe's?" Garrett asked. Eric shook his head. "Of course not. So why bring it up? There are only a handful of people on all of Osa that could land in the positions we're in. Do you see what I'm saying?"

Eric looked up directly at Garrett. "It's splitting hairs."

"Exactly."

4

Thirty minutes later, the seven joined the other four envoys in the elevator lobby of the nineteenth floor. They were still making small talk when Dr. Christine Paige emerged from around the corner and said, "Room 1908, follow me," in a good-humored voice. They walked the short distance to her office, which was large and bright, with the exterior wall made entirely of glass and letting in plenty of daylight. Her desk was small and tucked away in the interior corner opposite the door. In the back of the office, parallel with the windows, was a large conference table, which she circled with her hand out, inviting them to sit.

"Please sit anywhere you like," she said. Garrett watched Joe select a chair and intentionally sat opposite him, across the table, wanting to communicate with him visually if needed. He counted himself fortunate that he had a confidante. Dr. Paige sat down, placed a blank notepad in front of her, and laid a pen on top of it.

"I have no curriculum, as this is an extraordinary situation. So, I elected for our time together to be in this format. I will not preach to any of you about something that I know nothing about and never will," Dr. Paige said. The attendees were all looking at her, and a few nodded in agreement.

"This is a roundtable; I will get the conversation going, but we are all just going to talk about everything and anything you want to. Pooling our thoughts can only help better prepare all of you for this… adventure." She seemed uncomfortable using that word to describe the enormous tasks set out before them, but most of them laughed a little, and she relaxed.

"Fear, I think, will be a large part of your lives going forward. Does anyone want to talk about any fears you've had upon deciding to accept the role of envoy?"

No one said anything at first, but then Eric Thomas, from the cafeteria, spoke. "I feel a little dumb saying this, because of everything that we will have to do… this one seems the easiest because we do it here all the time. Maybe because it's the first thing that we will have to do? Anyway, I'm a little afraid of the launch. No one here has ever left Osa, so that's a little nerve-wracking for me." There was no laughter.

"Is anyone else apprehensive about the launch?" Dr. Paige inquired.

A dark-haired man, and the youngest of the group at only nineteen years old, Kyle Gellar, spoke up, "I'm not really concerned about the launch as much as I am traveling through the solar system and interstellar space. I'm afraid that at some point in the journey I'm going to smash into something out there that we didn't plan for."

A few of the other guys nodded, but Joe spoke up. "Compared to the space we'll be moving through, there is nothing out there to hit. Statistically, any of us hitting anything? We'd have a better chance of winning the lottery ten days in a row. Except for hitting all the trash orbiting Osa, that is," Joe said. There was a flutter of laughter.

"No," Garrett once again spoke the word without preparing to talk. It was a topic he knew about, and he spoke up reflexively. "There's a launch window. No satellites. No trash. Nothing," he said. They were all looking at him and no one said anything, waiting for him to continue.

"My mother is an astrophysicist. These are the conversations we had at the dinner table when I was growing up," Garrett said.

Joe looked puzzled and asked, "Everything orbits at different speeds. How is it possible to keep a 'window' open?" Garrett laughed to himself and looked down at the table.

"LWMDs. Launch Window Maintenance Drones," he said and looked back up at Joe. "They aren't drones, though, they're satellites themselves. They all have solid fuel packs and eventually run out and have to fly back to the surface to be refueled. But there are about a dozen launched each year for that purpose alone." He looked around to find the group still staring at him.

"Well, I'll be damned. I never heard of such a thing," Joe said, and looked at Dr. Paige. The others followed suit.

"That's fascinating, Mr. Rhodes. Does anyone else have questions about the launch window?" No one said anything right away, so Joe took the opportunity.

"I think I have a lot more questions about it, especially why they use solid fuel," he said. Garrett smiled. "But none on topic for the psych roundtable. Garrett and I had lunch together, though, and I'd be mad at myself if I didn't bring up a topic that we started without all of you. He asked me what I thought I would do at the end, after the fifth." Dr. Paige frowned, confused, but everyone else was nodding. Joe, pleased with himself, sat back to hear what others had to say on the topic.

"I plan to just finish life on the fifth. I can tell you I have no desire to die on the Lance—none. I want to die in a cabin, by a lake, breathing fresh air." It was Phillip Jonas speaking, which surprised a few of them because he was an alternate. Position eleven. He was a small man of twenty-two years, with a copper complexion and jet-black hair in a flattop. "My job will be done at that point. If I make it that far, I'm going to want to relax." A ruffle of laughter and a few guys said "yeah." By that point, Dr. Paige had caught on to what "after the fifth" meant.

"That's a pretty big jump from being concerned about the launch, Mr. Burkman," Dr. Paige said. She had been writing notes until then but put her pen down. "I suppose it's something you're all thinking about, though, so who else wants to talk about their plan for after it's over?"

A tall, slender young man who had a sharp jawline and light blonde hair bordering on white leaned forward. "I can't say I know for sure what I will do on the fifth," said Randy Vila, position six. "But I know I'm going to have a transport built." A few of the others nodded. "It depends what happens there. If I like it, depending on the conditions once the Lance is gone. But one thing is for sure: I agree with Phil. I will not be *on* the Lance," Randy said. More nodding.

"I don't want to sound naïve. I've spent a great deal of time being briefed on the details of these missions, but I feel like they did not provide me with much of the nomenclature associated with it. That said, a few of you have referenced the 'Lance?'" Dr. Paige inquired.

"They don't exist yet. The Lance is a design plan for the interstellar vessels that we all have to commission on each planet we visit. The ships that will take the marks to Orris," Randy said. Dr. Paige nodded.

"I do, actually, plan on boarding the Lance on the fifth." It was Tom Holly. "I think I want my remains to end up on Orris."

"I had that thought, too," Garrett added.

"What about you, Mr. Burkman?" Dr. Paige asked. "You asked the question, but you haven't given your plan yet."

Joe stirred, still sitting back in his chair. "Yes, forgive me, but my view is a bit," he paused, and looked up at Garrett, "pessimistic."

"You don't think you'll make it that far?" she asked.

"No," Joe said. His attitude then brightened. "But hey, if I do, then I'll happily admit I was wrong and figure out what I'm going to do then."

5

The next morning at ten, the envoys and Dr. Paige took their seats in the dark conference room with Arthur Sterritt. He was opening the blinds to let the daylight in, and there was a whiteboard set up behind his chair. The addition of bright light revealed powder blue walls and multiple chalkboards containing everything from advanced chemistry to grocery lists.

"I want to start by apologizing for how yesterday's meeting ended," Arthur said with his back to the group, still opening the blinds. "To say I'm fundamentally torn on this project would be exactly accurate." He turned to the group and sat down in his chair. "There are times that I'm excited to be a part of it and others that I'm fearful for your wellbeing." He stopped and stared off into the distance.

"There can be no great achievement without great risk. You of all people know that, Arthur," Garrett said, seeking to ease the tension he had helped create the day before.

"Yes, Mr. Rhodes," Arthur was smiling uncomfortably. "But I find it much easier to stomach when that risk is on my shoulders alone."

"We're an extension of you, Arthur," Garrett said. "We are eleven grown men who have accepted extreme jobs with extreme risks, fully aware of what those risks are." Every envoy was nodding in agreement. "You were the first to take that risk, but it would all be for nothing now if we didn't risk our lives in turn to get our marks." Dr. Paige looked around, but all eyes were on Garrett. "The marks all have to give up their lives and risk everything, even their children's lives, to get to Orris. And Orris," Garrett sat back in his chair. "The entire population will risk everything when they make the move to beat the collapse. The Orris Project is nothing but risk after risk after risk, and to what end? Life beating a universal cycle for the first time since time began. You are the architect, Arthur. Your risk was only the first. But without it," Garrett gestured to the rest of the group, "none of this would be possible." He pointed toward the ceiling. "None of that would be possible." No one misunderstood. Garrett was pointing at the sky and not the ceiling, an obvious reference to Orris under construction in Osa's orbit.

Arthur was nodding. "I understand, Mr. Rhodes. But it's a heavy thing on a man's conscience. An architect of achievement or an architect of death? It's my conundrum," he folded his hands in his lap.

"Everyone dies, Arthur. Eventually," Garrett said and nodded toward the whiteboard. "What's that?"

"Ah, yes!" Arthur stood and walked around to the whiteboard behind his chair. "This is the dosing guide. I want to go through it with all of you so you understand how to measure and administer, but more importantly, how to read the guide."

After going through the details of the prescription placard and how to read it, and then how to administer the prescription itself, Arthur asked if there were questions.

"What happens if you swallow some of it?" asked Ken Chase, position nine, and the one Arthur had suggested might fall through a floor.

"It would be a problem only in the respect that any of the liquid that made it to your stomach would mix with gastric juice, stomach acid. It would be chemically altered and rendered inert. So, if your plan was five hundred years and ten percent of the liquid made it to your stomach,"

"Four hundred and fifty years, got it," Ken finished, then frowned. "On that topic, Arthur, cellular activity is suspended, but I can't imagine chemical activity would be. Will we all wake up with horrible ulcers?"

Arthur chuckled. "No, no, Mr. Chase. You're right to say that Sterilex does not suspend chemical activity, but it stops your parietal cells, which make the acid. Any residual acid in your stomach will naturally neutralize in your stomach lining over time, but not so badly that it would cause an ulcer. Excellent question, Mr. Chase."

Garrett was staring at the whiteboard with a question forming in his mind. He was about to ask, when Jonroe Daniels, position four and an athletic but short man with longer than average black hair, asked the exact same one.

"What about our skin, Arthur? What happens if some liquid gets on our skin? Say, when we have no intention of going under." Arthur raised his eyebrows and looked from person to person, each eager to hear the answer.

"How devious, Mr. Daniels," he said. The envoys focused on Sterritt, but Dr. Paige looked perplexed. "The answer is yes, gentlemen, to the question that you did not ask, not directly anyway. Christine, I'm afraid this one might be a bit uncomfortable for you, but these gentlemen were asking if they can use Sterilex as a weapon."

Dr. Paige shifted in her seat. "Can you explain what you mean?" she asked. The envoys grew uncomfortable, embarrassed by what they understood to be a potential necessity, but nonetheless, a horrible act.

"I warn you, it is very unpleasant," Arthur said. She nodded as if to say, "go on." "If I were to see that a tiny droplet of Sterilex came into contact with your skin, you would feel tired shortly after the contact. You would then lie down wherever you were, because you would not have the strength to support yourself. And you would die. In most civilized societies, they would bury you. Unfortunately, if it were a truly advanced society, and they did an autopsy and went through an embalming process, that would be it, dead forever. Also, unfortunately, if it were not so advanced, you would wake up buried, just in time to suffocate and die all over again, this time from asphyxiation."

Dr. Paige lowered her gaze, then stood up and said, "Excuse me," and walked out.

"Gentlemen, if you have any other questions that you may deem unsavory, now is the time to discuss them." Arthur looked around the room for a moment.

"The marks. These people will undoubtedly have completely different DNA than us. Can we expect that Sterilex will work the same way?" Joe asked.

"Yes," Arthur said. "First, the DNA of these marks, I think it will surprise you to find, will be remarkably similar to ours. But more importantly, the basic mechanics of Sterilex are very simple. It's had the exact same effect on every species of animal my team has experimented with, from rodents and flowers to bacteria and fungus. There was only one exception. Viruses. It kills viruses permanently."

"That could be useful," Stan Richman added.

"Yes, my team is working on it now."

"What about the autopsy? Could a death by Sterilex be traced back to us?" Stan asked.

"It's hard to say, but I would lean towards 'no,'" Arthur said. "It will be the first thing tested for here on Osa and on Orris once Orris is populated, but I imagine elsewhere they would only find things they were looking for. Sterilex has nothing close to the signature of any poison, and if they detected it, they would have no way of knowing what it was or what it did. I never want to say anything for sure, but my guess would be that these cases would likely be deemed natural, cardiac arrest or something of that sort."

6

Mercy Daniels sat at her kitchen table, still in her nightgown, even though it was an hour past lunchtime. She had eaten nothing since breakfast and was staring at the kitchen table, which was empty except for a wooden basket containing paper napkins, and six bottles of prescription pills. They were her pills, and she had promised Jonroe she would take them when he left their modest apartment six hours before. She had not moved from the chair in those six hours. Her hands were kneading each other in her lap, and her eyes were staring at the front door to the apartment, wet with tears.

Mercy was a widow of seven years and had only one child. Her son was her entire world, and he was preparing to leave her forever. Leave her with nothing. He had no children of his own, not even a girlfriend, and he said his job was going to send him away for a long time. He assured her the Orris Project would take care of her, but it was not a comfort for Mercy.

Her prescription bottles stared at her like she was a criminal. She had *promised* Jonroe she would take them, two for blood pressure, one for cholesterol, and the other three were a cocktail that her therapist had come up with to treat her depression and anxiety. She had been taking the cocktail since her husband, big Jon, had died from a pulmonary embolism he suffered after slipping in the shower and breaking three ribs on the edge of the tub. The doctors said he had a lot of blood clots and that the fall and subsequent injury had freed one of them and it traveled to his lung and killed him. Mercy did not believe them. Jonroe Senior had worked in the launch facility for a company subcontracted by the government called Delman Rail Works for his entire adult life. Although the last job he held before passing was head of maintenance, Mercy believed he had died from radiation poisoning. Both Jonroe Senior and Junior assured her there was nothing radioactive at the launch facility at least a hundred times, but there was no convincing her. After all, space travel involved a lot of radiation, and where did all space travel start? The launch facility.

She slapped the six bottles off the table and sobbed. After thirty seconds, she calmed down and walked to the balcony of their apartment. She stepped up onto a chair that stood next to the railing and stared down at the street below. It seemed a simple enough answer, a conclusive answer. It would solve every one of her problems, and the awful feeling of dread that coursed through her veins and pressed into her bones would disappear. She bent at the waist and gripped the railing so hard that the color drained from both hands. After several minutes, she stepped down from the chair and relaxed her grip on the railing. She breathed deeply and slowly and thought, *I need a glass of wine.*

7

The envoys were collecting their things and exiting the room after their meeting with Arthur Sterritt had concluded, but Garrett stayed back, waiting for the others to leave. He asked Arthur if he had a minute to talk privately, to which Arthur nodded. "Of course, Garrett. What's on your mind?"

"It's not a serious question, but it's one I haven't been able to get over. And I certainly wasn't going to ask in front of the others. I didn't think it was appropriate."

Arthur grinned. "Can I guess what the question is before you ask it?" he asked. Garrett nodded. "You want to know why it is not 'Dr. Sterritt?'"

Garrett laughed. "Yes! That's exactly it! You're brilliant. Yes, it seems silly to call you *Mr.* Sterritt."

Arthur smiled. "It's simple, Garrett. I'm a businessman, not an academic. I couldn't wait to finish with school. As soon as I got my degree, I left school forever. I started my company three days after that and set up Sterritt Compounds Incorporated in my father's garage, which he graciously allowed me to use. At least, he let me use the back wall to set up my 'glass factory,' as he called it. I suppose if you're not a chemist, all of that glassware just looks like a lot of bottles and jars."

"How did you come up with the idea for Sterilex?" Garrett asked. It fascinated him. He had wanted to know the story of Sterilex since he first heard what it could do, but he was not sure if he should ask in the group setting.

"What it does, or what I had intended for it to do when I theorized the compound?" Arthur asked. Garrett turned his palms up and raised his eyebrows. He wanted to know it all.

"Right," Arthur laughed. "Well, it was originally supposed to be a marker to identify cells that were cancerous. It did not do that at all, as I discovered when testing it on mice. It simply killed them all. Or so I thought. My next task was to figure out what dose was lethal to the mice. I found that any dose was lethal, except during the last round. The mouse with the smallest dose—and when I say smallest, Mr. Rhodes, I mean microscopic doses— woke up after two days." Arthur sat back down.

"Wouldn't you incinerate the dead mice after discovering that they had died? Or do an autopsy?" Garrett asked.

Arthur's face brightened. "Yes, we did autopsies on the first dozen but could not find a cause of death. So, we labeled them all as 'cardiac arrest,' not because we didn't know what killed them, but because we could find no affected organ or damaged tissue."

"So, how did you know not to incinerate the last of the test subjects?" Garrett asked, wondering if it had been sloppy practices or if it was just dumb…

"Luck," Arthur said. "We administered the doses to the last six mice in the trial on a Friday. When I got to the lab on Monday morning, they were all still dead. I got my coffee, started my paperwork, and when I went back to the mice, the one that had received the smallest dose was breathing! The second smallest dose, and I'm talking a difference of a nanogram here, woke up three hours later. By the next day, all six were alive and well and living normal mouse lives. Like magic," Arthur finished. He had an enormous smile on his face. Garrett said nothing, just stared off into the distance and shook his head in slow, short arcs.

"Your next question is 'How long did you study it before giving it to yourself?' And that answer is eight years," Arthur said. "The first time, I went down for two days, then I went down for two months, but they didn't write about those in the news. My mother had passed away when I was fourteen from skin cancer. I was not married, no children, nor did I have a love interest. While I was under for the two-month stint, my father had a stroke, a bad one. It killed him."

"That's when you decided to jump?" Garrett asked.

"Yes, I had no one left, and thanks to a few other projects we had going, my company was making money. I promoted my number two to number one and went down for a hundred and fifty years."

"That's an amazing story, Arthur. You should tell the rest of the group."

Arthur smiled and stood up. "I will, in one of our meetings. I'll go over the birth of this substance that everyone will rely on so heavily. It's only fair they know where it came from. Anyway, I think it's time for lunch."

8

That evening, Jonroe Daniels unlocked the door to the apartment he shared with his mother to find prescription pill bottles scattered on the kitchen floor beside an empty wine bottle. Alarm rose in his mind as he recognized the items for what they were and what it could mean. He charged into the apartment in search of his mother. He walked through their unused dining room and into the only bathroom first, which was empty, and circled through his mother's empty bedroom to the living room. With no sign of her, Jonroe was on his way to his own bedroom when he registered movement through the glass doors that led to the balcony. Although it was dark, his mother was still wearing the same white nightgown she'd had on earlier that morning. She was standing on a chair near the edge, with her weight on her back foot on the chair and her other foot resting on the balcony railing. She had another wine bottle in her hand, and she lifted it to her lips. Jonroe understood how badly the depression was affecting his mother, and it had crossed his mind that she could become or even had become suicidal. He was careful to keep track of her medication and how she administered it. That morning, he was running late and asked his mother to take her pills. She seemed like she was in a good mood and was eating her breakfast. "I'll take them as soon as I finish eating, Jon, I promise," she had said. "Now, you get going, you're already late!"

Their apartment was on the twenty-eighth floor of the building, and his mother was one strong breeze away from taking the fastest trip down possible. She was swaying so much that Jonroe did not think he could get to her in time. He ran to the double doors but opened them gently and did not call out, not wanting to startle her. His plan was to grab her before she even knew he was there.

"Hi Jon, please go back inside. I'm…" but she trailed off. She turned to him. Her head dipped and her eyes closed. Jonroe was immediately in motion. She fell backward over the railing as Jonroe reached for her and wrapped both of his arms around her waist. With all his strength, he pulled to get her back up. Jonroe was a strong young man, but he had no way of knowing that most of the wine had spilled onto the smooth tile floor of the balcony. Both of his feet slipped out from underneath him, and physics took over.

9

Garrett walked into the OPM building at 8:42 the next morning. A somber Dr. Christine Paige and two other envoys greeted him as soon as he was through the double doors. His pace slowed and his brow furrowed. He did not wish them a good morning.

"What's wrong?" Garrett asked. He was looking at Dr. Paige.

"Jonroe, um, Daniels," she said, "We lost Jonroe. He passed away last night. He and his mother." Tears were running down Dr. Paige's cheeks. She covered her face with both of her hands. Garrett looked to the other two in the group and raised his eyebrows. Ken Chase and Stan Richman exchanged a glance.

"They think it was an accident. The two of them fell from their apartment balcony. It was not survivable," Ken said.

Garrett noticed the other envoys filtering in. He turned back to Ken. "Does Terry know yet?"

Ken shrugged. "I don't know how he could. They didn't release the names of the two victims yet. We only know because once he was identified, the authorities thought it best that OPM be notified immediately." Terence Stone, position ten and first alternate in the event of a position opening in Group 1, walked in at just that moment. Although younger, he was the only envoy taller than Tom Holly, and he had the same light blonde hair but wore it slightly longer and combed fiercely to one side.

"What's going on?" he asked. Dr. Paige put a hand on his elbow.

"Please follow me up to my office, Terry. We have a lot to discuss." The two walked over to the elevator bay. The rest of the envoys were discussing the situation amongst themselves, and Joe looked up at Garrett.

"What is this going to mean for us?" Joe asked.

Garrett looked at him with a humorless expression. "I don't think it will mean much for us, but Terry just lost a whole year on Osa," Garrett said.

Joe's eyes grew wide. "That's right! I hadn't even thought about that. I was thinking about the launch order. They'll have to shift it all around, at least the back half. We just got bumped, buddy."

Garrett was nodding, but he had not thought about it until Joe brought it up. Before this tragedy, the launch order put Garrett last and Joe second to last. It was only a loss of four days, but a day to spend with your family was important.

Garrett felt a hand on his shoulder and turned to find Dr. Alex Murray. "Hey guys, horrible news." He stood, shaking his head. "Have I missed Dr. Paige and Mr. Stone?"

"They got on the elevator a few minutes ago," Garrett said.

"Thanks guys, keep your heads up." He turned to walk to the elevator bay.

"Hey, Alex?" Joe said, stepping around Garrett. "Do you know how this affects the order?"

Dr. Murray nodded, "Sure, the protocol in place will slide Tom into Jonroe's spot, you'll go into Tom's, and Garrett into yours. Terry will launch last." He raised his eyebrows and nodded as if to say "okay?" Then he walked off to the elevator bay.

Joe turned back to Garrett with a solemn look. "Did you know him well? I got to know him over the last two weeks. He told me about his mother. Poor woman, he said she had a lot of mental health problems, that he was worried about her. He even said he might have to quit the program," Joe said.

Garrett shook his head. "Horrible. Come on, I'll buy you a cup of coffee."

10

Nine hours later, Dr. Christine Paige unlocked and walked into her empty apartment. She was still happily married to her husband of thirty-seven years, but Roger was an ambitious man, and even though she thought him crazy for it, at sixty-six years old he was orbiting the planet, working on Orris. "There's no way that thing can exist in my lifetime, and I don't at least put my hands on it..." Roger had said. He promised to retire for good when he returned eleven months from then. She was sixty-one herself and had told Alex Murray she would give him three more years. The moment the twenty-seventh envoy escaped the atmosphere, she would be retired, officially. Alex had agreed with thanks.

It had been an empty nest for the last fifteen years; they had two children, the storybook boy and girl. Their son was a physics teacher at a high school about an hour from her apartment. Ever the daddy's girl, their daughter was with her father in orbit around Osa, also helping to build Orris.

The day's events had torn her limb from limb. She offloaded her bag, keys, and jacket onto the kitchen counter and pulled the whiskey out of the liquor cabinet. It had become a daily ritual with Roger and Marti in space. She had gone from one drink on hard days to three or four, and without her family, they were all hard days. She had a call scheduled with them that evening and she looked forward to it, but she smiled knowing she had a little time to unwind first.

She was on the couch with her third drink when the large screen in the living room lit up with the Orris logo. Small numbers in the lower left-hand corner displayed the countdown until the connection would become live. Seventeen seconds. She got up and, with only a little stumbling, made her way into the kitchen and dropped the empty glass in the sink. She walked back to the couch and put on her "everything is fine" smile and waited. Her daughter's face filled the screen a second later, with her hair going off in every direction. "Hi Mom!" she said. Christine could hear her husband's voice faintly in the background, and Marti said, "Dad's here too!" She backed up and Christine could see them both.

"How are things down on Osa?" Roger asked. She went through the events of the day with them. The alcohol made it easier.

Chapter 5

Clotz Farm

1

It took a long time to come back from a three-billion-year stint, and like on Telraed, the Envoy could not believe he was still alive. He was again mind-locked, with no senses at all. In his darkness, he walked through the fields of Distria, his first mission planet, as the first thirty minutes there before they picked him up were so peaceful and pleasant.

From there, he went back to the tidal islands on early Earth. He laid on his back, watching the meteorites flash across the sky and letting the waves lap against his feet and up to his thighs. It had been a pleasant experience, despite his hunger and general fatigue.

After that, his mind went to Rhett, the second mission planet. He had a small cabin on Donner Lake and had built a short dock for fishing. There was always time to kill between commissioning the Lance and the actual building project. The Envoy would only jump when he was positive the project was on track and that the builders understood how to interpret the instructions. The Donner Lake fishing and game commission stocked the lake with only four different species of fish, and he usually…

Genuine alarm rose in his mind when he first felt the muscles in his chest moving. It was not like the previous times; they were straining. He felt his diaphragm relax and then snap into a hard rock, attempting to force the air out of his lungs. *There's nothing you can do until you can move*, he thought. *Stay calm*. His heart was racing. The feeling was coming back to his arms and legs, and he could feel something surrounding him; not everywhere, but pressing in multiple places along each limb, and on his back and his gut and chest. He could feel a slight pressure on the back of his head, but not at all on his face. *Don't jump to conclusions*, his mind said, but he could not help believing time had buried him.

His sense of smell had come back. Soil. Not just soil, but damp soil, rich with organic matter. He was there; he had made the big jump, and he was alive. His chest still heaved; his heart still pounded. He tried to move and found that while he had some range of motion, it was extremely limited and painful. His left hand was up by his face, and his right was down at his side. He could hear his breathing, and it was as labored as he thought. He tried to reach up above his head with his left hand and was able. The action took some time, as he passed out twice from the pain during the effort. His hand finally poked out of the blanket roll and crashed into loose soil, but it was not just loose, it was cold. He had been buried alive, as he suspected. *I can't be deep if it's that cold*, he thought. He continued with the fingers of his left hand and used the small amount of energy he had to scratch and claw at the near-frozen soil. He could feel it tumbling down around his wrist, and as he dug, he noticed that it got colder and colder, almost frozen solid. The evil touch of what could only be a droplet of recently melted snow tracked its way down the underside of his forearm. He paused and felt around with fingertips that were becoming numb. He was touching snow, not soil. As he recognized the feeling, he could feel something else on the back of his fingers: a breeze. He quickly pulled his arm back into the blanket roll and turned his face up to the opening. Pain flooded each of his bones and his joints were in agony; but the cold, beautiful, oxygen-heavy air coated his face. He breathed deeply. It was the first satisfying breath he had taken since leaving Telraed.

He laid there breathing in the exquisite air until his nose was numb with the cold. He had more energy than he did the last time he woke up on Earth. A lot of oxygen goes a long way. He opened the bottle of water leaning on his chest and drank the whole thing. The global itch on his skin was rearing its ugly head, and drinking the water could not have been timed more perfectly.

The Envoy did not want to freeze to death, but he also needed oxygen and wanted to be freed from the cocoon of his blanket. Twisting in place, he was able to loosen the blanket, which was all he was hoping to achieve. He pulled it down around his chest, and the cold air pooled around his head and shoulders. The cold was uncomfortable, but the oxygen it brought with it was so welcome, he could not help but smile. He had left his bag six inches from his face and could easily access it. The pain was intoxicating, and he knew one bottle of water would not be enough. He drank one and a half more bottles before the cold and the pain were too much to bear. He took cover once again under the blanket, but not before cycling in the cold, oxygen-heavy air to mix with the warm, stale air of the blanket. Once he was back under cover, he closed his eyes, breathed deeply, smiled, and slept.

2

The Envoy woke up feeling better than he had since arriving on Earth. He was starving, but he had energy and his spirits were high. There was no sign of joint pain, and the itch on his skin was mild. He emerged from his blanket and smiled at the dim daylight beaming in from the fist-sized hole. He reached into his bag and pulled out the food he had left. There was not a lot, but he thought this might not have such dire consequences at this point. He tore open a packet and chewed the old meat. It tasted like nothing and broke apart in his mouth quickly, having lost its original toughness. It was like eating bland powder. He relaxed again and waited for the energy to come. It took almost an hour, but eventually his muscles became jittery and he only wanted to move.

He pushed his bag down close to his waist, which was as far as it would go. There were roots all around him mixed with the loose soil, and he imagined his bag had pinned itself against one of these. Reaching up with both hands, he scraped the soil away from the opening, enlarging it. He used the place where his bag had been as a staging area for the displaced soil. Once he felt his rib cage could pass through, he kicked and pulled and birthed himself from the Earth.

3

The Envoy shivered as he stood on the surface in three inches of snow. Sparse evergreens stood in every direction. He surveyed his surroundings, amazed at what time could do. The plateau was gone. Wind erosion, water erosion, or geologic activity, something had destroyed it, transforming his prison cell into a pocket within the soil of the new world.

He reached into the hole for his blanket, thrilled when it got stuck. His bag had come with it and pinched the blanket in the hole. With a firm grip, he yanked and freed them from the potential grave. He kneeled down in the snow once the blanket was around him, satchel around his neck, bag on his back. He placed his right hand in the hole. "Thank you." A tear rolled down his cheek. He could not believe he was still alive.

He observed the trees to get his bearings and turned south to escape the cold. The snow was a blessing, as it recorded tracks, and he could get an idea about the size of the wildlife he may have to contend with. After two hours, he saw only the markings left by small game.

He reached an open meadow of frozen wild grasses and got his first full look at the sky. He was astonished to see the crescent moon in the clear blue, but so small. So far away. "We're going to lose you," the Envoy said to the white hook floating above the tree line. He frowned and continued walking.

The path he chose bisected the meadow, and he was back into the trees when he smelled smoke. It was a fantastic smell. He pressed forward through the wooded area on a mild declining grade. As he approached the base, the trees were thinning, and he could make out a patchwork of sky. Through one of the canopy windows, he saw a thread of black rising. He adjusted course.

4

As the Envoy came upon the source of the smoke, he smiled. The marks were not yet in any advanced technological stage based on the humble farmstead that stood before him, but at least they were out of the caves. Surrounding a dozen pens that contained a variety of livestock were three buildings. He could see a dwelling to his left, a barn directly in front of him, and one other enormous building to his right with no obvious purpose except that it had a water wheel fixed to the narrow side. The water wheel was curious, as the Envoy could see no waterway anywhere close to it. The pens were square but organized in a rectangle, four wide and three deep. Large and small grazing animals wandered lazily in a huge, fenced-in field behind the barn, always searching for the next mouthful of grass. There were signs of agricultural activity, including wagons, plows, rakes, shovels, pitchforks, sickles, and hoes.

He heard footfalls to his left, but before he could even turn to look, they stopped and ran in the other direction. It was a young boy of nine or ten years old; a young boy who had spotted him. In his best effort to appear as nonthreatening as possible, he laid his gear on the ground, including his blanket, and waited for whoever the boy was running to.

5

"The wood needs to be split and stacked, all of it, before it freezes. The pigs need more hay in the pen and that gate needs to be fixed." Luca Clotz finished his lunch and wiped the crumbs out of his dark beard. He was speaking to his eldest son, Mateo. "I need you to brew the next batch as well, but I think you will not have enough time today."

"I don't think I'll have enough time to split all the wood. We had a great haul this morning. Three loads? A lot to split in one afternoon," Mateo said, concerned. "Can't you go to Udine tomorrow?"

His father laughed. "Mateo, we have no empty barrels. This is good, it means everything is full or moving, but if we stop, we could lose our position in Udine. And when you consider how much we lose already, we have to go as fast as we can, or someone else will."

"I understand, father. I will do my best to get everything done," Mateo said.

"Not just you, use your brother for whatever you can. I'll tell him before I leave that he is to do…" At that moment, the door of the kitchen crashed open and Marco, Mateo's younger brother, was standing in the doorway trying to catch his breath so he could speak.

"A man," Marco was still breathing hard. "A man in the woods."

Luca stood and grabbed his younger son by the shoulders. "What are you saying, Marco? What man?" Mateo stood and picked up the knife they had used to cut the pork they ate for lunch. Marco had regained his breath enough to talk.

"I was going to see if I could find any berries we hadn't picked yet. But before I got far, I saw a man in the woods, just standing there, staring at our farm!" Marco said.

Knife in hand, Mateo strode through the house and out the front door before his father could stop him.

"Marco, get the sickle, or the pitchfork. Get both and come meet us up on the hill," Luca said. Marco was nodding and bolted out the front door.

When Luca was Mateo's age, he had spent six years as a soldier, and he still had his sword. The army issued weapons to most of the infantry, but Luca's family had money. He had his sword made by a blacksmith who was also a friend of the family. Because he went to the army with his sword in hand, he left with it, and it was leaned up in its scabbard in the corner of the bedroom he shared with his wife. His wife was in the bedroom mending the hem of one of the girls' dresses when he walked in.

"Elisa, get the girls and go down to the cellar. Now." His wife looked alarmed but did not argue or ask questions.

"Bria, Luna! Come to me right now!" she said. Luca heard the laughing in the girls' room stop, pulled his sword from its sheath, and walked out the front door.

Once out of the house, Luca spotted the place where Mateo stood, brandishing his kitchen knife in front of what looked like… a man? Barely a man, more like a skeleton wrapped in tight skin. He had a thick beard, and his hair was long and dirty. The man was kneeling in front of Mateo with his arms spread out to his sides, fingers splayed, palms up. He was naked from the waist up, the easiest way to communicate that he was starving, literally on the brink of death.

6

The Envoy saw the young man approaching with something in his hand, probably a weapon, and felt it would be important to make sure the young man knew that he meant no harm. He stripped off his shirt, fell to his knees, and put his arms out to either side, palms up. No weapons. No threat. *Look at me, I'm dying. Please don't hurt me.* The fit young man with the curly black hair slowed his pace at the sight but kept approaching. The Envoy waited for the words that he would not understand.

"Quis tu, quid agis?" The young man looked angry, not scared. The only thing the Envoy knew of that would immediately communicate the language barrier was to talk to him in his native Osan language.

"I don't understand your language. I am hungry. I will work." The young man flinched, as if he expected to be able to communicate. An older man, bald but with a thick beard, joined them.

"Quid vis? Cibum?" the elder asked the younger.

The young man answered loudly. "Nescio quid cupit; sed si non impetro off terram nostram i et jugulatus!" In the older man's right hand was a sword, slack and at his side. He reached his left hand gently out to his son's, which bore the knife.

"Advena exiges civem ferro fili," he spoke softly. His son dropped the blade to his side and slowed his breathing. The father looked at the Envoy again and spoke, but made an eating motion with his free hand, down and up to his mouth, back down and back up to his mouth. "Vos volo manducare?" The Envoy understood at once and tried to communicate without using words. He placed both of his open hands over his face and bowed to the men, nodding.

The father grabbed one of the Envoy's bony elbows and led him down to the water-wheel building. The young boy, the one who had discovered him, ran up holding two farming tools and the father yelled to him with what sounded like instructions.

"Marco, et vade in domum aliquam panem et carnes porcinas, aliquam faba quoque. Educ illos ad bracino." The young boy turned at once and ran awkwardly back to the house, dropping the two farming tools as he went.

There were two large doors on the broadside of the waterwheel building facing the courtyard of the farm. The men led him through a smaller, man-sized door on the wheel side that faced the forest and into a dimly lit space that caught the Envoy off guard. It was a brewery or a distillery. He could smell it as soon as he breached the door jamb. Sweet smelling grain and what smelled like a thousand intermingled herbs and spices and an after-note tang of alcohol. Just inside the door was a rough wooden table and two benches, large enough for six adults. They let go of him and pointed to it. The Envoy sat, interlaced his fingers, and rested his hands on the table.

"Hic opperiri," the older man said, and the two left. The Envoy reached to his chest, relieved to feel the satchel. He waited for only three minutes before curiosity got the better of him and he got up to explore. Stacked barrels almost completely obscured the far narrow wall opposite the wheel. He spied the shaft coming through the wheel wall, but it appeared to drive nothing. A grand idea that never carried water. There were large metal kettles suspended on arched frameworks of wood and iron, with cold ash beneath them. A hundred different tools and jigs were scattered throughout the place. The back wall, the long one, had a string of tall bunkers with doors on them. *Grain*, the Envoy thought. He could hear whistling above his head and realized they fluted the roof ridge to let the smoke escape, but also noticed a second floor to half of the building. It was simple, a long floor that bordered the long back half of the building above the grain stores. It rested on an overkill of support posts, some enormous slabs of wood alternating with built up stone piles. The Envoy supposed the wooden runway could support a parade of cattle. *This is one of the most interesting places I've ever been in,* he thought, and that included a lot of technically advanced places on Osa. The door banged open, and he rushed back to his place at the table.

It was the young boy, with a mop of black hair that matched his older brother's. He had a pitcher in one hand and a basket in the other. He stopped once inside the door and spoke. "Ego cibum habeo ad te. Et non nocuerunt mihi placet!" He stood still, waiting for his eyes to adjust to the dark room.

7

Marco was nervous to enter the brewery housing the strange man without his father or brother. His father had told him the man would not hurt him; he was starving to death. He needed food badly. Marco kicked the door of the brewery open. He shouted into the brewery, "I have food for you. Please don't hurt me!" He waited for a reply while his eyes adjusted to the darkness. Nothing. He stepped into the building and let the door swing shut behind him. He could see the man hunkered down at the table and placed the basket and the carafe of water on the table.

The thin man looked at him and said, "Tapadh leat." He devoured the food: pork, bread, and beans. After he finished eating, he sipped the water and started crying.

"Tapadh leat, Tapadh leat." Marco had learned his first Osan words. He understood that the man was saying "Thank you."

When the man stopped crying and was wiping his eyes, Marco tried to communicate with him. "My name is Marco. What is your name?" The man looked confused, so Marco pointed at his own chest, "Marco," and then pointed to the man, who smiled, understanding.

"Tosgaire," he said. "Ach chan e sin m 'ainm ceart." Marco was more confused than ever. The man smiled, "Tosgaire." He touched his chest, and then reached out to the boy, "Marco." Marco smiled at the sound of his name from the exotic voice. He stood and walked deeper into the brewery. He turned and beckoned to the stranger. The man rose and followed him to the far side of the front wall, where there were two large, framed bookends that held stacked wood. Next to the far bookend was a heap of tarpaulins. Marco stopped and pointed at them.

"You can sleep here." Marco placed a hand against his ear and rocked his head to the side, briefly closing his eyes.

"Tapadh leat," the Envoy said, "Marco." He sat on the pile of cloth and laid back. Marco walked out of the brewery toward the voices of his brother and father outside the large doors.

"I'm off. Both of you mind our guest. But we need all this work done before dark. Marco, do as your brother instructs you to. He is in charge until I return. Do you understand?"

"Yes, sir," Marco answered.

"Mateo, the wood is the most important task. Leave Marco to tend the pigs and the pen. I'll be back after supper," Luca said and climbed aboard the wagon loaded with full barrels of ale. He clicked a signal to the two horses charged with pulling it, and the wagon creaking into motion.

"What do I have to do in the pen?" Marco asked his older brother.

"It's a mud pit. Spread hay down into the mud and make sure you use a lot. After that, you must figure out what's wrong with the gate. It shouldn't be so hard to close. And be careful. It snaps open hard."

"Okay. I know his name, he told me."

Mateo looked uninterested in the topic. "I don't care what his name is, I just want him gone. Now go tend to the pigs."

Disappointed, Marco dipped his head, and walked down to the barn.

8

Mateo kicked the woodpile, relieved to find it had not frozen. He walked to the big doors on the brewery's face, lifted the pin on the left one, and dragged it open. He had a bitterness about him because the task seemed impossible to complete before dark, and he did not want to disappoint his father. On top of it all, there was the beggar to deal with. Mateo slammed the door open and tore the axe from its hanging place on the inside panel. He walked to the pile and picked up a medium-sized log and brought it to the old oak stump they used as a chopping block. He stood the log up on the stump and swung the axe down, clean and hard, splitting it in one swing. Back to the woodpile, back to the stump, one swing, back to the woodpile. He had split only six logs when the beggar came outside. Mateo observed that the man still had no shirt on, only the small fabric bag on the curiously fine metal chain hanging around his neck. Frustrated, Mateo did not speak to the man because he would not understand him, so he tugged at his own shirt and pointed up to the hill. *Go get your shirt.* The man understood at once and walked off.

Mateo had finished splitting his tenth log when the eleventh appeared on the stump before him. The beggar stood there, fully clothed, with an empty right hand, which had contained the log now on the block, and another in his left. Mateo gasped, and at first meant to chase the beggar away, but thought better of it. He could use all the help he could get. He pointed to the ground next to the stump, and the beggar dropped the log and returned to the pile. With twenty logs split, Mateo began gathering the product of his labor off the ground and walking it into the brewery to stack it. The beggar did the same. When it was all stacked, they walked back out to the chopping block and saw Marco standing next to it. Before Mateo could say anything, Marco spoke.

"I can stack! You two split it all and I'll stack it! We'll be done way before dark! And then you can help me finish the pen and we'll still be done early!" Mateo inhaled, intending to tell his brother to get back down to the pen and do what he was told, but the simple logic of it won him over before he could get a word out.

"Okay, Marco. I like your plan. Can you keep up?" His young brother's face lit up.

"Yes!" Marco moved to the far side of the chopping block. After only fifteen minutes, they were already through almost a quarter of the wood. Mateo could not believe how fast it was going, but his arms and back were on fire from swinging the axe. While he stood stretching his muscles, the beggar walked up to him and tapped himself on the chest, then made an axe-swinging motion. Mateo held out the axe to the stranger.

One swing. Over and over again, one swing. He was just as skilled as Mateo at the task, and the man looked like he had one foot in the grave. After twenty minutes, the stranger had to swing twice to make it through the log, and the two brothers laughed. Mateo took the axe back, and the man gave it up happily, even smiling at the exchange.

They finished the whole pile in one hour, and the rack in the brewery was full, with a small stack in front that would not fit. The trio walked down to the pen, finished spreading the hay, and had the gate opening and closing smoothly and easily in only ten minutes. Mateo had a wide smile on his face.

"Well, this is a big problem!" he shouted. His brother frowned. "We have at least two hours of light left and nothing to do!" Marco laughed. "Father is concerned about the next brew. We don't have enough time to do it today, but let's go back up to the brewery and get everything set up so we can finish by lunch tomorrow. Then father can tell us what to do for the rest of the day." Marco nodded and ran back to the brewery. The stranger was standing still, smiling, not understanding anything, and Mateo motioned to follow him.

They spent the next two hours cleaning, weighing out ingredients, staging wood for the fire, and placing equipment. When they finished, Mateo took three wooden cups from a shelf near the table and walked over to a lone barrel near the back wall in the corner and filled them.

"Tosgaire," Marco said. The stranger flinched at his name. Marco beckoned him over to the table, and they both sat. Mateo placed a cup in front of each of them and sat himself.

"Drink up, boys." Mateo held his cup out in front of him. Marco and the stranger copied the gesture. "This turned out to be a great day." They all drank, and the brothers both laughed at the stranger's reaction to the beverage: pure joy. "That's right, friend, we make good ale here at Clotz's."

"When it isn't terrible," Marco added, and both brothers laughed again. Mateo finished his ale and gathered the cups to go back to the barrel.

"Marco, go up to the house and fetch us all some supper. Our guest should have company while he eats. And bring back a few candles. We're losing light fast and I think we have none in this place," Mateo said. Marco stood up at once and turned to leave. "Marco?" Mateo stopped his brother, who looked at him. "How do you say his name?"

"*Toss-geh-deh*," He separated every syllable, "and try to get him talking in his language, it's funny sounding." Marco disappeared out the door.

9

Marco brought back three candles, a loaf of bread, and enough pork and potato stew for six men. He also brought an empty pitcher, which they filled with Clotz Ale. They ate and drank, and instead of having the normal conversations of people meeting for the first time, they passed the time holding up objects and pronouncing them in their native tongues. Mateo stuck a finger into his ale and pointed to the drop forming on his fingertip…

"Cervisia," Mateo said.

The stranger did the same. "Lionn," he said.

Marco tapped the table with one finger. "Mensa."

The stranger surprised them by slapping his hand down on the table and exclaiming, "Bòrd!" They all laughed.

After fifteen minutes, Luca walked in, grabbed a cup off the shelf, and poured himself an ale. He sat down next to the stranger and drank half the cup.

"So, how did it go?" Luca asked. Mateo ran down the details of the day, and his father looked pleased. "Very good, Mateo. I knew you would manage this well. You will do well as the head of this operation when I'm gone. And thank you too, Marco, and you," he gestured toward the stranger. Marco told his father how to say the name.

"So, father," Mateo asked, "How was your trip to Udine?" Luca tore off a chunk of bread and dipped it into his stew. Once he swallowed, he finished his beer and refilled his cup.

"I guess that depends on how you view our current situation," Luca said. "I delivered fifteen barrels. I received orders for another fifty-eight. That part is fine. We have one hundred and fifteen ready. But I have to deliver thirty-five more this week, and I only brought back eight empty barrels." He looked from son to son. "I should have had fourteen, so those buffoons broke or 'lost' six of our barrels. This is a problem."

"You already have an order in with Monteprato for more barrels, father?" Mateo asked.

"Yes," Luca spoke between mouthfuls of food. "Forty more, but they won't be ready until the end of next week, and at this rate I'll have to order forty more when he delivers."

10

It was still dark when Mateo came into the brewery the following morning. Dark, but the birds were chirping, forecasting the sunrise. "Tosgaire," he said as he came through the door. "Surgere: nos autem ut incipiat." He walked to the large doors, which he must have unlatched before entering the building, because he simply pushed and they both opened easily. Marco walked into the building as the Envoy was putting on his shirt. Mateo loaded wood from the pre-stacked pile into the fire pit but paused and turned to Marco. "Marco, tollant plaustra iumentaque adfer aquam et octo dolia." He turned back to the fire pit and continued his project. Marco ran to the far wall and rolled a barrel out of the colossal building. The Envoy retrieved his own barrel and rolled it out. Mateo looked up from the fire pit and smiled, confirming it was the correct response. Marco was struggling to get the barrel up into the wagon, and the Envoy dropped his own and helped push it up. He then swung his own on board the wagon. They repeated the procedure three more times, and Marco climbed aboard.

"Tosgaire, veni mecum ego postulo vestri auxilium," Marco said. He tapped the bench next to where he was sitting with an open hand to better communicate his request. The Envoy understood and climbed aboard. He was excited. Back on Osa, he had been an amateur brewer himself and had learned much about the craft. It was not work for him; it was a pleasure to carry out the tasks of an ancient brewing operation. He expected he could help with some of the more scientific principles. Most of the first brewers in a civilization didn't understand how fermentation worked, they just repeated the same steps and sometimes it worked and sometimes it did not.

The path they rolled down stretched through a slow-moving waterway, a wide and deep stream. Marco drove the team through the body of water to the other side. He then artfully turned the whole parade back, pointing toward the brewery again, and stopped when the horses were neck deep and the two men were ankle deep. *Brilliant*, the Envoy thought. *Fill the barrels and then use their buoyancy in the water to aid in loading them back on the wagon. Brilliant.* Marco dropped the reins and climbed into the back of the wagon. He lifted the lid out of one barrel and tipped the open mouth into the river. After only a few gallons had entered the barrel, he tipped it right side up again and began swirling it. He dumped the slurry back into the river. The barrels were the ones that Luca had brought back with him the previous evening. The Envoy realized that to the Clotz family, the process was simply rinsing and reusing the barrels, but they did not understand the value of what they discarded. "Marco!" the Envoy yelled. Marco looked up in surprise. The Envoy moved to the next barrel in line and took the cover off. He lifted it over his head and walked it to the barrel in the front of the wagon. He removed that barrel's lid and dumped the old beer sludge into it. He replaced the cover and brought the empty barrel back. Marco rinsed and filled the barrel. The two of them repeated the process for the last six barrels, but the Envoy would not let Marco touch the barrel that had all the accumulated sludge in it. "Yeast. Save it," he said, but Marco gave him a strange look.

They drove the wagon back up to the brewery. Instead of following the path to the two large doors, Marco drove the horses up a hill to the far, narrow side, opposite the large water wheel. He opened a smaller set of doors and returned to the driver's seat. It amazed the Envoy to find himself rolling into the brewery about fifteen feet above the ground along the back wall. It then made sense why they had installed all the support for the second floor. Mateo climbed a crude ladder, and he and his brother tipped barrels over the side and down into the large kettle below.

When they finished with the seventh barrel, Marco pointed to the eighth and spoke to his brother. The Envoy assumed he was explaining why it had not been filled with water like the others. Mateo looked up at the Envoy, "Quid enim salvum facis? Est quisquiliae inclusae sint." He lifted the lid to the eighth barrel. The Envoy hopped up onto the wagon and reached down into the barrel. When he brought his hand out, the brothers could see his fingertips coated in a light beige film that looked almost like paint.

"Yeast, for the beer." He recalled the word they had used, "Cervisia." Mateo looked confused but turned and told his brother what to do next. Apparently, that was getting six more barrels of water.

11

The following morning, Mateo opened the brewery door to find the stranger standing next to the ten barrels they had brewed the day before.

"Coipeadh," he said. Mateo did not understand what it meant. The stranger was leaning on an eleventh barrel and removed the top from it. "Yeast." He reached down and pulled out a handful of the stuff and pointed to one of the new barrels and looked at Mateo. It only took a moment for the young Clotz man to understand what the stranger meant to do. He held out his hand and extended his thumb up toward the ceiling.

"One, only one barrel. We usually lose two or three every batch anyway, so I'll give you one." Mateo pulled the bung from the bunghole and allowed the stranger to pour in the slick, sand-colored stuff. He replaced the bung and could not help but laugh when he looked back up at the stranger, who was standing there with his hands on his hips and grinning. They added the last of the ingredients to all ten barrels and as Mateo pressed the bungs back into place, the stranger followed him and loosened each of them. Mateo shook his head and smiled.

Two days later, the barrel they had added the yeast to was foaming over and hissing. The other nine were silent. Mateo, Luca, and the stranger were standing there, watching it. The stranger was smiling. Luca shrugged, "I guess we'll see how it turns out."

12

The Envoy had one primary goal while he was on the Clotz farm and one secondary. Teaching the Clotz family better brewing practices was just something to do for fun during his time there. The primary goal was to get meat on his bones again; he had flirted with starvation, and he wanted to get as close to his normal weight as possible before the next stint. The second goal was learning as much as he could about how far advanced these people were, so he could gauge how far into the future to jump. Without the ability to communicate, the latter goal would have been difficult to achieve.

After seven months on the farm, the Envoy was in excellent health and speaking conversational Latin. The Clotz family had also moved him into their house. They had offered room and board and even a little money for as long as he wanted to stay and work the farm and brewery with the Clotz men. During those months, he had shown them how to sanitize their "bad" barrels using steam, the benefits of adding yeast to a drink you intended to ferment, and how to make and use rudimentary air locks to prevent the fermenting beer from becoming contaminated and spoiling.

The major project, the one he was excited to have helped with, was building the wooden aqueduct from the stream on Tenna hill down to the brewery. The water wheel then made sense, and the days of hauling barrels of water up the hill in the wagon were over.

He had learned a great deal from the family once he could freely speak with them, and he was getting ready for his next stint. He had planned to tell them he would soon leave in the following days, but it came up naturally while they ate their dinner in the house one night.

As Luca's wife, Elisa, was portioning out the chicken and vegetables, she asked, "Tosgaire, I'm interested in your name. Is that your given or your family name?" She smiled as she asked the question. The Envoy sat up straight and leaned back into his chair.

"It isn't either of those, actually. Tosgaire, in my language, means 'Envoy,'" he said. The family members looked back and forth at each other, confused. "My home was called Osa, as Marco knows. He's learned a little Osan since I've been with you folks. I left Osa to go in search of the men I was asking you about last week, the men that know about the sky. But I had difficulties and almost starved. Without you and your wonderful family, I would have," he was looking at Luca. "And that is why I will take your advice and travel to Rome."

"Will you go back to Osa?" A rare question from the dark-haired Luna, one of the seven-year-old twin girls and youngest of the Clotz tribe.

"Osa is gone now. It was burned up by Sochee." Luna looked sad. Her sister, Bria, with a single braid running down her back that matched both her sister and mother, asked the next question in a whisper.

"Is Sochee a monster?"

The Envoy smiled and wanted to say "yes," but knew that he could not because the girls would have nightmares. "No, Sochee was a fire, but it went out. Now it's gone forever," he said. It was mostly a lie, but not completely.

"We got off topic," Mateo said. "What's your name?"

The Envoy took a deep breath. "Garrett."

Chapter 6

Lauren

1

Six months after Jonroe Daniels died, the envoys had concluded their initial classes with Arthur Sterritt, the transport field compression drive class, the on-board electronics class, and the galactic navigation class. They were about to begin the next set of classes, communications with Dr. Olive Francis and acquisitions with Dr. Lauren Astor. The psych roundtables with Dr. Paige were a daily event that would continue until the launches began.

The communications course was a setup much like the psych roundtable, in which they all sat at a big conference room table with Dr. Francis at the head. For the first meeting, she stood up, reintroduced herself, and mentioned how sorry she was to hear about Jonroe. After a complement of nods, she continued. "This is the communications section of your training; this will be fairly simple for all of you. We will meet every day for the next two weeks, another two weeks later this year, and for one final week leading up to the start of the launch cycle," Dr. Francis said. There was genuine interest in the faces of the envoys. Once they left, they would treasure the limited communication they could have.

"We have no plans to communicate from Osa. All Osan communications will be directed through Orris for as long as it continues to orbit Osa, and also once the solar burn is complete and it's orbiting Sochee." She looked up at the group for any uncertainty on their faces and found none. "The communication stream from Orris will start once the command center is online, which is currently estimated at four months from now."

One envoy laughed. It was Tom Holly. "If they send signals in four months, there will be no one to hear them," Tom said. He smiled and looked around.

"Tom, every one of you has a reception planet, right?" Olive said. Tom realized his mistake. Osa had already communicated to every reception planet, and they would expect each envoy.

"Yes, I feel dumb, and I apologize for interrupting. Please continue."

She winked at him. "No problem, Tom," she smiled, and with the smile lent further credence to the rumors that she and Tom Holly had "secretly" been seeing each other.

"The communication will start on only one channel and will be a simple statement of mission status. Over the course of the following eighteen months, fifty-three channels will exist. Each envoy will have an exclusive channel, and communication on that channel will be looped continuously. If you miss a part of anything, you will only have to wait a short time until that communication is rebroadcast," Olive said.

"What if we're in another galaxy?" It was Eric Thomas. "We'll never get the communications."

Dr. Francis nodded. "Yeah, they'll only go so far. They plan to ramp up the power on the comms over time, but they will only be so strong," she shrugged.

"So, we'll just be out of luck?" Eric frowned.

"Eric, I'm not an astrophysicist, but like all of you, I am a space junkie. If you go that far, there would be no way for Orris to recover your marks before they make the jump, so chances are, this will not be a problem for you." Dr. Francis was trying not to sound condescending, with little success. Eric nodded. "Stay in the sector guys, five galaxies, ours and the four that surround it. All of your work will be for nothing if you go outside of it." She was talking about the small sector of the universe where it was possible for crafts from other planets to travel to Orris.

"Is there a time limit on any parts of the sector?" Ken Chase asked.

"Yes, although I'm not qualified to answer that, but yeah. The universe is expanding, everything is getting farther away from everything else. You will lose the edges of the sector in less than four. Really, more like three and a half." Billion years. She did not say the words, but that is what she meant. "Dr. Estes will go over all of that with you. He is qualified to talk to you about it. I am not. I want to make sure you all know that." She glanced around at the group and seemed satisfied. "By the time your training is over, you'll know way more than I do about this stuff. I love learning about it, though, it's fascinating!"

"You said there will be fifty-three channels. How will we know which is which and what to listen for?" Stan Richman asked.

"Good question; twenty-seven of the channels will be dedicated to the envoys individually, the other twenty-six we will go over throughout the course of our meetings. Once the others start broadcasting, the Mission Status channel will also list the frequencies and details of each channel."

2

They attended the acquisitions class in a more traditional classroom setting. There were simple chairs with a writing board attached to each, and they all faced the same direction.

The class was scheduled for 15:00, at which time each envoy was in their seat, but Dr. Lauren Astor was not yet present. At 15:07, Randy Vila asked, "How long are we going to wait?" Before anyone could offer an answer, a thin-framed young woman with large curls of red hair dropping to her shoulders walked into the room, apologizing.

"I'm so sorry, gentlemen," she said, and strode across the room to a steel desk pushed against the far wall. "It's been a hell of a day," she offered, saying the words in a manner that sounded rehearsed. She put down the armload of files and a small box she had been holding, presumably writing utensils, and walked front and center to address the group.

"Again, I'm deeply sorry that I was not punctual." She stopped and looked back at the wall behind her students.

"And Jonroe… horrible," she said in a way that was this time clunky and unrehearsed.

Garrett remembered meeting her, along with the rest of the board, six months prior, but he did not remember finding anything particularly attractive about her then. He could not put his finger on what it was, but he felt differently in that moment. Her hair was down, and he could not remember if she had worn glasses at the earlier meeting, but she wore none now, and he found her pale blue eyes to be exceptionally beautiful. He thought it hard to believe that only these two slight differences had such an impact, but the more she talked, the more he realized a part of it was also her awkwardness in the role of instructor.

She leveled her gaze. "Acquisitions," she said, and looked from man to man. Garrett was anticipating the moment her eyes would fall on his. "It cannot be as simple as looking for volunteers. There will probably be a lot of volunteers, as long as you can communicate the mission and fully convince the public that what we are doing is real and important." Randy, Jim, Ken, Eric… never Garrett. He thought it was a mistake, so he maintained a lock on her eyes. "Each Lance can hold up to eighteen-hundred people, and that leaves room for expansion over the course of the journey for families, but you have to start with at least four hundred." Jim, Eric, Tom, Terence… still not once had she looked at Garrett.

"What is the maximum number we should start with?" Kyle Gellar asked.

"Good question, Kyle, but like everything else on these missions, it depends," she said. She was looking at Kyle and not shifting her eyes. "You'll have access to a beacon from Orris, so you'll know before they leave about how long it will take to travel there. If it's less than two generations, you can start with up to six hundred. If it's more, I would recommend you stay right at the minimal four hundred, to give them the best chance." She looked around again. "There is nowhere to expand on that ship. Controlling their numbers from the beginning is the only thing we can do to give them the best chance of surviving without having to resort to," she gave a small look of discomfort, "unpleasant resolutions to overpopulation."

Tom Holly chuckled under his breath and said at half volume, "They'll have to kill the dumb ones." It became apparent that Dr. Astor had exceptionally good hearing.

"Do you think that's funny?" she asked, glaring at him.

Deep red flushed through Tom's face. "No. I apologize." Tom said.

Dr. Astor neither winked nor smiled at his apology. "Over the next two weeks, we will go through the details that you all must know for acquisitions, and…" she continued, but never during the two hours did she look at Garrett.

3

Each floor of the OPM building had an elevator bay, and each bay had two steel-framed benches to sit on. During the busier periods of the day, it could sometimes be a substantial wait before an elevator could retrieve a caller. Garrett sat on one of them and, for the first time in a long time, was not thinking about his future missions. He was thinking about Dr. Lauren Astor. In his mind, he was arguing with himself about how stupid and futile it would be to ask her out. *I'm leaving Osa forever in ten months,* he thought. *Why start a relationship with a woman when I know I will have to end it?* He wanted to, and that was the only answer, no matter how stupid or futile. Moments before the elevator bell chimed, he decided he would ask her out to dinner. If she said no, then that would be the end of it. After the chime, he thought through the different ways he could approach the question. He recycled the thoughts and methods during his descent in the elevator, going through them when the doors opened and during his first few steps toward the OPM building's front doors. After those first steps, he looked up and was staring at the back of his subject, just before she reached the doors herself. He knew if he waited, she would disappear into the turbulent foot traffic of the city outside, so he yelled, "Lauren!" She froze in place and then turned slowly toward him as he caught up with her.

"Yes, Mr. Rhodes?"

All the ways that Garrett had been thinking of asking her to dinner left his mind at her unexpected formal reception. The envoys and the instructors in kind had always been on a first name basis.

"It's Garrett, and I want to take you out to dinner." A remarkable thing happened at that moment: as he felt the hot flush of blood fill his face, he witnessed the same thing happen at the same time on hers.

"Um," she said, "Don't you think that would be..." she trailed off and looked down at her hands, "Pointless?" Garrett risked touching her elbow, and although she shivered at first, she did not pull away.

"Maybe, but I still want to. If you would, that is."

She looked up at him. "When?"

"Now, tomorrow, next week, as soon as possible," he said. For the first time, she smiled, and it was a big smile. He found it hard to believe he had not noticed her appeal at their first meeting.

"I can't tonight," she said. "I have to go to my sister's place. I promised I would sit for her." The look of regret on her face pleased Garrett. "Tomorrow?"

Garrett offered his own big smile. "It's a date," he said. She returned the smile and escaped out the door. Something she had said triggered an alarm in his head that he had to think about for a moment to see clearly. *Sister*. His own sister was in the hospital, having just given birth to her and Rodney's first child. Garrett told Brenia he would visit and saw the good fortune of having his dinner request pushed by a day.

4

The hospital was huge, and it took some searching before Garrett found the maternity ward. Once there, an exhausted-looking but sweet receptionist gave him the room number. When he arrived, it confused him to see his father sitting in a chair turned so its back was to the hospital bed. As he approached the door and his father looked up and started speaking, he realized why and stopped before reaching the doorway. "Hey Gar, if you don't want to see your sister's boobs, you might want to wait a minute before coming in."

He heard his sister react loudly. "Dad! I told you I'm all covered up!" Garrett's mother walked up to him, rolled her eyes, and hugged him.

"Come on in, honey, your dad is being ridiculous." The cramped room had little standing room, but there were several chairs tucked into corners and along the one wall with a window. Brenia was lying on the hospital bed and had multiple blankets in a twisted mess upon her chest. A small yellow blanket that she was paying special attention to suddenly revealed a tiny foot. Garrett could not help but smile. He took two more steps into the room and stared at the little foot with the toes so tiny they were almost hard to see. Rodney stuck out a hand and Garrett took it; he shook twice, wincing at how hard his brother-in-law shook hands. He was a large man with short, dark brown hair and an enormous beard.

"Thanks for coming, Gar, Breni was missing you."

"Rod, I think he's done. Can you take him so I can get buttoned up?" Brenia said. Garrett's brother-in-law picked up his son and draped him over his chest and onto the folded towel on his shoulder. The contrast between the tiny baby and the enormous man was comical. "Gar, can you give me one sec?" Garret spun one hundred and eighty degrees, but it was only a few seconds before she said, "Okay, I'm all set."

Garrett turned back around to see both of his sister's arms extended toward him and walked over to hug her. She hugged him weakly and kissed his cheek twice. She leaned back into her pillows and closed her eyes. "You have to meet little Rodney," she said. Big Rodney smiled while he patted his son's back.

"Maybe after he burps," Rodney said. "I'm sure Gar doesn't want any messy surprises." But Brenia was already asleep. "So, how is space-man camp going, Gar?" Garrett took no offence to Rodney dumbing down what he was doing. He and Rodney had always gotten along well, despite coming from different backgrounds.

"It's intense, but it's going really well." Garrett did not want to expand into any detail, and he expected Rodney would not be interested anyway. "How are things going at your shop? Did you get the specs yet for the drive systems?"

Rodney rolled his eyes and spoke softly, glancing at his wife. "Yeah, we got them, and we've already started building one. These things are insane. The windings in just one blade will use more copper, gold, and silver than I thought existed on Osa. When you get on board that machine, man, you could start a country with the amount of money going into these things."

"Eighty percent the speed of light without losing time doesn't come cheap, Rod," Garrett said, smiling.

"I guess," Rodney said. "You should hold the baby. Breni will ask when she wakes up." Rodney passed the tiny person to Garrett, who took him with more than a little anxiety. So small, so delicate, and Garrett thought, *I have no idea how to do this.* His mother spoke before he got too anxious.

"Don't worry, Gar, you won't break him. Just be gentle and bounce a little." Before Garrett had bounced three times, he heard his sister.

"Aww! Little boy is with his uncle!" Brenia was smiling, but she already had tears welling in her eyes. A moment later, she was crying. She had her arms out to Garrett again. "Mom, take the baby," she said between sobs. Garrett carefully handed the baby to his mother and went to his sister again, holding her as she cried in his ear. "I'm so mad at you," she whispered.

"I know, Breni," Garrett whispered back. "But you're going to have your hands full with that little guy. You don't have to worry about me anymore."

She let go of him and spoke in a normal volume, "I'll always worry about you, idiot." Garrett retrieved a tissue from the nightstand beside the bed and handed it to his sister.

"Breni, did you tell Garrett the baby's name?" Their mother asked, knowing that she had not. Brenia blew her nose and tossed the tissue into the wastebasket in front of the nightstand.

She took a deep breath. "His name is…" her eyes filled, and she started sobbing again. Rodney took over.

"Rodney Garrett Kane," he said. Garrett's heart sank. "It kills the 'junior' thing. My middle name is David, but I think I'm going to call him 'junior,' anyway."

5

The acquisitions class the following day went much like it had the day prior. Dr. Lauren Astor did not once look at or acknowledge Garrett, and he made no effort to be acknowledged.

"Qualifications. This will probably be the uncomfortable part when you first solicit volunteers," she said as she paced in front of the class. "I'll start with the children first. Children younger than ten years will not be accepted, as their aptitude cannot be accurately measured. The places you go may have their own intelligence tests, but they will not be accepted as a substitute for ours. This is important for both consistency and predictability." She glanced at a few of the faces before her but saw no misunderstanding. "Children between ten and fifteen will be accompanied by one or both parents, who must also qualify. Anyone sixteen and older can go unaccompanied."

Tom Holly spoke up, but for once he was not making a joke. "Each planet we visit will have different annual cycles. The aging on the planets won't match ours here on Osa," he said.

She took a deep breath and let it out slowly. "Yes, Tom. But I'm fairly sure that each of you is good enough at math to get around that problem." Tom blushed again, and Garrett smiled. He had a feeling that Tom would be quieter in the future.

"They will also need to pass fertility tests, all of them. The success of the journey will rely heavily on the marks reproducing, as none of them will make it to Orris themselves. Any sterile person would be a wasted seat," she paused as if expecting a comment or question, but there were none.

"Keep families to a minimum. We need diverse gene pools. That also means it will be important to accept marks from distinct races, as evenly as you can. It will give them a good chance at maintaining the diversity in their pools." She paused again, but still nothing.

"No women over thirty years old, no men over thirty-five. The women need to have healthy child-bearing years left, and we can't have the men dropping dead from cardiac arrest two years after they leave," she said. Finally, someone made a comment. It was Terence Stone, more somber and focused as the newest member of Group 1.

"I feel like that will cause a lot of problems in a society advanced enough to build a Lance."

She smiled, and Garrett thought it a beautiful smile. She answered sweetly, unlike the way she handled Tom Holly. "Yes, Terry. You're right. I'm just scratching the surface of the details and disqualifiers today. A lot of the rules and guidelines and methods will seem unfair to the marks. That's the reason you will each need to take great pains to explain everything to them. It will not be fair. It will not be equal. Certain people will be given preferential treatment, but it is all by design. We do it this way to give the entire group the best chance at survival; the best chance of succeeding in their mission," she said. Several in the group were nodding. "If we let them do it their way, everyone would be dead in a hundred years. Orris would either receive a ship full of corpses or their Lance would just drift through space until the collapse." Garrett found smart women attractive; he felt the same about grounded women, and at that moment, he was finding Dr. Lauren Astor irresistible. He looked at the clock more and more often, and the butterflies in his stomach were in an all-out war.

6

When the class concluded, Garrett went slowly about his business. The others hurried out, eager to get to their homes or their evening plans. Dr. Astor had walked to the metal desk against the wall after dismissing the class, and when she turned around, she looked surprised to see that Garrett was the only one left.

"Wow, I thought we would have to be more covert than this. Well, I'm yours. What are we doing tonight?" Her words reignited the butterfly war in Garrett's stomach. He was extremely relieved that he had mentally walked through the moment a hundred times the night before.

"Well, we have two options. There is a really nice place on Seventh Ave. It's a fusion restaurant and offers many types of food, but it is very high class. We could both go home and get changed into our finest eveningwear, or…" he paused. She was giving him a playful scowl. "Or there's a steakhouse on 42nd Street and we can go as we are." She smiled. "Steakhouse it is," he said.

"That sounds great," she said, gathering her things and stowing them in her bag. "There's a bus stop across the street, right outside the front doors. I don't really want to put a lot of effort into keeping this a secret, but we probably shouldn't walk out together. Go to the bus stop and I'll meet you there in a few minutes."

Garrett was only standing at the bus stop for what felt like two or three minutes before he saw Lauren emerge from the OPM building and stride across the street. She was wearing a dark red button down top and a black skirt that stopped at her knees. Garrett couldn't help but glance at her legs as she traversed the crosswalk.

"Ready?" she asked. She was smiling, and Garrett once again felt a warm feeling in his chest.

"Yes, let's walk. It isn't that far," he said. They walked together and although Garrett felt it inappropriate to reach for her hand, he felt hers gently grip his elbow after only a few steps. He smiled. They did not speak for the one-and-a-half blocks it took to get to the restaurant. There was still an awkwardness about them, and Garrett felt it was the awkwardness that fostered the silence and was glad for it. When he spoke to her, he did not want it to be while they were walking, but while they sat across from each other and could read one another's expressions.

They arrived at Glenn Barron's Steak & Ale minutes after leaving the bus stop. Their table was a thick slab of wood, sanded and lacquered to a glossy finish. The chairs were equally heavy and well-made, also smooth lacquered wood with an embroidered leather cushion nailed into the seat. The whole place was dim, but each table was lit individually, giving the impression of a more private experience.

"I've never been here before," she said. "But I like it. I prefer places like this to the more upscale restaurants. I feel more comfortable."

Garrett nodded. "Me too. I've been here a few times, but the first was when my father decided I was old enough to drink. I think he was sorry he did that, because I learned how much I love beer, so much that I even started brewing it in his garage."

She laughed. "Really? So is the great Garrett Rhodes also a master brewer now?"

"I excel at making bad-tasting beers, so no, not that good."

She furrowed her brow. "They're all bad?"

"No, I'm exaggerating. They're usually drinkable, but I'm not going to enter any competitions. And I have made a few that were downright disgusting."

They both laughed as the young waiter, probably a few years their junior, approached and asked Lauren what she would like to drink.

"I will have whatever that man is having." She smiled and stared at Garrett with anticipation.

"Are you sure you want to do that?" he asked. Smile firmly in place, she nodded.

"I'll have a Henson's Dopplebock." His eyes never left hers.

"Twelve, twenty, or thirty-two?" The young man asked. Garrett smiled wider; gaze still fixed on Lauren.

"Two thirty-twos, please." The waiter nodded and walked off to the bar to get their order. The smile faded from Lauren's face.

"Are you trying to kill me?" she asked.

Garrett laughed. "I just wanted to give you the experience. It's the same order my father put in when he first took me here. I guarantee it will be interesting, for better or worse."

"Okay, I'll try it, but if I don't like it, you have to finish mine," she said.

He smiled again, but it was a small smile. "If I drink a half gallon of that stuff, you'll have to roll me out of here." As he finished his sentence, the waiter was placing the two enormous glass mugs of midnight black ale in front of them. Lauren's eyes grew wide.

"I think I understand now," she said. The waiter asked for their dinner order and Lauren again deferred to Garrett, who did not torture her, ordering two modest steaks with the house sides.

When the waiter left, Lauren changed the subject. "When we're in class, do I make it extremely clear that I don't like Tom or just moderately clear?"

"I think everyone understands. Why is that? It seems like it predates our classes with you." He lifted the enormous glass to his lips and sipped the strong beer.

"It does. It's Olive. She wants to start a family, and she's already thirty-six years old. And now that rat has her wrapped around his finger, and he's leaving in ten months!" She slid the glass close to the edge of the table so she could take a sip without having to lift it. "Ready?" She took the sip. Garrett observed the fluid level in the glass as it declined, confirming that she had made a serious effort at her experiment. Her brow first shot up high on her forehead before settling back down rather quickly, and she smiled.

"I can't believe it, but I like this. It's so strong, though!" she said.

Garrett laughed heartily. "I'm impressed. That is not a beginner's beer."

She squinted at him. "I'm not a beginner, but I've never had anything that strong." They both took another sip.

"The whole thing with Tom and Olive, and us talking about them; it kind of shines a pretty bright spotlight on what we're doing right now. I leave eight days after Tom," Garrett said.

The smile melted from her mouth but not her eyes. "That's true, but there is one major difference. I'm twenty-three years old, and I honestly don't even know if I want to have children. But I have a lot of time to figure that out." Their food came as she was finishing her sentence. Garrett understood they were approaching the topic of their relationship and the butterflies came back. He had never felt less like eating. He went to his beer again to help soften his nerves. As he put his glass down, he noticed she was doing the same, and that put him more at ease. He cut into his steak.

"So, what does your father do?" she asked, and the duration of their meal comprised her asking and him answering questions relating to his family, their occupations, his own history, both academic and otherwise. He did not know if she was intentionally preventing him from asking questions about her family or not, but she was doing an artful job of it. His revelations took them all the way through the meal, and once they finished, Garrett took inventory of their large drinks. He had consumed two-thirds of his and could feel it. To his surprise, she had finished almost the same amount. When he looked back up at her, she was smiling and had a touch of blush on her cheeks.

"Is this all we have planned, Mr. Rhodes? Or are we doing something else tonight?" Her smile never wavered. If it were not for the alcohol, the butterflies would have reentered the scene.

"I'd love to continue the evening, but I regret not planning anything else." He was disappointed in himself, a thing that sober hindsight would eventually remedy.

"Do you want to go look at Orris?" she asked. His expression must have been a priceless blend of confusion and excitement, because she laughed at his reaction. "You took care of the first half of the date. Let me handle the second half." They stood up, both leaving their remaining beer. They left the restaurant, Garrett stopping at the bar to pay and leave a large tip, of course, with his badge.

As they walked out, he asked, "Where are we going?" She smiled and tilted her head, indicating that he should follow. They walked two-and-a-half blocks and Garrett read the text carved into the stone wall of the enormous building she was leading him toward.

DINESTA CENTRAL OBSERVATORY

OPM—Dinesta, Rep. of Korrah

"How are we going to get in?" Garrett asked. She chuckled and looked at him as though he were crazy.

"Who do you think you're with?" she asked. As they reached the doors, she lifted her own badge to the radio receiver and Garrett heard a loud *thunk*, which could only have been the bolt disengaging. A small red light on the receiver blinked out and relit green. She pushed the door open, and when it shut behind them, Garrett heard it relock. The entrance to the building was a cavern, the ceiling four stories high. To both the left and right were large banks of elevators, the back wall lined with heavy wooden double doors. Garrett suspected they were conference rooms or one large auditorium. Above, hanging from the ceiling, was a model of the Orris operations center. Not as it was, but what it would look like when complete. The model was enormous and beautifully detailed. As they walked to the security desk, she pointed up at a specific node protruding from the ring-shaped model.

"Do you know what that is?" she asked. The echoes from her heels clicked loudly through the cavern as they drew closer to the security desk.

"Command?" Garrett asked.

She nodded, smile never fading, and said, "Hi Wade." They had reached the security desk. "This is…"

"Garrett Rhodes," the security guard, Wade, stood and extended a hand to Garrett. "It's a pleasure to meet you, son." Garrett shook hands with the man, who looked old enough to be his grandfather but fit enough to be sturdy in his age. His grip was firm, and his smile seemed genuine.

"The pleasure is all mine, Wade," Garrett said. The security guard laughed and sat back down.

"Yeah, sure it is. What can we do for you and your friend, Lauren?"

"We're going up to the observation deck." She glanced at Garrett. "We're also going to make a stop on thirty-four," she smiled at the man.

"What? This thing isn't big enough for you?" He glanced up at the model. "I imagine you'll be up there for more than an hour?" She rolled her eyes and nodded. "Okay, I only ask because I'm off in an hour and Earl is taking over. Maybe leave through the back or the side exit."

"Ugh, okay," she said as she leaned over the desk and hugged the man. The hug took Garrett by surprise, but she walked off toward the elevators to the right of where they were standing, as though it were completely normal. Garrett followed.

"So, you know our friend Wade pretty well then?" Garrett said once they were in the elevator and the doors had closed. She laughed and nodded.

"He's my mother's older brother. He told me and my sister not to call him 'uncle' anymore once we were adults, so we don't," she said. Garrett nodded. "Why? Are you jealous?" Alcohol or not, Garrett blushed. He *was* jealous, but before he could say or do anything else, she embraced him. Her hair smelled amazing, like some flower that he could not think of but was familiar to him. He gently returned the embrace to find her frame thin and delicate. Her cheek was smooth against his closely shaved neck, and as she released her grip, she kissed the underside of his jaw.

"There," she said. "Jealousy abated." Garrett's legs were jelly, and he hoped he could walk normally when the elevator doors opened. Fortunately, the elevator was not as fast as the one in the OPM building, and they were going all the way up to the thirty-fourth floor.

When the carriage stopped, and before the doors opened, she said, "Close your eyes." He looked at her. "Quick! Trust me!" Garrett closed his eyes. He heard the doors slide open and felt the fingers of her left hand interlace with the fingers of his right. She led him out of the elevator. "We have to walk a little, but keep your eyes closed, you won't regret it." He did as she asked. After an eternity, she stopped and said, "Okay, step up. Ten steps, ready?" He did his best to ascend the stairs without tripping. When they were at the top, she let go of his hand, stepped behind him, and put both of hers on his sides, just above his belt. She steered him around a corner. "Stop," she said, and he felt her place each of his hands on a railing directly in front of him. "Okay, OPEN!" He opened his eyes.

What he saw shook him to his core. "Is that…?" he said, but he could not finish. He just stared.

"Orris," she said. It was nothing like the modest model down on the first floor. That had only been the operations center, the section under construction at that moment in Osa's orbit. He was looking at the *whole thing.* The finished craft, as they expected it to look when it made the jump to escape the collapse. The model consumed the entire floor of the building, minus the elevators. Garrett had to squint to see the operations center as they had represented it with the model. It was the size of his thumbnail. His knees finally buckled, and he fell to them on the floor.

"I never thought I'd see it!" He had a tear running down one cheek. Lauren squatted to help him back up. "It's… I can't, I don't…" he drifted off as she helped lift him back to his feet. He braced himself on the railing again and breathed deeply several times. "This is everything. It's what will be left when Osa is gone, when Distria is gone, and all the others. This is why we're here." Tears had run down both of his cheeks, and from his right side, she embraced him again. He draped his arm over her shoulders and pulled her close to him. He had never experienced such a hurricane of emotion.

Still locked in each other's arms, she looked up at him and said, "I think it might get even worse." Garrett burst into a mix of tears and laughter.

"I'm ready!" he said, smiling through the tears. "Let's do it!" He pulled her close again before releasing her.

7

Once they were in the observatory, Garrett's face twisted in confusion. "I don't understand how this can work in the city." He was looking at the enormous optical telescope at the top of the observatory building and shaking his head.

"Curfew, 26:00," Lauren said. "Then the city goes dark. It's 24:30. In an hour, this place will fill up." Garrett still could not believe they could darken an entire city enough to reduce light pollution to levels required by such a massive telescope.

"How?" he asked.

She didn't laugh but dipped her head with her perpetual smile. "Ninety-eight percent of the light is controlled by the city. At 26:00, they turn them off. Any external light not controlled by Dinesta is mandated to be off by 26:00. If it's not, they get fined."

"How does the city's population not revolt against this?" he asked.

She looked up at him with a beautiful innocence. "They know it's for Orris. They adjust their lives to give us our eight hours of dark each night. At six in the morning, they can go back to doing whatever they want."

"What about crime? Police?" Garrett could not wrap his mind around the curfew. He had grown up and lived almost thirty miles away, so other than work, his family rarely ventured to the city, and never in the late-night hours.

"Any criminals are in the dark and the cops have infrared. The bad guys are at quite the disadvantage. Crime is actually very low in Dinesta," she said.

Garrett nodded and shook his head. "Amazing."

"Anyway, we can't use the big one for a number of reasons, but mostly because I don't know how. I can use these, though. Come over here." She took his hand and led him to a large, heavy metal door and pushed it open. Outside was a narrow, long observation deck with much smaller telescopes dotted along its length. Each of them had a bench assigned to it, four feet back from the devices. The telescopes, although small compared to the monstrosity inside, would still put any home hobbyist to shame.

Lauren selected one of the small optical machines and began spinning dials and checking the viewfinder. After she finished the adjustment she said, "It's not perfect, but look, and hurry." Garrett bent over the viewfinder and could see a rounded segment of steel tube framing, one third clad in sheathing, all floating in nothingness, drifting across the viewfinder's field. Its angular awkwardness was such that it could be nothing but real. No good movie director alive would allow for the framing to be that awkward. After the segment escaped from view, he sat hard on the bench behind him. She stepped back and sat next to him, closely. He noticed she had intended for their thighs to touch. She leaned back and then over onto his shoulder, with her hands clasped in her lap. Garrett instinctively and without reservation put his arm around her. The butterflies were gone. He was sure she was as invested as he was.

"I'm not sure I have the words for tonight." He turned his face to hers. "I've never been an emotional man, but this experience has turned me inside out. Twenty-eight hours ago, I was sure I wanted to spend time with you. Five hours ago, I realized my feelings were much stronger than that, and now I'm enamored with you. But even though we both love this stuff... it will ultimately tear us apart." He breathed in and looked up at the sky. "I'm not sure what to think or what to do. It's not a paradox, it's a conundrum, and I'm not sure I understood the meaning of that word until this moment."

She placed a hand on his chest. Her expression was blank, as if in deep thought. "There is no solution," she said.

He took her hand from his chest and kissed it. "Well, there has to be something," he said. She turned her face into his chest. Garrett looked down at her. She looked up, and they kissed, truly, for the first time. "I want to spend every minute I have left here with you."

She offered him a small smile. "I told you before, I'm yours."

Chapter 7

Roma

1

Coming up from a thirteen-hundred-year stint was nothing compared to the longer ones he had already done on Earth. The Envoy had not needed to look for a cave; he knew of four from his exploration with Marco Clotz on the few days they had off during his months with the Clotz family. On their various expeditions, he had revealed to Marco his true story. Garrett confided in him on the condition of absolute secrecy. He enjoyed talking at length with another person about his true history, his true time on planet Earth, and his true intentions for the future.

The Envoy had selected the furthest cave from the Clotz farm, as it was also the deepest, and close to the road to Rome, which was his next destination.

Even before his eyesight had returned, and without water, he could sit up. He heard a whistle and assumed it was wind blowing over the mouth of the cave, some eight hundred feet from where he sat. He knew it would be important to get hydrated, no matter how good he felt, so he located his bag by touch and pulled it onto his lap.

Alarm rose in his mind when he uncinched the throat of the bag. It did not feel right. He always put a loose knot on top of a tight one, but the bag had only one loose knot. When he reached in, he discovered the reason. The first object his hand touched was foreign. It was an object that had never been in his possession before. It was weighty, had hard edges and corners, and was a bit... sticky. Curiosity exploded in his mind. No one knew where he was, not even Marco. He desperately wanted light so he could inspect the object. *I suppose I would also need sight for the light to do me any good.* He chuckled at his own joke. He concluded that his sight *had* returned, but that it was pure darkness where he was.

He drank a bottle of water, waited for fifteen minutes, and stood. He found he could carry himself well. Possessions accounted for and strapped in place, he listened and felt the walls and spent the next hours navigating out of the cave.

His sight had returned, as confirmed by the soft moonlight in the cave entrance. He walked out into the cool night air and sat in the dim, white light. The foreign object from his bag was a bundle of papers, folded twice and coated in something sticky. He brought the pack close to his nose and breathed deeply, hoping to identify the substance. It was mostly odorless, but he thought it may have been wax.

With the papers deposited back in his bag, he pulled out a fresh bottle of water, drank all of it and laid down on his back. Staring at the night sky, he waited for the sun.

2

When there was enough light to read by, he again withdrew the papers and carefully unfolded them. As he did, flecks and flakes of the sticky substance separated and fell to the ground. When the papers were open and he could gaze upon the script, he recognized Marco's hand at once. He read the date at the head, and the words *'I found you when I was twelve years old.'* It went on from there, but Garrett refolded the papers and put them back in his bag. There were a lot of pages and a lot of writing on each, and he wanted to save them for a time when he had a lot of waiting to do.

He got to his feet and walked down to the path below, turning southwest. The path was a faint track when he had gone under, but he stepped up onto a wide and cared-for road. In the east, the sunrise assured him he was traveling in the right direction. The Clotz's had told him that if he intended to walk to Rome, it would be an eighteen- or twenty-day walk if he walked all day, every day. Garrett had no intention of walking that much and would hitchhike as much of the distance as he could.

Three hours into the morning daylight, he came upon a horseless wagon loaded high with barrels on the side of the road, pointing in the direction he was traveling. The barrels looked brand new, each branded with the name *Monteprato.* About twenty yards off the road were the horse and the man, the horse drinking from a small brook.

"Hello!" Garrett said in Latin. The heavy, balding man looked up the shallow incline but did not speak. He reached down and grasped the reins on the horse and led it back up the slope.

"Latin?" the man said as he crested the incline. "Can you speak Italian?" Garrett shook his head. The man nodded. "You may have some trouble in this area. What other languages can you speak?" Garrett shook his head again, knowing that Osan, Destrian, Rheeta, Bordell, and Temura would not count. "Nothing? What? Are you a thousand years old?" The man squinted hard as he was facing the sun. He wore humble clothing with a large, brimmed straw hat and looked as though he were in his sixties.

"I've traveled far and come from a place that only speaks Latin."

"Sardegna?" the man inquired.

"No, it is far to the northeast." The man shrugged his shoulders and asked where he was going. "My destination is Rome."

"Rome? Well, you may find some there that you can speak to. You're lucky you ran into me here. I taught Latin for thirty years before I retired to my farm. I'm only delivering these barrels as a favor to my brother." He led the horse to the front of the wagon and began fixing the buckles. "You can ride with me for part of the way. I'm not going that far, but it will save your feet for a while." Once finished with the buckles, he walked up to Garrett and extended his hand. "My name is Francisco Monteprato."

"Garrett Rhodes."

They rolled along the road for about two hours. During the time, they passed through beautiful hills and orchards. There were several vineyards dotting the countryside, and one apparent timber operation. The scenery differed greatly from the bleak desert Garrett had remembered from what felt like only months ago. They had to pause once to wait for a herd of sheep to cross the road but did not have to wait long. As they approached a town, or even a small city, Garrett could see a gaseous white column rising high into the sky. Before they reached the oddity, the driver tensioned the reins of the single horse and spoke to it in a kind voice. The horse stopped.

"Well friend, if I take you further, it would be in the wrong direction," Francisco said, and pointed to their right. "This is the road you will want to continue west, then south to Rome." He extended a hand toward Garrett again. "It has been a pleasure traveling with you."

"The pleasure was mine, Mr. Monteprato. Can I ask you, though? What is that?" He pointed to the column of what he assumed to be a blend of smoke and steam and then lowered himself from the wagon to the earth.

"Oh, that's the mill. Lumber. They have one of the newest steam engines there. The world is changing, son, it is changing for sure! Good luck in your journey, Mr. Rhodes." Garrett waved as the wagon once again rolled along the hard-packed road. Once he had fixed his gear, which was revealing the effects of age, he set out on his western course. Dory-10, synthetic or not, the material was beginning to fray and split. The company had claimed it would last for ten billion years, and it took Garrett just over eight billion to prove them wrong. The thread in his bag had also become useless, as he had discovered on Clotz's farm; it would snap every time he tried to draw a length to mend with.

3

After two hours on foot, a caravan of three horse-drawn, covered wagons approached him from behind. Although none of the drivers spoke the dialect of Latin that Garrett knew, nor any Latin at all, they understood *Roma* and gestured an offer to travel with them. Garrett climbed aboard the lead wagon, seated to the right of the driver, and with the failing daylight decided he had enough time to read at least the first of Marco's letters:

April 4, 563 -

Garrett,

I found you when I was twelve years old, about three years after you left our farm. As the years passed, I reflected on our tireless conversations as we roamed the countryside. My older and matured twelve-year-old mind realized that although you had set off for Rome, you had also said you would go into a long sleep before reaching it. It took me three years to understand that the reason you expressed so much interest in the surrounding cave systems was because you intended to use one. So, I searched, and then I found you. As you may have guessed from the date on this letter, that was ten years ago. Although I found your body, and you were gone to all of us forever, I was still too immature to understand that I could communicate with you, and so only now am I doing so. I also speculated that you may have made up all your stories to entertain a young boy's mind; but I have visited you twice since, and never once did I get the scent of death. Because of that, I choose to believe you were telling me only the truth of your adventures.

I will write and keep these letters, and if I am so fortunate to live a long enough life, I will deposit them among your possessions before I die. As a reminder to me, and based on your unintentional guidance, folding them, and coating them in wax, to preserve them through the years.

During your time with us, you had become like family, and so I thought it would be prudent to update you on our family's histories as they become apparent. I am very happy to report that there is no sad news. Mother and father are well, and father, although having surpassed his fiftieth year, is still as active on the farm and in the brewery as he ever was. Mateo married shortly after you left us and now has four children of his own! His wife is Cerelia, and she is a very tired woman. Ha! It was my great fortune to meet a girl who is now my wife. Her name is Marquesa, a beauty who also carries my first child. We no longer live on the farm, but for a price that my father helped put up, we purchased a small tract for ourselves only up the hill.

The twins have set themselves on very different paths. Bria is betrothed and set to marry in the summer, and then she will go to live with her husband in Bordano. Luna has asked to live with me and Marquesa, if only to get away from all the children on the farm. We are worried about her. She is a beautiful young girl, as you may imagine, having known her, but there is an affliction about her we cannot understand.

The brewery is nothing like you might remember. Father had another building put up behind it, just to store the barrels, and now Monteprato supplies us with ten times as many new barrels as you would have known. There are no other major brewers for a hundred miles, as we've used your guidance to make Clotz Ale the finest in the region.

I will write you again, but for now I will say goodbye, and Godspeed,

M. Clotz

Garrett placed the first letter behind the rest, folded them, and placed them back in his bag. The light was no longer sufficient for reading, and he had to strain to make out the last of Marco's first letter. He smiled at the thought of the boy he had befriended and was glad he spent so much time and effort communicating with him; a man who would never know how much meaning and good cheer such letters could possibly bring to the Envoy. He was also happy when the caravan broke for the night, and he could sleep.

4

The sun had not yet come up when the lead driver began rousing them from their rest. The youngest driver, as he had done the night before, gathered the horses and led them to a small creek thirty yards from where they camped to water them. He was more of a boy than a man; probably thirteen, with long, curly black hair and a deeply tanned complexion. He was a younger-looking version of the other two drivers, who Garrett suspected were all a part of the same family.

Garrett could see that they had a fire the night before, and the lead driver was now resuscitating the flames. The young driver finished watering the horses, then handed the lead driver a kettle laden with water from the brook. The older man placed the kettle on a metal rack suspended over the small fire. He spoke to the others in a language that was unfamiliar yet similar to the Latin he had learned from the Clotz's. He pulled a satchel from his bag, opened the kettle, and poured the contents into it, replacing the kettle lid after the satchel was empty. More chatter before the young driver emerged with four metal cups, each with a small handle. The lead driver poured the kettle off into the four cups and took one for himself. The young man handed the single cup left in his right hand to the other driver, separated the two in his left hand and offered one to Garrett. Although he did not know what the beverage was, he took it and sipped. It was hot; it was delicious; it was bitter; it was aromatic; he loved it… whatever it was. When he finished, he handed the cup back to the young driver.

The lead had already stamped out the fire and was checking the harnesses on the horses. "Andiamo!" he said, and they were off again. Soon after they pulled away from their camp, Garrett took the notes from the bag again and read the next two letters:

December 11, 575 -

Garrett,

I'm afraid we've suffered a major tragedy earlier this year. Both of my sisters are gone. This past May, while giving birth to her fourth child, Bria passed, and I'm sad to report that the child did not survive the bad pregnancy either. Upon the news of her twin, Luna's already fragile mental state became insufferable for her, and she disappeared. We discovered her body the next day, as she had cast herself off the north side of Tenna Hill, where we sourced the water for the duct all those years ago. The drop was sheer, and as you must know, fatal. Bria's husband allowed for us to bury them next to each other, on his family's land in Bordano.

Mother and father are still with us, though father is not as active on the farm as he once was. Mateo has taken over fully for years now and runs the entire operation. All of his children now work on the farm as well as my oldest boy, whom I named for myself, and my second boy, whom I named for you. Young Garrett is now the age I was when I met you! I have one other, a young girl of six years who is named for her mother, Marquesa.

Except for the sad news of my dear, sweet sisters, we are all healthy and happy.

Godspeed Tosgaire,

M. Clotz

May 17, 586 -

Garrett,

Father passed away two days ago. He had been ill for over a year. He was seventy-three. A good, long life for a man. I should be celebrating him, but I admit I am just heartbroken.

I am now myself at forty-five years, older than you and my father both when you spent that summer with us. I am beginning to feel the age in my joints and muscles. My wife insists my mind has also become soft. I love her for many reasons, but her humor pleases my soul. I have begun an experiment with a more and more popular beer seasoning. It's a flower that grows on a vine. I have only three hundred plants, but if it proves itself over time, I plan to

Garrett shivered at the revelations and felt sad about the death of the elder Luca, whom he admired. *Silly, though*, he thought. *They are all long dead now*. He placed the two letters he had read to the back of the pile and found there were only two left. As he lifted the first to glance at the second, he frowned. The handwriting on the last letter of the series was not Marco's. He decided he did not want to know, then. He would let it be a mystery for a while longer.

The convoy rolled along the dusty road for many more hours, and Garrett took in the scenery. As the hours passed, he considered the number of vineyards they spotted, a rather unbelievable quantity. When he tried to come up with a number, he was at a loss. It was becoming clear that this was a wine-drinking culture, as he saw almost no small grains being grown, other than a few wheat fields, and not one of barley. Grapes everywhere.

5

Garrett traveled with the convoy for three days. On the morning of the third day, he took the occasion while in solitude on the driver's bench to peek into the wagon. He saw a wild variety of chests, crates, sides of meat packed in what he supposed was salt and wrapped in heavy cloth, and assorted machinery. He realized the convoy was an early shipping company, with no obvious specialty.

Twenty minutes after passing through Bologna, the eldest driver turned down a smaller, rougher road and stopped the trio. He stepped down to the ground and motioned Garrett to do the same. He pointed back to the road that they had just turned off in the direction that they would have gone.

"Roma," he said. Garrett nodded and shook the man's hand. He then turned and began his long walk. He had no other offers to hitchhike, and it took him eight more days before he reached the magnificent city.

6

Rome was beautiful, but it was clear to Garrett that it was ancient. For every pristine new structure, there were five dilapidated ones, some with a look of a thousand years having passed. *How much of this was here when I was on the farm? A lot, I think.* He walked the streets, surprised to find how many of the inscriptions he could read. The language he spoke was, at one time, the language of the land. He approached a few people and spoke to them, but most hurried away. One young man, though, understood him and stopped to engage with the Envoy.

"Hello, do you understand my language?" Garrett asked, the same way he approached every person he attempted to talk to. A young man with close-cut black hair, black robes, and no other adornments stopped at once and furrowed his brow.

"Latin? Are you of the cloth?" the young man asked. Garrett understood the words, but not the meaning.

"I don't know what it means to be 'of the cloth,'" Garrett said.

The young man smiled. "Then you are not. Do you not speak Italian?" Garrett shook his head. "Only Latin, then? Interesting. How can I help you?"

"I need work and a place to stay. I also have a lot of questions that I need to find the answers to, and eventually I will need to travel again, maybe far. Can you help me with any of this?"

"Well, I suppose I'm uniquely qualified to help you, as I am both a man of the cloth and one of the few who can speak with you. My name is Pietro. I am a deacon of the church, in training for full priesthood."

Garrett understood little of what Pietro said, but he understood his name. "So, Pietro, you can help me?"

Pietro, a thin young man of average height, stepped back and looked the stranger over. "You asked for a lot of things, but not a meal. It looks to me, though, like a good meal would help you more than any of the other things you named," Pietro said. He looked back up at Garrett, who smiled. He was not as badly starved as he had been upon reaching the farm, but he had eaten little over the last week, and it showed in his cheeks and thin frame. "But I ask one thing in return. Your name?"

"Yes, my name is Garrett, and you are right. It would be a great help," he said. Pietro motioned for him to follow, and they walked together in the direction he had been traveling. They walked in silence for ten minutes until arriving at a large dormitory. Pietro approached one of the ground level doors, opened it, and walked into the humble apartment. Just inside the door was a small wooden table sized for two adults, with as many chairs.

"Please, sit here and I will fix us something to eat," Pietro said. Garrett sat and watched as the young man drew two plates from a cupboard and some items from a pantry. While he prepared the plates, Garrett took the notes left by Marco Clotz out of his bag and reread the few from the back of the pile. A question lit up in his mind.

"Pietro, if you don't mind, what is the date today?" Garrett asked. Pietro was walking to the table with two plates, each with chunks of bread, three slices of cheese, and some cured meat. He set them down on the table and returned to the kitchen.

"May the sixteenth? Yes, the sixteenth," Pietro said. He had returned with two glasses and a carafe of wine. After pouring the wine, he raised a hand and spoke a blessing, then lifted his glass in the air, a custom that Garrett had grown familiar with on the farm. Garrett lifted his own.

"To long life and a quiet soul, thanks be to God," Pietro finished. They both sipped their wine, and Pietro sat.

"If I could trouble you further," Garrett thought of the third letter from Marco, the one that brought the news of Luca's passing, dated May 17, 586. Pietro nodded. "For the year?"

Pietro finished chewing and said, "You don't know what year it is?"

"Forgive me. I've been traveling for a long time and had no use for the day or the year. Now I am curious."

"Well, it is the year of our Lord, eighteen hundred and seventy-five," Pietro said. With that, he tipped his glass again and drank. Garrett glanced down at his bag, which lay open on the floor. He had laid the unfolded papers inside and could see them.

"Thirteen hundred years," he whispered to himself in Osan. While he was not new to jumping time, losing those he cared about stung. He felt as though the passage of time were not real. In his mind, Marco Clotz had not yet reached his tenth year, let alone having been dead for centuries.

"I will ask around about work so you can support yourself, but I'm afraid I won't be able to help you find lodging. I am leaving the day after tomorrow, bound for France, first Avignon and then Paris," Pietro said, and refilled both of their glasses. "Now, what were the other things you had need of?"

"Information. I need to speak to men who understand the stars. I need to learn about scientific advancements and where our current discovery is regarding the science of the physical world. Last, I imagine I will need to travel again, and to learn a modern language," Garrett said, and Pietro laughed.

"That is for certain!" Pietro said. "No one speaks Latin anymore, except the church, and yours is old, a much more classical version. I have been studying classical Latin since

I was a child, but I think even many of those from the church would still have trouble conversing with you."

Garrett nodded. He finished the last of the food on his plate and sipped from his remaining wine. "Thank you for the food and drink. You are very generous," Garrett said. Pietro lifted a hand from the table for a moment and let it settle back, as if to say no thanks was required. He sat in silence for a moment and watched the liquid as he swirled it in his glass.

"You should come to Paris with me. I need an assistant for the duration of the trip, and I can pay you a small sum. My youngest brother is scheduled to go as a favor to me, but with little interest outside of that, and against our mother's wishes. If I take you in his place, it would appease them both and may put you closer to your goals. I will teach you the French language as we travel. No need for Italian if you are leaving Italy."

"Paris. I may find my answers there?" Garrett asked with excitement.

"I imagine it is one of the best places. There are others, but Paris is no worse than the rest. It is also close to some other cities you may want to visit. Munich, Berlin, London – all, I think, would help you with your discoveries. That said, it would also be helpful for you to learn German and English. English, especially, if you make the long journey to New York, or other places in the United States."

"How far is it? New York?" Garrett asked, only mildly interested, yet he was curious what it would entail should he find the need to make the trip.

"Thousands of miles. It's a world away, and there is no land! You would have to book passage on a ship. There are steamers, though, that are much faster than the old sailing ships, but it would still take ten days, maybe nine, to traverse the Atlantic," Pietro said. He finished the last of his wine and wiped his mouth.

"These steamers, they're ocean-going vessels that are powered by steam? Do I understand you?" Garrett asked. Pietro nodded. "Do they use paddles or screws?"

Pietro's face slackened. "I don't know. In fact, I don't even know what that means." Pietro looked down at his empty plate.

Garrett leaned back in his chair and smiled. "That's not a problem, friend. All of your information has been helpful already. I can tell you I am excited about our journey together, and I'm even more excited to see Paris!"

7

"We could have had a driver," Pietro said, "but I thought it might suit us better to have a little freedom with our travel." He lifted a small chest into the wagon and turned to walk back to the apartment. "I'll need help with the next one." The next chest was absurdly heavy. Garrett winced as they both wrestled the monster up and into the back of the wagon. He looked at Pietro, who shrugged. "Wine, food. Come on, there are two more. We will be traveling for weeks. We need these things."

They walked back into the apartment and into the only bedroom where the remaining two chests were. Besides the bedroom, kitchen, and pantry, there was only the small sitting room near the front door where Garrett had slept the night before. On the bed was one neatly folded and stacked outfit. "After we get these two into the wagon, come back here and change. You will be much more comfortable," Pietro said. "We are about the same size, so they should be a little loose on you until you fatten up. Don't forget to pull the door closed behind you. As soon as you're done, we're off."

"Thank you. I have always preferred cotton clothing," Garrett said. They loaded the trunks into the wagon and Garrett changed, pulling the heavy wooden door closed tightly behind him.

Pietro was checking the rigging on the single horse and called to him, "Did they fit?"

"Yes, thank you. Much better than what I had." Garrett placed his own bag in the wagon behind the driver's seat and climbed aboard. Pietro handed him the reins. He was thankful in that moment that Marco had taught him how to drive not one horse but a team back on the Clotz farm, thirteen hundred and twenty-five years before. Garrett clicked his tongue in his cheek twice and snapped the reins. The horse lumbered forward.

"Très bien monsieur, continuez," Pietro said.

Garrett at first looked confused, but understanding poured over his face and he smiled, "The French language."

"Oui, monsieur," Pietro answered. "We don't have enough time for me to teach you to speak it well, but I will familiarize you with it as much as possible. After living there for a while, your French should improve."

8

They traveled for seven days and made camp about twenty miles after passing through Genoa.

"We will cross into France tomorrow, and then only two days' travel to Avignon," Pietro said. It was dark, and he was poking at the fire with a large stick in his right hand and holding his wine in his left. The clearing they had set up in was just off the road, but still remote and small. Except for the road, heavy forest surrounded them. Garrett heard several ominous sounds in the wooded area, branches snapping, leaves rustling, but had become used to curious critters over the years and paid them no mind. What he did alert to when he heard them were foreign footsteps. Close footsteps.

A tall, thin man with long, gray hair and deep lines pressed into the features of his face emerged from the darkness. In his right hand he held a metal object that Garrett could barely make out, but he could see the sparks of light glinting off it as the fire burned. Garrett shot a look at Pietro and stood as he saw the alarm in his face. The man spoke gibberish, and Pietro answered in similar gibberish. Pietro looked at Garrett. "Sit! Sit back down!" Garrett did as instructed. The thief walked backward, waving what could only have been a firearm. He reached their vehicle, mounted the wagon, and drove the horse forward down the road. After getting the horse into motion, he turned around and pointed the gun at Pietro and Garrett.

"He said if we followed him, he would kill us. Argh! We're ruined!" Pietro threw his hands up and back down to his hips and stamped a circle around the fire.

"We're no such thing. I'm afraid that man just made the last poor decision of his life," Garrett said, but did not move. He only stood still, staring after the thief who was driving away with all his possessions on board, including the notes from Marco. The Envoy's right hand absent-mindedly reached up to his breastbone, where he was happy to find the satchel.

"He'll kill you!" Pietro tried to reason with Garrett.

"I doubt it. There is no moon, there are barely any stars out with all the clouds. He won't see me. He'll get one shot, but only one, and I don't believe he'll hit me," Garrett said. Pietro was pale and sat down hard on the ground.

"If he kills you, he'll come back and kill me." Pietro's jaw was slack, and a look of horror had malformed his face.

"I doubt that, too. If he could kill me, which he can't, he would be happy he got away with it and run to whatever hole he's heading toward now. But if it makes you feel better, walk back up the road in the opposite direction he drove, about thirty yards, and hide in the woods. When I'm back with our possessions, I'll call out to you." Garrett walked over to the pile of brush they had gathered to use as fodder for their fire. He snapped off several twigs and further trimmed them until they were long and straight, between six and eight inches long.

"All right, Garrett, I'll do as you say." Pietro stood and stared at Garrett, who smiled back at him. Once the Envoy had the straight sticks ready for action, he bundled them and placed them in his left hand. He turned and sprinted after the thief. Pietro got up quickly and hurried off to his hiding place.

Garrett breathed long, slow, and deep breaths that made no sound. He ran first on the hard-packed road, then in the soft vegetation on the shoulder and back to the hard-packed road, judging that it was quieter. He caught up to the thieving driver quickly and slowed his pace. The horse was slow with poor night vision, and he determined there was no need to risk climbing aboard the wagon. He jogged up along its right side and kept pace behind the rear wheel. Once he isolated the longest stick he had, he shoved the rest in his back pocket. Using the index finger and thumb of both hands, he loosened the cinched throat of the satchel and withdrew the bottle of Sterilex. Cap off, he stopped walking long enough to drip a bit of the liquid carefully onto the end of the stick. With the cap back on, back in the satchel and cinched tight, Garrett walked up to the bench where the thief sat. The gun was still in his right hand, an awkward shot. He could smell the man; a blend of whiskey, vomit, and the sour stink of sweat.

Simultaneously, with his right hand, he shoved the stick coated with Sterilex down into the thief's boot, and with his left, threw the sticks from his back pocket into the old man's face. The thief yelled out in surprise, and Garrett dashed into the woods, shielding his eyes from wayward twigs and branches. The thief got off two shots before dropping the gun and sitting heavily on the bench. Neither of the two shots were close to where Garrett crouched.

He emerged from the wooded refuge only a minute later and approached the wagon. The thief was awake but lethargic. Garrett pulled him down to the dusty road and dragged him into the forest, watching as the man's face twisted into anguish brought on by horrific dreams.

Eight minutes later, Garrett rolled back up to the camp and whistled. "Pietro, my friend! We are avenged!" He yelled so he would be heard by the cowering man. Pietro appeared, jogging up the road moments later.

"What did you do? How did you retrieve our wagon?" His look of relief and confusion made for an interesting expression.

"I think it's best for me just to say that I will need to do a confession," Garrett said. Pietro sat down hard for the second time that night.

"What about you? Are you alright?"

"Yes."

"Is he dead?"

"Yes."

Pietro blessed himself and broke into prayer. Garrett walked back to the wagon and got a bottle of wine from the food trunk. He did not bother with a cup.

9

Their wagon passed through the ramparts and into Avignon three days after the attempted robbery. Garrett marveled at the sights. An old city, but also an important one. They rolled through streets bustling with shops and others with dark facades and no activity. Deep into the city, Pietro told Garrett to stop the horse and hitch it to a post nearby. They would go on foot from there.

"We both have business here; I will first attend to your confession and then I will deliver my letter. We shall stay one night and be off to Paris in the morning," Pietro said.

They walked through a large cobblestone courtyard toward a series of four steps leading up to more courtyard. It was exceptional.

"What is this place?" Garrett asked.

"Palais des Papes. This city was the seat of all of Catholicism in the thirteen-hundreds, for many years. This is where the popes lived. But we are going to the cathedral." They climbed the four steps and continued toward the cathedral.

"Pietro," Garrett stopped walking. Pietro stopped, confused. "You must know by now that I have no religion. I know of confession because of our many conversations, but I do not know what to do." Pietro walked two steps back to Garrett and took both of his hands in his own.

"Do you believe in our Lord, God, with all of your heart and soul?"

Garrett did not withdraw his hands from Pietro's but looked in his eyes with sincerity. "I believe I am a humble man who does not now, nor ever will understand, the true nature of our world, nor its creation. It may be our Lord God, it may be someone else's, or there may be no God at all. I do not possess the arrogance to claim that I above all others know the truth." It was the same sentiment Garrett had offered to all the different world's peoples as he encountered their varied religions. Pietro's look of anticipation fell into one of disappointment.

"Don't say that to the Priest. Let's go, better you confess than not," Pietro said. They continued across the courtyard to the steps of the cathedral.

They ascended a ramp, and the imagery at the top moved Garrett. Above them, he could see a man nailed to a wooden cross, or at least a statue representing it. They ascended the stairs, and then he walked around so he could face the statue. Four stone women with wings surrounded it, flanked by two, a man and a woman, with their hands clasped in prayer. The man on the cross wore a crown of thorns and only a loincloth for clothing. Metal spikes had been driven through each hand onto the cross, and one large spike through both feet and into the base. Garrett marveled at the image. Pietro was speaking to him, explaining the image he was gazing upon. Beyond the statue, high above and mounted to the top of the spire of the Cathedral, was a golden woman with her hands outstretched. She wore a halo of stars.

"Who is that?" Garrett pointed high to the golden figure atop the spire.

"That is His mother, the Virgin Mary," Pietro said.

Garrett looked confused. "That doesn't make sense."

"That's the point. You have much to learn," Pietro said, smiling. He walked away, "Come, follow me."

They walked into the cathedral, and when they entered the main chamber, its beauty shook Garrett.

"Wait here, I'll be back soon." Pietro disappeared into the building. Garrett looked into the massive interior space with its large support pillars and enormous vaulted ceilings. Four columns of seating pews occupied the space, and the walls were adorned with sculptures. It was a vision.

Pietro returned moments after he left and beckoned Garrett to follow him into the room next to the sanctuary.

As Garrett followed him, he whispered, "When you enter the closet, first say, 'Forgive me father, for I have sinned,' the priest speaks Latin, so you will not have to struggle with French. He will lead you from there, and when he gives you your penance, say only, 'Yes, father.' Nothing more. Come to me and tell me the penance he assigns you." Pietro motioned for him to enter the small wooden closet.

After only ten minutes, Garrett emerged from the wood-paneled confessional and walked across the room to Pietro, who was waiting for him.

"So, what is your penance? What did he say?" Pietro asked in a loud whisper.

"He asked me to repeat the story two times. I did, and he sat quietly for some time. After that, he said that this was not a murder, and he told me to say the Lord's Prayer. That is all," Garrett said. Pietro slapped his own forehead, wiped his face with both hands, and shook his head.

"Okay, wait outside for me while I attend to my business here. I will collect you shortly and we will find our lodging."

10

They traveled north the following day, bound for Paris. The night before, Pietro had walked the Envoy through his penance after they ate and before they had laid down to sleep for the night. Once complete, Garrett told Pietro that he felt better, and it was an honest sentiment. The complexity and elegance of Pietro's religion touched Garrett.

The ride on the first day up to Paris was much quieter than from Rome to Avignon. Pietro would engage in conversation, but not with the enthusiasm he had on the first leg of their trip. Garrett recognized his reservation, and the next day he tried to make amends with the holy man. As they pulled away from their camp Garrett said, "I would like to offer you a sincere assurance." Pietro looked at Garrett and nodded. "The would-be thief, just outside of Genoa, is not actually dead."

Pietro shook his head. "What?" he asked, surprised. His look of confusion was exactly as Garrett had expected.

"The solution that I used to put him down is not a poison, but a powerful intoxicant. I have administered it to myself before, to help me sleep. He is only sleeping and will surely wake again in the future."

"Why are you only telling me this now? Why did you confess? I don't understand," Pietro said. Garrett stared straight ahead, out in the direction their horse was pulling them.

"I expect he will die. I felt as though I assigned him a death sentence and treated it as such. He will sleep for a long time, very long. But as long as no other ill presents itself to him, he will assuredly wake up." Garrett said, still looking into the distance, but Pietro was staring straight at him.

"How long?" Pietro asked. "How long will he sleep?"

Garrett shook his head. "I have no way of knowing. I don't know the size of the dose he took in; some of the solution soaked into his stocking, some into his boot. I do not know how much made it to his skin, except that it was enough for us to make our escape." It was, of course, a lie. Garrett knew it would be between half a million on the low end, and thirty or forty million years on the high end. That knowledge, he would keep to himself.

"I feel much better, though, despite that," Pietro said. "You did not kill the man, you simply subdued him. A perfectly acceptable response to such an assault. I feel much better about this now. Thank you for giving me the details of your actions. I understand fully now why the priest prescribed the penance that he did." Pietro had a smile on his face, and Garrett had no plans to say anything that would change that.

They rolled on down the road, through the French countryside, with Pietro exuberantly reengaging in his French language lessons and Garrett eagerly learning. They set camp, continued the lessons, broke camp the following morning, and still maintained the lessons. On the morning of the fifth day, Pietro told Garrett that he would no longer speak to him in Latin. He would only communicate in French until they reached Paris, which was only three days from that morning.

Though it proved difficult, years later, Garrett reflected that it was the fastest he had ever learned any language, and that included an extensive catalogue.

11

They entered Paris in the afternoon of the seventh day, which Pietro had predicted even before they left Avignon. They had crossed the Seine several miles back and entered the city along its southernmost edge. Almost as soon as they had crossed into the city, Pietro jumped down off the wagon bench and told Garrett to keep going. He jogged over to a young boy peddling papers and purchased one. He easily caught back up to the wagon and boarded. Garrett took some enjoyment from the knowledge that they were traveling north on Avenue d'Italie, having spent so much of his time in the country.

"Take a left here, on Rue de Tolbiac," Pietro pointed with his left hand. "I have been to Paris three other times in my life, but they only opened the ossuary for public viewing last year. I must see it." Pietro stared ahead with conviction.

"I don't know that word, 'ossuary,'" Garrett said.

Pietro looked at him and nodded. "Yes, it is a place to store the old bones of the dead, long after their internment in a more appropriate grave. A hundred years ago Paris was absolutely teeming with the dead, and their graves were consuming so much of the land…" he looked at Garrett with a half smirk of shame. "Sorry, I don't mean to speak of the misfortune with enthusiasm, but I expect the ossuary to be a magnificent sight."

"They could bear no more dead? They had no space for graves?" Garrett was genuinely interested in the topic, though morbid.

"Precisely. They had to find a solution, and the solution they arrived at was to build an ossuary in the abandoned limestone mines beneath the city. It already existed, so there was no need for excavation. It was a perfect solution. I have been told it was done artfully and with much respect to the dead. I need to see it with my own eyes. Take a right; we will be there in a moment."

After hitching the horse to a post near the entrance, Garrett found he had to make an effort to catch up with

Pietro. They were up and into the small building that served as the entrance point to the catacombs in only a minute.

Once below, fully among the bones, the grand nature of their surroundings moved Garrett. Pietro wept. The cramped space was dim, but the available light was enough to view the bones. They buried most of the odd bones behind and out of view, but all the facades were intricate works of art featuring skulls and femurs.

"I am in awe at the," Pietro hesitated, "enormity. It's beautiful, it's horrible, it's…" he drifted off.

"Real," Garrett finished for him. "And it is the consequence of time. I will admit it is heartbreaking to see them and know there was an entire lifetime of stories for each. But it is just time, Pietro. Time is unforgiving, it is rude, and above all else, it is caustic."

Pietro looked at his new friend. "It's God's will."

"I suppose it is. Let's go. Staying here longer will not do either of us any good."

12

Once in the comfort of their prearranged lodgings, one of several small apartments procured by the church, they settled in. Set against the far wall, away from the door of the kitchen, a small wooden table and two simple wooden chairs sufficed as their dining amenities.

"We should stuff ourselves tonight. The last of the food we brought with us will not last another few days," Pietro said. Instead of making up plates, he placed two empty ones on the table and the now much-lighter food chest on the floor beside it. Wine, cheese, pork, beef, and lamb.

When both men could eat no more, they sat heavily back in their chairs. Sunset was still not close, and they sat and talked and opened a second bottle of wine.

"Tell me, Garrett. I have traveled with you and spoken with you a great deal over these last two weeks. I find you a curious person." Pietro tapped a finger on his lower lip.

"That isn't a question," Garrett laughed.

"That is to say, I find it hard to believe that you are from any part of the lands around here. You look like a man but do not resemble an Italian nor any other European, nor even an Asian or African. Your interests match few other men's interests, and your ambitions seem wholly odd." Pietro stared at the floor behind the mostly empty food chest.

"A little insulting, perhaps, but still no question," Garrett laughed again, but lightly.

"I say all of that to ask you this: who are you, where are you from, and why are you truly here?" Pietro asked.

The smile drifted from the Envoy's face. He met Pietro's eyes with a look that he hoped communicated sincerity. "I can tell you some things, but not everything," Garrett said. "I promise you that everything I tell you will be true, and that I am not insane. However, I fear that if I told you my complete story, you would conclude that I was a liar, or mad. Worse than either of those things, were you to believe me, it would offend your faith, and I have no intention of offending the faith of a friend." Garrett sat up in his chair and Pietro poured them both another glass of wine.

"My name is Garrett Rhodes, as you know. The place I was born and raised was called Osa. It was farther from here than you could imagine, and it doesn't matter now, because it's been gone for a long, long time."

"But where was this, this Osa? And how can a place just be gone? We are an advanced people now; we know all the reaches of the Earth. Was it in Asia or Africa? The Americas? Was it in the Atlantic or the Pacific or Indian Ocean? I don't understand. How is it now just… gone?"

"Fire."

"So, it is still there, but it has been destroyed?" Pietro asked with conviction written on his face.

Garrett shifted in his seat and appeared to think. "We are getting close to the border of what I can tell you and what I cannot. But it is gone. Osa is gone. There remains no burned up landscape, and it is gone forever," Garrett said. Pietro's brow furrowed in confusion, but he did not press the matter any further.

"I have been traveling ever since I left Osa, for so many years that I have lost all sense of time. I stayed for a while in northern Italy, and I even made some friends there, but they're all long dead now."

"Long dead? How? And how could you know?" Pietro asked. "You're such a young man yourself. You can't be over forty years old."

Garrett laughed loudly. "My friend, I am much older than I appear. But again, to give you the full story about that would be to flirt with offense." Garrett expected Pietro to tire of the excuse, but evidently he still had not. "As to why I am here: I am trying to gauge how advanced the science and technology are in this part of the world. Osa was extremely advanced, and they commissioned me as an envoy to penetrate deep into the world and assist with this advancement, among other things."

"What other things?" Pietro was stirring in his seat and poured another glass of wine.

"I cannot say."

"For fear of offense?"

"Yes."

"What if I said that I did not care? That I would hear the entire story, and any offense was my business only? Are you a demon?"

"No," Garrett said. "Who I am, where I'm from, and what I'm here to do… these things lie so far outside your knowledge of the natural world that if I were to tell you, you would be convinced I was mad. Or, you would go mad yourself, and either of those things would surely damage our friendship."

"I'd like to risk it, with the assurance that I will not abandon you even if I question your sanity. You have never threatened me nor given me any cause to be concerned for my safety while with you. Quite to the contrary, actually. So yes, please do tell me, and I will deal with any offense on my own, and vow to stay with you until you are ready to move on without me."

"If you are sure, then I will continue," Garrett said. Pietro nodded and sipped his wine. "As you wish. First, Osa was not a city, a country, or a land… it was a planet."

13

When Garrett finished speaking, he refilled his own wineglass and noticed the window in the kitchen had grown dark. Pietro sat with a slack expression. He closed his eyes and put his hands over his face. Without removing them, he said, "Well, you were right to warn me." He revealed his face again and crossed his arms on the table. "You are most definitely impaired in the mind."

"I would prefer you believed me mad than think I was lying to you," Garrett said.

Pietro shrugged. "I don't believe you're lying. You have given me no reason to think so. It's clear to me you believe all that you say, but it is all so much nonsense."

"In biblical times, if people needed to traverse a waterway, they would rely on a simple wooden skiff. Now you fly across the oceans on steam-driven crafts. You understand that with time comes advancement. How do you think people will travel across the ocean in one hundred or one thousand more years? In skiffs? In steamers? I assure you, they will not. And I think you know that just as well as I do."

The look of skepticism on Pietro's face fell off, and he said, "Did you know of the Treaty of the Metre? Of course you didn't, because I didn't tell you." Garrett shrugged and shook his head. "The Treaty of the Metre, signed two weeks ago in this very city. I read about it in the newspaper during our trip here from the ossuary. Seventeen nations agreed to adopt a standardized form of measurement, the metric system," he spoke about it enthusiastically. "Before now, measures were scattered and differed from region to region. It makes trade difficult across great distances. Maybe now things will be easier."

"Do you not see what I mean, then?" Garrett said, smiling. "That is advancement, remarkable advancement. No longer will this troubling confusion of weights and measures complicate business transactions. These countries that signed, are they all minor countries that are regionally close together, or powerful and spread wide?"

"They encompass the planet. Some are the most prestigious countries in the world," Pietro said.

Garrett nodded. "Then others will follow. It will become global, and you will do business on this side of the planet or the other, with no confusion. It is even more exciting in scientific disciplines! Collaboration will be much easier." Garrett rocked back and forth in his chair, grinning widely. "This is exactly the kind of thing I need to know! Thank you, friend. This now is the time of the kindling, but this world is about to burst into a bonfire of advancement. Mark my words, Pietro, you are a young man and have a great many years left. By the time you are approaching your final year, this world will not resemble the one you were born into." Garrett raised his glass before finishing the contents in one swallow.

"I do believe that to be true," Pietro said. "I have already seen amazing things, and talk of what is on the horizon is heavily buzzing in a city such as Paris. But, I have come to the end of my efforts for today. I'm going to bed." Pietro stood up and walked out of the small kitchen.

Garrett yelled out to him, "I encourage you to maintain your religious studies, but also entertain my madness!" He laughed and went to his own small room.

14

Shortly after their arrival in Paris, Garrett found a small tavern within walking distance from their accommodations and had grown comfortable in its atmosphere. He met a few regular patrons of the establishment and used them to both improve his French and to hear their entertaining tales. Garrett enjoyed his visits to La Taverne du Pont-Rouge and became a daily regular. His cohorts were three retired professors named Henri, Jacques, and Marcel.

Having had the experience of a young planet on Telraed and to a lesser degree on Katya, the Envoy knew he would need to amass at least a small amount of gold early in his mission. In addition to the small wage that Pietro paid him for his assistance, he had found work as an assistant in a small printing enterprise around the corner from the tavern. The job at the printer paid much more than Pietro, and so he disciplined himself to only spend the money he earned from Pietro at the tavern. He exchanged all of his earnings from the printer for gold coins, buying each as he had saved enough to afford them. The gold coins had an important meaning; unlike the money he had made on the Clotz farm, gold stood up to inflation. When he jumped to the future, he could exchange it for the money of that time, maintaining its value.

On the afternoon of his eighth day in Paris, and only after his fourth day working at the printers, he walked into the stone and mortar building that was La Taverne du Pont-Rouge. Although early in their relationship, Henri recognized Garrett and called to him. They sat at a round, squat table, pushed deeply back into the tavern and closest to the fireplace, but still only ten paces from the bar. The atmosphere was dark, but a candle burned at each table, and the light from the fire only added to the pleasant nature of the establishment. The floors were rough planks smoothed over time by foot traffic, and a good deal of sawdust helped with cleaning the inevitable spills.

"Garrett! Come! Sit with us," Henri said, and Jacques and Marcel both looked up with enormous smiles. They were all sharing a bottle of blood red wine. "No wine for Garrett!" Henri laughed. "Only beer for our traveling friend! Anton! Please bring our friend a pint of ale!" The bartender pressed a straw-colored liquid from the cask into a pint glass.

"Merci," Garrett said when Anton placed the glass in front of him and relieved the stack of coins Garrett had placed on the table of the fee.

"Garrett should decide," Marcel said. "He is far smarter than any of us old men, especially in the sciences." The three men were old friends and all had been instructors in their younger years. Garrett had already discussed the known scientific advancements of the time with them and had dispelled many of their lifelong assumptions in detail. In only a few days, they had grown to respect the opinion of a man thirty years their junior.

"What is the question?" Garrett asked, and sipped his cool, pleasant beer. Marcel took two pieces of paper, one in front of Henri and the other before Jacques, and placed them on either side of Garrett's beer glass.

"Two tables, one from Lothar Meyer of Germany, and one from Dmitri Mendeleev of Russia," Marcel said. "Two tables of the natural elements of our world, but a vastly different telling from each. I will not divulge to you which one each of us thinks is the most accurate, but I will tell you we are at odds. Once you answer us, the loser is buying the next bottle of wine!"

Garrett laughed at the competition, humbled by their reliance on him as the expert in all matters of the scientific world. He studied the first table carefully and with curiosity, and then the second with the same scrutiny. Before he answered the men, he asked for translations on multiple details of each document. Finally, he tapped with his left index finger on a space devoid of writing on the Russian document.

"This one," he said. Marcel stood and cheered while the other men sat back in their chairs.

"Why?!" Jacques asked enthusiastically.

"The spaces. You have made many discoveries, but not all of them. Mendeleev recognizes that in his table. He has left room in the correct places for the missing pieces," Garrett said.

"I believe you gentlemen need to procure us a fresh bottle! Off with you!" Marcel said, vibrant and animated. Henri tossed a coin to Jacques, who stood and walked up to the bar. Garrett laughed and took another sip from his glass.

Before Jacques returned, Garrett spoke to the others. "I greatly appreciate our friendship, but I need to ask another favor as we continue it."

The two remaining men nodded. "What can we do for you, son?" Marcel asked.

"I need to learn German and English. And I think of the two, it is more important that I learn English, because I plan to travel to the United States." Garrett looked apprehensive, but Marcel laughed.

"Is that all?" Henri asked. Garrett nodded.

Marcel yelled to Jacques at the bar, "Jacques! English only at the table from now on, so long as Garrett is with us!" Jacques answered in a language that Garrett could not understand. Marcel turned back to Garrett and slapped his shoulder twice.

"No problem, my friend, we'll have you speaking that devil tongue in no time!"

"Devil tongue?" Garrett asked to no one in particular.

"The French and the English have not always gotten along," Henri explained.

15

Four weeks into his Parisian experience and after his third payment of wages from the print shop, Garrett took his earnings to a banker and exchanged his bag of coins for three gold Napoleons, twenty-franc pieces. A day after they had arrived in Paris, he had used some money paid to him by Pietro to purchase appropriate clothing and two satchels. The satchels were large enough that he could fit both of his fists in each. He used the first to put all the loose coins he had gained from the Clotz's employment, which before had just pooled inside his large bag among the rest of his supplies. It surprised him to find they filled the first satchel completely, with a great number still remaining loose and pushed into the back corner of his drawer. The huge number of coins he had accumulated during his time with the Clotz's did not amount to much in total, as the denominations were small. The second satchel he carried with him and used to keep the printing house wages separate from Pietro's, which he would typically keep in the front pocket of his pants.

Besides his three new gold Napoleons, he had eleven francs and twenty-five cents left, which he put back in the satchel with his new gold pieces. Upon arriving back at the apartment, he transferred the gold pieces to the stacks of left-over Roman coins in the back right corner of his clothing drawer.

He had little of the money that Pietro paid him left that day, and so he skipped the tavern after leaving the print shop. Having eaten a small meal upon arriving back at the apartment, he sat on his small cot with nothing to do. Daylight still shone through his window. He thought of the farm, and that naturally led him to think about the letters from Marco, so he went to his bag and retrieved them. He first reread the initial three letters to refresh his memory of the goings-on among the Clotz's that led up to the fourth and ominous fifth. After he had digested this material a second time, he read the fourth:

February 12, 613 -

Garrett,

The last time I wrote you, my father had recently died. I am unhappy to admit that was almost thirty years ago. In the time that has passed since I last wrote, we have experienced many tragedies. First, as you may have imagined at this late age, my mother left us almost twenty years ago. She had no ailment, just slipped away one night, and I'm sorry to report it was my precious granddaughter who found her. We interned her upon Tenna hill next to father.

Mateo passed last year. He missed his eightieth by only three days! His heart was the cause, I'm afraid. He had experienced many chest pains leading up to his final day. I spoke with him for hours every day until his last, at his bedside. Although many years have passed since you told me your stories, I did my best to recollect them for him as he lay dying, if for no other reason than entertainment. He did not question their authenticity but laughed with true joy in his eyes. I told him of the letter that I would write you, and he asked me to say hello, so now, to you, I say, Hello! From Mateo.

As for the people who you never met, Mateo's wife, Cerelia, still lives. She was younger than him but is several years older than me. She is a strong old bat! I expect she will outlive me by ten years!

I lost my beautiful Marquesa nine years ago. We never truly knew what ailed her, just that she had painful headaches that got worse over the course of three months, and then did not wake up. It was a terrible time for me. If not for my own children, I may have cast myself off Tenna hill so I could rejoin her. My daughter, my youngest, and her three children brought me back from the brink. I live with her and her children because of what happened in August of '99, a few years before we lost her mother.

I told you of Luca, not my father but Mateo's boy, and his rotten wife, the Monteprato girl. The two of them had only one child, a girl they named Luna after my sister, and only after their marriage had aged. She was just twelve when all of this happened. Luca's relationship with his wife was horrible. Everyone knew it. They fought openly and violently, no matter who was near to witness it. Maurice, a great childhood friend of Luca and the eventual son-in-law of myself, as he was married to my daughter, interceded many times in their arguments. Alas, on a Thursday afternoon in August 599, we all discovered Luca murdered in the brewery, with countless wounds inflicted with a knife or dagger. His wife was gone from the farm, and Maurice immediately concluded she had murdered him. That very night, he traveled to the large Monteprato estate. He broke into their home, found Luca's wife in her childhood bedroom, and removed her head from her neck with a sickle he had brought with him from the farm. The men from the Monteprato house descended upon him, alerted by her dying screams. With Maurice dispatched, my daughter a widow, and my brother a new father to his granddaughter, the madness concluded. Mateo and I met with the Monteprato family many times over the next three years, and we finally returned to friendly relations.

I am sorry to bring you this news, Tosgaire. I imagine it all matters to you very little, as you would have known that by the time you wake, we will all have passed by one set of means or another. If you are not interested in our history, you can toss these letters into the fire.

I did not write you for almost thirty years, but I write now for a reason. I have a deep pain in my right side; it is persistent, and I fear my time here is very short. My youngest grandson knows of your story, and many years ago, we even ventured off to the cave where you sleep. We visited you a few times, as it was an excuse to get out of the house and adventure together. I showed him so that he would understand your story is real and not just mistake my interest as the mumblings of a feeble old man. If I cannot deliver these letters, he has promised to do so in my stead.

I want to thank you, Tosgaire. Our time together was short, but you were my greatest childhood friend. Your stories amazed me, and I carried your teachings with me throughout my entire life. I pray these messages and my best wishes find you and find you well.

Godspeed Tosgaire,

Marco

Garrett knew the tears that had dropped to the surface of the papers might degrade them, but he could not help himself. He intentionally hid the fifth and last letter behind the rest because he knew it would contain the details of Marco's death. He assured himself he would read it in time. At that point, he was coping with a loss that had occurred centuries ago, but the wounds were fresh for him.

He refolded the papers and placed them back in his clothing drawer with his money. Although the daylight still poured in through the apartment windows, he laid down and closed his eyes.

16

Pietro and Garrett had come to the agreement that although he was not convinced of all Garrett claimed, Pietro would operate under the pretense it was true, so long as they remained together. Garrett took advantage of the service, as he was able to learn more about the world from Pietro to help guide him in determining the next step in his plan. Pietro told him all he knew over several months, and Garrett absorbed all he could from Pietro and his trio of friends at La Taverne du Pont-Rouge in that time. Advancements, technologies, medicines, travel, and power systems were all discussed at length as well as the different parts of the world: Asia and Australia, Africa, Eastern Europe, and the Scandinavian countries, to the different western European countries and the Americas, and even Greenland and Antarctica.

A month after ringing in the new year and as they approached the end of their seventh month in Paris, they ate a modest dinner together in their apartment. "They have called me back to Rome, and I'm afraid you will have to decide what you will do upon my departure," Pietro said.

Garrett wiped his mouth and sat back in his chair, smiling. "I'm surprised it has taken this long." Garrett had abandoned the Latin months before, and they spoke in French, as Pietro's English was weak. "Honestly, I have expected that you would return for months now. I counted each additional day I had with you to be a blessing. When do you depart?"

"I'm not quite finished with my work here, so I will be here through this week and the next. The following week, I will depart for Rome," Pietro said.

"Excellent! That is more than enough time for me to settle my accounts and make preparations for my own departure." Garrett stood and began clearing the table.

"Where will you go? Have you decided? You are always welcome to come back to Rome with me. You have been a great asset to me since the day we met; though I suspect you have seen the last of Italy?"

"I have. Although our separation will be a sad one, I am bound for America," Garrett said.

"America! It will be a difficult voyage in the winter months, but you'll be happy to find that the fare is cheaper than when the weather is pleasant." He poured himself another glass of wine and offered one to Garrett, who refused. "Better that you'll have a warm cabin to stay in. I can say with all honesty, I am not looking forward to my trip. Paris to Rome in the middle of February!"

"If there is anything I can offer you to make your trip easier, please ask," Garrett said. Pietro shook his head, and with that, Garrett retired.

17

Three days after his conversation with Pietro and after leaving the print shop, Garrett walked into La Taverne du Pont-Rouge. He found two of his three friends sitting by a table near the large stone hearth and the fire at the back of the establishment. With his large glass of ale in hand, he walked back to join them.

"Where is Jacques?" Garrett inquired, as he took a seat at the table.

Henri looked at Marcel with apprehension. "We do not know. Jacques is always the first of us to arrive, and I'm afraid he may have fallen ill." Henri spoke in English, as the older men had been working with Garrett to get him as fluent as possible.

"Well, I'm terribly sorry to hear it. I come with news. Just yesterday I booked passage to New York!"

"Ha!" Marcel said. "Well, that is wonderful, Garrett. When do you depart across the icy Atlantic on this hellish voyage?" Henri and Garrett laughed.

"I travel by rail in three days to Havre, and the following day the ship departs, bound for America."

"I'm very happy that you will realize this dream now, Garrett," Henri said. "But I am sad that we shall no longer have your company. I'm sure I speak for all three of us when I say that our time together has been enlightening, fascinating and, most importantly, hilarious." Henri raised his glass as all three men laughed loudly.

"I assure you I will also miss the time I have spent here, and I thank you all for the help you have given me with my French and English alike. It is valuable beyond measure, and I know I can never repay you."

"I would accept gold," Marcel said simply, and the three men laughed again. "In all seriousness, Garrett, it was our pleasure. You have contributed to our lives greatly as well. It has been a very interesting and entertaining year."

18

The Sunday before his departure, Garrett packed his belongings into his bag, which was falling apart. Just as he had started his effort, Pietro appeared in the doorway of his room.

"I am sorry to part ways with you. You have turned out to be a great friend," Pietro said. Garrett stopped packing and stood up straight.

"I agree completely, Pietro. You have given me so much, but I'm afraid I cannot think of a way to repay you."

Pietro laughed briefly. "Yes, well, saving all of my possessions that night in Genoa was far more pay than I could ever expect. But I do have something for you. I first thought I would give you one of my chests to make your travel easier. But after thinking about that for only a moment, envisioning you trying to walk great distances in America dragging a chest behind you, I thought better of the offer." Garrett smiled as he envisioned it himself, dragging a chest down a dusty American road. "After I left the Cathedral the day before last, I remembered a vendor I pass every day that deals in leather goods, and so I made a purchase for you." Pietro disappeared out of the doorway, only to return holding a large leather bag. "I thought this would provide you more utility, and you can now discard that disaster you were about to pack up with your possessions."

Garrett walked to Pietro and took the bag from him. The leather was soft, and the bag itself had weight. Instead of the two straps he was used to, the bag had one long strap that he could throw over his head.

"I can't thank you enough! This is wonderful!" Garrett undid the large outside button and turned the flap covering the main opening at the top to examine the interior of the bag. It had no fewer than six pouches sewn into the inner wall, all with their own flaps and buttons to fasten them closed.

"Just promise me you will discard that awful thing you have been carrying with you for all of your years," Pietro said, smiling.

"Ha! No promises. That bag has been with me since before I left my family. It has meaning."

"Very well, then. God bless you, Garrett, wherever your travels take you."

"Thank you for everything, Pietro. It has been an honor knowing you." Pietro smiled and disappeared again. That was the last time Garrett ever saw him.

19

The next morning, when Garrett awoke, he walked through the empty apartment. Pietro had already left for the Cathedral. Thirty minutes later, washed and dressed, he inspected his room and drawers for anything he might have missed while packing. He repeated the process in every room of the apartment but Pietro's bedroom. While inspecting the kitchen, he heard a gentle rap at the apartment door. He went to it and opened the door enough to find an old man hunched over a cane and holding a book. He looked up, and Garrett immediately recognized him. It was Jacques from La Taverne du Pont-Rouge.

"Forgive the interruption, Garrett," Jacques said. "I'm glad you are still here."

Garrett opened the door wide and stepped back. "Come in, Jacques! It's freezing out there." Jacques ambled into the small apartment kitchen and sat at the table. "Can I get you anything?"

"No! No, nothing for me. I just came to give you a proper farewell. Henri told me of your escape, but I'm afraid I took a fall and hurt my leg. I was in bed for two days after!"

"I'm terribly sorry to hear that, Jacques. Are you sure there is nothing at all I can get for you?"

"Well, I suppose a cup of tea, if it's not too much trouble. That would warm the bones. Are you racing off to the rail yard now?" Jacques asked. Garrett prepared the kettle and put it on the stove.

"No, I have another two hours yet before I plan to leave this place for the last time. My train does not depart until noon."

"Ah, then I hope this isn't too much of an interruption."

"Not at all. I'm thrilled that we can say a proper goodbye," Garrett said, and went to the cupboard, retrieving two teacups.

"Have you ever traveled on a vessel such as the…"

"It's a steamer, and I can tell you I'm quite excited about it. It is called the *Amerique*. But no, I have never traversed an ocean in my life, and never set foot on a vessel of that scale." Garrett did not expand to include which vessels he had traveled on, nor did he say that he had traversed entire galaxies.

"I hope you have a strong stomach. The Atlantic in the winter is ornery," Jacques said. Garrett smiled and nodded, remembering his launch from Katya and the intensity it brought.

"I can only hope my stomach will survive the trip." Garrett placed the cups of tea on the small table and sat.

"I brought you a gift! I don't know if you'll have the ability to read during your voyage. Some people get terrible vertigo, but I thought if you could, this might help pass the time." Jacques slid the book across the table. Garrett looked at the front cover, *The Count of Monte Cristo,* by Alexander Dumas.

"It's an excellent tale. You have not read it, have you?" Jacques asked. Garrett shook his head. "Even better, it is a long tale. So long as you can read without vomiting, this will help you get across the Atlantic in a flash! The setting is in France and Italy, your two favorite countries!" Garrett picked up the book and felt the weight of it.

"I can't tell you how grateful I am, Jacques. In truth, I have only old letters, and no books other than your gift."

"You are in good hands, then. This tale will consume your mind for hours and days! I only hope your cabin contains the light to read by." The two men made light conversation while they finished their tea, and after fifteen minutes, they wished each other well and said their final goodbyes.

20

The train ride was brief, but Garrett took the occasion to begin reading *The Count of Monte Cristo.* He had barely skimmed the surface of the tale before the train slowed and halted, preparing for the passengers bound for Havre, of which he was one, to disembark. He stowed the thick book in his soft leather bag and moved to exit the train. Once on the platform, he walked toward the docks and gasped when he set his eyes on the *Amerique.* It was impressively large, with a black hull that seemed enormous in that simple time and two stacks rising off the general center of the deck, slightly favoring the great ship's bow. Three tall masts with all their rigging rose from its length. Although it was a steam-driven craft, it still possessed the ability to capture the wind. It was a sight to behold, and Garrett found it an impressive achievement for an age that was only just beginning to discover the benefits of thoughtful and advanced engineering.

Once on board, his general impression only grew stronger. He could feel the subtle movement of the ocean in the decking beneath him, and the view from its height drew a large exclamation point on his previous observations. After perusing the deck for ten minutes, he thought it smart to find his cabin and settle in for the voyage.

As he swung the door of his cabin open, he had two immediate and simultaneous thoughts: the space was so tiny he thought it absurd, and he had a porthole. It had a latch and hinges, and unlike the cabin itself, it was larger than he expected. Having viewed them externally from the dock made them look so small he was afraid they would not provide useful light.

Upon further inspection, there was a cutout for his possessions, with a few shelves at the base and a rod with hangers at the top. The hangers looked strange, as the wire hook was no hook at all but bent fully around the rod. *Smart*, Garrett thought. *Rough seas will not spill all your clothes to the floor*. He unloaded his new bag onto the shelves and hangers. In the small nightstand with its one drawer, he placed his most treasured objects: his Sterilex satchel, his letters from Marco, all of his accumulated coins, and his copy of *The Count of Monte Cristo*. A steel bolt and a wooden peg served as a latch to prevent the drawer from opening in rough water.

With all his possessions stowed, he traveled back up to the deck to get more acquainted with the ship. After taking a lap around, he settled on a spot along the rail to observe the sunset. Although it was February, the weather was calm and unusually temperate. The sun was low in the sky and would set upon the French coast twenty minutes later. He intended to observe it and then return to his cabin to sleep. It was early to sleep at that hour, but he wanted to get as much as he could before the ship set sail, not knowing how well sleep would find him once they were rolling amongst the waves.

"Evening," a voice said. A young man of about thirty years with light blonde hair pressed down around his ears by a cap leaned against the rail next to him. "Do you speak English?" His accent was thick, and he was clearly a native speaker of the language.

"I try," Garrett said, not hearing his own strong French/Osan accent in the words, and extended a hand to the stout young man, who shook it quickly.

"Alexis is my name. This is my first trip across the pond, you?"

Garrett smiled and nodded. "Garrett, and yes, I have never been to America, nor have I ever sailed a distance such as this, and this is the first time I've been on a steamer." He shuffled his feet and leaned against the rail, turning so he could converse with the young man without being rude.

"I took one across the channel to get here four years ago. I thought I'd be going home to Croyden, south of London. But two weeks ago, my father sends me a letter and this ticket to New York. I'll be there for at least a month before I can finally go home." Alexis lifted his cap and ran his fingers through his hair.

"What is your industry?" Garrett asked.

"Printing. My father owns a large printing press just outside of London. He bought a small print shop in Lisieux four years ago. That's why I'm in France, and now he wants me to bargain for the purchase of another small press, this one in Brooklyn. Stupid me, I thought I could go home." Alexis was rubbing his hands together slowly. "What about you? Are you traveling alone as well, or do you have family aboard?"

"Alone, with only a book gifted to me by a dear friend as a companion."

"Ah! And which book is it?" Garrett told him about the gift from Jacques. "Excellent! An excellent book. It is a captivating tale." Genuine excitement shone on Alexis' face before disappearing again. "I only hope you can read on the waves. It's troubling for some."

"I've heard," Garrett said, and looked at the sunset as it was fading beneath the horizon. He did not mention his own experience in printing, as he did not want to stir the possibility of an offer of work. Once landing in New York, he had to prepare for his next stint, and that was all.

The light was draining from the sky, and Garrett stepped back from the railing. "It was a pleasure meeting you, Alexis, but I am going to retire to my cabin. I'm sure our paths will cross again on our voyage."

Alexis nodded. "Good evening, Garrett. It was a pleasure meeting you."

21

Two days into the crossing, Garrett had learned three things. The first was that space travel and travel by sea were very different things. He had no trouble traversing massive distances in space. The second was that vomiting was reserved for those who had eaten, so after the first day, he refrained from the activity, as his first day was messy. The third thing was that once the nausea passed, and he could walk about the deck in the daytime, he loved breathing the sea air. It differed greatly from the first time he had encountered oceans on Earth; it was vastly saltier, and the introduction of near-infinite life and its influence on the chemistry of the water and surrounding air were pleasing to his senses.

He stood alone at the starboard railing of the ship, shortly after noon of the second day, with the dull but persistent pain of hunger in his stomach. Tucked under his arm was the copy of the book that Jacques had given him, and he took it to the bow, where there was a large storage cabinet. He sat on the deck, leaning back on the cabinet, and opened the book to see if he could read while rocking about. Though it took some getting used to, he found he could do it, and as he dug deeper into the story of Edmond Dantès, he lost his sense of time. The sky grew dark, and he at once had the false impression that a storm was closing in. It surprised him to find the setting sun to be the cause. He marked his place in the brilliant book and hurried to his cabin to sleep as quickly as he could, eager to resume the story he had found himself in.

The third day disagreed with his ambition, as now there really was a storm they had to pass through. He stayed in his cabin, as did most passengers, for the entire day. He tried to read by the light of the porthole in his room, but the skies were dark with clouds and his attempts were futile. His hunger was getting worse, and he feared he would not sleep.

The fourth day at sea differed completely from the third. Bright sunshine hailed all day, and the ocean surface was almost glass. The only breeze came from the ship naturally passing through the atmosphere. Garrett took advantage of the conditions and ate and drank heavily in the morning. He was able to read for the largest part of the daylight hours. Exhausted, having not slept much the night before, he forced himself to stay awake during the tranquility.

Garrett's fifth day on the ocean began pleasantly enough but deteriorated throughout the course of the afternoon. There was no storm, but the clouds crept in and brought wind and the waves it birthed. The clouds were not heavy, though, and he retired to his cabin, where he read by the dim light of his porthole. He even took the occasion to open the window, as the wind was somewhat warm, having come from the south.

The waves had calmed throughout the night, and Garrett fell into a deep sleep. When he awoke, it was daylight through the porthole, and he opened it to better see the conditions. Surprise overtook him as he felt the first of the frigid air touch his face, along with a considerable number of snowflakes. In the moment before he slammed the porthole closed again, he could see nothing but a mass of snowfall. A dark patch in the lower half of his field of view had to be the ocean water itself. He thought, *is every day going to be completely different?* Although the skies were overcast, there was significant light flooding his cabin, and he read. After several hours, his hunger returned, and he risked going up to the dining room to eat. Storm or no storm, it brought no wind with it, and the sea was still relatively calm.

22

The *Amerique* arrived in New York on the morning of Valentine's Day, February 14th, 1876. Repacked and prepared to disembark, Garrett reached the deck to set his eyes on America for the first time. The visage was enormous and packed with people and buildings as far as the eye could see.

He exited the ship and used the tips he received from Henri to navigate through immigration. Finally, they turned him out onto the streets of New York. He walked south. Several times, he stopped people he ran into for directions. On one of every three attempts, he received helpful information and navigated his way west across the Hudson to New Jersey. A cornfield was his accommodation for the first night, and the next day he continued walking west. He had stashed food from the *Amerique* in his bag, flatbreads, dried meats, and hard cheese, anything that would last, wrapped in wax paper. While on the Amerique, he drank only what they provided, saving the water bottles he had filled in France for the walking journey in America. It was the French water he sipped on as he made his long trek. His goal was to spend none of his accumulated money until after his time jump. During his trip across New Jersey, he stopped other travelers to get information, and found that if it were mountains he wanted, he ought to continue west to the Appalachians.

The mountains rose from the ground as he approached Pennsylvania. When he had found a well-beaten trail, whether an animal trail or one created by humans he was unsure, he left the road and began his ascent. He reached a clearing and sat on a rock, ate, drank, and stared out east across the New Jersey plain that he had crossed over the previous two days and smiled. He had traversed an enormous distance to set himself up for success. The last piece of the puzzle was to find a quiet place to lie undisturbed for some number of years.

Over the course of the next three days, he found two locations, but only one was deep enough to prevent him from freezing to death in the winter. Once he crept into the second location and settled in with his things, he faced a difficult question. For how long did he go under? He thought about all the progress he had witnessed throughout his journey and decided on one hundred years. After he finished administering the one-hundred-year dose, he thought better of it and added fifty more. Wrapped and drugged, the Envoy was down once more.

Chapter 8

Decision

1

Garrett tossed and turned for the second night in a row. After leaving Lauren at the end of their date, he spent the first night sifting through possibilities he did not want to entertain but that he had no power to dissuade. The second night, having not seen her since, was no better.

Written into their contracts, any envoy could pull himself from the program at any time without penalty. When Garrett signed up as the first, he never thought he would have a reason to question that decision. Since then, he'd had a few mild reservations, but Lauren was the first big one.

He had not slept at all and could see the window in his bedroom brightening with the sunrise. Lauren would arrive at his apartment at 12:00, and he had not slept well in almost three days. He feared the fog in his mind would cloud his judgement, that his extreme feelings might sully his relationship with her. He clamped his eyes shut again and prayed for sleep, even a little, to no avail.

2

The knock at the door came at 11:59. An exhausted Garrett, showered and deliriously tired, answered the door. When he pulled the door out of his view, he saw a young girl buried in a sweatshirt with its hood up and a look of exhaustion on her face.

"You look like death. Did you sleep last night?" Lauren asked.

"Not for the last two," he said. She walked into his small, one-bedroom apartment without invitation, taking his hand as she walked past.

"Me either. Can this date be sleeping?" Garrett had never heard a more wonderful question in his life.

"Absolutely," he said. She led him to the couch in his modest living room. She stopped and pointed at it. "That isn't going to work. Don't get the wrong idea, but let's go to your bedroom."

"I get it, let's go." They went to his bedroom, and both of them laid down on his bed. Although they were close together, they did not embrace. With her ankle draped over his, they both fell deeply and immediately asleep.

3

A comically loud kiss on his cheek awoke Garrett at a time he could not fathom.

"I feel much better, but we have a little problem," Lauren said. Garrett sat up, fully clothed in his bed, and wiped his eyes.

"What problem?" He recognized that it was dark in his bedroom.

"We both slept the entire day and most of the night. We have to be at work in four hours," she said. Garrett picked up the clock from the nightstand next to his bed and read 5:04. Lauren was smiling, but she looked a little drunk, with her sweatshirt twisted awkwardly around her and her hair disheveled.

"Well, okay. How much time do you need to go home and get ready for work? Do you have to leave now?"

Lauren sat up on the bed and smiled at him. "Well, knowing how tired I was, and being a little presumptuous, I brought a bag with all my stuff. I can get ready for work here, if that's okay with you."

Garett laid back down on the bed and smiled. "Of course. So, we can have a little date while we both get ready to go in?"

She bent over and kissed him hard on the lips, "Yeah, I'm going down to my car for my bag."

Before she could get out of the room, Garrett said, "Car? Fancy!" She turned in the doorway, smiled widely and squinted at him.

"That's right, slouch!" she said, and disappeared.

Garrett got up and walked into his kitchen. Although he was a bachelor, he kept a fair amount of food in his apartment and started making a decent breakfast for them both. He never bothered buying a kitchen or a dining room table and typically ate his meals at his computer desk in his bedroom. There was a narrow island that divided the kitchen and the empty dining room with two stools at it, and he set it as though it were a normal breakfast table. Lauren came back into the apartment a moment later and dropped her enormous bag on the floor.

"What? Are you making us breakfast?"

Garrett laughed. "Is it so unbelievable that I can cook?" He set down his spatula and walked to her, gently placing his hands on her sides. "I'm a pretty smart guy. I can cook eggs and toast."

She smiled. "Hey, smart guy, your eggs are burning."

Garrett turned around to see the smoke and rushed to the stove to address it. He then turned to her and said, "I'm so smart, I can make new ones!"

Lauren rolled her eyes. "You do that, I'm going to shower." She walked to the bathroom with her bag, and Garrett restarted making their breakfast.

When she emerged from the bathroom, she was wearing oversized shorts and an equally oversized tee shirt. Her sweet, perpetual smile still held firm. "I decided to dress sexy for you."

Garrett laughed. He placed their plates of unburnt food on the kitchen island and they both sat. "I have a question for you," Garrett said. "And please don't take it the wrong way. I think you already understand how I feel about you, but you are less than a year older than me, and…"

"I'm twenty-three years old, and I already have my doctorate," she said, and nodded. She looked up at the ceiling and smiled. "What you don't know is what age I was when I got it." She raised her eyebrows and looked at him. Garrett shook his head and imitated her. She laughed. "Guess!"

Garrett thought. A doctorate typically took eight years after the undergraduate work, which would take four. At that rate, it would put her graduating from high school at eleven, but it had to be even earlier than that, because she had already established a career. He did not know, so he guessed. "Twenty-one?" he asked.

She smiled a big, beautiful smile and whispered, "Seventeen." She squinted at him again and turned her attention back to her food. Garrett had felt a certain amount of intimidation when he spent time with her, but he thought he was becoming comfortable with it until she uttered that number. She was not merely a smart woman; she was one of the smartest people on the planet. "Nothing to say about that, huh? Smart guy?" she asked. Garrett felt his soul melt a little.

"I told you last night, I'm enamored. There is nothing above that. You are remarkable beyond measure, and if you are after my affection, you have it," he said. Lauren blushed. Garrett tried to lessen the blow, leaned in, and kissed the corner of her mouth. She relaxed.

After Garrett had showered and they were both ready to go, they walked down the three flights of stairs to the parking deck. Lauren led him to her car and unlocked it. "Hey, after we're done at OPM tonight, let's go to my apartment. Yours is terrible."

Garrett laughed but thought about the implications. "Are you committing to us?" he asked.

She placed her hands on the roof of her car and looked at him sincerely. "You have to go. You have to. As long as you commit to that, then I commit to you." Garrett nodded. The question that had so bothered him faded to obscurity.

4

As the two-hour acquisitions class ended that day, instead of strategizing covert relations with Garrett, Dr. Astor took a different approach. "That is all for today, gentlemen, but I have one quick announcement. Garrett and I are seeing each other. I would prefer that it was not a rumor that you all gossiped about. Yes, we know it's silly; yes, we know it can't last; and yes, Garrett is leaving in less than ten months. We both understand all of that. But if any of you see us together outside of work, don't get worked up about it." Jaws dropped. Garrett, having stood, was a statue. Lauren walked to her desk, gathered her things, walked to Garrett, took his hand, and led him out of the classroom.

After they were out, Garrett reeled her in and kissed her hard. "Wow, you just dropped a bomb in there!" he said.

She looked at him innocently. "Do you care? Because I don't. I just want to go home, and I want you to be with me."

Garrett embraced her. "Me too. Let's go." They walked to the elevator and stepped in. As the doors were closing, Garrett said, "I am completely unprepared. I have to go home and get my things." The elevator descended.

Lauren frowned and looked up at him. "What makes you think you're staying the night?" Once the look of surprise registered on his face, she burst into laughter. "I'm kidding!

Go home and get your things. I'll get dinner and we can meet at my place."

"You're kind of a jerk," he said, but smiled through the insult.

She kissed him. "Lighten up, slouch. Remember, it will be important to keep this relationship light. It is, by design, going to crash and burn." She lightly slapped his side and kissed him again.

"As someone who will be flung off this planet at thousands of miles per hour, can we refrain from the 'crash and burn' talk?" he asked.

She frowned. "Sorry," she said. "Do you know where I live?"

"If I did, that would make me a stalker, but yes, I know where you live," he said. She frowned, and Garrett laughed just as hard. "No! I have no idea. You have to tell me!" She gave him directions to her apartment, and they walked out of the building, holding hands. Before they reached the large exterior doors, they heard a voice.

"Lauren?" It was Cecilia. "Are you two…?"

Lauren looked at her and said, "Yeah." She never broke stride, and then they were out into the evening stampede.

5

Garrett knocked on Lauren's door ninety minutes later, hoping the bouquet he had picked up on the way to her place would surprise her. "Be there in a minute," he heard through the door from deep within the apartment. She opened the door and was wearing large red gym shorts and a black, oversized tee with the letters 'OPM' printed on the chest, with the Orris logo beneath the text. "Are those for me?" she smiled at him. "So sweet." She took the flowers from him without inviting him in and walked away from the door. He stepped in and closed it. She had produced a vase from somewhere and was arranging the flowers in it. "I don't want you to take this the wrong way," she said. "I genuinely love the gesture, but I would rather have had the ten minutes it took you to get them than I would the flowers."

The sentiment warmed Garrett's heart. "I understand. And you were right, your apartment is much better than mine." He was standing in an entryway that she had placed a table in to mock a dining room. To his left was an island similar to his, separating the space from her much larger kitchen. He scanned deeper into the apartment and spied a small telescope pointing up through the glass pane of one of her living room windows. He laughed and pointed at it. "You're such a nerd."

She finished with the flowers, walked over to him, and embraced him. "You can see Orris with it," she whispered into his ear. The snarky smile melted from his face. "Now who's the nerd?" she said, kissed his neck and walked into the kitchen. "I just got takeout. It should be here any minute." There was a knock at the door as she finished her sentence, and Garrett answered it.

Lauren served the food on proper plates and with proper silverware, and they ate at her "dining room" table. While eating, they only made light conversation about the other Envoys, and Lauren described her schooling adventure and her almost unbelievable journey to her doctorate. When they finished eating, he helped her clear the dishes, and they went to the kitchen to clean up. He used the casual opportunity to ask about the one thing that had been picking at his mind since that morning.

"I have another question," he said as he washed and rinsed, while she dried and put away. "This morning you told me I had to go, like you had put a lot of thought into it, like you knew I was second guessing my decision. What was that about?" He handed her a fork, the last of the dishes. She dried it, dropped it into its place in the silverware basket, and hung the towel up to dry.

"I didn't know." She was not looking at him but took his hand and led him into the living room, which again was massive compared to his, and sat on the couch. He sat on the opposite side and faced her. "I suspected that if it went far enough between us, you might consider backing out and living on Osa for the rest of your life," she said, rubbing at her temple. "I've only had two relationships in my life. You are my third. Both of the first two started out great and ended badly after a year or two. I can't bear to think you would give this up for me, just to have our relationship flame out in a couple of years, with you wondering what might have been."

Garrett shifted in his seat and offered her a small smile. "First, you need to stop the references to failing flight equipment," Garrett said. He breathed in deeply and exhaled slowly. "You're right. As much as I want to disagree with you, I can't." He shifted again in his seat. "There is just no way either of us can know for sure. Especially this early in the relationship, and honestly, we won't even have a year together. There is no way that we can *know*, especially after less than a year. You really are smart." Lauren shifted herself over to him and kissed him.

He laid back, and she laid on top of him, her head resting on his chest.

"It's hard for me to believe that once you're gone, before you even get started, I'll be gone. We'll all be gone. Does that tear at you? Not about me, but about your family?" she asked. He pulled her tightly to him.

"Yeah. About my family and about you, too. About everyone I know. If I'm honest, I expect to be in tears about it shortly after the launch. How does anyone console themselves from losing everything and everyone in one action? We've talked about that with Dr. Paige," he said.

Lauren closed her eyes. "Hmm, I love Christine."

"Yeah, she's a great person," he said.

She climbed up far enough to plant a kiss on his neck and then looked at her watch. "Ugh, it's too early to go to bed."

"Let's find something to watch. If you want to sit on the floor in front of me, I'll rub your shoulders," Garrett said.

She sat up and smiled. "That sounds great!" She put on a cooking show and sat between his legs. He rubbed her shoulders, and they watched and learned about proper grilling and smoking techniques. Twice, he felt her head bob down to the back of his hand. The third time, it stayed there. She was out. Garrett got up carefully, picked her up, walked into her bedroom, and put her into bed. He walked back into the living room, stripped down to his shorts and tee-shirt, and laid down on her couch. It took almost an hour, but he eventually drifted into a light, uncomfortable sleep.

After what seemed like hours, another one of those loud kisses on his cheek woke him up. "Hey, dummy," she whispered into his ear. "What are you doing out here on the couch?"

Garrett yawned and sat up. "Um, I wanted you to sleep well," he said. She sat down by his knees. "What time is it?"

"It's not even midnight yet," she said, and put her hand on his cheek. "And my sleep would be far better if I knew you were with me. Would you really rather sleep out here?"

His eyes still closed, he said, "Let's go," and he reached for her.

"Okay, no funny business, just sleep." She took his hand, stood, and led him into her bedroom.

6

The following evening, at Garrett's request, the two went to Brenia and Rodney's small house for dinner. Garrett warned Brenia that he would bring Lauren with him and had spent the larger part of his lunch break on the phone with his sister, explaining the details of their relationship. The whole affair confused Brenia at first, but upon understanding, she assured him she supported the decision. There were two other things, though, that Brenia specifically did not do. She did not inform Garrett that she had also invited their parents to dinner, and she did not inform her parents beforehand of the news about her brother's love interest.

When Garrett and Lauren arrived that evening, Brenia walked out to meet them before they even reached the door.

She hugged her brother first and then hugged Lauren, who smiled with surprise at the unexpected affection.

"It's so nice to meet you!" Brenia said. "Please, come in!" The couple followed her through their front door and living room into their large kitchen, where Rodney was chopping vegetables. He wiped his hands off and extended one to Lauren.

"Hi, I'm Rod, Breni's husband." Lauren shook his hand, and Garrett found it humorous watching Lauren's small hand be swallowed up by Rodney's.

"I'm Lauren."

Rodney stepped over to the refrigerator. "What are you two having to drink? Beer, Gar?"

"Yeah, make it two. She's the first girl I've ever met who drank the good stuff," Garrett said. Rodney nodded and pulled out two bottles. He opened them and handed them out as Brenia walked in with the baby.

"Awww!" Lauren exclaimed in a pitch that Garrett believed only females could produce.

As the girls got acquainted, Rodney said quietly, "Good-looking redhead man, cheers." Garrett smiled and lifted the bottle to his lips. As soon as he felt the liquid touch them, he heard his mother's voice.

"Where's my baby boy!" She had just come through the front door with his father in tow. Garrett shot a look at Rodney, with Brenia on the other side of the room.

"What, man?" Rodney said in response to the look. Garrett closed his eyes and breathed in. "Oh, they don't know about her yet?"

"No! And Breni didn't tell me they were coming!" Garrett said. He could think of only one potential solution to ensure the meeting would not end in a disaster. He put his beer down on the counter and walked into the living room where his parents had entered. He took his mother by the hand and led her straight back out of the house again.

"Garrett, what in the world is going on?" his mother asked.

He spoke quickly. "Breni didn't tell me you and Dad were coming. There is a girl in the house who I'm with. We're dating, and I was going to talk to you and Dad about it tomorrow night. But now you're going to meet her without us having discussed the details, and I just want..." His mother's face lit up when she understood what her son was saying. She didn't wait to hear more.

"That's great! I want to meet her!" and she made off for the house. Garrett followed and called out to his mother, but she strode into the house, then the kitchen. As soon as she set eyes on Lauren, she stopped and said, "Hi! I'm Cynthia, Garrett's mom. So, are you here to save him from this stupid adventure he wants to go on?" There was a look of excitement and anticipation on his mother's face that broke Garrett's heart. Cynthia caught Lauren by surprise, and it took her a minute to put together what was happening.

"Um, no. Actually, the opposite," Lauren said. Cynthia's face went slack at first and then grew angry.

"So, you're a whore?" Garrett's heart sank. He grabbed both of his mother's elbows and pulled her back into the living room. He only stopped when he heard Lauren call his name.

"Garrett!" she said, "Stop!" He stopped. "I understand why your mother would say that." All the idle chatter in the room had ceased. The house was silent but for the cooing of the baby. Lauren clutched the beer bottle with both hands in front of her. "I assure you, Mrs. Rhodes, that we will not marry. I will not gain a single cent from your son's departure, and I will be heartbroken when he leaves, as will you."

Garrett's mother had tears running down both cheeks. "Then why?"

Lauren glanced at the floor and then back up at Cynthia. "Because I fell for him the moment I saw him. I can't stay away. And I understand completely…" Lauren's composure broke at that point, "that it will torture me for the rest of my life. But I can't do anything about it right now." The two women wiped their tears and regained control of their emotions.

"Do you want a beer, Alan?" Rodney said at half volume.

Garrett's father leapt at the opportunity, obviously to get away from the drama. "Yeah, what do you got?" He walked over to the refrigerator with Rodney.

Cynthia focused her attention on her grandson. "Give me my baby boy!" Brenia handed her son to her mother, who took the child into the living room.

7

They ate dinner at the round kitchen table, drama free. Brenia updated everyone on all the curiosities of a newborn and all the complications that went with being a first-time mother. Rodney gave the details of their struggles with the new transport drives they were building for OPM, and after some prodding by Garrett, Lauren divulged the story of her unlikely doctorate at seventeen.

After they finished dinner, Lauren shocked the room by standing up and inviting Cynthia to take a walk with her. Cynthia agreed and stood, and the two of them disappeared out the front door. Brenia took the baby, who had been near the table in his bassinet, into the bedroom to nurse. Rodney spoke up once all the girls had evacuated. "You're in trouble now, Gar."

Garrett laughed nervously, but Alan answered, "No, he isn't. Gar, I know this is the last thing you want to hear, but after meeting Lauren and talking to her a little, man, she is exactly like your mom was when we were young. I'm not kidding. It's scary. Brilliant, strong-minded. It's uncanny."

Garrett got another beer out of the fridge. "You were right. I didn't want to hear that," he said. Rodney laughed. At the same time, they all heard Brenia yell his name from the other room.

"Sorry guys," he said, and disappeared to help his wife.

"Seriously, Gar, you and I are a lot alike," Alan said. "It's not a huge stretch to imagine we'd have the same taste in women. Lauren is great, but come launch day, it will make things difficult. More difficult than they need to be, I think." Garrett breathed in and shrugged. "I'm not telling you what to do, Gar, I'm just afraid that your launch date will come a lot faster than you expect, and it will crush your soul if she's still in the picture. I know it's going to kill mine." They both drank deeply from their beers at that moment, and Garrett shrugged again.

"Everything about this will be painful. I signed up for a lifetime of pain. At first, I had comfort knowing how much of the future I would see, but honestly, the reality of it all has been a growing stress," he said.

His father nodded. "But you will still go?"

"Yes. It's fair to say I'm less enthusiastic about it, but I'm not less committed. The reasons I wanted to do it in the first place have not changed."

"And Lauren?"

Garrett finished his beer and immediately got another one. "She doesn't want me to go, but she knows I have to. She's brilliant, as you know. That can be a curse. Do you think so?"

Alan received the question with a small smile. "I don't think so, I know so, Gar," he said, and refreshed his own beer without explaining further.

"What about you, though, Dad? I know Mom and Breni don't want me to go, and I know that you've said how much it will hurt when I leave, but what do you think? Should I go?"

Garrett's father leaned back on the counter next to the fridge. "There are a lot of life's questions that a father feels it necessary to address with his children. I imagine most impart their own life experiences onto their children, either to give warning or to offer comfort. Garrett, I have no idea. What you are asking me is so far from my pool of knowledge or experience that whatever answer I could give you would be nonsense." Alan took a swig from his bottle and continued. "I can tell you only one thing, because I thought about it a lot after they selected you. As your father, and to be the best father I can be in this circumstance, the only thing I can do is support whatever decision you make. I know that's not what you wanted to hear, but it is the full truth of the matter. I am your friend and ally, and I will help you in any way I can. But I cannot decide for you."

8

Cynthia and Lauren had walked down to the road and almost to the next block before either of them said a word. Finally, Lauren spoke.

"I was afraid that meeting you would go badly," she said. "Garrett was going to talk to you and your husband tomorrow night and schedule a day for us all to meet. I'm sorry it happened this way."

Cynthia raised her eyebrows. "Well, I understand now. I love my daughter dearly, but she is a scatterbrain. She arranged this whole evening, had all the information, but did not connect any of the dots."

"She is really sweet. I met her an hour and a half ago and she has already hugged me twice," Lauren said.

Cynthia laughed and stopped walking, turning to face her. "I apologize for what I said earlier, but despite that apology, I feel that you are going to make this entire process twice as hard on my son, or more. I don't even want him to…"

"He has to go," Lauren said, cutting her off.

"If you're not in it for the money, then why is it so important to you that he goes?" Cynthia asked. Lauren started walking again, and Cynthia followed. She gave

Garrett's mother the same explanation she had given him when he asked her the same question. "So, what's the difference if you leave him now or wait for the launch? If you do it now, he'll be over it long before he leaves!" Cynthia said.

Lauren had been looking at the sidewalk, then looked up at Garrett's mother. "For two reasons. First, I don't think it's my place to decide for him. That might seem contradictory, since I told him I would only commit to him if he fulfilled his role as envoy, but that goes back to the reason I don't want him to quit. If he wants the relationship with me for these several months, I will not tell him it's the wrong thing to do. It's not my place to tell him how to feel.

"The second reason is that as long as he feels that way, I am all in. He is one of the most, or *the* most impressive person I have ever met. He will affect more people and more cultures than anyone else in the history of all things. He is magnetic, and it is my wish to support him all the way up to and even after the launch," Lauren said.

Cynthia frowned. "How can you possibly support him after the launch?"

"Comms," Lauren said, not knowing what reaction to expect when she answered, but not expecting the reaction she got. Pure elation.

"Comms!" Cynthia yelled triumphantly. "I'm so stupid! How in the world did I not think of that before?!"

Lauren smiled, relieved by the reaction. "They will only be one-way, though," Lauren said. "You know, he won't wake up until... well..." This fact did not discourage Cynthia in the least.

"Yes, I know. But I can talk to my baby. I can talk to him as much as I want all throughout the rest of my life! And he will get all my messages, someday, he will get them all! Thank you, sweetie!" She hugged Lauren, and Lauren understood where Brenia got the habit.

9

Twenty minutes after they left, Cynthia and Lauren walked back into the house and then the kitchen, where Garrett and Alan were discussing the survival mechanics he would have to employ once out among the stars.

"They're back! Have you two girls come to a truce?" Alan asked.

Cynthia lightly slapped him on the side and said, "I have to drive home, don't I?" She snatched the beer bottle out of his hand and took a sip.

"Not necessarily. It depends on how badly you want to get there alive." Cynthia shook her head and rolled her eyes.

"So, Mom," Garrett said, "where do we stand?"

Cynthia took a moment and breathed. "I still don't think that what you two are doing is smart. You will be the architects of your own misery," she said. Alan was nodding behind her. "But you are both adults, and if you decide to go on this way, I will not cause either of you any more grief about it. We're about to have a hell of a year." Garrett hugged his mother, a moment later reaching out and pulling Lauren into the hug. Alan laughed quietly behind them and reluctantly tipped his bottle up to the heavens.

10

Lauren unlocked her apartment door, and they both walked in. Garrett sat down hard in one of the dining room chairs.

"That was rough," he said. "I'm sorry it all happened that way."

Lauren put down her bag and keys and put her arms around him from behind. "It's fine, it's over. All of that stress is over."

"This half is over, my parents. What about yours? You've never even talked about them," Garrett said. Lauren's demeanor lost all humor. She walked around and sat on his lap.

"There's not a lot to tell," she said. "My dad passed away when I was four years old. There was an accident where he worked. My mother died when I was twelve. When my dad… it crushed her, and she started taking pills to manage her depression. She ended up taking a lot of different medications. My sister, Denise, is convinced that mom waited until she turned twenty, because that was the legal age at which my sister could adopt me, but one night, she took them all. She swallowed a mix of pills… over two hundred. She didn't wake up."

"Wow, I'm so sorry, Laur. That's horrible," he said.

She leaned into him. "It was so long ago now; I came to peace with it a long time ago. But if you notice Denise 'mothering' me, you'll understand why."

Garrett hugged her. "Yes, I certainly understand why she would." Lauren lifted Garrett's hand from her thigh and placed it on her side, under her shirt and just below her ribs on the bare skin. She stretched up and kissed him. She then moved his hand to the small of her back and kissed him again.

"Let's go to bed." She stood up and walked toward the bedroom. After getting a few steps away, she stopped and turned to him. "You can get the wrong idea this time." She turned and started walking again, removing articles of clothing as she went. Mesmerized, it was only after she was out of view that Garrett got up and followed her.

Chapter 9

D.C.

1

The fourth and shortest stint Garrett did on Earth was the easiest by far. From the time he awoke to the time he was up and crawling out of the small crevasse within which he had gone under, it had only been ten minutes. He was pleased to find the temperature pleasant and see daylight as he approached the opening, but he realized it was fading into evening when he emerged.

He took full advantage of the remaining light and descended the mountain on the remnants of a trail he could still see. After half an hour, the last of the light was already dimming. The motor traffic that he could hear below encouraged him, and he resumed his descent, hoping to reach a road before it was too dark to go on. Another half hour passed, and he slowed his pace. He was afraid of impaling an eye on a barely detectable branch. It was much darker, but the traffic was also much louder, and he could see artificial, electric lights smoothly passing before him. *If I can at least make it to the road,* he thought, *I can walk by the moonlight.* Garrett pressed on at a slower, more careful pace until he reached the edge of the wooded area, when his feet first landed on mechanically cut grass. He was at the road, save having to climb a rather steep embankment. Once reaching the summit of the small hill, he came up against a sturdy metal rail meant to prevent wayward vehicles from sliding out of the lane. He climbed over it so he could walk on the level surface, observed the traffic for a moment, and then walked in the same direction as the vehicles on his side of the road. Traffic in the opposing direction had their own separate road, which ran parallel to the one on which he stood.

Garrett walked west for another hour, watching the sun set before him as he went. He passed a blue and red sign with no information but the word "Interstate" printed in a narrow red band on top and "78" in large print in a blue one below. On a separate metal placard was the word "west."

Many times while he walked, he heard the louder engines of trucks and busses approach and then pass him. Around the end of the first hour, he heard a new sound, a low, guttural noise that sounded loud and almost panicked. A large truck, appearing to be a cargo transport vehicle, passed him, but it was slowing at a rapid pace. Near to where he walked, it had pulled over into his path, and several lights on the back of it blinked continuously. A man dropped from the cab of the vehicle and walked along the side of the truck toward him. He said something, but Garrett could not make out any of the words. Finally, once the man was closer and only visible by the oncoming lights from the traffic behind him, he said again, "Hey man! You're gonna get yourself killed out here! You can't walk on a highway!" He was a heavyset man of thirty-five or forty years. His skin was pale, and he had a beard trimmed close to his face. He wore a shirt with a pattern, corrective lenses, and a cap.

"Should I walk on the grass, then?" Garrett asked, and pointed to the other side of the guardrail. The man put his hands on his hips and rocked back in his posture.

"No, man! I'll give you a ride. Where are you going?"

Alarm rose in Garrett's mind, because he had no answer to the question. He hoped that a generic answer would suffice. Riding in the truck with the man could be beneficial. If he was good enough to stop and help a stranger, he might be helpful in other ways. "I don't know. I can tell you that my name is Garrett. I have money, but none that will do me any good here. Ultimately, I need a place to change my money and then find lodging." The look of confusion on the man's face turned to a grimace, and then back to confusion, mixed with suspicion.

"That's weird, man. You aren't running from the cops, are you?" he asked. Garrett did not know what cops were, but he was not running from anyone.

"No, um…" he gestured to the man.

"Bill."

"No, Bill. I'm not running from anyone. I arrived here from France many days ago and have been walking since. I have not had the occasion to change my money yet and have a great need to."

"Jesus, man, you could've just changed it at the airport! And who only carries cash anymore? Don't you have any cards? The exchange rate gets applied automatically. Whatever, we have to get off the road. Come on back to my truck," Bill said, and turned to walk back to the vehicle. Garrett followed. After making a feeble effort at opening the door, Bill opened it from the inside and Garrett climbed into the cab.

"What in the hell are you wearing?" Bill asked. He looked at Garrett with more of his signature confusion.

"Forgive my dress. I know it is not period appropriate, but it is all I have at the moment. I can't buy anything more modern until I can change my money." Garrett reached down into his bag to retrieve one of the coin satchels. He opened it. Each of his two satchels contained half of his oldest Roman money, topped off with the dozens of gold Napoleons he had received in exchange for his printing wages. He plucked a few of the coins from the purse and held them out in the bright cab light for Bill to inspect. "This is the money I have."

"Well, damn." Bill leaned in closer to examine them.

"You can touch them, Bill. It is all real money." On Garrett's palm were two gold Napoleons and a copper Roman piece he had received from the Clotz family, almost fifteen hundred years before. Bill picked up the pieces, surprised by the weight of the Napoleons.

"Jesus, man, is this gold?" Bill asked, gazing at the pieces in amazement.

"Of course, I told you it was real."

Bill shook his head. "You don't change this kind of money, man, you sell it. These two both say twenty francs. I'm no expert, but I know that twenty francs, at least before France changed over to Euros, were worth about four bucks American. These are worth a couple hundred bucks each, at least. What the hell is this other one?" Bill held the Clotz coin up to the light.

"It's Roman. Very old," Garrett said.

Bill studied the coin. "I'll say." He dropped the coins back into Garrett's hand. "Well, man, you need a jeweler, or a pawn shop, or something like that. Trust me, sell them. They are worth a good deal of money." With that, he put the truck into gear and pulled back onto the highway.

2

Garrett was smiling subtly, happy to be in motor transport again with all its creature comforts. The scenery rushed by, cloaked in darkness but with fleeting moments of illumination from the electric light at the front of the truck and the other vehicles that surrounded them. It had been years, both in actual time and Garrett's realized time, since he had traveled a fast-paced and mesmerizing highway. That it was raining only added to the illusion, and he realized he had been in a trance, no conception of time passing.

"How long have we been driving?" Garrett asked. Bill was guzzling drinks from aluminum cans and had a determined look on his face. He had tuned the truck's radio to a channel that was only men talking, with no music to accompany it.

"Since I picked you up? Ah, three hours, a little over three. Why? Do you want to get out?"

Garrett straightened up in his seat to get more comfortable. The men on the radio were talking about vampires, a term he was unfamiliar with. "No, no, certainly not. It's just that I feel like I have no idea how much time has passed. The road can put you in a trance, I find."

Bill smiled and glanced at Garrett, then back to the road. "Hell yeah, it can. That's why I have these." Bill held up a mostly empty can. "They keep you awake, focused. I don't know how long we'll be together, Garrett, but I'm headed to Yuma, Arizona. And I can tell you right now that's almost on the other side of the country and driving at night is the only way to go."

"Well, I can tell you I am very happy that you are awake and focused as the operator of this large, heavy vehicle." Garrett said.

Bill chuckled. "I'm gonna drive until the morning, man. I gotta stop at 6:07 a.m. or this thing will rat me out." He tapped on a small digital console on the dashboard. "That will put us in Virginia, anyway. After we stop, we can figure out what you're gonna do. If you want to keep going, that's fine by me. I enjoy company, but I have nowhere for you to sleep, so it might get complicated."

They talked during the next few hours, Garrett asked a lot of questions and Bill answered them. They talked about the radio program they were listening to with all its macabre topics. A few times, they sat in silence and watched the miles roll by.

3

At 5:52, by the clock on the dashboard, Bill steered the large truck off the highway. After only five minutes and two more turns, he pulled into a large empty lot with painted markings on the ground but no other vehicles.

"We can park here for the day. I've done it several times before and had no problem. The best thing is there's a diner across the street," Bill said. "Wait here for a bit, I'll be back in a minute." Bill pulled a clipboard from the floor next to his seat and a pen from his shirt pocket. He exited the truck and Garrett observed him inspecting multiple places all around the truck and trailer. After he finished, he opened Garrett's door and motioned for him to climb down.

"You can leave your gear in the truck, I'll lock it, but why don't you bring one of your gold coins with you? Maybe someone in the diner can tell us where you can sell it," Bill said. Garrett retrieved one of the Napoleons from a satchel and climbed down out of the truck. When he swung the door shut, he read the logo emblazoned below the window. "Big Bill Little," it said, and beneath that, "Service with a purpose." "Follow me, I'll buy you breakfast and we can go from there." Bill strode across the street when it was clear of traffic, and Garrett followed.

The two men ate their breakfast in the old diner. The age of the establishment showed in its linoleum floor, deeply worn from foot traffic, and the torn upholstery of the diner bar stools. They showed the coin off to the waitress and two old men drinking coffee at the counter. One of the older men told them to try the jewelry store, which he referred to as "Ray's place." "You can even walk there from here. It's but two blocks, but he won't open for another two hours. I think he opens at nine." The old fellow looked at the man next to him, who shook his head and shrugged. Bill thanked the two men, paid the bill, and walked out of the diner.

Garrett followed and once they stood outside the diner said, "I appreciate all you've done for me, but I don't want to burden you any further."

Before he could finish his thought, Bill interrupted him. "Don't worry about it, man. This is interesting. Driving a truck for a living can be interesting, but it can also be boring as hell. I usually don't turn in until about noon, and then up at eight and right back on the road, so we have some time. Let's see if we can get you some new duds for cheap. There's a department store down this way a little. I'll cover you, and if we can get you some cash, you can pay me back, but if we can't, don't sweat it. It won't break me."

Garrett opposed taking any form of charity, but the prospect of being able to pay the man back made it easier to accept. "That's generous of you, Bill. I can't thank you enough for all this help."

Bill bought Garrett two pairs of blue jeans and three t-shirts. Two of the shirts were plain colored tees, but the third was in a bargain bin and had the word "Virginia" printed on it in heavy italics. They walked around the store for over an hour, killing time while they waited for "Ray's place" to open for business.

After they left the department store and returned to the truck so Garrett could change and get more of his coins, they made their way to Ray's. As they approached the store, Garrett read the correct name of the establishment on a hanging sign above the front door: *Raymond Heller's Fine Jewelry and Antiques.* Garrett smiled at the simplification of the name as espoused by the old man at the breakfast counter.

A small-framed, middle-aged man in a black business suit was walking up the sidewalk toward them from the opposite direction, holding a briefcase and fumbling with a set of keys. When he looked up at Bill and Garrett, he smiled and said, "Good morning, gentlemen."

"G'morning, are you Ray?" Bill asked.

The man found the key he was looking for, slid it into the lock, and turned it completely around twice, which produced a low, metallic *thunk*. He chuckled at the question. "Yes, most people call me Raymond, but Ray doesn't bother me. What can I do for you gentlemen this morning?"

Bill stepped back and gestured to Garrett. Garrett pulled one of the gold Napoleons out of his satchel and held it out. Raymond lifted his glasses away from his eyes to inspect the piece with more focus.

"Ah! Very nice. I rarely deal in coins, but if you want to come in, we can take a closer look and maybe determine its value." He raised his brow and his glasses slipped back down in front of his eyes.

"That would be excellent," Garrett said, and they followed him into the store.

When turning the corner, Raymond flipped up several switches, and the room illuminated with electric light. Glass cases lined the room, with four more artfully placed in the center. Ray walked to a counter on the far side of the shop, which appeared to Garrett to have computer equipment on top of it. The top of the counter was unlike the others in that it was an opaque polished stone where the others were glass. Ray pulled a stool up to the counter and a bright light over to the center of the unencumbered part of the countertop. Garrett placed the coin under the light and the satchel it had come from about a foot back from it. As the weight of the satchel relaxed on the surface, it made the sound that only a satchel of coins can. The sound caused Ray to pause. He gestured to the satchel. "What's that?"

Garrett slid the bag toward the light. "More of the same, and some others. It's all fairly old."

Ray tilted the satchel on its side and six more Napoleons spilled out, with two dozen assorted silver and copper Roman pieces. "Is this," Ray paused as he looked at four of the well-preserved silver, bronze, and copper Roman coins. "Are these all real?"

"Yes," Garrett said. "And I have another satchel of them just like this back in Bill's truck."

Ray's jaw dropped. He emptied the satchel under the light and spread the coins out, separating the French gold coins from the Roman ones. The collection was enormous; it occupied almost half of the free counter space.

"This is remarkable. How on earth did you come to collect all these, and so many more?" Ray asked.

Garrett had thought a question might arise about the exotic monies and parroted his mentally rehearsed answer. "A relative of mine in France passed three months ago. He had no other kin and left everything he owned to me. It didn't amount to much, but I found the two satchels of coins among his possessions."

"Oh, you didn't tell me that's how you got them," Bill said.

Garrett offered a small smile. "You didn't ask."

"Well," Raymond said, "I can tell you a few things. First, the French money, the twenty-franc pieces, those will have a pretty well-defined value assigned to them, as they aren't that old, especially compared to the others." He picked up one of the gold coins, inspected the front and back, put it down, and walked over to his computer interface. He typed in some information and appeared to read for about a minute. "It looks like they value the twenty-franc gold pieces at about three hundred and fifty dollars each."

"Nice," Bill said.

Garrett did not understand the value of three hundred and fifty dollars. He knew their breakfast had cost fourteen dollars, and the total of his clothing had come to sixty-three dollars and some number of cents that he could not remember.

"That brings me to some other things I can tell you," Ray said. "The value of anything is only what you can find a buyer willing to pay. Like I said, I rarely deal with coins, so as a general statement, I'm not interested in buying any of them. *But*," he held up an index finger, "if you have time for me to make a phone call, I might be able to arrange the sale of one or two."

Garrett looked at Bill, who shrugged. "We definitely have time for a phone call, yeah," Bill said.

Ray smiled and knocked twice on the counter. "Great, just give me a few minutes." He took his phone from his pocket and made the call. It was less than a minute before he put the phone down against his chest and addressed Garrett. "My brother will pay you six hundred dollars for two of the

Napoleons, if you accept, we can do the transaction right now and I'll settle up with him later."

Bill said, "Hell yeah, dude," under his breath.

"I trust that is fair," Garrett said, and extended a hand for Raymond to shake. Ray shook it, took the two coins his brother wanted, and walked back into another room, informing his brother of the good news as he went. When he came back, he made six stacks of five twenty-dollar bills on the counter. Garrett wiped up the cash and put it in his satchel on top of the coins he had gathered and put away while waiting for Ray to return.

"Thank you very much, guys, that was wonderful." Ray waved goodbye and the two men were back on the street.

As they walked back to the truck, Garrett counted out four of the twenties and handed them to Bill. Bill took them and said, "This is eighty bucks, man, you don't owe me that much."

"The clothing was over sixty-three, and breakfast was fourteen, plus the tip you left our waitress," Garrett said. "I owe you exactly eighty, if not a little more. And this way, I bought you breakfast this morning for offering me so much help." Bill nodded and put the money in his pocket.

"Ok man, if you're okay with it, then I am. You want to have a beer before we turn in? There's a restaurant on the way back to the truck. I've eaten there a couple times and I'm pretty sure they open at ten, which is in twenty minutes."

"I am dying for a beer," Garrett said. Bill smiled and pointed forward.

4

Once seated at the bar in the completely empty restaurant, the two men had to wait a few minutes as the bartender was finishing with her opening procedures. Except for the natural daylight spilling in through the several windows that lined two walls, there was little effort put into lighting the establishment. The bar was a large rectangular island in the middle of the massive dining room, with tables surrounding it and booths fixed to three of the walls. "So, what's your poison, Garrett?" Bill asked.

Garrett scanned the room and found a chalkboard that said, "On Tap," but was otherwise blank. "I'm not sure until I know what my options are," he said. Bill looked up at the tap handles and pointed. Garrett read through the writing on each tap handle with general disregard as he knew none of the names, until the second to last one. He read, "Clotz Ale, Est. 540AD." Garrett felt a chill down his spine. "I can't believe it. Fifteen hundred years?"

Bill looked at him with curiosity. "What, man?" he asked. Garrett pointed at the tap handle. "Oh, yeah. That stuff's been around forever. It's European, though, so you'd probably be into it."

A middle-aged woman with a deep brown complexion, black pants, and a matching vest with a white dress shirt beneath appeared and wished the men a good morning. She looked at Bill and squinted. "You've been here before, right? Truck driver?"

Bill smiled, "Yes, ma'am. A few times." He looked at Garrett and nodded, "We'll take two Clotz, we're not eating." She smiled and turned to get their drinks. Bill then turned to Garrett, "So, you still haven't told me what you're doing in the states, man. I know about the money and looking for a place to stay, but you gotta be here for a reason. Is it a vacation? Or a holiday, like the Brits say it?"

"No, nothing like that. I am here for a purpose, though. And honestly, I'm never going back to France. I have no reason to. Let me ask you, Bill; this will seem like a strange question, but please bear with me. Have men ever touched the moon?" The bartender placed two napkins in front of the men and a large glass of Clotz Ale upon each. She had heard Garrett ask the question and shot Bill a look that said, "did he just ask that?"

"Yeah, man, hell, they did that before I was born. A lot of cats out there will tell you we never been there, but they're all just conspiracy nerds. Those types think they fake everything," Bill said.

Garrett was grinning. He nodded and picked up his glass of Clotz Ale, fully prepared to be disappointed at what fifteen hundred years of recipe alterations would add up to. He was not. Although the beer tasted nothing like it had when he drank it on the farm, it was cold and refreshing and had a flavor that packed a punch. He smiled and resumed his interview.

"Was it this country or another that achieved it?" The bartender shook her head and walked to the chalkboard to update it with the current draft selections available for that day.

"It was us, man. The good ol' U.S. of A. And damn, that was back in sixty-nine!" Bill said.

Garrett slapped the bar once, but loudly. "Excellent, Bill! Who was in charge of it? Where can I find them? That is where I need to go!"

Garrett's animation startled Bill. He shifted in his chair and leaned back. "Um, I mean, NASA is in charge of all the space flight. But I'm not sure where they really are. They launch in Florida, but they must control everything from Texas, because you know, 'Houston, we have a problem,' and such. But I think they launch from Texas sometimes, too," Bill said.

In an unexpected twist, the bartender who Garrett saw was wearing a nametag that read *Charlotte* spoke up. "NASA is like any other government operation. It may have buildings in a lot of places, but the main place, headquarters, is in D.C."

Bill's face lit up when she finished. "Oh, yeah man, that makes sense. Probably D.C. is where you want to go," he said. Garrett smiled. It was all excellent information. "And you know what? Damn it! We just drove past there last night, probably around twelve-thirty or one o'clock." The missed opportunity did not discourage Garrett in the slightest. He had a good understanding of the enormity of the landmass that made up the continental United States, and if they had been close to his destination only a few hours before they stopped driving, he was close.

"It's close. How long would it take me to walk there, Bill?" Garrett asked, still smiling.

"Walk? What the hell? It's like three hundred miles, man! Jesus, take a few of the dollars out of your bag and buy a bus ticket." Bill said, laughing. As they finished their beers, they discussed the details of the bussing plan with

Charlotte. Once she recommended a motel that would accept cash without a credit card, they made their plan to both separate Garrett from Bill's care and then get him to Washington, D.C.

According to their plan, Garrett would go back to the bar at ten the following morning and Charlotte would arrange for a car to pick him up and bring him to Roanoke, where he could get a bus ticket to D.C. The two men left the restaurant after their plan was devised and walked back to the truck, where Garrett collected his belongings. They then walked to the motel, which was only one block from the diner. Once they had the motel accommodations taken care of, Bill and Garrett said their goodbyes, with Bill handing Garrett one of his owner/operator business cards with his information on it. "If you ever get a phone, call me and let me know how you make out," he had said. On the back of his card, he had written the four letters Garrett would need to know when reaching D.C., *NASA*. The men smiled and shook hands, and Garrett thanked Bill again for everything he had done for him. "Be safe, and good luck!" Bill concluded.

5

Garrett woke up late that evening in the motel bed that Bill had helped him secure. He took a long shower and changed into fresh clothes. He counted the American money he had left after paying the motel, four hundred and sixty-five dollars and some coins.

After sleeping for the entire afternoon and evening, Garrett decided he would deviate from the original plan. It was eleven o'clock at night and he had no intention of waiting eleven straight hours just for Charlotte to arrange a ride for him to travel eighteen miles.

He checked out of the motel ten minutes later and started walking for Roanoke. Knowing that the time he had ahead of him and the distance he needed to travel did not line up, he took his time.

The sky was brightening when he finally arrived in Roanoke. He passed an establishment with a sign that had the time and temperature on a rotating display, and he could see that it was 5:14 in the morning and 68°F. Garrett found the abundant signage in the U.S. to be helpful, as he never had to stop once to find the bus station. He did, however, stop at a gas station to purchase an enormous bottle of water and two bags of beef jerky. The selection was incredible, but he did not know what anything else was. All the packaging was bright and colorful, but the food it contained was unrecognizable as edible.

He arrived at the bus station only four minutes after leaving the store. Two hours later, he was on the bus, en route to D.C. two full hours before he had been scheduled to meet Charlotte about the ride to Roanoke.

After a brief, fruitless attempt at sleep, Garrett withdrew his copy of *The Count of Monte Cristo* from his bag and began reading. He barely got through a page before thoughts of Marco's letters forced him to lose enough focus that he put the book back in his bag and withdrew the letters. He again reread the four from Marco, then placed the dreaded final letter on top, so he could finally read it:

March 21, 613 –

My grandfather asked me to script this brief letter and gave me detailed instructions about what to do after. I will honor his request, as I promised him I would, regardless of my own personal beliefs.

He died last night at the age of seventy-two. He had been complaining of intense pain in his right side. Yesterday had been his worst day yet, and we could see the life draining from him. As the sun was setting, he took his last breath. He reminded me three times of my promise to him, to write this letter and then prepare and deliver them all to you. While I don't believe anyone will ever set their eyes upon these words, I loved my grandfather dearly and would not betray the promise I made to him.

He walked me to your location many times when I was a child, and I remember it like I remember my own name. He already took care to point out your shoulder bag and even showed me how to open it. My apologies if either he or I did not retie the throat as you would have. I remember he had a good deal of trouble opening it the first time.

You remember him as a young boy, but I only ever knew him as an old man. I will tell you he lived a good, long life and is leaving behind a whole team of grandchildren, many of whom are working to build up and strengthen the Clotz name. Although I am not a Clotz myself, as I was a son of Maurice and Marquesa, I too am focusing my efforts on the farm and brewery that you helped build.

As I close this note, I'd like to say that I just took it upon myself to read the four letters that my grandfather wrote to you. While it was heartbreaking to read the summary of the death of my aunt and uncle, let alone that of my beloved father, I am glad I did. My grandfather had a deep love and respect for you. Although my more mature mind has criticized my belief in the stories he told me of you, it has brought me happiness to read them. I can say that I will travel to you with a happy heart and a refreshed sense of purpose. Once this task is complete, I will kneel at my grandfather's grave with fond remembrance, knowing that I fulfilled my promise to him. Maybe, in the distant future, you will read this letter. I can't imagine what a fantastic world that will be.

Farewell, sir, and Godspeed.

Renato Marciano

The sadness of Marco's death so shortly after he had written his last letter to Garrett affected him less than he thought it would, possibly because of the thoughtfulness of his grandson's words. Having completed the letters, he found it easier to resume his consumption of the world of Monte Cristo and continued his reading undisturbed.

6

Once in the city, the Envoy struggled for three hours to get directions and then walk the distance to the NASA headquarters building on E street, southwest. He had never experienced roads, streets, and avenues named so unconventionally. He must have talked to fifty people from the time the bus dropped him off and the time he reached 300 E St SW, but as he got closer, the answers came with more confidence. Finally, a young lady pointed to a building diagonally across an intersection, and said, "That's it right there." Garrett thanked her no less than five times and hurried across the street as he had taught himself to do, by watching others.

Once in front of the building, he gazed at the letters carved into the stone of the exterior wall:

National Aeronautics and Space Administration

He let out a deep breath of relief, as he was now a little closer to completing the last mission of his life. He continued walking along the face of the building, surprised to find a few shops in the façade, including a coffee shop. Finally, equipped with American money, he walked into the shop and ordered a coffee, which took some conversation because of the specialized nature of the coffee shop. An exceptionally forgiving barista, a short, cute girl with black hair up in a loose bun and multiple tattoos on her arms, helped him, and he was soon served the best coffee he had ever tasted.

He sat at a round, high-top table in the shop's corner that had excellent visibility through the glass panel exterior walls to the street outside. The high-top tables lined the dining room with a dozen larger, squat tables centered in the space. The lighting was dim, and Garrett liked the mellow sound of the music playing from speakers somewhere in the ceiling.

Once he finished his coffee, he walked back up to the counter to purchase another and asked the barista if it was okay if he remained as long as he continued buying coffee. "You can stay as long as you want, sweetie," she said. "It never gets busy in here on Wednesdays." He thanked her and took his fresh cup of coffee back to his table.

Thirty-five minutes later, he got what he was waiting for. Two young men in their twenties entered the shop, greeted the barista by name, received their coffee and sat at a table within earshot of Garrett. Both men were wearing I.D. badges with the NASA logo. He could read their names as they approached the table they selected. Their first names were large and bold, and their last names were beneath and in small print, so Garrett just read "Harold" and "Michael." The men both sat at side profile in relation to Garrett, so neither had his back to him. Harold was shorter, with a dark complexion and equally dark hair that was painfully close to receding. Michael was a tall, skinny young man with light brown hair, gray eyes, and a mass of adolescent acne scarring on his face. Garrett listened closely to their conversation and waited for an opening.

When they sat, they were discussing a project that they were both working on, and Garrett could not make heads or tails of the conversation. They moved on to what he determined to be a science fiction book or movie, and they argued about the qualifying reality of it. Finally, that discussion devolved into one of the universe, and they argued about current astrophysics.

"It's not that simple, Mike. Remember that dark energy will keep pushing everything out! The bigger everything gets, the stronger the dark energy gets," Harold said, and sat back in his seat, having made his point.

"How the hell can that be possible? If it's energy, why isn't it bound by conservation of energy? The bigger it gets, the *less* influence it should have," Michael said. He was leaning forward on the table and getting animated. He had a deep voice that did not match his lanky and boyish appearance.

"It doesn't work that way," Harold said. "The space between the filaments gets larger as space-time expands, so there is more room for the energy to expand!"

Michael slapped his forehead. "So, you're telling me that if I push another table up to this one, doubling its surface area, that two additional cups of coffee would manifest because there was now more room?" Michael asked. Garrett stood up, holding his own cup of coffee, and took a step toward the table.

"So, what's the answer, Mike? I'm arguing from the side of all the top astrophysicists and theoretical physicists on the planet. You're arguing from the side of no one but you," Harold said.

Michael settled back in his posture. "I feel like as soon as we realized that dark matter existed and we didn't understand it, we slapped the 'dark matter' name on it, shrugged our shoulders, and gave up on physics. It pisses me off." Michael sipped his coffee but continued, "Especially when we discovered the redshift! Now we just say, 'oh, something else we don't have an explanation for? Let's just arbitrarily make up something else! Let's call it dark energy!'" When he said "dark energy," he exaggerated his speech and waved his hands about, so as to make it sound mystifying. "Oh, and by the way, none of these things are bound by the laws of physics." Michael shook his head, crossed his arms, and sat back in his chair.

Garrett listened closely to their conversation, as it was his first glimpse of modern astrophysics as it existed at that time on Earth. From the context, he determined they called eflix *dark matter* and misunderstood its effect on the universe. He finally approached. "Please forgive the interruption, but are you speaking of the universe?" He looked from man to man, who both nodded. "May I?" He placed a hand on the back of an empty chair at their table. Michael held out a hand to the chair, and Harold said "Sure." Garrett sat, placed his coffee on the table, and smiled. Though the two men were both agitated, neither seemed upset that he had joined them and just stared at each other with disdain from their respective seats.

"Harold, you're wrong about dark energy. It doesn't exist. It's a fictional anomaly to help explain something you don't understand," Garrett said. Michael laughed and pointed at Harold, who smirked and pointed at Garrett as if to say, *who the hell is this guy?*

"Michael, you're wrong about dark matter, if that's what you call it. That absolutely does exist, although where I come from, we have a different name for it." Garrett stopped talking and took the moment to finish his coffee. Michael was the first to speak.

"So, there's no dark energy? Then how do we know there is dark matter?" he asked.

Garrett stood up and said, "The expansion," and walked to the counter to get another coffee. He had been awake for eighteen hours. He asked if the barista could give him something stronger. She gave him a big smile and winked.

As he approached the table where they had been sitting, he saw Harold stand up and gather his things.

"Sorry guys, I gotta beat-feet. Wife is pissed that I didn't come straight home after work." Mike made a whipping motion with his right hand. "Hey man, when you finally meet a girl, marry her, and get her pregnant, then we'll see who's whipped." With that, Harold left the coffee shop and Garrett sat back down.

Michael extended a hand toward Garrett. "Mike Potaglia."

Garrett shook it firmly. "Garrett Rhodes." He smiled and looked into Mike's eyes. "Are you ready to learn about the real nature of our universe?" He smiled to dispel any discomfort in the situation, but Mike did not look uncomfortable.

"Yeah, man, what do you got?"

Garrett Rhodes and Mike Potaglia talked for the next three-and-a-half hours about the universe, the planets, Earth, and its achievements, and the world's plans for the future. The conversation had also slipped into who Garrett was, where he was from, and his current situation, with nowhere to go after the coffee shop. Garrett did not tell him the actual story that early but made up something believable.

"I lost my bag with my credit cards and I.D., so I think I will sleep in the park tonight," Garrett laughed. "I'm just glad I didn't lose my real valuables." He showed a part of his coin collection to Mike.

"These are amazing," Mike said. "And so many! This must be worth a fortune!" Garrett hoped it was but did not say as much.

"They will be worth something to someone, but they were left to me. I don't collect coins. I'd rather they ended up with someone who wanted them. As for me, I could use the cash, since I don't have my credentials or credit," Garrett said. Mike frowned and looked up at Garrett.

"Yeah, but you were joking about the park, right? You have a place to stay?" he asked.

Garrett shrugged and shook his head. "It's summer, though, so I'll be fine. It's not like I will freeze. Tomorrow, I'll see if I can sell some of my coins and straighten out my affairs," Garrett said.

Mike's eyebrows rose, and he looked like he'd just had an idea. "I know you said you don't have a lot of cash, but you should be able to get some once you can sell the coins, right? How long do you plan to be in D.C.?"

Garrett saw where the conversation was going and was having a hard time believing it would be so easy. "Well, yes. I have some cash, but not much. And yes, these coins should pay off, as long as I can find a buyer. As far as how long I plan to be here, I'm not sure, but I imagine it would be at least a year and a half, if not two."

"I live alone, and I can barely afford it. It was the cheapest apartment I could find without having to drive for hours one way just to get to work, but it is not cheap. I need a roommate. If you're interested, come back with me now, and when you can, split the rent with me. It solves your problem, and it will be a lot cheaper than a hotel, anyway. Plus, it will be a big help to me once you can pay," Mike said. Garrett could not believe it. Mike Potaglia had fallen into his hands as easily as a drop of rain.

"That sounds perfect! Wow, I thought it would take months to find a place."

"Well then, let's go home," Mike said. "I just need to stop on the way and pick up some cat food. You're not allergic to cats, are you?"

Garrett had little experience with cats, except at Clotz farm, where they had three resident cats in the brewery to fend off rodents that were interested in the grain. "No, I'm not. And I like cats quite a lot."

Mike led Garrett out of the coffee shop and down into the parking garage beneath the NASA building. They got into his mid-sized sedan and drove up the ramps and out onto the streets of D.C. As they pulled into the small parking lot of the gas station near Mike's apartment building, Garrett asked, "Do you like beer, Mike?"

They got out of the car and Mike tilted his head to the side, thinking. "I could take it or leave it. Honestly, I haven't really experimented much with different beers. I'm a scotch man, myself. Or a good bourbon," Mike said. Garrett did not know what bourbon was but knew that scotch was whiskey.

"Can I buy us some beer here to celebrate our new agreement?" Garrett asked as they walked into the store.

"Knock yourself out."

7

When they walked into Mike's apartment, its scale and general lack of furnishing shocked Garrett. Mike held his arms out to his sides. "See what I mean? Awesome apartment, no money left over to buy anything other than a little food." He tossed his keys on one of the three glass shelves screwed to the wall next to the front door. The entrance opened into a short hallway, then immediately into the living room, which, save for two still-packed boxes, was empty. Mike beckoned him to follow. They moved through the living room into another hallway, much longer and with four doors. Mike opened each door as he passed it: first was Mike's room, the door with a curious foam plate screwed to the bottom, and the only fully furnished room in the apartment. Second was the bathroom, which was simple but large with a glass-panel shower, toilet, sink, and two tall shelving units. The third door was either a tiny room or an enormous closet and contained two sets of stringers with five wide, white shelves hanging from each set. Next to the shelves was a stacked washer dryer combo, the kind made for small spaces. Mike pointed to the washer/dryer set.

"This is why I finally accepted this place. There's nothing I hate more than having to drive all of my clothing to a laundromat and spending hours there washing and drying everything. I had to do it the whole time I was in college, and when I got out, I promised myself I would never do it again. This is the best feature of the apartment, trust me," he said, then took two more steps deeper into the hallway, opened the last door and flipped on the light. It was empty. The square footage of the room, like the others, was substantial. It had three windows, two on the long wall and one on the short, and also had a walk-in closet. The entire apartment was painted a dull, off-white color, except for the high-sheen, industrial gray bathroom. "This one is yours. It's a little smaller than mine, but you have more windows and a much better view. You also have a big closet instead of two small ones."

Garrett set his bag on the floor and pulled two of the beers free from the six-pack. He opened both and handed one to Mike. "This is fantastic. Cheers," Garrett said. Mike clinked Garrett's bottle with his. "Well, now that I'm unpacked, should we retire to the kitchen?" Mike laughed and nodded. The two walked to the kitchen, which had a large central island and four stools. The only thing on the island was a laptop computer and a small pile of unopened mail. Garrett put the remaining four-pack of beer into the refrigerator and sat on a stool. Mike sat on the one in front of the laptop, opened it, and pushed the power button. "I would like to buy one like that. Can you tell me about how much they cost?" Garrett asked.

"The laptop? Oh, this one is ancient. I've had this since I was in high school. It was expensive years ago, but they're much cheaper now. You can get a simple one for four or five hundred bucks. Do you want cheap or good?" Mike asked, sipping on his beer.

"A cheap one now, a good one later. Actually, later on I might need one of the best that money can buy. If I can get the signals I'm after, I'll need it to process them." Garrett drank from his bottle and waited for Mike to ask…

"What signals?" Mike asked, as predictable as the sun rising.

"Signals that I'm very interested in studying. Are you familiar with radio signals that originate from deep space?" Garrett asked. He could tell he was getting Mike's attention.

"Um, yeah, like FRBs? From way out in the universe?"

"Exactly like that, but FRB?" Garrett asked.

"Fast Radio Bursts," Mike said.

Garrett laughed loudly. "Well, yes, if it's from a surion, they would be very fast," Garrett said. He did not know the word in English for quasar, so he substituted the Osan word, *surion*, which meant the same thing, without realizing it. Thankfully, Mike did not question him about it. "Excellent. Anyway, what if it wasn't a burst, but a stream? An uninterrupted stream. Would that capture your interest?"

"Hell yes, like a communication?"

Garrett nodded, stood up, and swapped his empty bottle for a new one. "Precisely. Once I can get my hands on one of those," he pointed to the laptop, "I can get my orientation and figure out the coordinates for the radio stream interception. After that, I will need to embark on the arduous task of finding some people with a powerful enough radio receiver willing to point it at the coordinates I suggest. And once they do, and I have my data, that is when I will need a much more robust computer to process it all."

"You can use this one whenever you want," Mike suggested.

"That's very kind of you, but if they're as cheap as you say they are, I think I'd like to keep all of my work on one of my own. I'll probably even purchase one tomorrow, as long as I can sell some coins."

Mike's expression brightened, and he muttered an "ah," sound. He looked down at his computer and started typing. "There's not much around here, but hang on," he said, reading. "Yeah. Why don't you come to work with me tomorrow? There are a few places you can probably sell some coins, and there's also a store where you can get a laptop for a decent price. If you can get some good money for your coins, we can go get some furniture for your bedroom after I get out of work."

Garrett was nodding, "Yeah, that sounds great."

"This weekend, I'll take you down to the subway and get you set up. Once you have your card, you'll be able to go anywhere in the city you want."

8

The following day, Garrett set off on foot from the NASA headquarters building and into D.C. He knew that pricing the Roman coins would be a much more delicate and complicated matter, so he only brought with him the thirty-six gold Napoleons he had remaining after the sale of the two to Joseph Heller. He knew their general value; he did not know the value of the others but could research that once he had his computer. As for the Napoleons, the full retail price was just over three hundred and fifty dollars American, but that was the retail price. He calculated that twenty percent less than retail would bring him about two hundred and eighty-eight dollars each and decided he would accept two hundred and seventy-five for them but would not go lower. Mike had given him three addresses: Duvraise, which was mostly jewelry but also dealt in rare coins; the Jack Cann Pawn shop, which dealt in a lot of gold and silver; and Tim McInnis Coin Exchange, which, of course, dealt exclusively with coins.

He had a lot of time, and the three places were only a fifteen-minute walk from each other. He went to Duvraise first and was told they would purchase all, but only at two hundred and forty dollars each. Garrett kindly declined and moved on to Jack Cann. Jack was not there, but the young man who helped him said he would pay the two hundred and seventy-five that Garrett wanted, but only for five. The clerk thought it too big a risk to take all of them, as he was not sure how long they would take to sell. Garrett asked if the deal would still be good if he came back later and the man assured him it would be, so he left in search of Tim McInnis Coin Exchange.

The storefront and the space inside were tiny. Between the door and the single display case that doubled as the service counter, there may have been enough room for six people to stand comfortably. The merchandise in the display case was lit brightly, but the rest of the room was so dark that Garrett was unsure the lights had even been turned on. The size of the store did not surprise him, but the size of Tim McInnis did. Garrett thought him a giant. The man had to be seven-foot-tall or just under, mostly balding, but with a few gray strands of hair that he still combed over the top of his skull. His eyes were a bright, piercing blue, and although his forehead was smooth, he had deep wrinkles around his mouth and eyes. He wore a black button-down shirt, partially covered by a white apron, which surprised Garrett, not understanding what could be messy about the coin trade.

"Good morning, sir. How can I help you?" Tim's voice was so deep it rumbled through the small room, seeming to arrive at Garrett's ears in a series of sharp pulses as opposed to a smooth tone.

"Good morning to you!" Garrett said, and approached the counter where Tim stood. "I have some coins I wish to part with. A lot of them, actually, but this is a selection of them. May I?" Garrett held the satchel of Napoleons open, above the counter, but thought it appropriate to ask before carelessly dumping them on the man's glass countertop.

"Sure! Let's have a look," Tim said. Garrett slid the thirty-six gold Napoleons onto the glass and Tim put on a pair of reading glasses. "Watch your eyes, this is bright." Tim yanked on a pull-chain and the counter exploded with bright white light. He leaned over and looked at the four rows of nine coins. He flipped each of them over and a few times shoved his reading glasses out of the way so he could use a magnifying loupe he produced from a shelf behind him. Without speaking, he walked over to a computer and typed in some information. He returned with a small digital scale and placed it next to the coins. First, he gathered all the coins and placed them on the scale. "Hmm," he muttered. He took them all off and weighed a sampling of them individually. Satisfied, he put the scale away and said, "Well, these are all real. Now that we have that out of the way, what do you want to get for them?"

"I sold two of them earlier this week for three hundred each," Garrett said.

Tim smiled. "You sold them to a collector. They pay more. You probably could have got more for them. I'm a reseller, so I have to make money on them. I'll offer you two fifty each for the lot."

Garrett gave the appearance of thinking it over. "I can't do that. I know what they're worth, and it's just not enough. I will move on my price, but not that far." Garrett put his hands in his pockets and relaxed, giving the floor back to Tim.

"Ok, well, I can tell you I truly despise shady dealers, and I always do my best not to be one. These particular coins will not be hard for me to sell. But with that said, I will still have to do a lot of work to get them all sold. It needs to be worth my time. Give me a better number."

"I would do two-ninety each. That leaves you a good amount of room to make some money," Garrett said. Tim put his phone on the counter and opened the calculator application. He punched in the numbers at two-ninety and shook his head.

"I'll go up to two-seventy, and that's a big jump. That's also a nice little stack of cash you'd be walking out of here with."

Garrett didn't just give the appearance of thinking it over this time; he truly was. "I would meet you in the middle, two-eighty each, and you got a deal," Garrett said.

Tim went back to the calculator again, shook his head again, and punched more numbers in. Finally, he said, "This is my final offer. I'll give you ten thousand in cash for all of them. That's almost up to your two-eighty. It's…" he keyed some more numbers into the calculator. "Two hundred and seventy-seven dollars and seventy-eight cents each."

Garrett put his right hand out for Tim to shake. "Deal," Garrett said. Tim shook his hand.

Thirty hours later, Tim had sold all the coins for a profit of $2,510. The profits steeled his positive opinion of Garrett, and the next time they met, Tim was happy to see him.

9

Surprise rose on Mike's face when Garrett asked him how much his share of the rent was. They sat in the same coffee shop where they had first met the day before.

"Well, rent is twenty-three hundred a month. Can you pay half?" Mike asked.

Garrett nodded and said, "I can, but I thought about it a lot as I was walking. I can give you eleven fifty, and that would be yours. You can keep that and my position in the apartment will be secured. Or, I can give you double that amount, and we can go to the store and spend it furnishing the apartment. That way we'd be spending half of your money, and half of mine."

Mike's expression changed as he thought, interested in the idea. "That's not bad. Will you have enough left to get a laptop too?" Mike asked. A small smile appeared on Garrett's face. "Oh! Wow, you got paid, then?"

"I sold all the Napoleons, and I got a little more than I had hoped to for them, so yes, you could say that I did well today." Garrett waited for the questions about his credit and credentials, but they did not come, so he did not bring them up.

"I already paid rent for this month, so what the hell, let's go shopping!"

Two hours later, they had finished their shopping spree and drove back to their apartment with all of their purchases in Mike's car, except for the items scheduled for delivery. In addition to furniture and kitchenware, they had purchased Garrett's brand-new laptop. The one he decided on, with some urging from Mike, was the most expensive of the three he was considering and would be the only one he would need for everything, including signal processing. They spent more money than they had planned to, but Garrett covered the difference.

Once back in their apartment, and with everything unpacked, Garrett opened his laptop and set it up opposite to Mike's, all while Mike was setting up their new sound system. As Garrett waited for the computer to boot up for the first time, he heard a haunting but pleasant sound coming from the living room, soon after, followed by Mike walking into the kitchen. "Music?" Garrett asked.

"Yeah, it's a new album. This band hasn't released an album in thirteen or fourteen years, so I was excited to hear it," Mike said. Garrett listened to the music, surprised by its complexity but also by how satisfying it was.

"I like it," Garrett said. "Can you show me how to use this? I have a lot of experience with computers, but none of this type." Mike showed the basics of computer usage to Garrett, who picked it all up quickly, as this was not dissimilar to the computers he had used growing up on Osa. The doorbell rang, and Mike received the food he had ordered for their dinner.

Garrett ate and perused the internet, asking Mike a lot of questions at first, but fewer and fewer as he got the hang of it. After some time, he searched for the Clotz Ale website, and once he found it, he parroted a colloquial term he had learned from both Bill and Mike, "Damn it."

"What's wrong?" Mike asked.

Garrett pointed to the screen with the Clotz Ale website spread across it. "It's in Italian. I don't speak Italian." Mike grabbed the mouse and slid the pointer to the upper right corner where the language selections resided and clicked on "English."

"Better?" He walked back into the living room.

10

Twenty hours later, Garrett had received and staged all the furniture, and Mike was getting home from work. When he walked in, he yelled out with joy and raised his arms up above his head. "This is awesome!"

Garrett got off the stool in the kitchen and joined him in the living room. "Good?" Garrett asked.

"Yeah, man. This is great. I ordered us some Chinese on the way home. You don't have a phone, so I couldn't call you, but hopefully you like beef lo mein. If not, I ordered a few other things." Mike dropped his bag on the floor and marveled at all the fresh additions to the apartment.

"I'm not a picky eater. I'm sure it will be fine," Garrett said, remembering the threads of dried meat he had eaten upon arriving on Earth. He walked back into the kitchen. "I found the coordinates."

Mike joined him in the kitchen. "Speaking of the coordinates, I have a gift for you," Mike said, and dropped a folded piece of paper on the island. "Open it."

Garrett opened the folded paper and saw the name "Becky Ferris" and a ten-digit number. Garrett did not understand and conveyed his confusion to his roommate.

"Becky is in charge of a massive radio telescope in Alaska. She can get you your signal, if it's there," Mike said.

Garrett stood back up at once. "Call her!"

Mike smiled and nodded. "After dinner. It's impolite to call at this hour, and we have a lot of work to do here. Let's get as much done as we can before dinner gets here. After we eat, we can call Becky, then hopefully finish with everything before it gets too late."

They set up the furniture, and the bell rang with their food delivery. Once they finished eating, Mike picked up his phone and dialed Becky's number. As soon as he pushed "send," he shook his head and said, "I forgot about the time difference, it's only…" Garrett heard a faint voice say "hello?" on the other end of Mike's call. "Hi, is this Becky?" Garrett could hear small sounds from the phone but could only understand Mike's side of the conversation.

"This is Michael Potaglia, from NASA in D.C. I got your number from a mutual friend of ours, Vanessa Tolland?" Mike smiled. "Yes, she's great. I've only just met her, but she's already made my life at NASA much easier." Another pause, and another smile. "Well, thank you. I hope it will. Anyway, the reason I'm calling is that I have a cousin of mine visiting from France. He's an astrophysicist, and he's telling me he has high hopes for a radio signal from a set of specific coordinates, and he wanted to know if it would be possible to work them into your rotation?" He walked through the kitchen, listening for almost a full minute. "Ok, sure, well if you would like, I'll put him on. He's standing right here next to me, but he is unnaturally shy." When he said it, he winked at Garrett. "Ok, yes, one moment." He covered the microphone with his hand and said, "She's not sure when she can do it, but she wants the coordinates now." He handed the phone to Garrett. Garrett put it up to his head the same way Mike did, and before he could say a word, Mike laughed and spun the phone a hundred and eighty degrees.

"Hello?" Garrett said.

"Hi! This is Becky Ferris. Michael told me you had coordinates for me?"

Garrett quickly moved over to his computer. "Yes! Yes, I do. I apologize, please bear with me for a second." Garrett clicked through the different applications he had open until he found the writing pad file he had relied on to store the numbers he did not want to forget.

Once he had read the numbers off to Becky, she thanked him and said that it would probably be four or five weeks before they finished their current scan. Garrett thanked her and handed the phone to Mike, who ended the call. The two men then resumed their efforts to set up the apartment with all the new furniture and gadgets.

11

Mike Potaglia hated interruptions while he was sleeping. He hated them so much that he made a couple of practices a part of his everyday life. One of them was to lock his cat out of his room while he slept. He even screwed a large piece of foam to the base of his door and covered it in double-sided tape. She hated sticky things and did not scratch at it. The other was his cell phone; he turned off the ringer and put it on the kitchen counter and charger every night before he went to bed.

The night of the call to the Denali State Radio Telescope Array, the call to Becky, was no different. Garrett and Mike were both deeply asleep, Garrett in his new bed and new bed linens, Mike in his familiar and comfortable lodging.

The repetitive rattle of Mike's vibrating cell phone on the kitchen counter that started at three fifteen in the morning did not disturb either of them.

12

That Saturday morning, Mike woke up to a newly furnished home with all the amenities of the western world. He happily walked into the living room, turned on his new TV, and tuned it to a typical morning news program. As he set the remote back on the coffee table, he heard Garrett's bedroom door open. He walked into the kitchen and prepared the coffeemaker. Once the coffee machine started to creak and groan, he walked to his phone and picked it up. He misread the notification bar the first time, so he set the phone down and made his best effort to wipe the sleep out of his eyes. The second was no different. Nineteen missed calls. Concern for his parents immediately welled up in his throat as he navigated to the call history, but before he got there, he heard Garrett's voice, "Mike? Come in here now!"

Phone in tow, Mike walked into the living room and finally recognized what they were actually saying on the news broadcast, "…a radio stream from far outside of the Milky Way galaxy. The Alaskan radio telescope has heard many fast radio bursts in its history, but they say this is the first radio stream. Truly, an intelligent communication and not just a cosmic anomaly," the reporter said.

Garrett looked at Mike, "I need to t…" Mike's phone rang in his hand as Garrett was speaking. Garrett nodded as if to say, "answer it."

"Hello? Yes… That's amazing… yes, he is, one moment." Mike held the phone out to Garrett.

"Hello?"

"Are you the one who gave me the coordinates last night?" Becky asked.

"Yes, my name is Garrett Rhodes." Garrett paced about the room as he talked.

"Well, Garrett. It paid off, big time. I sent the coordinates into the office last night and asked my team to put them in the rotation. They were frustrated with the scan they had been working on and your submission piqued their interest, so they turned the equipment to your spot. Apparently, they were flooded with signals, a lot of them, and they were constant, or I should say they *are* constant," she said. Garrett smiled. "We have seventeen more locations in the northern hemisphere tracking the signal. I think we're getting all of it."

Garrett's smile grew as wide as his facial muscles could achieve. "That's excellent news! And you're getting fifty-three unique frequencies?" Garrett asked. There was silence on the other end of the line. "Hello?"

"I'm sorry, how could you know there would be fifty-three?" Becky asked.

Garrett thought for a moment. He had made an error in revealing his detailed knowledge of the signal from Orris. It was the first time he had made the mistake since he left Osa. He let it be the opening salvo. "I know a great deal about the signal, and everything I know will soon be revealed to a select few people. If you want to be among them, you will need to travel to Washington." Garrett observed a blend of concern and curiosity blooming on Mike's face. "The most important thing, though, is that the uninterrupted signal is recorded, and that the data gets to me by way of Michael."

"Your cousin, Michael Potaglia?" Becky asked.

"No, he is of no relation to me. That was a story he crafted to get you to search for my signal. He is, however, an excellent friend of mine."

There was another pause on the other end of the line. Quietly, Becky asked, "Are you even an astrophysicist?"

Garrett laughed at that. "I am an amateur study in a wide range of disciplines, and yes, astrophysics is one of them."

"I don't know what to think, where to go from here… This is all so new, and strange," she said.

Garrett softened his voice, not wanting to add to her stress. "This will change the world as you know it, Becky. I believe you would like to be one of those at the forefront of that change. If I'm wrong, do nothing but get the data to Mike. If I'm right, then plan to get to Washington as soon as you can. I will ensure that you are among the first to learn about the signal. You have helped me a great deal." Garrett handed the phone back to Mike, who put it up to his ear again. Garrett walked back to the television to hear what the reporters were saying.

It was another ten minutes before Mike ended the call with Becky. He then went to the kitchen to get coffee. When he walked back into the living room, he said, "So, what the hell, man? How did you know about this? Why did Becky just ask me a thousand questions about you?" He handed a cup to Garrett.

"This is premature. I would normally have the signal translated before I revealed my identity and plead my case for the future," Garrett said. "But it appears I have lost that luxury. Anyway, I need a book and some software. If you would be good enough to drive me to a store where we can purchase these two things, I will tell you my full story. You will not believe it at first, but in time, as I reveal more and more, you will eventually come around."

"What store?" Mike asked.

Garrett looked surprised. "I have no idea. I need the software to write a program that our laptops can use and a book on how to write a program in that language."

"Oh, okay. That shouldn't be a problem. Is this software for the signal?" Mike asked. Garrett winked and nodded.

Chapter 10

Final Instruction

1

The final session with Arthur Sterritt was illuminating. It had little to do with Sterilex, as they had covered that extensively in their first meetings.

"I can't imagine what more we can discuss about Sterilex and its process, but OPM mandated these final review meetings. I suggest we spend the time combing through every question you might have about the topic," Arthur said, and looked from envoy to envoy, with no reaction. "This time doesn't have to be about Sterilex... we have talked at length on many topics. Is there anything else that we have talked about that you want to discuss?"

Stan Richman immediately spoke up. "Yeah, the marks." A few murmurs of agreement. "You said we shouldn't be surprised if they resemble us, that their DNA wouldn't be drastically different. How could you possibly know that?"

"That's a good question, Stan, but I have to be honest when I say that this is my assumption and that I don't truly know. No one on Osa knows; all we can do is speculate, but allow me to walk you through my reasoning." The entire group shifted in their seats. "First, and I think most importantly, they will have exactly two eyes. I'm positive about that, at least. Why am I positive?"

"Depth perception, binocular vision," Joe said. "They would need to focus with their vision, not just respond to movement." No other envoy said anything, but many of them were nodding.

"Excellent, Joe. That is exactly right. What about sound? What about hearing? Will our marks be mostly deaf, or will they have two effective ears? Or one, or three? What shape will their ears be? Will they be like ours, or will they be very different?"

Garrett took a stab at that one. "It will be two, and they will be fixed on either side of the head, like ours," he said as he continued to gather his thoughts about hearing.

"Why?" Arthur asked.

"They need to be able to hear to either side of them."

"Yes, but you said the ears would be fixed specifically on their heads. Why?"

"For the same reasons ours are. And for the same reasons our eyes and noses are. They are not close-proximity sensory organs. They can reach out into the world and generate a lot of information, so they are close to the brain to make that information known as quickly as possible." Garrett looked around at faces contemplating his answer.

"I believe that to be true, Garrett, all of it. But why the shape?" Arthur asked, "Why do we have this strangely shaped ear? I don't think anyone would argue it isn't strange. Does anyone have any ideas?" Utter silence among the group. "They are shaped this way for vertical location. Have any of you witnessed an animal rock their head to one side like this?" Arthur demonstrated. "It's because they can tell when a sound is coming from their right or left, but not if it's coming from above or below. By rocking their head to the side, they are artificially transforming their right/left ability to above/below ability. But we don't need to do that. I can blindfold any of you and clap my hands above or below your head, and you would all know which it was." The group was in deep thought, but all seemed to understand, and they didn't need a demonstration. They knew they could distinguish hearing from above and below.

"What about bi-peds or quadra-peds? Questions about that? Or is it absurdly obvious? Multiple fingers? Opposable thumbs?" Not one man reacted. "Evolution has led to the way we look, and when we discover peoples capable of doing what we need them to do, I think you'll find that the evolutionary steps will have tended to work out the same for all of us. One thing we're sure of is that they will be made of the same things, carbon-based, water, and so on. I believe that there will be differences. I just think they will almost definitely be few and small."

2

The final week with Dr. Benjamin Estes, Survival Theory, was more of the same, but things were much more focused on the young planets. As the first of the classes began, the envoys peppered him with questions.

"We will get to everything, guys, but remember, most of these things will be answered by your own research before you pick your next planet," Ben said. The chatter died down. "Radiation, temperature, O2 levels, these things and many others will contribute to your decisions. Tilt, proximity, star type; you guys all know these things." More questions and chatter sprung up, and Ben could not digest it all. "Guys, when you're picking your next planet, how many will you choose?" Murmuring, but it was clear they all knew it was three.

"When you arrive at your first choice, that will be the moment of truth. Your analysis from orbit will tell you yes or no, because the data will be much more accurate up close than from light years away. If it's no good, move on, and always adhere to the safe harbor protocol."

"What if there is no safe harbor?" Joe asked. "What if everything went wrong, or if you jump to another galaxy?"

Ben looked at Joe for a moment and then answered. "If you jump to another galaxy, then you know you should have prepared five target planets, since there will be no safe harbor. If the first planet is a no-go, that's one down. You will have three or four chances after that, and if you did your homework before selecting them, they should all be good chances." Ben walked back and forth in front of the group, structured in a classroom setting, much like Lauren's.

"What if it all fails?" Joe mumbled, staring at his desk.

"If it all fails," Ben said, "Then you have the pill. If you don't like that option, I would recommend taking a bit of the Sterilex and pointing your transport at the star. You won't feel anything either way." Dead silence pervaded the room after his answer. He continued in a lower register. "You guys already know all of this stuff. Make sure you bring water with you, and food. Make sure that when you leave, you're at least a little overweight. Fat will be important and may save your life. Make sure there is a sufficient magnetic field and that radiation levels are low. Make sure O2 levels are high, or at least high enough that you won't pass out. Make sure the atmosphere is mostly nitrogen and that the trace gases aren't toxic. It's fairly simple; you will have all the tools at your disposal." Once there was sufficient technology on any given planet, they had only to download the Envoy assistance application to have all of Osa's, and eventually Orris's, resources available for reference.

"We're just hacking through the same things over and over again, guys. If that's what you want to do, let's do it. But if any of you have an original idea, or question, or scenario, then let's hear it. Let's talk through it." There was general silence in the room. Eventually, one of them asked him if they could go through the preparation steps for a young planet again, and Ben obliged.

3

They completed the "Final Instruction" phase of the envoys' training in one-week segments from two of the disciplines each week. The current week was "Sterilex" and "Survival Theory." After the first day was over, Garrett went back to his apartment, which was Lauren's apartment, as he had abandoned his since becoming involved with her. Living together was her suggestion. "If we're going to be together until you leave, then let's be together," she had said. They also discussed the ease of leaving without having to give up an apartment. It was an unhappy discussion, but not a bitter one.

That evening, after they finished dinner and washed the dishes, they retired to the living room, where they laid together on the couch. The channel tuned in was one that discussed science, and the current program was one that touched on anything relating to the study of the universe. Interrupting the narrator, Lauren said, "We don't really know, do we?" It was such an arbitrary question; Garrett didn't understand what she was asking.

"Don't know what?"

"We're putting so much effort into the Orris Project. Building Orris, putting you and the other guys out there, but we don't even know for sure if it's all going to collapse; we're just guessing."

Garrett thought about his reply before making it but settled on a general thesis. "It's more than guessing; we know that the entire universe started from a singularity. We know the universe is still expanding, but we also know that is because of the eflix ring, which is slowing down. The eflix ring is the essence of gravity itself, and it is slowing down. It will stop, and all the physics we have ever learned tells us it will fall back in. When that happens," he looked up to the sky and shook his head, "The whole thing is going to collapse. That's why we're doing this. That's why I'm going to give up my life and our love to beat it." Tears appeared in Lauren's eyes. They had never used the word "love." Even in all the months preceding that moment, they equally believed it would only make things worse upon the eventual launch. Garrett could feel her tears saturate the cotton shirt on his chest and felt the sting of his own tears in his eyes. *There is nothing I can do about it,* he thought. *This is not flattery, this is fact.*

4

The following week, they had the final wrap-up with Dr. Olive Francis and Dr. Jack Abbott. Communications and general technology.

The communications course was repetitive; Dr. Francis recycled all the old information, and none of the envoys had questions. Garrett knew about how badly things had ended between Olive and Tom, and there was a coldness in the room that Tom, Olive, and Garrett alone recognized. With the meetings mandatory, but fruitless, Garrett and the rest, including the instructor, found them agonizing.

They could not say the same about the meetings with Dr. Abbott. The envoys, similar to the meetings with Dr. Estes, had hundreds of questions. Dr. Abbott was less agitated by them than Ben had been.

"Just remember that all the new technology you will encounter will be through the feeds you get from Orris once you're already landed. We stopped the development phase for the transports ten months ago. The only changes being made now are with either safety or efficiency. Anything new will be completely transparent to the operators, so I can assure you that what you have learned up to this point will be the reality of your launch experience. No surprises, I promise," Jack said. His office was a mirror image in design to Arthur's, but he kept it much brighter and had lined the windowless walls with whiteboards.

"Are they working on getting the drive better than 0.8?" Ken Chase asked.

"Oh, yes, of course. They can build a drive right now that will do 100c. But they know it would twist itself apart and kill everyone onboard the second it fires. They know how to do it, it's a matter of how they can do it successfully and safely." Ken nodded, satisfied with the answer. "What is one thing that worries any of you? Let's start there."

"Dying," Tom said. Everyone laughed nervously. Jack smiled.

"You won't die on my transport. I can tell you that. We've poured more time and effort into these tiny vehicles than anything else we've ever worked on. Our next project is the Lance. I imagine we'll spend a lot more time on that, but I would like to know that all of you are comfortable getting into a transport. I would be."

"The difference is that you will never have to," Randy Vila said, without looking up.

Jack nodded. "You're right, Randy. And I think I understand better now, the apprehension you all have, or may have. But I'll tell you, if you went to all the design, building, and testing meetings I have, you would all be much more confident. They are remarkable machines, extremely robust and capable." A general sense of ease washed through the room with Jack's confidence.

"I'm sure I haven't said it, and maybe I shouldn't need to, but I will anyway. You guys are extremely important to me. If any of you think I feel that you're only parts of the machine, I want you to all be assured that is absolutely not true. I have a strong attachment to each of your lives, and I don't take preserving them lightly." Silence in the room. "I'll have you know that I've had more than a few arguments with my teams because they think I spend too much time on safety. I've been told by more than one person that I'm beating a dead horse. When you strap into those seats, please know you are in one of the safest places in the world."

5

"Less than two months now," Lauren said once they finished dinner and were on the couch.

"Yeah, but a lot more than one month." Garrett kissed her on her temple, uncomfortably close to her eye. She swatted him.

"Stop!" He laughed as she pushed him over so she could lie down close to him. "I'm serious, Garrett. I'm afraid we made a big mistake. I'm going to fall apart when you leave."

Garrett spoke softly to her. "I don't think it would be better to end it the way Tom and Olive did. Do you think it would be easier if you hated me for the rest of your life? I am sincerely asking; I don't know the answer to that." Lauren shifted in his embrace multiple times until she had worked herself all the way around and was facing him.

"Of course not." She closed her eyes and rested her face on his chest.

"I'm just saying," Garrett said, "that the next seven weeks will be terrible if you only focus on the fact that it's our last seven weeks together."

"Then what am I supposed to do?" she asked. "It's getting closer and closer."

"So is death, but we all ignore that. We're programmed to ignore it. Just focus on what is happening right here, right now. It's the only way we will enjoy happiness for the last of my time on Osa." She stood up and took his hand.

"You're right. Let's go enjoy it."

6

The following week was with Lauren and Christine, acquisitions and psych. The psych roundtables had gone on throughout the entirety of the training, only suspended for the last two weeks during the focused final instruction periods for the other four disciplines. It would be their last week with Christine, the following week would be with Dr. Murray alone, and the week after that they would have off before the launches began. They would begin leaving Osa with either three or four days between launches, depending on weather and launch window timing.

There was little new material with Lauren and the acquisitions classes, but there were some questions. Terence Stone with the first, "We expect the drive technology to improve throughout the future. Won't the acquisition rules change as the Lances get faster?"

"No," Lauren said. "Remember that all the numbers are generated based on the estimated time it will take the Lance to get to Orris. So, on your first planet, if the Lance can get up to 1c, and Orris is 500 light-years away, it will take 500 years to reach it. The speed doesn't factor into the planning, only the duration. On the second planet, let's say the design improved and the Lance can now get up to 2c, but Orris is 1,000 light-years away… it will still take 500 years for the Lance to get there. You're doing the calculations based on the relative time, not the current drive technology."

"How long do you think they will have?" Kyle asked, "I mean, how long before life on the Lance becomes unsustainable. They can't last forever." Lauren's sober expression did not change, and she slowly shook her head.

"None of us really know. I have talked to Dr. Paige and some other instructors about it, and the consensus we reached is that the key is the first generation. If they can get past the first generation, then it will probably be equipment failure and not societal disillusion that brings about the end of the body; provided they don't make it to Orris first."

"Why is the first generation so important?" Ken asked.

"The first generation will be the only one experiencing a massive culture shock. And that will be in addition to the shock that comes from living on a tin can floating through space rather than a huge, welcoming planet. The second generation and beyond will know nothing else. We expect their brains to develop a comfort in being within the walls of the Lance. It will be the only home they've ever known, and it's not like they're all that small, anyway." The envoys all nodded. They had seen the blueprints for the first-generation Lance, or at least the theory of it. The design for the first commissionable craft would not be ready for another ten years.

"They will run out of fuel, I would think, before any major equipment deterioration," Stan said.

"That's more of a question for Jack, but as I understand it, they will recycle the fuel they leave with repeatedly until they get the last bit of energy from it. Before that happens, they will have to locate a source for new fuel. The protocols for Lance operation are extremely detailed and extensive."

"They will have to stop and mine other planets for fuel?" Stan asked.

"In an optimal situation, it would be asteroids or not at all, but yeah, they might have to if they're out there for a long time."

The room was silent until Stan said, "That's amazing. I didn't know that would even be a possibility."

Lauren nodded and shrugged. "We're trying to preserve these civilizations. It would be pretty dumb to lose one because they ran out of gas. I bet there are a lot of things you guys don't know about the Lance, because you don't need to know. You all have more than enough on your plates."

7

On the last day that week, and during the last psych roundtable, the air was thick with silence. Christine had asked a few questions but received little feedback. She took a different tactic, and instead of prodding responses out of the envoys, she talked about her feelings toward their departure.

"I can't believe this is the last one of these that I'll be doing with you as a group," she said. "You will all be together next week, but I won't be there. It's getting very real." Some nodding, but no other interaction. "I think I've told all of you that my husband and my daughter are up there," she pointed to the ceiling. "They will be back next month. That will put them at a year orbiting Osa. I can't imagine what it would be like to leave our planet for so long, and I can't imagine what it will be like for all of you."

She talked for another half hour, with no feedback, no reactions, and no questions. Finally, she reminded them all how to reach her for a one-on-one conversation and dismissed them.

8

"That was tough with Dr. Paige today," Garrett said to Lauren at their apartment later that night. They had just sat down to dinner, and Lauren furrowed her brow.

"Tough? Why?"

"I think it's because it's so close, everyone is wound up in knots. Including me. The last thing I wanted to do was talk about how I felt about this or that."

She nodded and smiled. "Right here, right now, Garrett."

"In that situation, we're forced to look ahead. I think that's why all the guys were so uncomfortable. I think everyone has been trying to ignore our imminent futures, at least while we can. That meeting just put it right in our faces. It's certainly not her fault, that's her job. So, that's what I mean… it was just tough." Lauren offered him a little smile and a nod.

After dinner, they fell into their usual routine of watching some program or other. At that point, the content had moved away from documentaries and favored comedies or dramas. Another part of their current routine was to go to bed early, which they did again that evening.

Restless, Garrett woke up and saw the clock read 3:04. He rolled over to find the other side of the bed vacant. Quietly, he stood and walked to the doorway of the bedroom. In front of the living room window without a curtain and with the small telescope in front of it, Lauren stood, naked, peering through the top pane up at the stars. Garrett thought his spying to be an invasion, as she clearly thought herself alone, and he took a step backward to return to bed so she could have her privacy.

"I know you're awake," Lauren said. She half turned toward him and held out her hand as an invitation to join her. He approached and wrapped his arms around her from behind, lacing his fingers over her belly. She placed both of her hands on his.

"What are you thinking about?" he asked. She rubbed both of his hands with hers and leaned her head back on his chest.

"You. And that," she nodded toward the sky, "and just how unbelievable it all seems right now." He breathed her scent in and kissed her neck. His hand then moved, and she shivered.

9

The envoys spent the last week before their break, in addition to equipment preparation, controls review, and their final course of oxygen deprivation conditioning, in a large, bright conference room with Dr. Alex Murray. Dr. Murray sat at the head of the long table, and the ten remaining envoys flanked him, five to either side.

"Good afternoon, gentlemen." He had only a paper notepad and a pen with him. He placed them on the table and sat down. "I planned these meetings with the group because I wanted each of you to have direct access to me leading up to the launches. I have no material to go over. These meetings are only to discover if we have missed anything, from your perspectives." He held up his notepad to show the group it was new and blank. "So, that's why we are here. If it's a question I can answer for you, or if it's an oversight that we can remedy before the first launch, that is what this time is for." He looked from man to man and waited.

Ken Chase lifted his hand and said, "We've gone over the launch protocols and the abort procedures a lot, but what if we have a problem when we wake up? When we're nowhere near Osa, or Orris?" Dr. Murray nodded.

"Once you're in the transport and the track energizes, you are subject to the capabilities of the transport. Every one of you is intimately familiar with the transports and their operation. If it's close to home and you can abort, great. If it's far from home, get into your orbit. That's the most important thing you can do in that situation. Once you're in orbit, you will be free to focus on other things. If a system fails, use the backup system. If that fails, then you will have to devise a workaround on the spot. You have a lot of functionality on those small crafts. Remember all seven solid fuel systems: they're there to bail you out. Remember your emergency thermo-gel evaporate pressure system, but only use that if you have no other recourse. Using that is a ticking time-bomb, but it could save your life in a pinch. If you have to use it, please remember to dump the plates out of the cells once you land. Remember your deceleration methods, your crush chutes, your drag chutes, and obviously your final descent chutes. They packed those little machines with functionality. Trust them, trust yourself, and trust your training." The recap eased the concern on Ken's face.

"Alex?" It was Randy Vila. Dr. Murray nodded. "Why is there an entire year between the first nine launches and the second? And then another year before the last nine?"

Dr. Murray smiled. "Because of the Sterilex. When Arthur brought us his formulation and method, we realized how painfully slow the production was, so when we designed our Sterilex lab, we made it capable of producing enormous quantities. Unfortunately, the designers of the lab didn't bother to include Arthur or his team, and there were two major oversights that rendered the lab extremely limited in its production capacity. The cost to fix these oversights was enormous, and once the technology team got wind of the problem, they told us to save our money. The extra time would make it much easier for them, since they had to get all the transports built, anyway. Jack Abbott proposed doing twenty-seven launches in groups of nine over three years, and that seemed to satisfy all parties involved."

"And you could keep up with the Sterilex production in that time?" Randy asked.

"Yes. You will each be provided with a thirty-one-milliliter bottle. The lab can make a little less than one milliliter per day, so it takes almost the entire year to make enough for nine envoys." With the question satisfactorily answered, a general silence settled into the room. Eric Thomas fidgeted in his seat and tentatively raised his hand. Dr. Murray nodded at him.

"This question doesn't really apply to our experience, but it is just a curiosity of mine." Dr. Murray nodded again. "Ten envoys, all men? Did any women apply for this role?"

"Oh, certainly, yes. Although the application rate was something around twenty to one, or twenty-two to one, I don't remember exactly. The next group has a woman envoy, Patricia Holland. She's number fifteen. There are two women in the third group, Wendy and Katrina, and they're both at the top of their class. You ten men scored higher than any of the other applicants, but if you measure against the ratio of applicants overall, the women are actually winning as far as acceptance rate goes." While the others were nodding, Garrett thought of getting the chairman's opinion of a question that had been the source of a lot of disagreement among the envoys.

"I have a question that I think a lot of these guys would like to know your opinion of, Alex," Garrett said. "What do we do when we're done? At the end of the fifth, if we can make it that far? What's your opinion?"

"Well, I would not do a sixth!" Dr. Murray laughed at his own joke, and the envoys joined him. "I apologize for joking. I know it's a serious topic. I guess this is something you all have thought about a lot more than I have, so I'm interested in hearing your thoughts. But honestly, if you get through all five planets, then you can do whatever the hell you want with the rest of your lives. You would have earned that right completely. You should be championed and held in high esteem as heroes of the universe." There was a heartier laughter throughout the room, though some of it was nervous.

"There are a few competing ideas," Garrett said. "The first is the simplest: fishing. Just settle on the fifth planet after the Lance is gone and find a simple way that you would like to live your life and do it."

Dr. Murray nodded emphatically. "Yes, that's great. Do it! You guys might have forty or fifty years left to live when you're done. Buy a nice place by a lake, soak up the rays, travel the planet, whatever you want. What other ideas do you have?"

"A couple of us had the idea to board the Lance, so they could lay our remains to rest on Orris."

Dr. Murray frowned. "I wouldn't. No way, not worth it. Life on the Lance will be terrible compared to a planet. None of you need to worry about Orris, anyway." He leaned closer to the group as though there were others listening whom he did not want hearing. "Once Orris moves to a solar orbit, they will begin construction of the first nation cylinder. This nation will be named Rhodes; it's already law. Shortly after construction is started, they will begin construction of the second, which will be named Burkman. Do you guys see where this is going?" Dr. Murray scanned the group. "The next two will be Holly and Daniels. You guys won't have statues and monuments named after you, you'll have entire nations named after you. It would be silly to squander half of your lives in a tin can just so your dead bodies could be buried in a nation that is already named for you." A general emotion washed over the group that Dr. Murray, at first, did not understand.

Garrett clued him in. "They're going to name a nation for Jonroe?"

Alex nodded. "Yes, there was no resistance to that measure." The envoys looked back and forth amongst each other, all pleased.

10

Garrett was snapped out of a trance while standing in his and Lauren's kitchen by the acrid smell of burning flesh. He had put the roast in the oven without setting the timer and burned it badly while he lost all sense of time, having escaped mentally to another world. He threw open the oven door and snatched out the pan, setting it on the stovetop.

With the oven turned off, he walked into the living room and opened all the windows. When he heard the key enter and turn the lock, he knew Lauren was home from work.

"If you were trying to burn the place down, you have more work to do," she said.

"Very funny, nerd," he replied, and continued opening all the windows he could. "Sorry, I never set the timer." She laughed as she landed her bag and keys on the kitchen island.

"Well, it looks like you're taking me out to dinner tonight!" She smiled radiantly, and Garrett stopped feeling guilty.

"Absolutely! Anywhere you want."

Once most of the smoke was out of the apartment, they closed up all the windows, discarded the failed dinner into the trash, and left the building.

With drinks served and their appetizers and entrees ordered, Garrett recapped the events of the day as experienced by the envoys. Specifically, he brought up the conversation about the eventual life decisions after their missions were all complete and how they expected to spend the balance of their lives.

"So, what's your answer?" she asked. The two had never talked about it, as they typically avoided conversations about any world where they were not together.

"None of them." He swallowed another sip of beer and wiped his mouth with his napkin. "I'm going to Orris. On my own. I'm going to have a transport built and I'm going as soon as I can."

She looked at him curiously. "Why? I don't understand," she said, as their appetizers came.

"Before I met you, I took advantage of this opportunity because it fit so well with who I am. I have to be engaged; I have to work toward something at all times in my life. Others might be content sitting on a dock, fishing, but not me. I want to go to Orris. I want to participate in the operation and the planning of the eventual course of the great machine. This story needs to come full circle for me. Even if I die before I get there, it will be worth it, because I can die knowing I was always in the pursuit of something great." Lauren blushed but was not sure why. "If I get there, I will insist that I be made no less than an advisor to Orris Command. At least I can have a voice among the group forging the path for its ultimate destiny." His words transfixed Lauren. She then spoke and caught him so completely off guard that he shuddered.

"Marry me," she said. Garrett looked back at her in a stupor. "I'll sign whatever I have to sign to disavow myself of the fortune afforded to family members of the envoys. If for no other reason than to keep your mother from thinking I was just a whore after all. I want to be able to call you my husband, but I don't want a penny for it. I just want the knowledge." With all the trials and stress and pain of the last ten months, it was a new cut; fresh, and painful.

"What? Why? Won't that... make everything so much worse?"

She smiled at him, a big and happy smile, without a hint of sorrow. "No, I think it will help. I think it will help a lot, for me, at least."

Garrett's eyes drifted from hers to the table in front of him. He was not putting the pieces together. He looked back up at her. "Why?" he asked in a whisper.

She breathed in deeply and maintained the smile on her entire face. "Because instead of this just being a fling with a guy that eventually left me, you would be my husband. We never divorce, we don't die and leave each other widowed, we would be two bound souls that distance couldn't affect. Twenty or forty years after you leave, I'll still know in my heart that you're my husband, and that you still live. That knowledge would improve my entire life." Tears welled in her eyes, and Garrett found the same was happening in his. They each blinked them away with some help from their napkins.

Garrett thought about the proposal and imagined what the future would be like in one case, and then the other. He cycled through his thoughts several times and thought about them again from his own perspective and with his own genuine feelings in mind. With every cycle, he grew more confident that Lauren was right. She sat there, picking at her appetizer. Her gaze alternated between her appetizer and his eyes, which were fixed on his half-empty glass of beer. Finally, he looked up at her. "Yes, I think you're right," he said. "But you're right about all of it. Get the papers tomorrow. Sign them and hand them off to me to sign. I would hate to live for the next five billion years thinking my mother hated you." Her smile, which was large to begin with, grew so big it distorted her face, and she started bawling. Garrett knew they were happy tears. He breathed in softly and smiled so she would know that he did not misunderstand the emotion. He then stood and walked around the small table to embrace her. It was a happy engagement.

Chapter 11

Acceptance

1

Mike and Garrett went to a diner to get breakfast before beginning their search for the book and software that Garrett needed. They sat in a booth, and Garrett began telling the story of his origin. He started with subtle references to his childhood and upbringing, but as soon as he revealed that Osa was a different planet and not just some place unknown to Mike on Earth, Mike stopped him.

"So, you're telling me you're an alien. Are you going to reveal your true form at some point?" Mike said, laughing. Garrett smiled and laughed himself. He knew it was coming and had been through it many times before. He leaned back in his chair and held his arms out.

"It would surprise you just how similar life is from planet to planet, all across the universe. I look like one of you, but if someone did a DNA test on me, it would not come back human. Close, but not human. One of my instructors, Art Sterritt, warned all of us that this would probably be the case, but I can't say I believed him until I witnessed it for myself." Garrett took another forkful of scrambled eggs. "Oh, and as far as the 'alien' thing, I feel like I am less of an alien than you and all the other people on this planet. I was here long before any of you." As they finished their breakfast, Garrett continued with his story: Osa, his family, Lauren, the launch, Sterilex, Distria, Rhett, Katya, Telraed, and finally, as they were walking back to the car, he told Mike of landing on Earth when it was just a hot rock.

Once they were in the car, Mike said, "I didn't know that mental patients could tell such entertaining stories." He pulled out of their parking space.

"I take no offense, Mike. As I said, it will take time before you fully believe me. But I'll finish the story up to where we are now, just so I can be done with it. Then there will only be questions."

Before he could resume, Mike cut him off. "How long will it take to finish your story?" he asked.

"Oh, I don't know, maybe an hour to summarize my years on Earth."

Mike nodded and said, "Do you want to tell this entire story, over and over again, to all of us who may want to hear it?"

"Not particularly, but it is important that I communicate the information so we can all move forward."

"How about this," Mike said. "Once we're home, you tell the entire story one more time, from the beginning, but then you won't have to do it again after that."

"A recording," Garrett said. Mike nodded. "Sure, that sounds great."

2

Once they were back at the apartment, Mike sat at Garrett's computer to install the software. Garrett could have figured it out at that point, but Mike noted it would be far faster if he did it. Garrett sat at the kitchen table and began reading his book on coding. Once the program finished installing, Mike made a mock recording space for Garrett to tell his story. He gathered every portable or semi-portable light and lamp in the apartment and arranged them in a crescent around the couch. Repurposing one of his moving boxes and a piece of cardboard, he made a stand for his phone. He placed the box on their coffee table and the stand on the box, opened the camera application, and turned on all the lights.

"Hey," Mike said. "Whenever you're ready." Garrett emerged from the kitchen with a smile.

"Couch? Can I get some coffee first?" he asked.

Mike smiled and laughed a little. "Sure, make two, also I'm probably just going to order pizza for dinner. Is that okay with you?"

Garrett had walked to the kitchen but called back, "Yeah, that's fine."

Once he had made the coffee and handed Mike's cup to him, Garrett sat on the couch and looked at the phone, which he understood also served as a video recorder. Mike nodded at him.

"Hello. My name is Garrett Rhodes. I was born in a small town called Dirividus, which is a suburb of the city of Dinesta, in the Republic of Korrah, on the planet Osa. This planet was in a solar system that no longer exists and was not a part of the Milky Way galaxy. It was one of the original solar systems in the Andromeda galaxy…" It took Garrett two hours and forty-five minutes to tell his entire story. He finished with, "And now I am here, in Washington D.C., on this couch. I still have a long way to go… *we* have a long way to go. But you will soon know more about the universe in which you live than you could have imagined possible in your lifetime." With that, he stood up, and Mike stopped recording.

They ate their pizza, Mike worked on editing the video, and Garrett continued to study his coding book and even started playing with the program.

3

Sunday was more of the same for Garrett. He buried himself in the programming language, and by the end of that day, he had finished the book and started reading it again from the beginning. Mike had left early that morning to visit his parents in Maryland, whom he told Garrett were about a ninety-minute drive away.

Later that night, after Mike had left his parent's house for the drive back home, his phone rang. It was Becky.

"Hello? Becky?" Mike said.

"Hi, Mike?" she replied. He was beginning to enjoy the sound of her voice. It was not just sweet and pleasant, it was also sane and grounded in reality, something he had recently felt himself getting further and further away from.

"Yeah, it's great to hear from you," he said, and she laughed.

"Well, I was just calling to tell you I have made arrangements to come to D.C. Whatever this is, I don't want to miss it. Were you able to find out anything more from Garrett?"

"Yeah, I found out he is one hundred percent crazy and should be institutionalized," he said. She laughed, but Mike could tell she clapped a hand over her mouth as soon as she started.

"Well? What is it? You can't hold me in suspense!"

"There is no way I could do his story justice over the phone. We made a video last night and you can watch it online if you have the password. Do you have a pen and paper?" She did, and Mike gave her the information she needed to view the video on the internet.

"Thanks, Mike, but are you worried? Do you think he's dangerous?"

Mike laughed. "No! Honestly, he's operating exactly as you would expect him to if his crazy story were all true. I think he genuinely believes it all." Mike's focus dropped from the call to the traffic as he merged onto a highway. After, he said, "Are you still there?"

"Yeah, I am."

In that moment, he realized the relief he felt when she spoke revealed he was experiencing the beginnings of an affection for her. "You were saying you were coming to D.C.?"

"Oh! Yes, on Wednesday. But I was calling to find out where I should stay, because I want to be close to you and Garrett," she said.

"Oh, sure, I'm driving now, but can I give you my email? Just send me a dummy message and I'll reply with our location and I'll send you links to a few hotels near us."

"That sounds great, Mike, go ahead." Mike rattled off his email address, and she repeated it back to him.

"That's it! I'll send the information to you later. I should be home in a little over an hour."

"Thanks again, Mike. I'm looking forward to meeting you." *The feeling is more than mutual*, Mike thought. "Same here. Take care," Mike said. She ended the call.

Over the course of the next hour, Mike grew more and more excited to get home so he could email the woman he had never met.

4

On Monday, Garrett made another trip with Mike into the city with the singular intention of visiting his friend Tim McInnis. When Tim recognized Garrett's face as he walked into the shop he bellowed, "Well hello there, friend!"

"Hello, Tim." Garrett removed the two satchels from his bag and placed them both unopened on the sales counter. Tim's eyes grew wide, and Garrett raised a hand, "I see the stress in your face, but don't worry. I am not here to sell you all these coins." They both laughed a little. "What I am here for is to ask your opinion. You are obviously one of the best men in the city to ask." Garrett began unknotting the cinch string on the two satchels.

"Sure, but can I ask your name again? I know you told me last time, but my memory is terrible."

"Of course, it's Garrett. Now," He spilled thirty or forty coins from the top of the first bag onto the counter and set the bulk aside, "I don't want any of these, but there are so many, I don't even know where to begin with them. I imagine they are all worth something, even if it's very little. What do you think?"

Tim looked confused at first, and then said, "Eyes," a moment before pulling the chain for the overhead light again. Producing the loupe, he studied the coins for several minutes. He eventually shook his head. "This is a hell of a collection you got here, and all that too?" He pointed to the two loaded satchels.

"Yes, that is why I see it as a problem, as much as good fortune," Garrett said. He emptied the first, and then the second satchel, revealing all his coins. They covered the entire counter.

"Holy Christ," Tim said. He did not bother with the loupe, he just stared and scanned from corner to corner around the counter. "Um, I'll tell you what. I can do these on consignment. They're all Roman?"

Garrett nodded. "The collection comes from shortly after the empire fell in the west, but they still used the coins for a long time after the fall. I'm sorry, I don't know the word consignment?"

"Oh, sure," Tim said. He picked up a single coin and held it up. "If you wanted to sell this coin on consignment, you would give it to me, but you would still keep ownership until I sell it. Before any of this happens, we would agree on a rate, a percentage of the sale that I would keep for the service of selling it for you. It works out for both of us because the more I can sell it for, the more money each of us earns on the sale."

"And you would do this for the entire collection?"

"I would, but I'll tell you, Garrett, it will take me a long time to get through all of these. Some of them may never sell. *A lot* of them may never sell."

"What is your rate for consignment?"

"Eight percent, typically. Sometimes I'll go a little higher or lower depending on the coin, but I don't see a need to do that here. Some places will charge ten or even more. I'm sure there are places that charge a little less, but I think eight is fair."

Garrett stuck out his hand. "I also think eight is fair, Tim. Do we have a deal?"

Tim smiled and shook Garrett's hand again. "First, we need to count all these, and I need to write up the consignment agreement. Let's both count. We have to agree on the sum, so do it carefully."

It took forty-five minutes before they had made stacks of ten, verified the stacks were each of ten, and counted out the total sum of coins, with the odd pile being of three. Tim wrote up the consignment form for four-thousand, three-hundred and seventy-three various old Roman coins, at a rate of eight percent, to expire in one year from the current date.

5

Having concluded his business in the city, Garrett opted to walk back to the apartment, knowing it would take over two hours but also looking forward to the exercise. He stopped at a diner on the way and sat at the counter among two old men that sat together and a young couple. Of all the things Garrett admired about humanity and Earth, he perhaps loved the stools and counters in diners the most. He found them informal, charming, and exceptionally friendly. After ordering his late breakfast; two eggs over-medium, rye toast and an order of home fries; he watched the news, though it had moved from the signal captured early Saturday morning on to other, more current events. He finished eating, paid, and stretched his legs again until he was back at his apartment, where he continued his reading and programming.

Mike arrived home that evening with a large white paper bag polluted with the spots and streaks of transparency that could only mean grease, and an enormous smile on his face. Garrett looked at him, concerned. "Hey, Mike. Everything okay?" Mike put the bag on the island next to their computers and went to the cupboard to get plates.

"Yeah, everything is great," he said. "I just got off the phone with Becky. She was able to get an earlier flight and she'll be here tomorrow. She told me she has fifty-one hours of the signal on a portable drive that she's bringing. Is your program ready yet?"

Garrett laughed. "No, but I expect it will be close by tomorrow night. I can't test it until I have the signal data though, so this all works out perfectly." Mike had not stopped smiling since he walked in the door. "Are you sure you're okay, Mike? You're the one that looks a little crazy right now."

"I'm just excited to meet her. I got burgers and fries for dinner," he said, and disassembled the package onto the paper plates.

6

Once Mike arrived at work the next morning, he waited until after eleven o'clock to text Becky. He sent a simple text message that told her not to bother with hiring a car, he would pick her up at the airport. He already had her flight information from their last conversation. She replied: *That would be so helpful! Thank you, Mike!* He reminded himself that once they met, it could go off the rails quickly, but at that point, he was still more excited than he could ever remember being. Mike was a bookish man and had little experience with girls in his first twenty-three years. He was smart, though, and knew that prudence was the best way forward. *Remember,* he told himself, *you might not even find her attractive!*

Later that afternoon, Mike stood outside the "Arrivals" exit from the secure area of the airport. He had even taken a piece of construction paper from work, on which he wrote "Rebecca Ferris" in big letters with an oversized permanent marker.

As her plane's passengers disembarked, he viewed the people coming through the secure exit point and out into the unsecured area, where there were a multitude of people waiting to receive passengers. He measured each female face to see if it fit with what he considered a "Becky" to look like. An airport employee pushed an elderly man in a wheelchair through the narrow exit. Behind him was a small figure, pacing the slow, lumbering train, waiting for them to get out of the way. At her first opportunity, she shot out from behind them and scanned the room as she walked. When her eyes met Mike's sign, she looked up at him and her entire face filled with joy. She jogged toward him.

"Mike?" she asked. The thought that he might not find her attractive disappeared instantly. She had wavy brown hair that spilled down past her shoulders, and she wore wire-rimmed round glasses. Her face was pretty, but when she smiled, it was divine. He smiled, and it was such a strong smile that he thought it might require a jackhammer to remove from his face.

"Yeah," he said. She wore a long gray knit sweater that gently revealed her features and fell halfway down her thighs with black jeans and boots that came up a few inches short of her knees. No one would call Becky Ferris a "short" girl, but Mike Potaglia was an unnaturally tall man, measuring six feet, four inches, and Becky only rose to just below his shoulders. She looked up at him with her beaming, bright smile, and Mike thought he might faint. Finally, he said, "Do you have a bag?"

"Just this." She had been pulling a small carry-on behind her. "I'm ready when you are."

He shook the ridiculous smile off his face in favor of a smaller one. "Okay! Let's go!" He took her bag from her so she could walk unencumbered and led her to the parking garage.

They drove to the hotel where she had made reservations, and Mike accompanied her to the front desk. She gave her name, and as the receptionist looked up her reservation, she turned to Mike.

"I've been a little nervous to ask, but I would like to check in here and then go with you so I can meet Garrett. Is that possible?" she asked.

"Of course. I never imagined that I would leave you here," he lied. His biggest fear since he laid eyes on her was that he would have to say goodbye. He assumed she would be tired, that she would say something like, "Okay, I'm going to get some rest, see you tomorrow, Mike!"

They checked in, and Mike accompanied her to her room. She spent only a few minutes placing her belongings and stowing her bag before announcing, "Okay, I'm ready. Let's go!"

7

As Mike and Becky approached the front door to his apartment, she pulled gently on his right arm to stop him. He turned to face her.

"I'm scared, Mike. I know that's silly. I understand that, but he said he's an alien, and we already know that he knows more than all of us. It's scary!"

Mike could see the fear in her face but let out a chuckle and led her a little further away from the door for privacy. "I can tell you a few things about Garrett: he's brilliant, he's nuts, but he's harmless." Becky's anxious look softened. "You will like him, Becky, and you won't be scared of him. He's fascinating." She rolled her eyes and smiled up at him.

"Ok. I believe you, Mike," she said. Mike turned back to the door, but just as he started moving, she reached up and took hold of his arm above his elbow. "I'm sorry, I'm nervous."

They entered the apartment and Mike announced, "Gar, someone here wants to meet you." Garrett came out from the kitchen and extended a hand to Becky.

"Garrett Rhodes. It's very nice to meet you." Becky shook his hand and reached behind her, retrieving the external drive out of her back pocket.

"I have fifty-one hours for you." She handed the drive to Garrett, who immediately looked at Mike for guidance.

"I got it," Mike said, taking the drive and walking over to Garrett's laptop. He installed the drive and called up the files. Once they were present in a window on the desktop, he showed Garrett how to access the folder.

"Okay, what do you two want for dinner?" Mike asked. Garrett announced that he did not care.

"Italian? I would love some spaghetti and meatballs right now," Becky said. Garrett leaned over and pulled on the refrigerator handle.

After a quick look, he said, "That's fine, but please have them bring some beer too. Clotz's. I'll pay for everything." Mike raised his eyebrows at Becky, who smiled.

After Mike called in the order, he joined Becky, who was looking over Garrett's shoulder. With the two of them watching his every move, Garrett turned around with a smile. "Guys, this will take a long time. Seriously, you would be far less bored going into the living room and watching TV. When dinner gets here, we can all eat together, but then I'm going to get right back to this." He smiled wider, and said, "And honestly, once I decode the signals and they're ready for playback, neither one of you will understand them, because it's all going to be in Osan.

Go watch TV." The two obliged and went into the living room. They found a show they both watched regularly and waited for their dinner to arrive.

8

A knock at the door thirty minutes later signaled to all that it was time to quit what they were doing and prepare to eat. Becky excused herself to go wash up in the bathroom. Garrett retrieved the food and paid the driver, and when he walked into the kitchen, said in a low voice to Mike, "You're quite smitten with her, aren't you?" Mike's face flushed with color, and he said, even lower than Garrett had, "I was trying not to be obvious!" They unpacked the food and Garrett put the beer in the refrigerator.

"You're not being obvious. I've just gotten to know you over the last week and noticed the subtleties." As he was finishing his sentence, they both heard the bathroom door open, and Becky reappeared.

Once Mike had temporarily moved the laptops off the kitchen island and the food was portioned out, they began with some light conversation about Becky's flight. As the topic concluded, Garrett asked Becky, "I know Mike told you about the video we made with my story. Have you had the occasion to watch it?"

Becky smiled and said, "Yeah, I watched it on the plane. I saved the file on my phone. I actually watched it twice. Anchorage to Denver to Washington is a long trip." She went back to her dinner.

"I assume you also think I'm crazy, at this point, anyway." Garrett asked, but she shook her head.

"I don't know what to think. That's why I'm here. I want to learn as much as there is to know."

Garrett nodded. "Excellent. Do you have questions for me?"

She thought about it, and then asked, "Why fifty-three separate frequencies? You didn't say anything about that in the video." Garrett nodded again. Mike watched and listened.

"Great question. Each channel is unique and carries specific information. The first is a general information channel about the Orris Project, and the last is a homing signal to help us prepare the Lances to navigate to Orris." Garrett took another bite of food.

"But still so many in between," Becky said. Garrett smiled and took a sip of beer.

"It really isn't, though. There is a channel dedicated to each Tosgaire, or I think the word in English is 'Envoy.' So, over half of the remaining channels are basically just our own versions of email, but it's one-way, of course."

"So, there are twenty-seven people like you out there in the universe?" Mike asked. Garrett lost all trace of a smile.

"Including me, twenty-seven launched over the course of three years. I don't know what happened to any of them. I doubt I ever will. But I did not know most of them. I went with the first group in the first year and all but one of them launched before I did. The others came later, or maybe not at all. I don't know."

Mike frowned. "But you said you each have a personal frequency. No one updated you on what happened after you left?"

Garrett wiped his mouth with his napkin and sat back in his chair with his beer in hand. "I don't know, I've never listened to mine."

The confused look remained on Mike's face, and he looked from Garrett to Becky and back to Garrett.

"Because it's nothing but pain. Nothing in those messages would be anything other than painful words from people who have been gone for a long, long time," Becky said. Garrett nodded slightly. Mike understood.

"I made a promise to my mother, though," Garrett said. "I promised I would listen to all of them in my travels. So, I told myself, if I made it to the end of the fifth, I would listen to all of it. It scares me, though. When I was on Telraed, the planet before Earth, I checked the refresh rate in my frequency stream. It took sixteen days to repeat. That's a lot of information."

"Did you have a big family? On Osa? Or do you not want to talk about it?" Becky asked.

"No, I don't mind," Garrett said, and summarized his family, including his whirlwind affair and marriage to Lauren, as they finished eating.

Mike stood up to clear the dishes. "Are the signals just audio? Or a combination of different things?" he asked.

"It's a combination of audio, video, and images on our personal channels." Garrett wiped down the countertop while Mike did the few dishes. "The others can have a wide variety of different file types, including computer applications. That's why I needed the software, so I could write an application and a driver for the signal data so it will work on the platform we have here on Earth. Then I can upload the signal to it, and it will become a huge file tree." He stood up and moved his laptop back to its former place on the clean countertop. "Speaking of that, I'm going to get back to it." As he set it up, Becky stood and stepped into the living room. Mike followed her.

"Do you want me to take you back to the hotel? Or do you want to hang out here with us for a while?" he asked. She laughed.

"The real question is, do I want to watch TV here with you or by myself in my room?" Becky asked, Mike laughed nervously. "As long as you don't mind, I'd like to stay. Garrett?" Garrett looked up at her. "How long do you think it will be before you have anything to show us? Even if we won't understand it?"

"Well, I have the application isolated from the stream. It's converting now, and then I'll add my driver to see if it works. If it doesn't, I'll have to troubleshoot, so my most honest answer is anywhere between two hours and two days." He smiled to communicate that he knew it was an unsatisfactory answer.

"Can I wait here with you, Mike?" she asked. "You won't have to drive me back. I can get a cab or a rideshare."

Mike smiled, "You can stay as long as you want, but I will still drive you back." They walked back to the couch. As they sat down, she surprised him with a question.

"So, do you have a girlfriend?" Mike blushed and said the first thing that came to his mind.

"I'm twenty-three, fresh out of college, and I work at NASA. What do you think?" Becky laughed. "Oh, and I live with an alien from the planet Osa." She laughed even harder at that.

"I might be an alien, but I have feelings," Garrett said from the other room. The comment brought both Becky and Mike to tears. When they both had finally calmed down, Becky was the first to speak.

"Seriously though, you're a smart guy with a great job. Why wouldn't you think that would be attractive to a great deal of women?" Mike blushed hard. He was grateful she did not notice, or at least did not make it known that she had noticed.

"I just haven't gone down that road yet. I've only been in D.C. at NASA for three months. I'm kind of just getting my life started." She smiled at him.

"That makes sense. I didn't mean to sound like I was giving you a hard time." She placed a hand on his shoulder.

"Well, what about you? Do you have someone waiting for you in Alaska?" Mike asked.

"I'm a twenty-five-year-old operations manager at a radio satellite installation," she said. Before Mike could respond, she interrupted, "In Alaska!" They both laughed again. "Seriously though, no. I've dated a few guys but I haven't found one yet who hasn't bored me to tears after only a few dates. And as far as dating goes, it's a pretty small pool up there." Mike nodded and picked up the remote.

"So, do you want to watch a movie? I don't think there's anything on TV now."

"That sounds great, Mike."

9

When the movie finished, Mike tuned the TV to a channel playing reruns of the show the two of them had watched earlier.

"Any closer, Garrett?" Becky said in a loud voice. Mike could tell she was half asleep.

"Certainly closer," Garrett said. "I think I'll have access to some of it tonight."

Mike looked at the clock. It was only a few minutes after nine. "Are you sleepy already?"

Becky closed her eyes tightly and said, "That flight sucked. I'm exhausted." She let her head rock forward until her chin hit her chest.

"I'll take you back to your room, Becky, so you can sleep," Mike said in a soft voice. She breathed in deeply, exhaled, and opened her eyes. She looked pleadingly at him.

"I don't want to miss it. I don't want to miss any of it. Can I just lay down here on the couch for a bit? After, I'll get a ride. You really don't have to bring me back, Mike, I know you have to work in the morning."

He wanted to take her back to the hotel so he could have more alone time with her, but she was so tired, he thought she would probably just sleep in the car. "Whatever you want, Becky. You are welcome here. I just don't want you to have to sleep on a couch. That guy doesn't drive, and even if he did, he's had about twenty beers at this point."

"Six." Garrett had exceptionally good hearing.

"It's not even that late, though," Mike said. "Take a nap if you want, but I will share the couch with you if that's okay, since we don't have anywhere else to sit in here."

She smiled at him. "You're awesome, I won't take much room." She laid down in the fetal position and closed her eyes. Mike slipped to the opposite side of the couch to give her more space. He thought it was less than a minute before her breathing pattern indicated a deep sleep.

10

Mike felt a gentle poking in his shoulder. It was Garrett prodding him. Apparently, he had fallen asleep. He could also feel a weight on his lap and realized that Becky was still sleeping but had stretched out so much that her feet were now resting on his thigh.

"It's ready," Garrett whispered, and pointed to Becky's feet and smiled. "That must be exciting for you."

"Shut up, man!" Mike said in a loud whisper, and Garrett went back to the kitchen. Mike tried to think of the least scary, least intimate way to wake her up and opted for touching the back of her exposed hand and saying her name.

"Becky?" She stirred but did not come to consciousness. He gently covered her entire hand with his and tried again, a little louder.

"Becky?" Her eyes fluttered, and she yawned and sat up. Her eyes remained closed.

"Yeah?" she asked.

"Garrett has something for us."

Her eyes shot open. "He does? What is it?"

Mike smiled. "I don't know, I fell asleep too. He just woke me up." Mike stood and offered a hand to Becky, who took it in both of hers and dragged herself to her feet. They both ambled into the kitchen. Mike yawned largely and loudly, which set off another yawn from Becky.

"What do you got, Gar?" Mike asked.

"Well, I had audio about an hour ago, but I wanted to wait for a video to load because I thought it might have more of an impact on both of you." Garrett clicked the file open, and the screen lit up with a congregation of people dressed in odd-looking clothes. They could hear mumbling, but no clear dialogue. The view from the obviously handheld camera panned around the crowd of people and then focused to a point of white in the distance, over the heads of a multitude of spectators. From the view of the camera holder, they watched as the videographer walked through the crowd to a guarded gate. The guard nodded at him and opened it. There were no others standing in this new place. He had it all to himself. He continued to walk toward the white object, which was becoming clearer and revealed itself as an odd vehicle. Once the man reached a railing that prohibited further travel, he must have set the camera on it, as the video then became sharp and steady.

"What is that? Where is this?" Becky asked.

"This is the launch facility outside Dinesta. The guy filming is my friend's father. This was the launch before mine. You can't see me, but I'm actually in that crowd somewhere. I was your age then."

"This is Osa?" Becky asked in a half whisper. Her eyes were wet.

"It was," Garrett said. The image zoomed in to the white vehicle, which appeared to have an external cage surrounding the glossy white capsule. A loud voice boomed over a PA system and spoke gibberish in a professional voice for a few minutes. On the far-right side of the craft, they observed a glass or plastic window, which revealed the head and shoulders of the craft's operator. The operator turned his head and nodded at the crowd. The mumbling from the group in the background got louder, and the craft moved from left to right. The camera followed its progression as it gained speed at an astounding rate. Just as it disappeared over the horizon, the white dot came back into view, lifting toward the sky. Once it was traveling vertically, an explosion of light appeared at its base, and it continued its vertical ascent until it was no longer visible.

The first audio they could hear well enough to understand came a second later. "Beannachd mac," a deep voice said. "Tha gaol aig d'athair ort."

Becky tapped Garrett on the shoulder with urgency. "What did he say?" She whispered.

"He said, 'Goodbye son, your father loves you.'" Becky reacted, her breathing audibly hitched.

Mike shook his head and walked around the kitchen. Finally, he said, "Come on, man." Garrett could tell that Mike was both frustrated and confused, still not wanting to believe. "That… that could be fake."

"Did it look fake, Mike?" Mike shook his head again and continued his pace around the room.

"No, Garrett. It didn't look fake. But if this is true, it shatters the whole world as I have ever known it!" He was getting animated. Becky sobbed. Mike went to her and wrapped his arms around her; not romantically, but as one human consoling another, as they learned for the first time that they were not alone.

"But it doesn't, Mike. Nothing is different, nothing has changed. It has always been this way. The only difference is that you thought you were the ladder, but now you know the ladder is much larger, and you're only a rung." Mike said nothing, and Becky continued to sob. "Mike, Becky, I know that you both still have doubts, but I promise you, this will not get easier. I will only convince you further, and beyond any doubt. But it's a good thing." Becky lifted her face from Mike's chest.

"How in the hell is it a good thing?" She said through hitching breaths.

"Because nothing changes. Earth has three or even four billion years left before your sun dies. When we make the selection and a few hundred of you leave the planet, you two will be so old that I would hope you smile at the accomplishment of humanity. All I bring with me are plans. Your kind have to build the thing." Becky looked up at Mike.

"Will you bring me back to the hotel now, please?" Mike nodded. They gathered their belongings and walked out of the apartment.

11

"I think we need a little break from Garrett," Mike said as he stood outside of Becky's room after the great video revelation.

"Yeah, what do you suggest?" she asked. Mike wanted to take her hand in his but resisted the urge.

"After work tomorrow, let me take you out to dinner. That way we can talk without the fear of being overheard by my alien-roommate." She laughed lightly and nodded.

"That sounds perfect, Mike. When you get done with work, come find me in Vanessa's office, I'll be working out of there while I'm here."

"Okay, that sounds good. Do you need a ride into work tomorrow, then?"

She smiled. "No, Vanessa is going to pick me up. We've had a hell of a night, huh? I have to go to bed. Good night, Mike." She hugged him and disappeared into her room.

12

Garrett was sound asleep the next morning when Mike left for work. When he got up, he was alone in the apartment and found a note on the counter in front of the coffeepot. It said, *I probably won't be back for dinner, eat without me. - Mike*

Garrett thought he knew what it was about and made his coffee. He sipped from his mug and sat back at his laptop, where he planned to spend his entire day. During the time he had slept, four hundred and ninety-three more videos had rendered. He clicked through the folders, carefully avoiding the one labeled "T1-Rhodes," and viewed many from the other folders. He glanced back at his folder and risked clicking on it to see how many files it contained. It was a mistake. There were dozens of files, and each had a thumbnail with the face of a past loved one printed in all-too-real resolution, among other faces he did not recognize. He clicked on a different random folder to get the images off the screen as his eyes filled with tears. It had been decades from his perspective, but the faces wrenched at his heartstrings as though he had only left Osa the day before.

13

After Mike finished his workday, most of which was composed of staring at the clock, he raced to the elevator bay and pushed the "up" button, excited to see Becky again. The doors opened to an empty car, and he boarded, hurting his index finger due to the amount of force he smashed the number 'six' button with.

Upon arriving on the sixth floor, he hurried to Vanessa's bright, spacious office and saw her behind her desk, but no one else. He walked up to her. "Hey Vanessa, is Beck…" Two hands folded over his eyes from behind. He froze. "Oh," he said, and smiled.

"You two make a cute couple," Vanessa said.

Becky left her hands over Mike's eyes, like this could somehow also impair his hearing and said in a whisper, "Vanessa? What the hell is wrong with you?" Mike gently removed her hands from his eyes.

"It's fine, Becky, she's just jealous that I'm not taking her out to dinner." Mike blushed immediately after, not knowing what had come over him. Vanessa had been nothing but helpful to him, and he instantly regretted the comment. He looked at Vanessa, who was smiling and even laughing a little, "I'm sorry Vanessa, I was just kid…" She waved a hand at him.

"Don't worry about it, Mike. You two go have fun. I never thought in a million years that you two would end up together." Mike and Becky both flushed hot red.

"We're not…" they both said simultaneously.

Vanessa laughed again and said, "Go! Just get out of here! I still have work to do before I can go home."

As they walked to the elevator bay, Mike asked if she had a specific place in mind for dinner.

"I think anything will be fine, but maybe a place where we can sit at the bar and eat?" she said. "I always liked that, because the bartender is always close if you need something." *That doesn't narrow it down. A lot of places have bars we can eat at*, Mike thought.

"Well, can I ask what you want to do after dinner? Do you want to come back to my apartment with me, or go back to your room? I ask because it will help me pick a place." He pushed the down button on the elevator panel and watched her think.

"I don't know. I'm sorry, I know that isn't helpful." They boarded the elevator. Mike thought more about the different places he could take her and decided that it didn't matter that much.

"There's a place right near my building. It's a pub, but they have great food. When we're done eating, we can go back to my place, or I can take you back to the hotel. It's not that big a deal either way, because the hotel isn't that far."

She smiled. "That sounds great."

14

Thirty minutes later, they were at the dimly lit but spotless and polished pub. After ordering their meals, Becky clasped her hands around her drink. "So, what do you think, Mike, about Garrett? Do you still think he's a loon?" Mike sipped his soda, which he had opted for instead of liquor, since he still had driving to do, and shook his head.

"I don't know. I'm afraid when I get back to my place tonight, with or without you, he will have a hundred or a thousand more videos, pictures, audio clips, schematics, and… and I don't know what else." Mike sipped his soda again. "What about you? What do you think?"

She looked at him with concern. "I think you're probably right. And where does that leave us? Where do we go from here?"

"You mean if everything he's saying is true? If he actually landed on Earth almost four billion years ago?" It was a genuine question, and Becky appeared to take it as such.

"Yes, exactly."

"If it's all true," Mike paused for several seconds while he appeared to think. "Then I think we do whatever he tells us to do. I mean, if he is actually who he says he is, then he knows so much more about the universe than us, we may as well know nothing. Did I tell you about our conversation the day we met?" She shook her head. For the rest of their stay at J.C. Reid's Pub, Mike took her on a journey of the cosmos through Garrett's eyes.

When they arrived back at Mike's car, he stopped and turned to her. "Have you decided?"

She smiled and looked up at him. "I decided I don't want to be a coward, and I decided I also didn't want you to have to go through it alone. So, yes, I'll go back with you to see what he has for us now." Mike smiled and even laughed a little.

"Great! Let's go!"

15

Garrett had eaten leftover Italian food from the night before for dinner and was halfway through his third beer when Mike and Becky walked in the door.

"Garrett? We're back," Mike announced. Garrett came into view from the direction of the kitchen.

"Hey guys, what have you two been up to tonight?" Mike put his keys and wallet on the shelf next to the door, as he always did.

"We went to the pub for dinner." Without waiting for Garrett to respond, he said, "So, do you have a thousand more videos now?"

Garrett ignored the question. "Did you have a nice time?" He was smiling. Mike looked at him without smiling. Garrett laughed. "Um, yeah. I wasn't sure you guys would want to see anything else, though. I know last night was tough on you." Garrett walked back into the kitchen.

"How many, Gar? How many videos do you have now? How many audio tracks? Photos? Other things?" Mike asked. Becky followed closely behind him into the kitchen.

"I'm not sure, Mike, probably several hundred videos, same as the audio files, thousands of pictures, and a variety of other files. But that's it, I'm done. I can't go further without more of the signal." Garrett looked from Mike to Becky. "Any idea when I can get the next part?"

The question took Becky by surprise. It hadn't occurred to her that he would ask for more of the signal. "Oh, um, no. I'll have to call tomorrow to see about that."

"Okay, that's no problem." Garrett stood up and pulled a second stool over to his laptop. "I'll tell you guys what. I'm going to sit in the living room this time. You two can peruse the files by yourselves, without feeling the pressure of me being there with you." He grabbed the mouse and selected his folder without opening it. "This is the only folder off limits, 'T1-Rhodes.' I can't bear to overhear anything in that folder. Promise me you will respect my wishes and the files are yours to look through." Mike looked at Becky, who smiled and nodded. "Ok, I will be on the couch." He turned to go into the living room.

"Garrett?" Becky called after him. "If we have a question about something?"

Garett smiled, "Sure, just let me know and I'll come and translate for you."

For the next two-and-a-half hours, Mike and Becky looked at photos and watched videos. They didn't bother with the audio tracks because Garrett would have to translate every word, and they wanted to be on their own as much as possible. On six occasions during their viewing time, they asked Garrett to come back and translate some audio they had heard on videos they watched, but aside from that, they left him alone. As they reached the end of their exploration, Mike opened the "T1-Rhodes" folder. Becky, not wanting to alert Garrett, grabbed his left hand hard and stared at him. Mike leaned over and put his lips so close to her ear that they touched. In the softest whisper he could produce, he said, "I won't open any of them, but look at the thumbnails." Becky nodded. They both scanned the tiny images of faces, and Mike put the mouse pointer over an older couple, and then moved it to the next image in line. An older woman, the one from the couple in the previous thumbnail, sat by herself. She appeared in many of the files. Mike mouthed the word "mother" to her, and she again nodded. They both looked further, and Mike put the pointer on a young woman and mouthed "Lauren?" Becky shook her head and tugged on her own hair. She mouthed the word "Red" back to Mike. He nodded, and they kept looking. He stopped at a photo of a little girl and looked at Becky with raised eyebrows. She shrugged and shook her head. At that point, they heard Garrett get up off the couch and Mike clicked off to a different folder and stood up.

"How are you guys doing?" Garrett asked.

"I think we're done, Gar. It's late, and I'm going to take Becky back to her room."

"Any new impressions? Do you still think I'm just a crazy person?"

Mike thought for a minute. "No, Gar, but I don't know where I am. I'm in a daze about it right now." Becky nodded. To Mike's surprise, she stepped forward to Garrett and kissed him on the cheek.

"Good night, Garrett." She walked to the door and waited for Mike. Garrett also looked surprised.

"Good night, Becky," he said and shrugged at Mike. Mike walked to the door, slapping Garrett on the shoulder as he did.

"I'll be back," he said, and they were gone.

16

In the hallway, Mike looked at Becky to find tears in her eyes. He took her arm and led her down to the elevator bay. "What's wrong?" Mike asked her. Becky shook her head but started sobbing. He pulled her into the elevator car and pushed the button for the parking garage. He wrapped his arms around her and let her cry into his shirt.

When the elevator stopped and the doors opened, he relaxed his arms, but hers remained locked around him. "We have to get off, Beck," he whispered. She finally relaxed and followed him to his car. As he drove, he could hear her attempting to get her breathing under control.

"Take your time, Beck, I won't leave you until you're ready." As he finished the sentence, it sounded corny to him, and he regretted it. Becky smiled, but Mike didn't see it as he was watching the road.

She sniffled hard, and in a breaking voice said, "Thank you."

When they were back at the hotel, Mike was silent, waiting for her to talk first, worried that if he said anything, it might set her off again. He walked with her back to the elevator bay, up to her floor, and then to her room.

"Will you stay with me for a while?" Relief washed over him, and he smiled.

"Of course, for as long as you need me." She smiled, kissed his arm, and unlocked her hotel room door. He followed her in and stood awkwardly as she milled about the room, preparing to go to bed. The room's furnishings included not just a bed and nightstand but also a desk and a love seat with a small table in front of it facing the TV.

After a few minutes, she seemed to have collected herself, and she pointed to the love seat and said, "Sit over there," smiling. "I'll be right back." She disappeared into the bathroom, but was out only two minutes later, and in pajamas. Mike felt a little uncomfortable, feeling like he was looking at a very intimate image every time he laid eyes upon her. She did not appear uncomfortable at all, and sat down next to him, even taking one of his hands in hers.

"I'm sorry. I owe you an explanation for my reaction to what happened, and thank you for helping me so much. You don't have any idea, do you?" Mike shook his head but was enjoying his current experience.

"It was the little girl. As soon as I saw her, my imagination took off." Mike was no closer to putting the pieces together, but he was enraptured by her every word. "He never mentioned a little girl, only his nephew. The girl you thought was Lauren was probably his sister. His nephew's mother. No little girl, Mike!" Tears formed in her eyes again, and her voice pitched up, "What if..." she broke off and breathed in and out several times before she tried again. "What if that was his daughter?" She started sobbing again. Mike put his arm around her, and she leaned into him. Through the sobs, "What if that was his daughter, and he's never even seen her before? What if he didn't even know he had a daughter? That would mean that we saw her before he did, and… and…" She broke down completely again. Mike rubbed her arm and kissed the top of her head. She let his hand go and wrapped her arms around him, crying into his chest. Mike felt a tear of his own form in one eye and blinked it away.

To comfort her, he said, "It could have been his niece. If his sister had another baby after he left, his niece could have sent messages to her uncle." She sat back up and nodded.

"Yeah, that makes sense. Do you think that's who she was?" Mike shrugged and offered a little smile.

Becky stood up and said, "Thanks, Mike, you're a hell of a good guy. I'm sorry I'm so disgusting and I'm sorry to keep you up so late." Mike stood and stepped toward the door.

"You are very welcome, and you are nowhere near disgusting. Good night, Becky." She smiled and blew him a kiss.

17

Mike walked back into the apartment at eleven thirty. Garrett was still awake and watching television on the couch. Mike went to the kitchen and got a beer.

"Done working on that for tonight?" Mike asked. Garrett looked up from the TV.

"I'm done until I can get more data. Hopefully, Becky can get me more of the stream soon." Mike nodded. Garrett was so casual and matter-of-fact about the answer that Mike was starting to believe everything. He was fairly sure Becky was almost completely in Garrett's world, but Mike wanted to see if he could find any holes while he still had such close access to Garrett.

"Can I ask you a question, or are you invested in this show?"

Garrett turned the volume down and turned to Mike. "Not at all. What's up?"

Mike noticed Garrett's weird, mixed accent was still present, but his lingo was getting more modern by the day. "In the very first video you showed us, that was obviously a launch?" Mike asked.

Garrett smiled and nodded. "Yeah, that was Joe Burkman. He was probably the best friend I had at OPM. The selection number wasn't supposed to be important, but it turned out to be, at least among the envoys. Joe and I were picked right next to each other, so we gravitated to each other pretty early on." Garrett stared off into the distance. "I only had four days left when that video was taken. What I would give to go back and see them all again."

"But you can't, can you? You and your people are much more advanced in physics than we are, but you can't go back in time, can you?"

Garrett shook his head. "Only forward. You can go forward slowly, you can go forward fast, you can lose time completely, and you can almost stop time. But you can never go back."

Mike was nodding and smiling. "I was arguing with Harold about that yesterday."

"Was that your question? Or did you have one about the video you saw?" Garrett asked.

"Yes, I do. The craft, the white one that launched," Garrett was nodding. "When it took off, it did so horizontally, and then changed course… and it was halfway up into the atmosphere before the rockets even lit up for the first time?"

"Yes, that's correct."

Mike relaxed his shoulders, which had been tense, and asked, "Why? How?"

Garrett smiled, stood, and walked to the refrigerator. "Efficiency, mostly. It's also more comfortable than the way you do it here. You know about the maglev trains in Japan?" Mike nodded, putting the pieces together. "The principle is almost exactly the same. The craft, we just call them 'transports,' slides into a carriage. We don't mount them to it, but the only direction they can separate is forward. Eighty-six percent of the escape velocity is achieved before the solid rockets even fire, and that's done on a massive maglev track that the carriage rides on." Mike was speechless. Garrett smiled. "Close to the end of the track, there are ten trigger blocks, each capable of starting the rockets, so that's all automatic. The operator doesn't have to do anything."

Mike sat on the arm of the couch. "But what are the g-forces? Wouldn't it crush you to death?"

Garrett shook his head. "I assume g-force is the gravitational multiplier?" Mike nodded. "No, we achieved the absolute speed before the ascent, and the ascent is gradual. We never break two times gravity until the rockets light up."

"What is it then?"

"About three, the same as here. But it doesn't last as long." Mike thought about it while Garrett sipped his beer. "Is your next question 'what do you do once you're in orbit?'"

Mike laughed. "No, my next question is, how the hell do you travel through interstellar space. How the hell do you live for four billion or ten billion years, or whatever it is? How the hell do you build a ship that's half the size of a solar system? And the worst one, how do you power a structure that big?" Mike exhaled and stared at the floor.

"You don't want those answers tonight, do you?" Mike shook his head. After a moment, he stood up and walked into the kitchen and put his empty bottle into the recycling bin.

As he walked through the living room en route to his bedroom, he said, "I'm sorry Garrett, my mind is fried right now. I have to get some sleep."

Garrett tipped his own bottle toward him. "Good night, Mike."

18

The inability to communicate with the handful of people Garrett knew in D.C. irritated him. His limited ability to travel was also a frustration. Relying on Mike driving or his own two feet pounding pavement further drove him to make it his mission that Thursday morning to both learn how to use the rail system in D.C. and acquire a cell phone. Mike told him he could get one prepaid and without credentials, he called it a "burner" phone and made a joke about criminals using them.

After speaking to a sweet woman with a nametag that identified her as Felicia, he had all the information he needed to get started on the D.C. underground rail system, which they called the "Metro." He spent two hours that morning getting on and off the trains and familiarizing himself with the process. Felicia had even given him a paper copy of the rail system map, which he studied as he traveled. He thought about stopping in at the *Tim McInnis Coin Exchange* to see how the big man was faring with the consignment, but he left him to his craft, as it had only been three days. Instead, he traveled to the same diner he had visited after seeing Tim that past Monday and ordered the same breakfast, but for lunch.

After lunch, he navigated his way to the same big-box store where they had made their many purchases the week before and wandered until he found the electronics department. A young but knowledgeable salesman named Alonzo set him up with a phone. After explaining to Alonzo what he wanted and the rather long conversation that followed, Garrett walked out of the store with the phone. "Hey man, if you need anything else, or if you need more time, come back here and I'll hook you up," Alonzo had assured him. With his two tasks completed, he took the Metro a final time that day back to the apartment.

19

Mike and Becky arrived back at the apartment that evening with dinner and news. Mike placed the fried chicken on the counter and said, "Garrett, we have a lot to go over." Garrett stood up from the couch and walked toward the two of them in the kitchen.

Mike nodded toward Becky. She smiled at Garrett and said, "We're not going to use the portable drive anymore for the signal. I have a login I.D. and password to the folder where we store the signal data at DSRTA, where I work in Alaska. It's read-only access, but there is no reason you would need anything more…"

Garrett was shaking his head and smiling. "No! That's perfect. So, I can access the signal as you receive it?"

"Basically, but that folder only refreshes every six hours, so four times a day there will be more for you to download," she said.

"That's great. How do I use it?"

She handed him a piece of paper. "Can I get onto your laptop? I'll make a shortcut to the site and put it on your desktop. That paper has your user I.D. and password, so don't lose it." Garrett walked to his laptop and signed on for Becky.

"Did you get a phone?" Mike asked. Garrett had left the bag with the phone and accessories on the kitchen island next to his laptop.

"Yeah, but I was hoping you or Becky would help me get started with it. I've used similar devices in the past, but they were different."

"Yeah, no problem," Mike said. "Let's eat first, though, while it's still warm." He portioned the food out and they sat down to eat after clearing the surface of the island.

"You said there was more to talk about?" Garrett asked. Mike nodded with a full mouth.

"Tomorrow, you have to come to work with me, or you can meet me there at ten o'clock. Some of the bigger dogs there got wind of the fact that an individual had predicted the signal, and it wasn't just chance or routine. They had to do very little digging to find out it was my roommate." Becky looked back and forth between Mike and Garrett. "Anyway, I spent the afternoon explaining to my boss what was going on and how it all happened. He called a meeting for tomorrow at ten and told me to make sure you were there." Mike went back to his food, and Garrett smiled.

"Yes, I've been to a few meetings of this type. I am familiar with them. Will it be an open meeting or private, behind closed doors?" Becky continued to glance back and forth as they ate.

"It will be an exceedingly private meeting, but that doesn't mean it will be small. I have no idea how many people will show up, but my boss invited his entire chain of command, and I'm sure additional members of top management will be there of their own accord," Mike said.

"Like I said, I've been there before. I have a good idea what to expect, so this is no problem for me. I'll be there, and I'll be early. If it makes you more comfortable, Mike, I'll go in with you, but I would prefer not to wait around for two hours," he said. Mike shook his head. "That's fine, I trust you. Just meet me in my office at nine-thirty and we can all walk up together. When you get to the building, tell the receptionist you have an appointment with me for nine-thirty." Mike picked up his phone and tapped on it relentlessly for several seconds. "There, it's in my calendar, so now she can verify the meeting and send you up. I'm on the third floor."

"Is that it? Or is there more?" Garrett asked. Becky turned to him.

"Just one more thing. I'm leaving tomorrow night. I have to get home." Garrett glanced at Mike, who was poking at his food, appearing to have lost interest in eating.

"Will you be back? Or no, probably not. It's a terribly long distance from here, I understand," Garrett said.

Becky, who sat next to Mike and opposite Garrett, frowned. "It depends. I don't really know. I would guess probably not, but there are a lot of factors at play." Garrett watched her glance at Mike, who was staring straight down at his plate and did not notice.

"You will be sorely missed. May I put your phone information in mine so we might communicate?" he asked.

She brightened at the suggestion. "Oh, yes! Absolutely." Garrett smiled and stood, clearing the dishes and cleaning off the shared eating and working space.

While Becky went over how to log in to the DSRTA VPN and access the single folder that he had permissions for, Mike set up Garrett's burner phone so he could communicate with all of them remotely.

Once Garrett was up to date on his signal access and how to use his new phone, stocked only with Mike and Becky's phone numbers, Mike took her back to her hotel room. As they were exiting the apartment, Mike stopped and turned to Garrett. "Hey, tomorrow, bring your laptop. I don't know if you'll need it or not, but I don't want to be dead in the water if they want to see something, and we can't provide it. There is a laptop bag in the coat closet on the top shelf. You can't miss it. Okay?" Garrett stuck one thumb up in the air, a communication device he had learned that he was rather fond of. He spent the rest of the night processing the new signal he had access to.

20

The following morning, Garrett left earlier than he needed to so he could make a stop before meeting Mike. He arrived at Tim's place only a few minutes after he opened at nine, and when Tim looked up at him, Garrett shook his head.

"I'm not expecting news, Tim. But I got a new cell phone and wanted to give you the number." He held his phone up so Tim could see it.

"Oh, okay. I do have some cash for you though." Tim brought a shoebox out from somewhere behind the counter and opened it, "Not a bad haul for only selling three coins." Tim took a rubber-banded stack of bills out of the box and handed it to Garrett. Garrett looked at the money.

"So, do I pay you out of this money? Is that how it works?" he asked. Tim smiled and shook his head.

"No, I already took my share. That's yours."

Garrett smiled and put it in his pocket without counting it.

"You don't want to know how much it is?" Tim asked.

"I still have plenty of money left from our first transaction, so it isn't that important right now. Why? How much is it?"

"Almost thirteen hundred dollars," Tim said. Garrett smiled.

"Excellent. Thank you, Tim. Let me give you my number so we can communicate remotely."

21

Garrett walked into Mike's office at 9:27 a.m. and was happy to see Becky sitting in a chair next to him, looking at something on his computer. Mike looked up at him and smiled.

"Thank you for getting here…" he glanced at the clock. "Early? Okay, great."

Before anything else happened, another man walked into the small office. "Mike? Are we all ready?" the man with short black hair and glasses asked. Mike and Becky both stood up.

"Garrett, this is my boss, Stanley Liang," Mike said. Stanley, about Garrett's height, looked at him, and then back at Mike.

"This guy doesn't look like an alien."

Garrett smiled. "What does an alien look like, Mr. Liang?" he asked.

Stanley looked back and forth between Garrett and Mike again. "Fair enough. Let's go, I want to be early." Stanley exited the office and walked back toward the elevator bays. The others followed him and the four boarded an empty elevator car together bound for the fifth floor. As the elevator rose, Stanley nodded toward the laptop bag Garrett was carrying.

"Is that the… evidence?" Garrett smiled and nodded. Stanley replied by looking up at the ceiling, nodding, and exhaling deeply. They walked out of the elevator and down a long corridor before turning right and then immediately right again into a large room with a long conference table. The wall near what Garrett guessed was the foot of the table featured a large rectangular white screen.

"Follow me," Stanley said as he walked toward the far end of the conference room. He laid his folder in front of the head seat, asked Garrett to sit to his left and Mike and Becky to his right. It was 9:36, and they were alone. The first person arrived at 9:52. By 9:56, the conference room table was full, and two minutes later, there were thirty people sitting in chairs set back from the table, lining two of the walls. At 9:59, a moderately tall man in his mid-to-late forties with salt-and-pepper black hair and round glasses walked in wearing a clean black suit, a dark blue shirt, and a black tie with the NASA logo embroidered on it. Mike closed his eyes, and Stanley shot up out of his seat and took two steps backward. The man walked right up to Stanley and shook his hand.

"Good morning, everyone. Thank you for coming. This is an exciting meeting to be in attendance for, isn't it?" the man said. A muttering of general agreement followed. "Well, Stanley, I don't mean to take your seat." He looked at the people sitting close to the head of the table. "Keith, I see a chair on that back wall with your name on it." An overweight man in his thirties with curly brown hair stood up, relieving the chair next to Garrett. "I'll sit there," he said.

"No, sir! No, please, sir. Sit here, I'll sit there." Stanley raced over to Garrett and sat beside him.

"Ok, well, thank you Stanley. Now, where is the man of the hour?" Stanley pointed at Garrett, seated between the two. "Ah, wonderful. Well, I'll be damned! You don't look much like an alien to our beautiful planet, sir." Garrett inhaled to regurgitate his rehearsed answer, but the man cut him off before he could utter a word, "My apologies, my apologies. You do not know who I am, do you?" Garrett shook his head. "I'm Jim Lambert, the administrator of NASA."

"Top dog?" Garrett asked, smiling. Jim winked at him. "Okay, Mr. Lamb…"

"Jim is fine," the administrator said. Garrett got a sense of deja vu. "Why don't you introduce yourself and give us a sense of why we're here today."

"Okay, Jim," Garrett stood up and addressed the entire room, looking natural and practiced in doing so, "My name, is Garrett Rhodes. I am an envoy from the planet Osa, in the Andromeda Galaxy." Garrett waited for laughter, but none came. "I'm here for three reasons. The first is to speak to you candidly about the nature of our universe. I'm here to convince you of the reality of our universe and its eventual fate if you don't already understand it, and based on my time here so far, you do not. I'm here to ask for the support of your people and their ability to understand and create exceedingly advanced technology; my own brethren on Osa commissioned a colossal machine that will attempt to preserve a sampling of the intelligent life in our corner of the universe, and that machine is called Orris. Maybe it would be better to call it a starship, based on the movies and television shows that I've watched here. So, the second reason I am here. I ask that you commission the construction of a transport vessel, to move volunteers from

Earth to Orris. I will provide the plans for the vessel. The third and final reason is regarding the volunteers themselves. If things go as planned, in the distant future, I will call on volunteers from Earth to board this vessel, give up their Earthly lives, and travel to Orris so that their descendants may arrive there." Garrett sat down.

"Well," Jim stood and said in a loud voice. He looked around the room before looking down at the table in front of him. "I'll be damned," he whispered. Addressing the group again, "Well, let's first talk about what brought us here today. The signal. We have been scanning the skies for decades with little to nothing to show for it. You pop out a few coordinates and we are inundated with an intelligent, repeating, and continuous signal. That one goes in your column, sir." Garrett nodded. "So, I guess my first question to you would be, if intelligent life is so prevalent in the universe, why is this the first time we've heard anything about it? We've been searching for over sixty years."

Garrett laughed. "I'm sorry, sir, for the outburst. The answer is simple, though. It is extremely hard to communicate across these distances. I can tell you honestly, that I don't know how Orris can generate the energy required to get the radio signals to us from its location, which is an unimaginable distance." Jim nodded and sat back down.

"Last night, I listened to this man's story in the form of an audio file. Has everyone had the occasion to hear the story?" Jim asked. There was little to no response in the room. "Well, if you didn't, it's your loss and you'll be confused a lot as we continue today. I know that Mr. Liang linked it in the meeting request, because that's where I accessed it from, so everyone had every opportunity." Jim removed a small, spiral-bound notepad from the breast pocket of his suit jacket. Garrett smiled at the two pins on Jim's lapel. A tiny American flag, and just beneath it, a silver cartoon rocket. He flipped the top cover back. "I have thousands of questions for you, Mr. Rhodes, but I will only allow myself three, so I can give others the opportunity to ask some. My first question, and forgive me if this is too broad, is what exactly it is that we have 'gotten wrong' about the universe? Stand, if you wouldn't mind, so everyone can hear you."

Garrett stood. "The first thing I'd like to say is that you have mostly been right. Everyone holds Albert Einstein in high esteem and for good reason. He was well ahead of his time. The major mistake is the focus on dark energy as being a separate and independent entity relative to dark matter when it is actually just a gravitational consequence of it. Dark energy only exists in the form of the collective gravity of the eflix ring. Eflix is what we called dark matter back on Osa. Any other mistakes or misunderstandings you may have pale in comparison to that one. It is also clear that you don't even know about the ring, which isn't surprising, as it is extremely challenging to detect and measure." Garrett expected comments or follow-up questions and didn't bother sitting. Stanley did not let him down.

"If it's so hard to detect, then how did your people do it in the first place?"

"I left Osa about 8.4 billion years ago. The ring was much closer to all of us then. Its influence was much more visible."

Someone in the back, out of view, said, "So, you're 8.4 billion years old?" Garrett laughed.

"No, I don't know exactly how old I am, but I would guess between 38 and 42 years old. The rest of the time I have spent in a form of suspended animation." At that point, Jim Lambert took control of the meeting back.

"Interesting. So, how far is this ring from us now?" he asked. Garrett shook his head.

"I don't know. We called it a ring on Osa, but it's actually more of a sphere, as most natural things are. I know when we measured it on Osa it was expanding rapidly, and I know it's still expanding, because if it weren't…"

"There wouldn't be a signal," Becky said. Garrett nodded.

"Exactly. When Orris detects the stoppage of the ring expansion, the protocol is to cut all non-essential energy expenditures. The broadcast will be one of these cuts, as there will be no more recoverable ships after the jump." Jim had dropped his notepad, apparently forgetting it.

"Where is Orris now?" he asked.

Again, Garrett smiled. "I don't know. The last time I tracked it, I was on another planet in the Milky Way galaxy, the only other one besides Earth that I've visited, but that was four billion years ago. One of the frequencies is a beacon, but I still don't have enough of it to reveal the present location." Jim nodded.

Another voice from one of the folks against the wall, "What was that planet called?"

"Telraed." Garrett looked at Jim, who was staring at the table again, silently.

Another voice from the back asked, "If you don't know where Orris is now, then how did you know where to look for the signal?" There was a flutter of agreement with the question.

"I knew where it was when I was on Telraed, and I knew its course. I corrected for the position difference between Earth and Telraed, which wasn't much, honestly. Then I calculated where it would be after traveling for another four billion years and subtracted the time it would take for the radio signal to arrive here."

The same voice said, "So you could make an educated guess where it is since we received the signal. It confirms that it maintained its course plan."

Garrett nodded. "Yes, that's true. But it would only be a guess. A much more accurate way to determine its location would be to wait for more of the signal. Once I have the updated course, my guess would be much more educated. At least within three million years instead of four billion. Understand, the signal we are receiving now has been traveling for over two million years." The entire conference room was silent.

Jim tapped the table lightly with one finger. "The drive," He continued, tapping the table, and thinking, "How can you travel such distances?"

"Yes, well, you have a rudimentary understanding of the technology here already. It's a flex drive, it manipulates the space-time around the body, rapidly," Garrett said.

Jim chuckled. "Rapidly, he says. You said you traveled to the Milky Way from Andromeda, that's two and a half million light-years away. How long did it take you?" Jim rocked back in his chair and looked directly at Garrett.

"I can estimate, but I was under for most of it. I left Andromeda after the Katya disaster. I had programmed the course for the star that Telraed orbited, and I dosed myself for 2,500 years. When I woke up, I was orbiting their sun."

"You traveled at a thousand times the speed of light?" Jim asked with skepticism in his voice.

"That's not exactly true. It isn't technically traveling through space. But yes, if you calculate the time taken to cover a given distance, you could calculate it to roughly 1,000c. Which is much better than the technology available to us when I left Osa, which put us at only 0.8c." Jim went stone silent.

Another unseen voice said, "What were you saying about a disaster?"

"My third mission planet was my last in Andromeda. The planet was called Katya. A jealous and bitter engineer there set off a chain of events that ended up destroying everything. I have since modified my construction and testing protocols to prevent anything like that from happening again. Telraed went smoothly."

"Should we have him show us what is in the signal?" Stanley asked. Jim straightened up and nodded.

"Yes, yes. Someone get him set up with the projector." Garrett, Mike, and a youngish girl with short blonde hair all walked down to the projector and set the laptop up. Once Garrett's desktop illuminated the large screen, Mike whispered to him before returning to his seat near the head of the table.

"Show them the launch first," he said. Garrett did, then showed another fifteen videos. From there, he went through thirty photographs, and the first few blueprint files for a class seven Lance. Never was a room with seventy-eight people in attendance so silent. When he finished, he turned off his laptop and someone flipped the lights back on. Jim stood up, stowed his notepad back in his pocket, walked up to Garrett, and shook his hand.

"Thank you for the meeting," he said, and walked out. Everyone else in the room filed out until only Mike, Becky, Stanley, and Garrett remained. Stanley gathered his things and ambled to the door. Before walking through it, he looked back at the group.

"Thank God it's Friday. I'm going home. I have a bottle of Jack that's calling to me." The other three followed him out and made their way down to Mike's office. To their collective surprise, Jim Lambert was sitting in Mike's desk chair.

"I'm going to borrow your friend for a little while," he said to Mike. "Will you come with me, Mr. Rhodes?" Garrett nodded, and Jim led him back to the elevator bay. Jim pressed the "up" button and turned to Garrett. "You're telling me you arrived on this planet *four billion* years ago?" Garrett nodded. Jim shook his head. "Wasn't it hot? There was no oxygen, don't you need oxygen to breathe?"

"Yes, it was miserable, but there was oxygen, just not nearly as much as there is now. And yes, it was so hot that it nearly killed me on many occasions." The elevator doors opened, and they both stepped in. Jim punched the button numbered seven on the control pad. The door closed, and the car lifted.

"What about the moon? What was that like?"

Garrett smiled. "I have fond memories of that. It was beautiful. It filled the sky for at least a part of every night. It was so bright that I traveled by moonlight at night, as it was so much cooler than trying to travel in the daytime heat. And it was so smooth, Jim. The craters came later. And I can tell you something else, I've never seen anything like it on any other planet I've visited." Jim nodded and smiled. The elevator bell chimed, and the doors opened. Garrett followed Jim out of the elevator and into his office. An older woman with a dark complexion and a mop of white hair tied tightly about her head sat on a couch with her hands folded in her lap. Jim spoke as he removed his jacket and hung it on a hook behind his desk.

"Garrett, the kid in me wants desperately to believe everything you're saying, and everything you've shown us. It's all fascinating and exciting, and I can't wait to hear more." The woman stood up and picked up a small white box that had been resting on the short table in front of the couch. "The adult is screaming at me to be more realistic. To stop believing in fairytales. So, since I'm caught in the middle of this, I have a final question for you. Are you a human being from Earth?"

Garrett laughed. "No. What is this? A DNA test?"

Jim smiled and nodded. "Mostly, we will take a sample of your blood with your permission. The major test we will do is DNA, but depending on how that comes back, we may have other questions. Do we have your consent to take a sample and study your blood?"

Garrett rolled up his sleeves and smiled. "Just leave me enough to stay conscious."

22

Later that afternoon, Mike accompanied Becky to the airport. When they arrived at the security checkpoint, they prepared to say their goodbyes.

"Well, this is it. Adventure: over," Becky said.

"I can't tell you just how happy I am to have met you, Beck. I hope we won't lose touch." She smiled in a way that lit Mike's emotions on fire. He was struggling with the loss.

"Remember when you were in middle school? Remember how the boys and girls used to pass notes to each other?" The question confused him, but he shrugged and nodded. "When you get home, look under your alarm clock. A girl might have left you a note." At that moment, she stood on her toes so she could kiss his cheek, and then she was off to the TSA agent to get checked in through security. He stood like a statue and watched her pass through the checkpoint, and every inch she moved after that, until she was out of sight.

Mike was a good and conscientious driver and rarely drove more than four or five miles per hour above the speed limit. When he drove from the airport back to the apartment on that Friday night, he would have had a hard time convincing anyone of that fact. It was only after he arrived home that he thought about the possibilities of what could have been a rather severe traffic ticket. Once out of the elevator, he raced to his apartment door, unlocked it, and raced to his bedroom. There was a folded paper under his alarm clock, and Mike could not help but laugh at the juvenile way she had drawn a heart on its exterior. He hastily unfolded the paper to read its contents:

Mike,

I apologize in advance for the adolescent way I'm communicating my feelings to you, but I think it would be too hard for me to do it in person. I hope I had the courage to tell you about the note at the airport, and that you will not just stumble upon it by accident at a later date.

I had more fun with you in the first ten minutes of our acquaintance than I have had with all the guys I've dated in my entire life. After the first two days, and all the emotional trials we shared, I found it comforting that you were with me through it all, and it only made my affection for you stronger.

Leaving you will be extremely difficult for me, even if I don't show it outwardly. I've picked up on subtle signs that you may feel the same way about me. I hope I was not just imagining things.

I'm on the plane now, and my phone is on airplane mode. I hope that when I reconnect to the cell network, that I'll get a message from you confirming that you read this note and communicating your opinion of it to me.

Becky

Mike fell over on his bed and heard the front door open. Garrett was home. He stood back up, note in hand, and walked out to greet him. As he approached the place Garrett stood, he held the note out to him, but did not talk. Garrett took the paper and Mike went to the cabinet where he kept his single malt scotch. He grabbed a pint glass, filled it with ice and topped it off with the scotch. Garrett laughed as Mike took his first sip.

"Mike, this is obviously exactly what you wanted, but do you see anything funny about it?" Mike snatched the paper back from Garrett and reread it in its entirety.

"Funny? No." Garrett did not attempt to take the note back. He just got himself a beer.

"She lives in Alaska. She traveled over three thousand miles to meet me and find out more about the signal. She learns all of it, she finds out that humanity is not alone in the universe, along with many other world-shaking things while she's here. But in your note, she doesn't even mention them. Any of them. It's all about you. She's crazy about you, Mike." He sipped his beer. Mike stood there, smiling stupidly, and staring at his drink. "So, when are you going to Alaska? Tomorrow?"

Mike laughed. "No, I wish I could, but no." He set the note on the counter and took another sip of his scotch. Garrett walked around the island to where he was standing and took the glass out of his hand.

"I'm going to do you a favor, friend. That note says she's expecting to get a message from you when she lands. Do you want that message to be a sober one or a drunk one?" Mike smiled and picked up his phone.

"Thanks, Garrett." He rapidly pounded the surface of his phone, pausing several times, then resuming. After a few minutes, he handed it to Garrett.

"I said all that sober Mike wants to say. To avoid drunk Mike from intervening, can you put that somewhere I won't find it until tomorrow morning?" Garrett laughed and took the phone.

"You got it, buddy, and congratulations. I like her a lot too. She's a great person. You hit the jackpot." Mike was smiling from ear to ear as he picked up the scotch that he hoped would dampen the sadness of Becky's departure.

23

On Saturday afternoon, Jim Lambert stood in the kitchen of his large apartment cutting up a cucumber. He separated the wheels in half and spread them on two paper plates and lightly seasoned them with salt and pepper.

"Kids!" he yelled into the living room, where his two children were watching TV. A girl of five years came ambling into the kitchen, holding a stuffed rhinoceros. She climbed onto a chair at the kitchen table without putting the plush toy, which she called "Henry," down. Jim placed one of the plates in front of her and called into the living room again, "James! Come on, I made you a snack." His son, eight years old and desperately thin, came to the doorway of the kitchen.

"I'm not hungry, Dad." Jim put the cutting board and knife into the sink and turned to his son.

"James, you have to eat more. You barely ate any of your lunch, and it's important that you get all the nutrition you need at your age." His son answered with a shrug. "I'll make you a deal. I'll let you get away with not eating this time if you promise me you'll eat all of your dinner. All of it. Deal?" His son nodded and walked back into the living room. "Words, James." He heard his son call back, "Yes, sir," from the living room.

Jim picked up a few of the cucumber wheels he had cut up for his son and was about to eat when his cell phone rang.

He picked it up off the counter. "Jim Lambert," he answered, as always.

Chapter 12

Launch

1

Garrett met his mother at a popular diner in Dinesta the afternoon following his engagement to Lauren. They sat in a booth and each ordered a simple meal, as it was an hour past the typical lunch time.

"This is so nice, Garrett. Thank you for inviting me to lunch!" Cynthia said.

Garrett frowned. "It's for a reason, Mom. Not that I wouldn't invite you to lunch without one, but it's hard to get away from OPM. This time it was important, so I forced myself out." His mother frowned and refolded the napkin she was fidgeting with.

"Important bad? Or important good?" She smiled for only a moment and then put on her concerned face.

"No, no. It's good, very good actually, at least from my perspective. But let's wait for Lauren. She's on her way, and I don't want to say anything else without her here." His mother frowned again but settled back in her chair to wait for Lauren.

Although only six minutes had passed since the conclusion of their introductory conversation and the arrival of Garrett's beloved, it felt like an eternity to him.

Lauren sat at the table with them, with a wide and bright smile on her face. Clamped in her two hands was a single sheet of paper.

"What is this?" Cynthia asked. Garrett drew in a breath, preparing to answer his mother, when Lauren cut him off.

"I am going to marry your son. And this is the proof for you that I'm not in it for the money." Lauren handed Cynthia the paper. Cynthia studied it, reading it twice.

"You filled this out and signed it, but you haven't filed it yet?" Cynthia asked. The smile fell off Lauren's face.

"No, but only because I wanted to show it to you first. I want you to be confident when you hear me say that I love him that it's genuine love and not a ploy."

Cynthia smiled and refolded the form. "Then you will be perfectly happy leaving this document with me?"

Lauren looked at Garrett, then back at Cynthia. "I don't know that you can file it on my behalf. I don't know how that works."

Cynthia smiled again and shook her head. "You said this document is only to put my mind at ease?" Lauren shrugged and nodded. "Well, then, it's no problem. Leave it with me and I'll do with it what I will."

"So, you won't…" Lauren again looked at Garrett, "Stop me from marrying him?"

Cynthia tucked the folded paper into the small bag that she carried with her. "I won't interfere at all." She looked down for a moment, then back up at Lauren. "I never hated you. I was only afraid for my boy. You producing this document proves to me beyond any doubt that your intentions are pure."

Lauren smiled and launched out of her seat, moving quickly to Cynthia and hugging her. "Thank you," she whispered.

2

Marriage on Osa was unlike on Earth. There were no large gatherings and celebrations. The engaged couple filled out a marriage license in the presence of an official qualified to witness the agreement. After the couple applied their signatures and the witness theirs, the marriage was legal. The local government would then register the paperwork with the appropriate state offices.

Garrett and Lauren went to the courthouse the next day on their lunch break and approached the counter of the civil affairs department. They filled out the license and each affixed their signature to the document in front of a pleasant older woman who introduced herself as Annie Martin. Once they applied their signatures, Annie took the license from them, checked several boxes on the form, and embossed it with her seal. Finally, she scratched her own signature at the bottom and initialed within the embossed area. She picked up the paper and looked at the two young people, smiling. "Congratulations, you're married." She turned and walked back further behind the counter and placed the document into a bin for later processing.

It was not standard practice on Osa to have wedding rings, though couples did sometimes purchase simple rings or other jewelry to commemorate the occasion. Lauren had wanted to do it, and so after work, they went to a jewelry store and selected a ring for her.

"I want you to have one, too," she said, smiling. He shook his head.

"I can't. I'm not allowed to take anything with me other than what they issue before the launch." She looked back at the display case and pointed.

"Get that one," she said, ignoring his refusal. "On your launch day, give it to me, and I'll wear it around my neck. It will be the best thing I have left to remember you by." Garrett smiled at her and nodded.

To continue the special occasion, Lauren requested they go to Glenn Barron's Steak & Ale for dinner, as it was the first place the two had gone on a date. Garrett agreed, and they had a fine meal, and both ordered the large beers that had contributed to their initial intimacy and eventual relationship.

"Next week is coming fast," Lauren said. She was referencing the fact that the following week was the envoy's assigned week off. The week after that, on Monday, Ken Chase would launch into space and start his decades-long job of convincing five peoples from five planets to build an enormous starship, select several hundred of their own kind, and send them on a lifetime commitment to deliver their descendants to Orris. The coming week off was something all the envoys were looking forward to. The training regimen had been long and grueling. Usually just five days a week, but sometimes six, and it had lasted the better part of a year. "Are you excited?"

Garrett laughed. "Yeah," he sipped his beer, but after a few seconds, he had drank almost a quarter of it. "The hard part will be balancing my time. With you, my parents, and Breni and Rod."

She smiled mischievously and shook her head. "Nope! You don't have to," she said, as she displayed an enormous smile. He looked back at her with confusion. "When you were in the shower this morning, I called your mom. We're all going to spend the week together, all seven of us, and for all nine days."

"What? Where? Rod won't be able to get the time off, I can guarantee you that. I love the idea, but how can you make that work on such short notice?"

She smiled her signature, sweet smile and laughed. "Me? No, I can't. But your mom can. Actually, she did. We discussed the plan while you were in the shower. I hung up with her as soon as I heard the water turn off, but she sent me a message an hour later that just said, 'all set.'"

"Amazing. Where are we going?" he asked. Lauren shrugged.

"I haven't talked to her since this morning, so I don't know. She said she had a few places in mind. I guess it will be a surprise."

They finished their dinner and went back to the apartment, where they settled into their normal routine. They still had two days of work left before the grand vacation.

3

The place turned out to be a mountaintop cabin large enough to house twenty-five, much too big for the six adults and one baby, but they all took the extra room in stride.

There was a massive sitting room with large windows that looked out over the mountainous terrain outside. The room featured a fireplace with a white and gray stone chimney that stayed cold, as it was summer on that part of Osa. Centered in the room was a large table between three oversized couches that all faced in on each other, and the lighting was all fixed to the walls instead of illuminating from above.

The family spent the week cooking, eating, laughing, and reminiscing. They played games, went on hikes, built small campfires in the evening, and enjoyed the small lawn that separated the lodge from the sheer drop of the mountain face.

On the last night at the camp, the men sat around the fire drinking beer while Cynthia, Lauren, and Breni were inside preparing their own drink concoctions.

"How long before you wake up, Garrett?" Rod asked.

"It will be about a hundred and fifty years before I get to Distria."

"Damn," Rodney said. "How long do we have left here?"

Garrett looked up at him. "You mean Osa?" he said. Rodney nodded. "Three billion years, anyway, before Sochee expands."

"And anyone left here will burn up?" Rod asked.

Alan laughed and shook his head. "No, there won't be anyone left at that point," Alan said. Rodney and Garrett both looked confused. Orris was not taking everyone. There would surely be a full population left on the planet long after Orris left the solar system. Alan looked at Garrett. "The core is slowing down."

"Oh," Garrett said. "How long?" Alan shrugged and sipped his beer.

"A billion, probably, before it fails," he said. Rodney had been a member of the family long enough to know when to be quiet and wait for one of them to explain what they were talking about. It was status quo with the Rhodes family. He was not a stupid man by any measure, but he did not have the interest in the topics typically discussed among the Rhodes' to have any idea what they were talking about.

Alan did not disappoint. "The core is liquid metal, Rodney, and it's spinning. The moving metal creates a huge magnetic field around Osa. That field protects us from of the better part of Sochee's harmful radiation. But the field is only there because the metal is moving. Once it slows down…"

"Osa gets fried," Rodney finished. Garrett and Alan nodded. "That's rough." They all laughed.

4

Lauren and Garrett arrived at the Dinesta Control Center and Launch Rail about thirty minutes before Ken's departure. When they entered the main lobby, they heard a female voice call out to Lauren. It was Olive.

"Hey! You guys are just in time. Ken will board in fifteen minutes, but he's meeting with his instructors and the other envoys right now." Olive beckoned to them, and they followed her through a heavy wooden door and down a long staircase. After passing through the control center, which impressed both Lauren and Garrett alike, they arrived at two large glass exterior doors that opened onto a fenced-in concrete patio.

Ken was not a large man, neither in height nor girth, but he looked impressive nonetheless in his flight suit. Jack Abbott had his arm around him and was talking in his ear. Garrett walked up to the soon-to-be ex-Osan and extended his hand. Ken shook it hard, with an excited smile on his face.

"Thanks for coming down, Garrett. I was hoping to see everyone before I left." Garrett used his free hand to slap Ken's shoulder.

"I wouldn't miss it for the world, Ken. You're the lucky one, you know?" Ken shook his head inquisitively. "In four days, we'll all be back here for Kyle to send him off. All of us except you, Ken. By the time I launch, it will just be me and Terry."

The two men heard Terry, who was only a few feet away, laugh and say, "I'll be by myself, so I don't want to hear it!" The handful of people keyed in on the conversation laughed.

A moment after the laughter died down, someone who Garrett did not know asked for a picture with Ken, and he spent the balance of time he had left being photographed with various people. While the photos were being taken, Dr. Alex Murray yelled through the small crowd to Ken.

"Ken? One minute, and through the gate." Ken nodded and announced that he wanted a picture of him with the other envoys. They crowded in around him while multiple family members took photos. As they dispersed, Dr. Murray took him by the elbow and led him to the gate. Upon exiting, he waved at all the people he was leaving behind and walked down the concrete path toward a party of four tasked with getting him into the transport. The moment he turned toward the vehicle, everyone on the patio streamed back into the building to get up to the observation pavilion.

Garrett climbed back up the steps and rounded the corner into the large, open-air pavilion with what must have been a fifty- or sixty-foot-tall ceiling. He cued in on one of the large displays fixed to the poles supporting the roof. It had Ken's face in the upper right-hand corner and a mass of information displayed about both Ken, the weather, the mission, and the countdown. The time was in large block print in the center of the bottom of the screen and it read 11:34… 33… 32. Garrett had Lauren's small hand in his and he led her through the crowd to the eastern wall, where there were only a few people congregated.

"We can't see Ken from here, we'll…" She cut herself off in mid-sentence and looked out at the landscape in front of them, which included most of the rail that Ken would traverse. "Oh, I get it. You're quite the thinker, Garrett Rhodes." She winked and tapped her temple. There was another one of the large screens near them, and they passed the time by reading all the details offered by OPM. To his surprise, the next time Garrett looked down at Lauren, she had tears in her eyes. She sniffed hard and wiped them with a tissue she had produced from her bag.

"You realize that it's Ken leaving, right, nerd? I'm still here for almost another month." Lauren smiled and nodded. Then Garrett noticed a new sound, a high-pitched whine that devolved into a much deeper, louder buzzing sound.

"I know, but it's still sad." The countdown timer read 0:13, and she approached the railing to watch. Garrett stood behind her and wrapped her in his arms.

The crowd counted down to zero, and Garrett heard a repetitive banging, loud followed by somewhat less loud. *BANG, bang… BANG, bang… BANG, bang…* like the world's loudest electro-mechanical heartbeat, and then he witnessed his near future. The transport, in its carriage, accelerated across the terrain so fast he thought it would crush Ken. It seemed to slow down as it got further away, but then, when it was on the horizon, it lifted. The vertical speed appeared slow, too, but Garrett knew better. The flash, although far away, was impressive, and after the rockets burned for a few minutes, the show was over, at least for the naked eye.

5

Four days after Ken launched, they repeated the same steps for Kyle Gellar. Three days after, Eric Thomas. With each launch, it was getting harder and harder for both Lauren and Garrett. His time was approaching. Randy Vila launched, and then Stan Richman.

They arrived back at the apartment after Stan left, and although they had not had dinner, Lauren's mood was so sour that he expected they would not. She tossed her bag on the dining room table and started taking off her clothes as she walked toward the bathroom.

"I'm going to shower," she announced, without waiting for a reply. With Lauren in the bathroom, Garrett shook his head and leaned on the kitchen counter. *Something is wrong with her,* he thought. Many times, during their relationship, Garrett had imagined how she would react as his launch date approached, but the wild tempers and emotional mood swings were never predicted. He went to the refrigerator for a beer and waited.

When she emerged, wrapped in a towel, she was a new woman. She smiled, kissed him, and said, "We should probably get something for dinner, it's getting late."

Garrett's first thought was to embrace the happy version of his wife and dive headfirst into the pleasant evening it appeared he would have. His better judgement interfered, and he asked her point blank, "Sweetheart, something has been wrong with you for the past few weeks. Especially this week. What is it?" Lauren's sweet, smiling face slackened into a somber expression.

"I know. But I don't know why. I thought I would handle it better than this."

Garrett wrapped her in his arms and kissed her temple. "Okay, good answer. What do you want for dinner?"

They decided on takeout from one of their favorite restaurants and had it delivered. Once dinner had concluded, they had a pleasant night playing a card game. After playing for almost two hours, Garrett's eyelids got heavy, and Lauren exclaimed, "Hey!" Garrett snapped to attention, and she laughed. "I think it's bedtime, slouch." Garrett smiled.

"Okay, nerd." She walked around the table and pulled him out of his chair.

"I'll clean this up in the morning. Let's go."

Garrett only slept for two hours before he woke up with a sense of deja vu. He turned over and found the bed, once again, vacant. He got up and walked to the dark living room. Instead of standing before the curtainless window, his naked wife was now sitting in the open window as though it were a seat, with comfort and safety to her left and certain death to her right. Garrett froze, not wanting to alarm her. Although she looked outside and up at the stars, she laughed.

"Are you going to join me?" she asked. He walked up to her and gently took her elbow in his hand.

"Are you okay?"

She turned to him and smiled. "Yes. I'm not suicidal. I just love feeling the night air on my skin." She lifted his hand to her lips and kissed it.

"I think there are a lot of eyes out there also liking the fact that you like the night air on your skin," he said.

She shrugged and smiled, "I doubt it, but I also don't care." Garrett looked at the clock. "Why? Don't look at that. Let's stay here for a while. We don't have to be anywhere tomorrow." She slid off the windowsill and down to the carpet in front of it and pulled him down next to her. "Just enjoy the air, the breeze. You're going to miss it."

Garrett did enjoy it. She was right. Feeling her pressed against him with both of their backs to the open air also felt good.

6

During the next week and before Joe Burkman's launch, Lauren and Garrett spent three evenings with his parents for dinner, and the last weekend with Brenia, Rodney, and the baby. Lauren's moods did not improve, but she and Garrett dealt with them quietly.

The morning of Joe's launch, Lauren felt sick and said she did not want to go. Garrett asked her to put her final decision off to the afternoon. She agreed, and when the afternoon had come, she announced she was better and willing to accompany him.

They arrived at the facility for the last time, such that they would also leave together, and made their way down to Joe's departure gathering. During the drive there, and even after they had arrived, all life appeared drained from Lauren's face. She was a statue. She stood and stared into the distance, not wanting to participate. As time with Joe grew short, Garrett asked her to say goodbye to him. Her stone face broke. She looked up at him, nodded, and walked over to Joe, placed her hands on either side of his head, and kissed him on the mouth. When she released him from her grip, she said into his surprised face, "Godspeed, Joe. We will miss you." Joe shot Garrett a look that said, *What the hell?* Garrett closed his eyes and shook his head.

In the observation pavilion, Lauren had returned to her statue form and Garrett watched as Joe's father scuttled through the crowd with his camera held high. Only a few minutes after that, Joe was gone, and Garrett was on deck.

7

The last days leading up to Garrett's launch were painful. Lauren cried a lot. The reality gripped him, and he often questioned his decision. The day before he left, he ate a large lunch. Protocol dictated that he could not eat twenty-four hours before administering the Sterilex, which he had estimated would be about 16:30 the next day. He ate slowly, knowing that his next meal would not be for about a hundred and fifty years.

For the same reason, Garrett skipped dinner. In its place, he drank two quarts of water over a four-hour period. Lauren had been in their room, crying. He visited her several times, lying next to her on the bed and holding her. She turned and kissed him on his third visit.

"This is our last night together, Laur. Do you want to spend it like this?" Garrett asked. She shook her head and stood up. Holding hands, they exited to the living room. Garrett sat on the couch and Lauren pushed him over to lie on his chest. He stroked her hair.

"Are you scared?" she asked.

"Yes. But less so now that I have seen the other guys do it. It seems pretty routine at this point."

Lauren laughed. "Routine? I couldn't imagine doing something like that. Just getting off the ground... strapped to a bomb? No thanks."

"It's not a bomb. Our trainers told us the acceleration training was worse than the actual launch, anyway. I guess I'll find out if that's true soon enough."

"Do you think you'll miss me when you wake up?" She had a standing tear in her eye, but she was not crying.

"Of course! I'm leaving tomorrow, but when I wake up it will be as though no time had passed. For me, I'll wake up tomorrow night, but it will be a hundred and fifty years from now. I'll have every memory and emotion that I had in the moment I went under." She hugged him tightly.

They laid that way, talking and enjoying each other's embrace for another hour. Garrett finished the last of his water and they both went to bed.

8

It surprised Garrett and Lauren both that, although it was not a perfect night, they both slept a good deal leading up to the life-changing morning. Garrett had showered upon waking, dressed in his OPM issued launch clothing, and went into the living room to go through his stretching routine while Lauren was getting ready. When she emerged from the bedroom, he handed her his ring. She removed a simple chain necklace and threaded it through his wedding band and rehung it around her neck. The couple hugged for what would have been an unusually long time under normal circumstances.

They left early and arrived early, as Garrett had planned. When they walked through the front doors, Dr. Murray and Dr. Paige were standing in the center of the lobby, talking. Dr. Murray looked up at the two entering and extended a hand to Garrett.

"Glad to see you, Garrett." The men shook hands and Alex turned his attention to Lauren. "Dr. Rhodes." Lauren smiled, few people called her by her proper, legal name and title. Most people did not know she was a doctor, and even fewer still knew that she had married Garrett. It had been a hell of a road from Ms. Astor to Dr. Rhodes. Christine approached her and kissed her cheek.

"Good morning, sweetie." She stepped back and hugged Garrett. She whispered to him, "Hard day, Gar. A really hard day." When she stepped back from him, he nodded. Dr. Paige returned her attention to Lauren. "How do you want to do this? Do you want to stay with us? Or, if you like, I can probably find you a vacant office with a couch if you want to take a nap while he gets ready." Lauren shook her head. "No, I want to be with him for every minute I can be." Dr. Paige smiled and nodded. "I thought that would be your answer. Ok, everyone. Let's go downstairs. We're early, but Arthur is already here and waiting for you." She walked away from them, and they all followed. Down the long staircase again, Christine pushed open a large door immediately at the bottom and they all followed her into a corridor that must have run beneath the pavilion. Another right, and they entered a room that had the door propped open. Arthur sat on a stool opposite an empty one in front of a large metal table pushed against the back wall of the tiny room.

"Garrett, excellent." Arthur stood and shook his hand. He smiled at Lauren and said, "Good morning, Dr. Astor." She smiled as Alex leaned in.

"Rhodes. It's Dr. Rhodes now," Alex said. Arthur looked back and forth between Garrett and Lauren.

"Oh! Well, that's wonderful. And a little heartbreaking." Lauren shrugged and smiled again. He held a hand out to show Garrett he should sit on the stool opposite his, and he picked up a gray canvas satchel that sat on the table next to him. "Garrett, this satchel contains your life. So, don't lose it." The two men sat, and Arthur emptied the contents first into his hand and then spread them out onto the table. Christine, Lauren, and Alex all chatted while Arthur went through the contents of the satchel in great detail with Garrett. After they had concluded, Arthur reloaded the satchel and hung it around Garrett's neck. They exited the small office and progressed to the next room over, which was much larger and much brighter.

When they arrived, Christine stood outside the door and gestured for them to enter. She said, "We will wait out here for this one. You'll understand in a minute." Confused, Lauren followed Garrett into a room that had one young man in it wearing pale blue scrubs and writing on a clipboard.

"You're the envoy?" the young man asked. Garrett nodded. He looked back at the clipboard. "Garrett Rhodes?" Garrett nodded again.

"Excellent, my name is Dennis. I will get you prepared to jump time." He walked over to the windowless door, swung it shut, and bolted it. "Take off your clothing, lay it there." He gestured with his pen to a single chair in the front corner of the room. "Is this your wife?"

"Yes, it is. Do I take off everything?" Dennis nodded, not looking up from his clipboard.

"Every stitch," he said. Garrett undressed, and Lauren realized why Alex and Christine had stayed outside the room. With Garrett standing as naked as the day he was born, Dennis said, "This is a little unpleasant, but once you're in your suit, you won't even notice it. Now, when you're out there, do this last. If you put it on too early before you take the Sterilex, it could kill you. An hour at the most is fine, but not four or five. Do you understand me?" Garrett looked confused.

"Not really. It will be at least two hours before I go under this time," he said.

Dennis nodded. "This time your suit will monitor your body temperature and adjust as necessary. In the field, you won't have that luxury." Garrett nodded. "Feet apart, arms out." Dennis demonstrated the pose he was looking for. Garrett assumed the pose, and Lauren watched as Dennis put on rubber gloves and then smeared a sticky, clear gel all over Garrett's body. Every square millimeter, including in his ears, nose, and other parts not mentioned in polite company. When he finished the application, he said, "You can wipe your eyes, but not too much. Just wait for it to dry. You can get dressed." Garrett wiped his eyes and squinted as he walked to the chair containing his uniform.

The next room was similar to the one with Arthur, and Jack Abbott was there with a large backpack. Much like Arthur, he emptied the bag and reviewed all the items with Garrett. Lauren noticed while they were reviewing its contents that Garrett seemed to be getting more comfortable with the process he had just undergone, as he was no longer squinting and looked more at ease. After the review, Garrett slung the bag over one shoulder, and Alex said, "Okay, let's get you suited up!"

For the next stop, they walked through a series of corridors in multiple directions until Lauren and Garrett alike lost any sense of their absolute location in the facility. The group walked into a room with rows of monitors and a team of two men and a woman charged with outfitting him for the flight. They first pulled up Garrett's shirt and applied several sensors to his chest and abdomen. They assisted him as he stepped into his flight suit. With the suit secured, they added his gloves, then showed him how to fix his helmet in place before removing it and handing it to him. The three of them nodded with smiles on their faces, and the group then walked through a set of solid double doors that led to the patio.

Garrett's parents were already there, as well as Breni, Rod, and baby Rodney. Lauren's sister, Denise, was there with her husband and their three children. Lauren had always found it comical that all of their children had bright blonde hair while their parents both had dark brown. Arthur and Jack were there, and Ben Estes. Lauren watched Garrett counting the people he recognized when Olive came through the glass doors with Terry Stone in tow.

They all took turns shaking hands, hugging, kissing, offering well wishes and calls for good luck. Garrett navigated through each person until Lauren finally seized his hand as she had been keeping track. She looked up at the flight display and was disappointed to find only minutes remaining before he would have to board the craft. She locked her arms around his waist, and Garrett dipped his head so they could whisper to each other. They did just that for several minutes. The rest of the group looked at them and felt some of the emotion that must have been occupying that small space between the couple's lips and ears.

Dr. Murray looked at the countdown timer and knew he had to break it up. He approached them with some extra time and put a hand on each of their shoulders.

"It's time," he said, and Lauren broke into a sob.

"Remember what I said," Garrett told her. She sniffled and nodded, trying to repress the tears. He kissed her temple, her forehead, and finally, her lips. He let go of her and stepped back. She unlocked her clasped hands and as he moved away, let her hands slide down his arms until they disappeared into his gloves. "I'll love you forever, nerd, I'll love you until the end of time."

She had stifled most of her tears and said, "It better be longer than that, slouch!" They both laughed the short laugh that one can manage during emotional times. Garrett let go of her hands and turned toward the gate. Once through, he blew her a kiss.

9

Garrett arrived at the transport and the four members of the launch team greeted him. One man took the bag off his shoulder and stowed it under the operator's seat, swung a panel up, and latched it. The four worked as a team in assisting him up and into the craft. Once seated, they strapped him into place and showed him the two release levers to undo all the restraints. The only woman on the team stepped up so she was half-inside the craft with Garrett, took his Sterilex satchel out of his hand, and stowed it in a small compartment.

"Do you need help with your helmet?" she asked. Garrett shook his head. "Okay, but put it on as soon as we lock the doors; the air is already on." Garrett nodded, and she stepped down.

"Godspeed, Envoy," one of them said, and waved. They all repeated the farewell, closed the large transparent door of the transport, and went through the external locking procedure. With the last step complete, they all stepped back, waving, then turned and walked back to the command center. Garrett put the helmet on his head and locked it in place. Only the back of the helmet was opaque, and he found he could swing his head left to right with a full view, only losing his peripheral vision at the extremes. The touch-panel of the transport exactly mimicked the simulators he had been in, and Garrett scrolled through the different screens and found them all where they should be. He settled on the launch screen and noted there were only eight minutes left. He looked out the right side of the craft at the observation pavilion and saw his family gathered on the private deck. Lauren stood at the railing, with her hands nervously rubbing at her belly. It was at that moment when Garrett first suspected she was pregnant with their child. He put a gloved index finger up to the clear surface of his face shield and pretended to kiss it through the space. He did the same thing with his other index finger, and then pressed the tips of both to the glass, both pointing toward her. She smiled but started sobbing. Seconds later, she was visibly working to get herself under control.

At the six-minute mark, a voice simultaneously crashed into the pavilion and Garrett's helmet alike. "Good afternoon, folks, this is Commander Mark Harris, and I'm the command supervisor for this flight. As always, we have this channel for the exclusive use of the command center and its various department heads, but also linked up to the pavilion speaker system so our observers can be closer to the action." Garrett's family were talking amongst themselves, but Lauren's eyes were fixated on him. The launch was imminent, and he knew he would have to drop his gaze from her soon. "Today's launch is the eighth such launch we've had for the OPM Migration Division. It is an interstellar flex-transport bound for the planet Distria, at a distance of 39 parsecs, or about 127 light-years. Our operator today is Envoy Garrett Rhodes, who will begin his journey to secure five alien civilizations to join us in our effort with the Orris Project. At this time, we will begin our system checks." The voice crackled out for only a few seconds. Garrett tore his gaze away from Lauren and stared down at the launch screen, illuminated with the system checklist.

"Rail maintenance." The voice roared back to life.

A softer voice answered it, but still loud coming over the pavilion speaker, "Rail maintenance is ready."

"Power."

"Power system is ready, sir."

"Navigation."

"Navigation confirmed, ready."

"Chemical propulsion."

"Chem prop is ready, sir."

"Engineering."

"Engineering is ready, sir."

"Flex drive."

"Ah, yes sir, the flex drive is confirmed, ready."

"Nuclear."

"Nuclear is ready."

"Systems."

"Systems check complete. Confirmed ready, sir."

"Operator." Lauren's heart sank. It would be one of the last times she ever heard his voice.

"Operator is ready, sir," Garrett responded.

"Power on…" The high-pitched whining started faintly and got louder and louder before settling into a painfully loud, vibrating buzz.

"Power? Confirm, please."

"Full power confirmed."

"Track clearance."

"Track is clear, sir."

"Launch window."

"Window is clear, sir."

"Ladies and gentlemen, we have confirmed this launch. Note the countdown on your overhead displays, and thank you for visiting the Dinesta Control Center today." The voice crackled out.

Garrett looked down at the timer to see only seventeen seconds left. He looked back up at Lauren; her gaze had never left him. He placed his right hand on the transparent door and stared at her. A moment later, he could read the lips of the crowd as they chanted *10, 9, 8, 7…* The whole craft lifted eight or ten inches and rocked back and forth. As the crowd chanted 3, then 2, he gripped his harness with both of his gloved hands as they had instructed him to do and forced himself to look away from her, straight ahead.

The banging sound was so violent that the whole craft shook for the first few cycles, but Garrett did not notice. His attention was focused on the weight of his torso being crushed into the soft back of the operator seat. The landscape first moved by, and in the next instant it rushed by; an instant after that, it flashed by and had become a blur. He expected to see the craft turn up toward the sky, but it seemed more like the planet fell away from him. As he raced toward the bright baby blue of the sky, he noted that he could not see the end of the track. He next heard a rapid snapping sound, like a fuse-less circuit shorting to ground, and the solid rockets lit. He thought the initial acceleration had pressed him hard into the seatback, but he was wrong. When the rockets lit, he could feel himself sink even deeper into it, and he was uncomfortable for the first time. He never witnessed the track ending, but only a moment after the rockets flared up, the sky's baby blue faded to an oily black. As his eyes adjusted, the stars became sharp and pronounced. He was in space.

10

When the light from Garrett's solid rocket faded out, most of the crowd dispersed. Lauren walked from the private deck into the emptying pavilion and sat on one of the many benches. The rest of the family members followed her slowly, concerned. Denise's husband, Brad, whispered into her ear, and she shook her head.

"No, I'm going to stay with her. Take them home, I'll meet you there." Brad shrugged and led the three blonde haired kids out of the pavilion after planting a kiss on his sister-in-law's cheek. The children all hugged their Aunt Lauren, and she kissed the tops of their heads.

Cynthia whispered to Denise, "Alan and I can bring you home later, if you want." Denise shook her head.

"I think I'll be spending the night with her." She gestured to her sister. Cynthia nodded.

The bench Lauren had chosen faced another, only ten feet from it. Cynthia and Denise flanked Lauren on the one, and Brenia, Rodney, Alan, and the young Rodney Junior sat on the other. As they got settled, the crackling voice flooded the mostly empty pavilion.

"Garrett, this is Commander Harris, can you still hear me?"

"Loud and clear, sir." Lauren's expression brightened.

"Excellent. Garrett, it looks like your orbit around Osa is right on target and you're approaching the start of the parabolic burn. Are you still wearing your gloves?"

"No, sir, gloves are off. Sterilex is in hand." Lauren looked up at the screen, which still displayed the photograph of Garrett in addition to his flight status.

"Excellent, Garrett. The navigation system has confirmed it is ready. I have an indication that the transport has reached vertical orientation. Can you confirm that for me?"

"Vertical orientation confirmed," Garrett said. Lauren was cherishing every word she heard from him. She did not want it to end but knew there was not a lot of time left.

"Great. Okay, Garrett, the rockets are going to fire in thirty seconds. You will have about forty-five seconds of sloppy gravity, so move quickly."

"Copy," Garrett said. Lauren took a deep breath and waited. Cynthia and Denise were comforting her. Alan was wide eyed and staring at the monitor. Brenia and Rodney were dealing with their child, who was becoming fussy.

After a minute, Garrett came back on. "Sterilex administered, packed up, and stowed. Apex approaching."

"Very good, Garrett. Select the nuclear controls screen and activate plate compression." A few seconds passed before Garrett answered.

"Plate compression activated. 30% power," he said. There was no response from the command center. Lauren grew worried and thought they had cut the pavilion off from the transmission. She looked up at her sister in alarm, but before she could say anything, "60% power, apex achieved. Beginning descent," Garrett announced.

"Confirmed, 60% power, beginning descent. We won't be able to communicate further. Godspeed, Envoy." They were the last words from the command center. Tense seconds passed; Lauren looked from person to person in the small group.

"90% power, eight seconds until the tangent. Preparing to engage flex. 95% power, Lauren, my heart is yours for eternity, I love you, nerd! 100% power, engaging flex." Lauren shivered. Fifteen seconds later, the loudest thunder any of them had ever heard crashed down on the pavilion, startling all its inhabitants. As Garrett passed overhead, the transport flex field had clipped the denser atmosphere of Osa, creating a shock wave.

11

Engineering and mechanics are complicated things. Fasteners, for instance, can be beneficial or detrimental depending on the type, application, environment, and any applied forces, either fixed or varied. This was also true for the launch rail, just outside of Dinesta, Republic of Korrah. A heavy, impact-resistant hard rubber bumper fixed along the entire length of the triple rail system used thick bolts and nuts as fasteners. The bumpers existed for the rare occasions when the carriage physically contacted the track. The large bolts were an inch thick and a foot and a half long. Track maintenance fixed each bolt and nut set with a locking mechanism to prevent the nut from loosening. Four miles off the ground, on the right side of the track, one of the locking mechanisms had an impurity in the steel, and when Ken Chase had launched, it finally cracked. When Kyle Gellar launched, it vibrated so badly that it fell off, all four miles to the ground below. The next four launches loosened the nut dramatically, and when Joe Burkman launched, the nut itself traveled the four miles to the ground, and the bolt shifted up seven inches.

Garrett's transport missed certain disaster by only one-and-a-quarter inch, as the proximity sensors passed over the exposed bolt head two hundred yards before the trigger blocks. The vibration and resulting harmonics from the passing body moved the bolt further.

The rail maintenance team was also responsible for inspecting the whole track the day before each launch. Three inspectors walked the entire level ground section of track, looking for any alarming failures or even areas of concern. They did the inspections in the morning when the sun was at their backs. If there were any issues, they would radio back and have a maintenance team sent to make the needed repairs. As the rail bent up toward the sky, a group of three drones went up remotely, with three operating inspectors monitoring them from the control center. The ground and drone inspections happened simultaneously. With the sun brightly illuminating the rail system, all three of the aerial inspectors missed the loosened bolt… twice. Had they done the inspection in the late morning or even at noon, they would have seen a long, awkward shadow cast by the bolt down the length of the track. With the sun at their backs, it was just a bright point of reflected light, among other bright points of light.

12

Denise stayed with Lauren for the first night and, after some prodding, convinced her to stay with her and her family for a few days. The arrangement pleased Brad, because when Lauren visited, his wife's daily stresses disappeared. Lauren helped with everything, including the children, and made life easier for both Denise and Brad while she was present.

As an instructor, she would attend the last launch of the year for the Migration Division. That, of course, was Terry Stone, who occupied Garrett's launch position due to the unfortunate death of Jonroe Daniels. Lauren had agreed to stay with Denise until Terry launched, and then she said she would have to begin living her new life.

The night before Terry's launch, Christine Paige called Lauren. Lauren answered the phone happily. She had an exceptionally good relationship with Dr. Paige, and although she was a little surprised to receive a call from her at that late hour, she answered anyway.

"Hi Christine!" Lauren said.

"Hi sweetie, how are you doing?" Christine asked.

"Well, I'm staying with my sister and her husband and three children, so you could say I'm embracing the distractions." They both laughed.

"Well, Lauren, the reason I'm calling is I talked to Terry this afternoon. He said that he understood the position you are in, and he would not be offended if you wanted to skip the launch tomorrow."

The idea had not crossed Lauren's mind. She thought about it only briefly. "No, but thank you. No, I'm definitely going. When Jonroe died, Terry found out that he had lost an entire year on Osa with his family. The least I can do is show up and send him off with my best wishes."

"Okay, sweetie. I had an idea that was what you would say. Come find me as soon as you arrive tomorrow. We can hang out together with Olive."

"That sounds great, Christine, thank you." They said their good nights and ended the call.

13

Olive was waiting for Lauren at the front door of the Dinesta Control Center and Launch Rail, not even inside the door but outside, as though she were the facility's greeter. When Lauren came into view, Olive called out to her, and she looked up and smiled. As soon as the two met, Olive embraced her with her substantial arms.

"Oh, how are you doing, Laur?" Olive asked. Lauren giggled as she found herself a hostage in the large woman's hug.

"Fine! I'm fine," Lauren said. Olive let her go and led her into the facility. They talked as they walked down to ground level to see Terry off. Lauren mentioned how much she had grown to hate that long staircase.

When Terry saw Lauren follow Olive out to the patio, his face lit up.

"Dr. Astor!" He shook his head, "I mean, Dr. Rhodes! I didn't think you would come." Lauren smiled and walked up to Terry, hugged him, and kissed his cheek.

"Of course I came. This is an amazing day for you and all of Osa, and you were my student for a year. I wouldn't have missed it," she said. He smiled and thanked her. "Do you have family here?"

"Yes, my uncle. I'm sorry to say he is the only family I have left." Lauren nodded, able to sympathize with his losses. A balding man of medium height with a large gut and glasses approached them, clapping a hand on Terry's back.

"My boy!" the man said.

"Dr. Rhodes, this is my uncle, Manny," Terry said.

"It's a pleasure to meet you, Uncle Manny." Lauren smiled and shook the man's hand.

"The pleasure is all mine, Doctor." Terry's uncle winked at her, Lauren flushed red and returned a small smile, embarrassed.

Alex rescued her, resting a hand on Terry's shoulder and announcing that it was time. Terry waved to everyone and hugged his uncle hard. It touched Lauren to see a tear in Manny's eye as he kissed his nephew on the cheek.

"I'm so proud of 'ya, Ter. I love 'ya, son!" Manny yelled as Terry walked through the gate.

The group moved up to the pavilion and waited for the countdown to start. Lauren led Olive and Christine to the spot where Garrett had taken her a month before, when Ken had launched. The three women chatted about their lives while they waited for the minutes leading up to the launch to pass. Once they hit the sixth minute, the voice of Commander Harris flooded the pavilion again, giving his normal speech and announcements. He went through his ready check, and when he finally finished, the crowd chanted the countdown.

Lauren, not participating in the countdown, nor even paying attention to it, jumped when she saw the craft flash before her eyes. She fixed her gaze on the white dot, watching the last of her students leave for what was sure to be a fantastic adventure. The dot rose. It moved higher and higher into the sky, and then Terry's voice filled the pavilion.

"I hit something. There was a loud bang and the whole transport shook hard." The craft continued to rise at an amazing speed, but the flash never came. "I'm off the track, and I do not have ignition!" Terry was yelling, panicked. A voice new to the pavilion PA system replied.

"Terry, we're going to light the rockets. You're still in the carriage, and we have to get you out of it before you can deploy the emergency parachutes. That's the red and yellow lever, right between your knees. Pull it hard as soon as you see the carriage slide back." Pulling the emergency abort chutes also ejected the solid fuel rockets.

"Copy, abort after carriage is jettisoned." The radio went silent. From the pavilion the observers witnessed the flash, but it was much dimmer than on previous launches, and it appeared to flicker.

"Terry? The carriage should be separated now. Can you confirm the abort?" Silence. Lauren watched the flickering light. She could sense that it was spinning and falling rapidly.

"Terry, can you hear me?" The radio silence continued. The next sound that came was a loud, high-pitched pop, as they disconnected the pavilion sound system from their radio transmissions.

Chapter 13

Alaska

1

Saturday evening, while Garrett was waiting for their Chinese food to arrive, he anxiously checked the DSRTA folder for an update to the signal. Nothing new was available, as he should have known. Mike had been on the phone with Becky, and he emerged from his bedroom and put his phone on the charger in the kitchen.

"Hey, I'm going to take a shower, but it's my turn to buy dinner," Mike said. He handed Garrett a ten and a twenty. Five minutes after he disappeared into the bathroom, there was a knock at the door, and Garrett received and paid for the food. As he placed it on the kitchen island, Mike's phone rang. The display said "Stan Liang." Garrett hesitated for a moment, but then answered it.

"Hi, Mr. Liang, it's Garrett. Mike's in the shower."

"That's fine, Garrett. I called him because I needed to talk to you, anyway. I need you to come back to NASA on Monday with Mike. Can you do that?"

"Sure, what time?" Garrett asked. The request piqued his curiosity. Never had things transpired so quickly on any other planet he visited.

"First thing, just go in with Mike. I'll come find you in his office."

"Can I ask what exactly I'm needed for?" There was a brief pause on the other end of the connection.

"I don't know, Garrett," Stan said, exasperated, "Jim Lambert called me at home and told me to make sure you were there first thing Monday morning, so I am just doing as he instructed."

"I understand, Mr. Liang. I'll see you Monday morning."

"Good. And stop calling me Mr. Liang, it's weird. Just call me Stan."

"No problem, Stan, good night." Garrett unpacked the food, and Mike emerged a few minutes later. Garrett filled him in on the call from Stan.

"Wow, that's something else. You said they took your blood, right?" Mike asked.

"Yeah, three vials. Enough to do a thousand DNA tests."

"They're probably doing more than just DNA tests, Gar."

Garrett nodded again. "I know. It's too fast though, Mike. I've been through this kind of thing before. It usually takes a week or more. At least three or four days. It's barely been one day."

"When the top brass wants something fast, they get it fast," Mike said, and smiled. He was in a good mood.

"So, the call with Becky went well?" Garrett asked. Mike had never stopped smiling. He nodded comically.

2

Sunday was uneventful. Garrett intermittently checked the DSRTA site and on two occasions got an update, which he queued for processing, and otherwise watched television. Mike spent most of the day on three separate calls to Becky. When he finally hung up with her late Sunday night, he joined Garrett in the living room.

"So, do you know when you're going to Alaska yet?" Garrett asked, only half-kidding. Mike shook his head.

"We've been tossing ideas around, but me going to Alaska serves no purpose. We decided to wait at least a few days and see what happens with you. There's a chance all of that will bring us together again and we won't have to pay for it out of our pocket." Garrett smiled, knowing it was a likely thing to happen.

"That's good, Mike. I know it's taxing not knowing when, but that is an intelligent decision. If I have the opportunity to affect her being called back, I'll do so with the permission of the two of you." Mike raised his eyebrows. "Hadn't thought of that?" Garrett asked.

"No, but that's awesome. Thanks, man."

Garret nodded and smiled. "Mike, you've helped me more than I could ever ask of anyone. I'll always do whatever I can for you, but I'll need more of your help in the future. With that said, please ask any time you think there is any help I can provide for you or Becky. I am at your service." Mike smiled and offered his hand to Garrett.

"Thanks, man, and I'll tell you, although I'm a lot more convinced of your story than I was, when everything else shakes out, you're just a good guy. I'm happy to know you." Garrett shook his hand. Mike stood up and walked to the hallway but paused and turned back to Garrett. "I know it's a long way off, but if one of my kids, or grandkids, wanted to travel to Orris, would you tell me that was a good idea, or not?"

"You understand that anyone who boards the Lance here will not reach Orris, right?" Garrett asked. "They'll live their entire lives on the Lance. Only their children, or more likely their grandchildren, will ever see Orris."

Mike shrugged. "Yeah, so don't do it. Not a good idea."

Garrett shrugged himself. "The ones who go will not just be committing their own lives, but those of their own blood to the cause. It's a difficult decision to make. Staying on your own planet would be vastly more comfortable, but you would miss out on the opportunity for your bloodline to be a part of the next cycle."

"But you left everything behind. Even though it wasn't to continue your bloodline, you did it to further the cause of making it to the next cycle. You have already done it. So, what would be your opinion if my grandson comes to me one day and says he wants to get on board the Lance?"

Garrett didn't hesitate, "I'd tell you to talk him out of it."

Mike's face went through a few different emotions but landed on perplexed. "But you're here asking people to go?"

"Not because we want them to subject themselves to life on the Lance, but because we want to preserve a part of them. As an envoy, I will do what they sent me to do, because it is important. But as your friend, I will tell you the truth of what it means to give up your life for a cause, because I know what it means. I've wished a thousand times I could go back in time and tell my younger self not to do it. I missed out on every part of being alive. I left my wife. I have no children, no family of any kind. I bounce from planet to planet, trying to bend entire civilizations to my will. It might sound like an exciting life, but I'd give anything to have a single minute with my wife again."

Mike did not react, just stared for a moment, and then dropped his eyes. "So, then, how do you stay sane? What do you do?"

Garrett smiled and leaned back on the couch. "I make friends. I enjoy their company while I'm with them, and when they're gone, I remind myself that they lived full lives, and not to pity them for dying. The same will happen with you, Mike, but it makes me happy to think that you will live a full life, and I'll enjoy every bit of time we have together while we are here." Garrett had a thought at that moment. "Are you going to sleep right now? Or do you have another minute for me?"

"Sure, whatever you want," Mike said. Garrett went to his room and retrieved the letters from Marco and brought them into the kitchen, which had a much brighter light. Mike followed him.

"I stayed with this family in Northern Italy for almost seven months. The man who wrote these letters was nine years old when I knew him. It's all in Latin, so you won't understand any of it, and I won't make you suffer my translation of the letters. But look at the dates." Garrett slowly paged through the letters, showing Mike the dates, relying on his ability to translate the Roman numbers into Arabic, and announcing Marco's relative age at each. "My friend Marco died one thousand four hundred and seventeen years ago. He was seventy-two when he died, but I still remember him as a nine-year-old boy. It's a strange life I lead. I wouldn't recommend it to anyone."

Mike nodded, "I think I get it, Garrett."

3

Stan was already in Mike's office when they arrived on Monday morning. He looked up at the two men as they entered the small office and stood. "Morning. Drop your things and let's go up," he said, and walked out to the elevator bay. Once the trio was on the seventh floor, they made their way to the administrator's receptionist, and Stan announced their arrival. A short, pale woman old enough to have retired five or ten years earlier answered him.

"Go on in, they're expecting you." Stan led them into the office of the administrator, which Garrett was already familiar with. Besides the large desk he kept for his own use and the couch that the blood-taking-lady sat on, there was also a circular table with six chairs near the far-right wall, the only one with windows. The couch and the large chair that paired with Jim's desk were empty, and there were three people sitting on one side of the table, Jim seated in the middle.

"Good morning, gentlemen." The three stood up to receive the newcomers. Beside Jim was a tall, thin man with carefully kept white hair, and a woman of thirty-five years with dark brown hair pulled into a bun behind her head. All three wore broad smiles and nodded to the trio.

"Folks, this is Stanley Liang. He's the lead buyer on our acquisitions team and this is one of his excellent employees, Michael Potaglia. And this fine young man is the reason we're here. This is Garrett Rhodes. Our visitor." They nodded and said hello. "Gentlemen, this is Congressman Brian Miller, Chairman of the House Ways and Means Committee, and this is Angela Bissone, from our executive management team. She is present because she oversees all large-scale projects, be it a NASA project or a third party we have an interest in. Everyone, please have a seat." They all sat down at the table, which had a large carafe of ice water and six overturned glasses set upon it. Jim did not produce his notepad.

"Well, Garrett, you were right about the signal, and now it appears you were right about your own DNA. The lab ran eight individual sequences on your blood, and all of them came up inconclusive. They could not identify you as human. This is the moment where everyone at this table except Garrett can get scared. We're facing the possibility that you're the real McCoy, Garrett. But my guess is that you're not surprised at all, are you?" Although Garrett did not know the colloquialism, he could infer its meaning from the context.

"Certainly not, sir," he said. Jim nodded. Garrett noticed he did not glance at either the man or the woman on either side of him.

"So, what's next, then? Where do we go from here? We're still doing some tests, but I expect they'll come back just as inconclusive as the others. So, from my perspective, I'm convinced, and I want to know what the next step is." Stan and Mike were so silent that Garrett wondered if they were even breathing.

"The next step is educating the decision makers and then getting them to make a decision. Will Earth be a 'go' for the Orris project, or will it not be?" Garrett was proud of his use of some NASA lingo he had picked up from watching movies and online videos describing the history of the government body.

"What if the answer is no?" Chairman Miller asked.

"It hasn't happened yet, but if the answer is no, then my next course of action would be to negotiate a deal. I provide you with the theory and the practical means for building a highly effective and efficient flex drive. You commission the construction of a small ship for me. After that, we will shake hands and I will be on my way."

"What the hell is a flex drive?" Miller asked. Jim looked at him.

"It's like an Alcubierre Warp drive." Brian did not look less confused. "It's Star Trek stuff, Brian, but it isn't that important at this point." At that, Angela Bissone gasped. "That's not to say it isn't important, but for our meeting today, we can kick that can down the road."

"There isn't one person who can make that decision, Garrett," Stanley said. "That's not how our country works. We have to bring it before congress. They will vote on it and then it will go to the Senate. If both bodies sign it, it goes to the President. But I suppose the reason Chairman Miller is here is to test the waters in that respect. Am I wrong?" Jim looked up at Stanley.

"No, Stan, that's exactly right." The room went silent, and Brian thought it his turn to ask a question.

"Well, yes. I only have a cursory understanding of what this project would entail, but my first question would be about cost. How much are we talking about and over what period?"

"Well, the exact amount is impossible to say," Garrett said. "But I expect if you fully commit to the project, it will take between fifty and sixty years. The expense would have to be a global effort. No single nation could afford the project on its own, unless it controlled almost all the planet's money."

"We may not be able to afford it on our own, but we could sponsor the effort, and lobby the other nations to commit to its cause," Stan said, and Jim nodded. They both had seen one set of blueprints for the Lance and knew the dollars required would be measured in trillions.

"That sounds like the only realistic option we have. Thank you, Stanley." Jim turned to Brian. "We'll need a sponsor for the bill, and one of us should let the President know what's going on. This would be a hell of a blindside for him if we don't."

Brian laughed. "I guess so. I'll tell you what, I'll get you a sponsor, but before I do, I want you to make a presentation worthy of going before the Committee. I'll review it myself first, and I'll bring along whoever I choose to sponsor the bill. After that, I'll schedule a time you can bring it before the Committee. As far as the President goes, you should call him, Jim. He likes you." Jim nodded and turned to Angela. "I want you to hand your other projects to your staff and assign each a lead. I want your focus to be on this project alone. It will be the biggest project anyone has ever managed."

She smiled. "Absolutely, sir."

Jim then focused on Garrett. "Every Tuesday and Thursday from noon until five. We go that way until the presentation is complete. If we have to add time based on what Brian can do for us, or what the President says, then we will adjust. Garrett, meet me here tomorrow at noon and we will get started. Angela, same thing." He stood up. "Thank you, folks."

4

Three full weeks later, on Tuesday morning, Garrett had received the last signal loop cycle, loaded it into his software, and converted it for general use. Once completed, he closed his laptop and loaded it into a new bag he had purchased for himself. He picked up his phone to send a text message to Becky, as he had promised to notify her when the signal was complete and repeating on all frequencies. To his surprise, he had a text message from Tim.

Tim: Hi Garrett, can you come to the store in the next few days?

Garrett: I can come tomorrow morning, but not before that.

Tim: That's fine. Bring a bag. Tx.

Garrett had gotten used to texting lingo. At first, the only people he had communicated with on his phone were Mike and Becky. Since NASA had accepted the project, he had communicated often with Angela and Jim, as well as the eight others who Jim eventually added to the team to write up the presentation for the House Ways and Means committee.

Bound for another session at NASA with the team, he stepped onto the Metro and realized that he had never sent Becky the message he had intended to. He glanced at the scrolling digital banner in the train and waited for it to display the time… 11:21 a.m. That would put Becky's time at 7:21, as Anchorage was four hours behind EDT. *Not too early,* he decided.

Garrett: Hello, Becky. The stream is complete. Every frequency is now recycling.

Becky: Thanks Garrett, I'll let everyone know they can move on. Will there be a reason to resume monitoring the signal?

Garrett: Yes, but not for about fifty years.

Becky: Lol k

Garrett made his way from the Metro up to the street and to the NASA building. When he walked into the small conference room on the sixth floor that had served as their permanent workspace, he hooked his laptop up to the projector as he had every other day prior. Jim walked in while he was setting up and said, "Are we there yet?" The entire team had been awaiting the last part of the stream, as it included the first half of the blueprints for the Lance and the most current flex drive plans.

"We are. I got the last of it this morning, and it's ready to go."

Jim clapped his hands hard. "Yes!" Almost as though on cue, the others poured into the room just after he said it.

5

The following morning, Garrett woke up after Mike had already left. Wednesday was his off day, so he had a cup of coffee and emptied his laptop bag onto the counter. With his coffee finished, he showered, dressed, slung his empty laptop bag over his shoulder, and went down to the street en route to Tim's place.

Once he arrived, he pulled open the heavy door to hear the familiar bells jingle and find the coin dealer sitting at his computer with a pair of reading glasses on. Tim's face lit up when he saw Garrett.

"Excellent! Garrett, I'm so happy you're here. I have money for you, and it's quite a bit. I was getting nervous keeping it here, even though it was in my safe in the back." Tim was coming around the counter as he talked, and he walked up to the front door and locked it. "Come around back with me." Tim led Garrett behind the counter and through a doorway, ducking to avoid smacking his head on the frame. They were in a tiny office that had no furniture, save for a stool and a wooden plank nailed up to the wall to serve as a long but narrow desk. Above the desk was the safe, built into the wall. It was an old safe, with a dial and tumblers instead of a digital keypad or other advanced form of electronic security. Tim spun the dial back and forth a few times, and when he pulled the handle, the door opened heavily. He withdrew a cardboard box and set it on the board desk before removing the cover. Inside were three stacks of rubber-banded cash.

"See why I told you to bring a bag?" Tim said. He stood up straight, and Garrett lifted one stack out of the box. He felt the weight of it.

"How much is here?" he asked.

"A little over a hundred and thirty grand. I wasn't going to bother you, but after last week, I got nervous when you didn't come in. That's why I contacted you." Garrett shuttled the money into his laptop bag. "If you didn't answer me by this afternoon, I was going to deposit it in my savings account, just so it was safe," Tim said.

Garrett smiled. "Does that account earn interest?"

Tim looked a little guilty. "Well, yeah, but not much, and I figured I was doing you a service by keeping your money safe."

Garrett laughed. "I agree completely, Tim. I was just poking fun at you. I appreciate your effort and your candor." He zipped the bag closed. "So, how many of the coins have you sold? I'm surprised you got that many people into your store in such a short time." It was Tim's turn to laugh.

"Oh, trust me, I didn't. The store is a just a place to hang my hat and keep my inventory. I do 99% of my sales on the internet." He walked past Garrett and back out onto the sales floor. He unlocked the front door and said, "I've sold almost seven hundred coins so far, but honestly, most of that money came from about fifty of them. There are a lot of fairly common coins in the collection you consigned to me, and they're worth about twenty-five dollars, but the rare ones are fun. I can whip up a lot of excitement on the web when I come across a rare one, and then I just let the bidding begin. The number of people out there who collect coins would surprise you, as would how much money they're willing to part with to get the ones they want."

Garrett smiled. That meant that Tim had only sold about a sixth of the coins passed along to him, and Garrett could not imagine needing any more money than what he already had. A safe place to keep it was a different story.

Tim and Garrett said their goodbyes, and as Garrett walked back to the Metro, he called Jim. By Friday, Garrett had a full set of credentials, including a U.S. citizenship, an I.D. card in lieu of a driver's license, and a checking and savings account.

6

The initial meeting and presentation took place the following Wednesday at NASA headquarters. The guests for the meeting were Chairman Miller and his selection for the bill's sponsorship, an older woman who had apparently been a professor at MIT for decades before running for congress. The gray-haired Helen Rigby was short and considerably overweight, the latter causing her movements to be slow and tentative. She was also exceptionally intelligent and easily digested the content of the presentation as quickly as they could throw it at her. Brian struggled with almost all of it. When the presentation was over, Jim, Garrett, and Angela spent another hour discussing the material with Helen and answering all her questions. At the conclusion of the meeting, Garrett felt confident Helen was on board with the proposal, and he felt exceptionally good about her championing it.

Once Helen and Brian left, Garrett turned to Jim. "So, what is the next step?"

Jim pointed toward the door from which the two had just exited. "The ball is in their court now. They will write up the bill and go through a series of steps internally, and they will notify us when they need something. That could be tomorrow or in two months. I really don't know, but I'll call you when they're ready." Garrett shook hands with Jim and Angela and gathered his things. As he made his way out of the conference room, Jim called out after him, "Garrett?" Garrett turned around. "You're not going to leave Washington for any reason, are you?"

Garrett shook his head. "I have no plans to leave, no. But if I need to, I'll let you know first." Jim nodded and waved goodbye.

As Garrett walked down the hallway to the elevator bay, he pulled his phone from his pocket to turn the sound back on. As the screen illuminated, he noticed he had a text message from Mike.

Mike: Hey, we both got tired of waiting. I bought a ticket this morning and I'm on my way to the airport now. Going to Alaska, as you may have guessed. I'll be back Sunday night.

7

Repeatedly in his mind, Mike could see himself and Becky throwing their arms around each other in their first act of physical affection. Reality though, as most people find in the first budding throws of infatuation, often gets in the way.

Not only did he not throw his arms around her when he left the secure area of the airport, he did not even see her. When the small crowd dispersed, he looked around for a sign that would tell him which direction to walk for the baggage claim. Before he found one, he noticed a girl leaning against a bright information kiosk and talking on the phone. The moment he recognized her, she smiled at him and waved. As he approached her, she pointed up at something behind him. It was a sign with an arrow and the words 'Baggage Claim,' printed on it. She walked in that direction and he followed her. He could not help but feel a little cheated out of his moment and wondered who she was talking to that was so important. He did not have to wonder for long, as hearing her side of the conversation revealed it was her mother. Mike thought she was adding the word "Mom" to her sentences just to communicate to him what was going on. As they arrived at the baggage conveyor, he watched for the single bag he had brought. Becky ended the call, with her words acting as a plea to her mother and a half-apology to him.

"Yes, Mom… Yes, he's here. He's been here for five minutes, waiting for me to get off the phone… I know… I know, Mom… I'm hanging up, Mom… yes… love you too, goodbye." She ended the call and closed her eyes. Without opening them, she said, "I'm so sorry."

He laughed. With the moment having passed, he thought diving in for a hug would be awkward. "It's no big deal. I called my folks last night to let them know I was going out of town. When I told them it was to come here to see you, my dad said, 'Go get her, son,' and my mother asked me about four thousand questions. So, yeah, I get it." She laughed, and Mike pointed at a green backpack several yards away on the belt. "That's mine." They waited a few seconds until it arrived, and Mike lifted it up and over his shoulder. She took the hand not occupied with the bag and pulled him toward the exterior doors.

"Follow me!" she said. They reached the door, and as she pushed it open, Mike expected a blast of frigid air. To his surprise, and not thinking about the fact that even though it was Alaska, it was still July, he found the air temperate. Once they were in the parking garage, he was astonished when she pressed a button on her key fob and the taillights of a big Ford F-350 blinked awake. The truck was a deep red with large, thick-treaded tires and a sleek, solid panel tonneau cover. Becky walked up to the back of the truck and dropped the tailgate. "You can put your bag in here. It's clean. I almost never use the bed for anything." Mike placed his bag on the bed, inside the gap between the tailgate and the liner. He inhaled to make a comment about it when she squeezed all the air right back out of him by clamping her arms around him, just above the waist. "Sorry, I've been waiting for a month to hug you," she said. His face lit up with joy, and he hugged her around the shoulders, resting his face gently on top of her head. He relished the scent of her hair, pleasantly familiar from her time with him in D.C. He was in heaven.

She relaxed her grip but did not let go. Mike watched as she tilted her head back with her eyes closed. He may not have had a lot of experience with girls, but he knew she expected to be kissed. He leaned in and kissed her for the first time. When they finished, he lifted his head, and she opened her eyes. "I'm so glad you're here," she said.

He smiled. "Why do you drive a monster truck?"

She burst into laughter, and he joined her. She placed her hand on the back of his neck and pulled him in for another kiss, and said, "My Dad insisted on it. He paid for most of it, too. He was afraid of me moving up here. We're from upstate New York, so it's not like I didn't already know how to drive in the snow, but he wanted me to drive a tank as long as I was up here."

"It makes sense. I think I'd probably do the same thing if it were my daughter," Mike said.

She offered him a half sly, half sarcastic look. "So, you don't think women can take care of themselves?"

Mike was not falling for it. "I think my daughter will take help from her father, whether she likes it or not. Are you saying you don't think a father should do everything he can to help his little girl?"

She smiled and kissed him again. "Touché. Let's get out of this parking garage." They got into the truck and started the hour-long drive back to the small house Becky rented.

8

Mike woke up on Becky's couch the next morning to find her sitting on the far end, in her pajamas, eating a bowl of cereal and watching the news on her small TV. She glanced over at him as he sat up and smiled.

"Oh, I thought you were dead," she said.

Mike shook his head and smiled. "Did you drug me?"

She laughed. "No, but I'm surprised you made it from the truck to the couch. That's a long flight. It takes a lot out of you."

He rubbed his face. "What time is it?"

She looked at her watch. "8:00 here, noon in D.C. Do you want coffee?"

He nodded emphatically. "A thousand times, yes."

She got up and went into the kitchen. "Are you hungry?"

"No, just the coffee would be perfect." A moment later, she was handing him a mug with a thin crown of steam dissipating off the top. He sipped it, and a look of surprise washed over his face. "Wow, this is fantastic!" He took another sip.

"I remembered you drink it black, not even any sugar. I tried to find the brand you have at your place, but I couldn't, so I asked around."

He finished the cup and smiled again. "Thank you, it was a big success." He tilted his head down, staring into his empty cup until she laughed.

"It's in the pot. The first one was on me, but you can get your own coffee from now on." He stood and walked into the kitchen. Mike heard his phone chime and thought he heard Becky's chime at almost the same time.

"Oh, you have got to be kidding me," she said. Mike poured his second cup of coffee and walked back into the small living room.

"What's going on?" he asked, as he sat back down on the couch.

She pointed at his phone. "You got it too…" she said, exasperated. Mike picked up his phone and could see it was from Garrett, a group text between the three of them. As he read the text, Becky's phone rang.

Garrett: Hey guys, I wanted to warn you, they want Becky back in D.C. for the hearing. It's on Monday. I had nothing to do with it.

"Hello?" Becky said into her phone. "Yes, sir. Yes, Garrett told me. I understand. Thank you, I'll make the arrangements. Yes, I'll keep a record. No, sir, not mad, a little frustrated, but that's life, right? No, sir, I wouldn't want to miss it. Okay, goodbye, sir," she said, and ended the call. "This is just Murphy's Law. Can you believe it?"

"It's a pisser," he said, secretly happy that he would have her company for the flight back.

As though she had read his mind, "Well, at least we'll be together for the flight back. Count your blessings, not your problems, right?" Mike smiled. He had never heard the expression but instantly liked it.

"Yeah. And as long as you're comfortable with the idea, you won't need a hotel room. Just stay with me and Garrett."

She frowned. "Where would I sleep?" Mike blushed hard, and she erupted into laughter.

"It's so easy with you, Mike! I'm sorry." She kissed him. That being the first time she got so close to him that morning, he grew self-conscious and asked her to show him to the bathroom so he could brush his teeth. She laughed and led him down a short hall and into her bedroom. On the opposite wall was an open door he could see was the single bathroom in the tiny house.

They spent the morning watching television and poking fun at those on the TV and at each other. Becky took him to a diner for lunch and while they were waiting for their food, a look of discovery appeared on her face. "Wait, Mike. We have to ask Garrett if it's okay that I stay with the two of you next week. What if it makes him uncomfortable?" she asked.

Mike smirked. "What? Why? He won't care. He's a guy. Guys never care about that stuff."

Her concern did not disappear. "He's a guy from a different planet. Maybe not exactly like every other guy on Earth," she said, and the waitress put their lunch in front of them. They both thanked her.

"I'll bet you lunch that he doesn't care," Mike said.

She met his gaze and said, "Deal. Ask him." Mike wiped his mouth and picked up his phone. He dialed Garrett and turned the speaker on. Garrett picked up on the third ring.

"Hello, Mike."

"Hey, next week, Becky is going to stay with us instead of getting a hotel room. Is that okay with you?"

"Sure," Garrett said. "But where is she going to sleep?" Confusion washed over Mike's face a split second before Becky burst into laughter, and he knew it was a setup. "You kids have fun," Garrett said, and hung up.

Becky wiped tears from her eyes. "I got the idea when you were brushing your teeth, and I texted Garrett. You're right, he's just a normal guy. Alien or not."

"Well, you two are hilarious," Mike said, and smiled. He also thought it was rather funny. "Even more hilarious is that I was right. You have to pay for lunch." She rolled her eyes and smiled.

For the rest of the afternoon, they drove into Anchorage and went to a large shopping mall called the Dimond Center. They perused the stores and talked about but decided against seeing a movie. After a brief discussion, they left to head back closer to where Becky lived and get dinner at a pub there.

They each ordered a burger at the pub, and after they had finished eating, they played darts. By the time they left, it was after eight o'clock, and Mike noticed it was still bright and shining daylight. The sun wasn't even threatening to go down. He understood the mechanics of the earth and the seasons and even understood the sun would not set until after eleven o'clock, but it was the first time he had witnessed it for himself.

Once back at the house, as they walked toward the front door, Becky blindsided him. "Can you believe this is the first night we're going to sleep together?" Mike stopped cold and flushed red, something he was getting used to while he was with Becky.

"Are you ready for that?" he asked.

She recalled the words she had just said and flushed herself. "Oh, crap! That's not what I meant. I meant actually sleep, like, in the same bed." Mike smiled awkwardly and hugged her, which also felt awkward, but he did it anyway. They went into the house and watched TV for a long time.

With both of them dressed for sleep, teeth brushed, contacts out, and in bed together for the first time, Mike accidentally touched her leg with his hand as he was getting comfortable. Upon feeling the touch, she leaned in to kiss him. Forty-five minutes later, they were both sound asleep, and Becky was pregnant with the first of their five eventual children.

9

Garrett sat in front of his laptop, his eyes fixed on the folder that read "T1-Rhodes." Everything in that folder was old. It had been old for billions of years by that point. Although the total time elapsed in his own mind was only perhaps twenty years, ages upon ages had passed since any of the sentiments in the messages there corresponded to anyone living. His gaze traced the folder icon, and he reread the name affixed to it a hundred or two hundred times before he ultimately got up and abandoned the effort. As he did, his shifting weight levered his finger on the mouse button in what must have registered as a double click, and it flooded his screen with thumbnails. In the same motion, he turned away, but the thumbnail images caught his eye and a small photo of his mother registered completely in his mind. He sat back down. Sitting still and leaning on the island, he stared fixedly at one of his shoes in the short hallway leading to the front door of the apartment. The shoe was meaningless. It was just a point in space at a comfortable distance upon which to fix his gaze while he remembered. Several times during his trip into his mental history, his binocular vision gave up, and he saw two identical right shoes.

He shook his head to snap himself out of it. Still with his back to the laptop screen, he decided. *Tonight is the night,* he thought, *but not without beer. A lot of it.* He picked up his phone off the couch and called one of the two places he knew of that would deliver beer in addition to food. He ordered a burger and fries and three six-packs of Clotz's ale.

"Sounds like a hell of a party," the burger shop employee, who had identified himself as Jeremy, said. Garrett laughed but did not reply. "It'll be about 45 minutes."

"Thank you." Garrett ended the call. Without thinking about it, he glanced at his laptop and was happy to see the screen had turned off to conserve power. He placed his phone on the island and returned to the couch to watch television until his order arrived. Nothing on television interested him, but a commercial about a cruise line triggered his memory of crossing the Atlantic on the *Amerique* all those years ago. He had never finished the book that Jacques had given him. He stood and walked into his room where he had laid the book on his nightstand but otherwise had not touched since arriving in D.C. Seated on the couch, he opened to the place he left off. As was his habit, he reread the previous page to reacquaint himself with the position of the story before he dove deeper into it. He read until his food and beer arrived, while he ate his burger, and while he drank beer, purposely leaving the empty bottles on the coffee table as an indicator of how many he had drank. Only after there were six empty bottles would he watch the content that his family and friends had made for him. It would make him more emotional, but it would also dampen the impact of the experience. When he reached that point, he gathered his six empty bottles, rinsed them, and placed them in the recycling bin.

With the seventh beer in hand, he sat down at his laptop. He touched the mouse gently, just enough to wake the computer up, and noticed his heart was pounding. After a deep breath, he sorted the files by date, thinking it would be utter chaos if he did not go in clear historical order through the messages. The first one featured both of his parents, and once he opened the file, he could see that the videos each had a date stamp and a timer. They recorded the first video the same day he had launched. The two sat on chairs in front of what looked like a gray sheet hanging from its long edge to create a solid background. The video was moving for Garrett, as he had not heard the voices of his parents in twenty years, and it lasted about twelve minutes. He did not scan the thumbnails, he simply clicked the next one, and the next one, using his peripheral vision. The first four were from either both of his parents, or from just his mother. The fifth one was Breni and Rodney with little one-year-old Rodney Junior bouncing on his father's leg and smiling. He was apprehensive about the sixth. As he double clicked the thumbnail, not looking directly at it, he knew. He registered the deep auburn of Lauren's hair in the tiny picture, and then her face filled his screen. His heart dropped, crushing into his stomach and making him feel sick. His eyes welled with tears so completely that her image blurred out of view almost as abruptly as it had displayed. He blinked rapidly through the whole video to clear them of the film, which would not stop coming. He could see a small smile on her mouth but deep sadness in her eyes.

"Hi, slouch. I'm sorry I waited almost four months to make the first of these videos, but it was for a reason." She looked tired. She wiped away a tear from one eye, but it was for naught, as they kept coming and the emotion rose in her voice. "I know… that you know." She looked down at the floor and cried. Finally, she looked back up, but not at the camera. She was looking at something, or someone, beyond the camera.

"How long do I have before I have to stop?"

Faintly, in the background, he could hear a man's voice say, "You're his wife, Mrs. Rhodes. Spouses and children do not have a limit." Lauren smiled at that and nodded. Garrett relished the happiness on her face, however brief it was. He was curious to find out if she would correct him, because her official prefix was "doctor," but she did not. She turned her attention back to the camera.

"Before you left, on your launch day, when you were in the transport waiting on the countdown," Garrett did not need her to recount it for him. The memory was so seared in his mind that he had only to close his eyes and recall every detail of those moments. "You held up both of your index fingers, kissed one and then the other, and blew them both to me. I knew in that moment that my deep suspicion was not a secret to you." She looked back up at the man. "Would you mind turning around for a moment? It won't take long, I would just like a moment alone with my husband."

"Of course, Mrs. Rhodes." She stared in the same direction for another second, and then looked back at the camera and stood. She was wearing a light, blue cotton skirt with an elastic waist and loose and light white button-down top. Garrett watched as she unbuttoned her shirt, starting from the bottom and working her way through half of the buttons before pulling the two halves apart like drapes and revealing her naked and clearly pregnant belly. Almost as soon as she had revealed the product of their love, she refastened the buttons, leaned back down to the camera without retaking her seat, and blew a kiss into it.

"I'll be back soon, slouch. I love you, no matter how far away you are." She stood so he could no longer see her face, just the re-clothed surface of her belly. "Ok, sir, I'm done for this one." One second later, the image froze. He spent his eighth and ninth beers watching that one video repeatedly. On the sixteenth viewing, he paused the video as she revealed her swollen mid-section. He dragged the tips of his fingers over the screen.

10

When Mike woke up, he was instantly aware of two things. First, he was naked under the covers of Becky's bed, and second, she was too, and his arm still rested on her waist. He could not believe that the awkward events of the previous night had concluded with them making love for the first time. She stirred under his arm and rolled over to face him. Based on her apparent mood and the smile on her face, Mike concluded that she had no apprehensions.

They showered, dressed, and moved to the kitchen to have coffee and breakfast. With Becky's bowl of cereal and Mike's large cup of coffee complete and set on the coffee table before the television, they tuned in to the news and watched with interest. Since the announcement of the hearing with the House Ways and Means Committee, information had leaked to the press, and it was all the national news wanted to talk about. Mike and Becky watched the news as though it were a comedy, laughing at the massive exaggerations and the complete lack of understanding of the events that had led up to the hearing. The speculation was the part they found so funny; at one point, Mike rolled off of the couch laughing, which made Becky laugh even harder. When he got control of himself, he said, "So, I guess they're holding Garrett in Area 51. What a surprise it would be if they found out he was hanging out in an apartment in D.C. Probably watching TV and eating a breakfast burrito!" They both burst into another fit of laughter.

11

Garrett never made it past the first video featuring Lauren the night before and woke up hung over and miserable. As the morning stretched into the afternoon and after several cups of coffee and even more glasses of water, he began to feel normal again. He laid on the couch until two o'clock. Boredom took over, accompanied by a deep hunger. He decided to travel to his favorite diner and order his favorite breakfast.

After finishing his breakfast at three in the afternoon, he strode back to the Metro. As he approached his building, he felt well enough to continue his efforts from the previous night and diverted to the gas station a half a block up. He purchased two twelve packs of Clotz's ale and hauled them back to the apartment. While he walked, he thought about Lauren and their baby. The knowledge that their lives had already long ago come to a close was painful, but he was happy to know for the first time that he had a child. He hoped that he or she had achieved all the dreams they could have imagined, and he was happy knowing he would find out at least the beginning of the story that night.

Later, with his dinner ordered and already four beers deep into his adventure, he started the videos again. Like the night previous, the first four were of his mother, sometimes accompanied by his father. His mother was so excited about the baby he thought she might claim it as her own.

The fifth video was heart-wrenching. Garrett's mother and Lauren had budded an amiable and lasting friendship, and in the fifth film clip, the two were together in a hospital room with Lauren so pregnant that he thought she might burst. She laid on her back in the hospital bed with Cynthia there, clasping Lauren's right hand in both of hers. Cynthia wiped the hair off of Lauren's sweaty forehead and leaned over to kiss it. Garrett's eyes stung with tears.

"That should have been me," he whispered to himself. He could hear his father talking but couldn't make out what he was saying. The camera angle swung to a heavily padded olive-green chair in which his sister sat, bouncing the one-and-a-half-year-old Rodney Junior. After focusing for only a moment on his sister, the camera view swung back to Lauren, who hauntingly addressed Garrett.

"Hey, slouch… I'm doing this for you. I love you, you idiot." She was obviously under a great deal of stress, and two or three seconds later lapsed into what must have been terribly strong contractions.

He heard his father clearly then. "Doctor!" he yelled. A short, bald man entered the room and kneeled beside Lauren, whispering to her.

She nodded emphatically and yelled, "Yes!" The doctor stood up and addressed the room.

"The baby is coming. Please, only her parents and husband should be present for the delivery." The announcement sent Lauren into a fit of hysterics.

Cynthia came to her aid, "I'm her mother," she told the doctor, "Everyone else out!" A voice came booming through the computer speakers. It was big Rodney, and Garrett realized that he had been doing the filming all along.

"Cyn, do you want this?" the camera angle flailed wildly for a few seconds until his mother took it from her son-in-law and pointed it at Lauren's stressed face.

"Nurse!" the doctor yelled, and then Garrett heard him ordering the delivery team to assist him.

His mother fixed the image on Lauren's face, and she was breathing fast, shallow breaths. Another round of contractions. The doctor yelled louder and the pain in Lauren's face melted a part of Garrett's soul that he thought he may never regain. A moment after it passed, he witnessed Lauren snatching up Cynthia's free hand in both of hers and clenching it tightly to her breast. A devastating sadness formed on Lauren's face as she plead to Cynthia, "I want him here! Why isn't he here!"

He heard his mother sob and say, "I'm sorry, baby." Lauren was trapped between screaming and crying. Garrett never expected to know what it felt like to have his entire heart and soul crushed.

Faintly, in the background, he could hear the doctor, "I need you to push, sweetie." Lauren wailed, and the view from the camera dropped into the blankets and effective darkness. Only audio from that point forward.

"I need him!" Lauren screamed.

"I know, angel," his mother said.

"Push!" the doctor yelled. Screams from Lauren, sounds of encouragement from his mother.

"Push!" the doctor yelled again. More screams and then immediate crying from Lauren. A longer and gentler stream of sweet and soothing words from his mother that he could not make out.

"You're close! One more! PUSH!" the bald doctor yelled. Lauren screamed so loud that Garrett thought the camera vibrated, and just as he thought he could take no more of the anguish, he heard a new sound. A tiny but loud cry that seemed to ripple and echo inside of the camera microphone.

"Yes!" the doctor yelled. He heard all the life go out of Lauren in one exhausted exhale, with his mother consoling her. The increasingly loud cries of his child were followed by loud scratching sounds. The video flashed back to life as his mother picked up the camera and pointed it toward the swollen, wet, beet-red face of his and Lauren's baby.

"Mrs. Rhodes? It's a girl, sweetie."

He heard his mother laugh, and then Lauren in a rough whisper, as though all the life had been beaten out of her. "Thank you."

Commotion as they tended the immediate needs of the baby, and then an unrecognized female voice said, "We will get her cleaned up and we'll be right back with her, okay?" Lauren made no reply, but Cynthia said "yes," and thanked her.

"Garrett, I need a few minutes with my sweet girl, we'll be back in a minute." The video ended. He furiously pounded the mouse button to start the next one. It opened with Lauren asleep. He could hear his mother's voice, but she centered the image on his exhausted wife's face.

"Hey Gar, she did great, and you have a beautiful baby girl." The camera image flipped and focused on his mother's face. "I love you, sweetheart. I'm sure it's hard for you to watch this, but I want you to know that your wife is my daughter, and your baby is my baby. I will sacrifice everything to make sure they are safe, happy, and healthy. Your dad will, too." The video snapped off at that point, and he again clicked on the next installation.

The next video started on Lauren's face again, but she was awake with the remnants of tears in her eyes. Her hair was a mess, and her swollen face was without makeup, but Garrett found her beautiful. He missed her deeply. Knowing he could never see her, kiss her, or touch her again carved out his very core. As he wallowed in his not-so-newfound misery, he heard an unfamiliar female voice.

"Mrs. Rhodes? Here she is! All pretty and ready to snuggle with Mommy!" The nurse held an impossibly small bundle out and gently laid it on Lauren's chest. Garrett witnessed her expression go from half-dead, to excited, to satisfied, to sleepy in only five or six seconds. With her eyes closed, she kissed their little girl all over her face. Garrett paused the video and broke down again.

Once recovered, he resumed the video. Lauren looked at Cynthia, and it was apparent that Rodney had resumed the filming duties, as he could see both women in full view.

"I can't ask Garrett, so I'll ask you. What do we name her?"

Cynthia did not break down, but the resolution on the screen was good enough that Garrett could see the tears coursing down his mother's cheeks. "Sweetie, that's not for me to decide."

Lauren seemed no more emotional than Cynthia had, but tears formed in her eyes as well.

Garrett then heard another female voice on the audio track of the video. "Oh no! I was too late?" It was Denise, Lauren's older sister. Lauren smiled at her, and Denise walked to the bed and kissed her sister's cheek. "Oh!!!" She took the baby from Lauren and rocked her in her arms.

"We're talking about what we should name her. It's important, and I can't get an answer out of her father." Everyone in the room chuckled. "So, what then?"

"We should name her after you, or Garrett, I don't know," Alan trailed off. Rodney zoomed in on the faces of Cynthia and Lauren.

"It's your decision, hon, think about Garrett and what he might have wanted, think about what you want, and if you can't come up with anything right now, that's fine, too. You have a day or so to decide," Cynthia said.

"I want to name her for her father, but Garrett is an awful name for a cute little girl." A flutter of laughter went through the room before the booming voice of Rodney-the-camera-bearer slammed through the speakers again.

"What about Hope? I like that name for a little girl. It's just a suggestion." Garrett smiled a split second before he saw the same exaggerated smile form on the face of his former wife. Lauren nodded emphatically, and Cynthia smiled.

"I love it!" Lauren said. "Thank you, Rod! It's perfect. I love it." She held out both of her arms to him and the camera view approached her and then passed her as the cameraman embraced his wife's sister-in-law.

Garrett paused the video once again. He was married to Lauren, and they had a daughter named Hope. He had a family. It was devastating. The last part of the video was just doting over the baby. Garrett did not re-watch any of the preceding videos but watched the part of the video with his daughter featured fifty or sixty more times. He drank more beer, got more and more drunk and therefore more and more emotional, and eventually passed out on the kitchen floor.

12

Later that weekend, on Sunday night, Mike and Becky walked into the apartment to find an emotionally drained Garrett laying lifeless on the couch.

"What the hell happened to you?" Mike said as they dropped their bags.

Garrett sat up and rubbed his face. "My comms, I've been watching them for the last few days." Mike and Becky looked at each other briefly and then back to Garrett.

"Do you want to talk about any of it?" Becky asked. The two new arrivals took off their shoes, and Mike emptied his pockets.

"No," Garrett said. "Not tonight. I imagine the two of you are pretty exhausted, anyway."

"Yes, we are. But we won't have time to talk in the morning. We have to be at Capitol Hill by nine," Mike said.

"There is no rush. I have barely scratched the surface compared to how much there is to watch and listen to." The exhaustion on his face momentarily melted away, and he smiled. "I had a daughter." Becky jumped, startled because her assumption was right. "She was so cute. I haven't heard anything from her yet. I'm only up to where she is an infant, and each new comm from Lauren is a struggle that ends up consuming my entire night." Although ending on a sour note, his mood appeared to have improved, and it showed on his face and entire body as he stood. "It's good to see you guys again." He hugged Becky and shook Mike's hand.

"Well, Garrett," Mike said. "It feels kind of rude now, but I think we're going to turn in."

"No problem at all. What time should we leave here tomorrow?" Garrett asked. Mike looked at his watch, as though that could help him answer the question.

"We have to be on the road by eight. Capitol Hill isn't far, but traffic is always murder. I can drop you two off, and then I'll probably spend another hour looking for a place to park," Mike said, visibly irritated. Garrett glanced at Becky. She was still standing, but her eyes were closed.

"Go," he said. "You two go to bed. It's 8:30 now so you have plenty of time to sleep and recuperate from your flight."

"Okay, Gar. Night," Mike said, and placed his hand on the small of Becky's back, which brought her back around. She smiled and walked toward Mike's bedroom.

"Good night, Garrett," she mumbled, and disappeared through the door.

13

They had written the bill in only three days. It left a lot of questions unanswered, and they left entire sections vague on purpose. Part of the reason was that there were a massive number of unknowns, at least to the bill's team of authors. Also, because they knew that if they used too many specifics, it would confuse almost everybody. They used little high-level scientific language, as it would all require explanation within the bill for general consumption. The bill itself, although it represented the largest project ever attempted in the history of humanity, was brief.

Mike dropped Garrett and Becky off close to a walking path leading up to the entrance of the grand building. Becky took Garrett's hand. She made it known she was nervous. Garrett had made it crystal clear that he had done this kind of thing many times before and was not nervous at all.

They went through security and followed one of the staff members to the House chamber. They finally saw Jim Lambert. He waved them to the witness table, where he was standing with his lead project manager, Angela Bissone.

The hearing started fifteen minutes later and lasted for two hours and forty-five minutes. Several times during the questioning, Garrett got frustrated and Becky would lean over and whisper to him, either words of encouragement or pleas for patience. Two things surprised Garrett: First, the number of educated, intelligently thought-out, and well-framed questions, which he delighted in answering; second, the number of questions that were so stupid and ill-informed it was as though a toddler were asking them. The latter were the ones that typically drew Becky's pleas for patience.

They got through it, and the day after, Becky left for Alaska without Mike, which hurt the two of them deeply. NASA hired Garrett full time to start the groundwork for the Lance and all the other associated projects to get the large-scale mission rolling. Jim made the decision after talking to Chairman Miller and Representative Rigby. The apparent chatter throughout the entire house was one of excitement, devoid of any partisan politics, and they thought it would pass the House, at least, easily.

"We'll have another hearing before the entire body, but I don't think it would be inappropriate for you to get started now," Brian had said. "I doubt we'll be able to get you in for another month, anyway. You may as well not waste that month." Jim had agreed with him and called Garrett right after to arrange the full-time employment of his services.

After two weeks working with the newly commissioned "Lance 5" team, Garrett boarded the Metro to find he had a voicemail. He always turned his phone's sound off while he was at work and always turned it back on when he was on the train. The train and street were loud, so he opted to wait until he was in the comfort of his apartment to listen to it.

Voicemail: "Hi, Garrett? This is Tim, um, McInnis. I've had excellent luck selling your coins. The cash in the shoebox just stopped working weeks ago, and I haven't seen you. I have accurate records of what I owe you, but I have deposited it into my bank account to get the cash out of the store. When you're ready to pick it up, can you call me first? I'll get a cashier's check for you. It's much safer that way. Okay, Garrett, thanks, I'll talk to you soon."

Garrett laughed. The last time he had seen Tim, he had received $130,000 in cash. He opened a bank account two days later, depositing $90,000 in a savings account and $40,000 in a checking account and had used little of it. He laughed because he could not imagine what the new total was up to if Tim felt the need to get it out of his store.

As a courtesy, he called Tim on his lunch break the next day. Tim told him not to worry about coming in for the check unless he needed the money, as he had many auctions going that had not yet closed. "If you get the check now, I'm just going to owe you more the next day," he said. "But it's totally up to you. Just let me know what you want to do." It was Tuesday, and they agreed to wait out the rest of the week. Garrett would go in on Saturday to pick up a check so that Tim's books would balance, and Garrett could invest the money.

That Saturday morning, Garrett walked into Tim's store and up to the counter. Tim looked up from his phone and greeted him. "Well! Hello there, millionaire!" Tim said. Garrett smiled and shook his head. He had thought it might be a lot, but not that much. Tim opened the register drawer and withdrew a cashier's check. Before handing it to Garrett, he dramatically sniffed it and said, "Whoa! Smells like a lot of money here." Tim handed him the check. Garrett looked at the amount, shocked: $1,408,619.13.

"You know what the amazing part is, Garrett?" Tim said. "I haven't even sold half of them yet! And just on this check that I gave you, I made more than I did last year, more money in a month than an entire year!"

Garrett stayed with Tim for another hour, asking him questions about money: how to keep it, how to invest it, and most importantly, how to protect it. It was a fruitful conversation by Garrett's measure.

14

Three more weeks passed, and an exhausted Becky walked into the apartment with Mike, who had picked her up again from the airport. She looked like death warmed over.

"Hey, Garrett," she said.

Garrett walked to her and hugged her. "I know this is tough on you, but it is really nice to see you again."

She smiled at him and brightened a little. "Well, this time will be better. I'm here for two weeks. No more of this two-day crap." The bill was going before the house as a body, and Jim had called her back once again in case they required her presence. "And the bill isn't going up for another three days, so I'm on vacation now." She walked into Mike's bedroom with her bag.

"Beer or booze?" Garrett asked Mike.

"Beer is fine. I don't want to drink too much tonight, she's going to sleep early and will get up early, and I'd like to get up with her." Garrett handed him a beer, and they clinked bottle necks.

After dinner, the trio sat around the freshly cleaned kitchen island talking about the events that had occurred since they were all together last. Becky's eyelids were heavy, and it was no surprise to either Garrett or Mike when she announced she was going to bed. Mike and Garrett talked and drank beer for another two hours, and then Mike turned in, too.

Alone in his apartment again, Garrett had drunk a sufficient amount of beer to return to his comms. Over the last five weeks, he had watched many of them, but any time

Lauren had made one with their little baby girl, he would watch it over and over again without moving on. On that night, he watched one from his mother and then he opened the next chronological video. It contained Lauren, but without the baby. She sat there with a small smile on her face, staring behind the camera. Finally, she nodded and looked into the camera lens. "Garrett, I've waited over a year to make this video, and it will be a hard one for you to hear," she said. After only her first spoken word, his own name, he knew it would be a grave message, and probably bad news. She never called him by his given name. It was always "Slouch."

"I asked everyone in your family to let me be the one to bring you this news, and I warned them it would be a long time before I would, for good reason. I wanted to have all the information and all the answers before I told you. With all of that said, and now that the official investigation has been closed, I can tell you that four days after you left, Terry Stone died." The breath went out of Garrett as though someone had kicked him in the chest.

"I was there when it happened," she continued, with more emotion in her voice. "The transport went up, but the rockets didn't fire." There were tears in her eyes, but she wiped at them, shook her head, and appeared to get herself under control. "They determined that one of the large bolts that held the bumper pads in place on the track came loose and rattled out. They think you must have just missed the bolt when you launched. When Terry's transport passed over it, it destroyed all the proximity sensors that could have triggered the rockets, and it also damaged the…" She picked up a stack of papers and read through a part of the top page. "It also damaged the SLO-4 rocket, rendering it inoperable." She set the papers down and breathed for a moment before continuing.

"I think I know the rest without having to look at the report. After he hit the bolt, it didn't just destroy the sensors and the rocket, but it hit the transport itself. When that happened, the transport became unnaturally wedged into the carriage. The command center fired the other three rockets manually to disengage the transport from the carriage so Terry could deploy the parachute, but it didn't work. They were mechanically fused together. The escaping gas from the rockets came out at wild angles. It created a spin, and…" She trailed off for a moment, staring underneath the camera. Without looking up, she said, "They think the centripetal force killed him." She looked back up but did not talk right away. She stared into the camera for several seconds. A tear formed in her eye and rolled down her cheek. "I could see it spinning from the ground." She wiped the tear away. "There's one more thing, unfortunately. I think he felt responsible, even though he shouldn't have. It wasn't his fault. Jack killed himself that same night. Jack Abbott. He hanged himself." She sat upright, sniffled, and wiped both of her eyes again. "I'm sorry, Gar, I love you so much. I'll be back tomorrow with Hope for a happier visit. I love you." She nodded at the camera operator and the image froze.

It was another night-ending comm for Garrett. He did not watch it again, but sat on the couch for another half hour, reminiscing about Jonroe, Terry, and Dr. Abbott and how their lives had each met their different, but equally tragic, ends.

15

The house passed the bill with overwhelming support. Only twenty-eight representatives dissented, with five abstentions. The Senate received the bill, and it went to a vote only five days later. It passed 93-7. The president signed it enthusiastically the day after, to a great deal of fanfare and ceremony. It was from that moment on, that Garrett had a small team of secret service assigned to him.

The United States pledged 30 trillion dollars over fifty-two years for the project and agreed to manage it through NASA. The U.S. would also have a team deployed around the globe to stump for support, both financially and for resources from the other resource-rich countries of the world. Garrett would be a member of that team and travel the whole of the planet with them, including nostalgic trips to both France and Italy.

In the evening, three days after the president signed the bill into law, and the day before Becky would fly back to Alaska, she emerged from the bathroom, walked to where Mike was sitting on the couch and whispered to him. Mike stood up and announced to Garrett that they would go out for a bit. Garrett nodded but said nothing.

She had whispered, "It's my last night here. Take a girl out for a drink!" When they got to the bar, she asked to sit at a small two-top table in the back corner, but near to the bar. Mike asked her what she wanted to drink, and she told him to get her a soda. He could get scotch and she would drive them back. He did so, and when they finally sat across from each other with their drinks, she dropped the bomb.

"I'm sorry to do this to you this way," she said. Mike thought she was breaking up with him. His heart dropped in his chest so hard he thought it was more than just a figure of speech. He broke into a sweat before she could even get the next word out. "Mike, I've been on the pill since I was nineteen, but I'm almost one hundred percent sure that I'm pregnant." Mike's emotions flipped so chaotically that he was not even sure what was happening. It finally dawned on him, having not fully absorbed the implications of them expecting: she *was not* breaking up with him. He said nothing, just sat there with a slack jaw, staring at her.

"A few weeks after you left Alaska with me, I missed a period. I got a pregnancy test off the shelf and it was positive, but you can never trust those things, so I made an appointment with my doctor to get a blood test. Before the appointment, Jim called me back here to D.C., so I had to cancel it. Mike, I missed another period, and I got another test from the drugstore, I did it just before asking you to take me here, and it was positive." Mike did not speak. He had a small smile on his face, and he was gazing into her eyes. "I went from being sure that it was a mistake to not being sure, to being almost certain it's true. Please tell me what you're thinking, this is killing me."

The small smile never disappeared from Mike's face, but he sat back in his chair and rocked his head back, looking at the ceiling. When he looked back at her, he had a pleasant, serene look on his face, the exact opposite of what Becky had expected. "I think that is wonderful," Mike said. "I understand that I'm only twenty-three and probably not ready to be a father yet, but I'm crazy about you, Beck. This doesn't seem like a devastating blow to me. I thought you brought me here to break up with me!"

The look of surprise on her face temporarily broke the trauma of the almost-certain pregnancy. She smiled and got off her stool to walk around their small table and kissed him. "No! No, no, no, no! I love you, Mike!" They kissed and hugged.

"So, in that case, will you marry me?" Mike asked. Becky's face flushed a hard-red color. She had thought it was possible that he might ask her that question when he discovered the pregnancy, but she thought it was a long shot. She was not sure how to answer. In her heart, she wanted to shout "yes," but the realities of their world crept into her thoughts.

"Is that smart? What… what would we do? I don't know, Mike, I don't know what to do," she said, struggling.

"Let me change the question a little. Do you, right now, *want* to marry me?"

The tension in her face melted away, and she burst into a bright smile. "Yes!"

"So, what we have is this: forget the pregnancy for a minute. I know it's important, but please hear me out. I want to marry you, and you want to marry me. Aren't the rest just details that we have to figure out?"

Her smile grew even wider, and she kissed him again. "Yeah, I guess so."

"So how about we do this for now: no commitments tonight, but we should start talking about how we could make it work in the real world, even if I have to become an Alaskan lumberjack." She laughed and nodded.

16

Mike and Becky's eventual solution to their problem was sloppy and even reckless. The solution was to get married, have a baby, and Becky would quit her job and move into the apartment with Mike. Becky was betting on her ability to get a job in the same building as Mike after the baby was old enough to go to daycare. Until then, they both had good credit and credit cards with high limits. They both knew Garrett planned to leave for his time-jump well before any of that would happen, so his presence would not be a problem.

Garrett had gone around the world with the NASA team over the course of three months and was able to help secure support from other nations totaling $78 trillion over the 52-year construction forecast. The commitments also included raw materials from China, India, Russia, Mongolia, South Africa, Australia, and thirty-one other nations, which the project depended on.

When Garrett got back to the U.S., he traveled with Jim Lambert to the three sites where they were building the rail launch systems. One in Texas, one in Arizona, and the heavy launch system built in Florida. When the first three visits were complete, they toured the four plants building the parts of the Lance. One each in Colorado, Michigan, Toronto, and Georgia. The progress pleased Garrett, and he had only one other trip scheduled before he prepared to go down… his bunker. The bunker they had made for him was in Virginia, and it would be the first time he would go under on Earth with complete confidence he would be safe for the duration of his sleep. It was a concrete structure, built almost like a pyramid but with a dome at the top, and it was climate controlled and sealed off from the environment. The only things in the single room it contained were a bed and a toilet, as Garrett had requested. Armed guards would surround the bunker for the duration of the time he was under.

For the next month, he reviewed the plans with the teams at NASA. The build team; the newly formed Acquisition team, which was studying documents drafted by his wife and translated to English by himself and a language-learning application courtesy of Osa; and the equally new team set up to put together the operations curriculum for the unborn operators of the Lance. Lauren's calculations pinned Earth's Lance population number at one-third capacity, as it would be a heavily multigenerational flight. It would include a "one to one" law internally in the Lance, meaning an individual could only have two children, one for each partner. The extra room in the Lance was there for generational layering.

Garrett felt good about the progress on Earth and decided to go under so he could reach the finalization of the project. He met with Jim and all the project heads to make the announcement, and they all wished him well. When he got home the night before he had scheduled himself to go under, he hugged Mike and made a forty-minute phone call to Becky to bid her farewell. He apologized no less than five times for not being able to attend their wedding and promised that he had a special wedding gift that would arrive on their wedding day.

He cleaned Tim out again, added the money to his stash, and signed off on the papers making Tim the full legal owner of anything left over from Garrett's original consignment. Tim hugged him. He ended up making over

$400,000 from the gift over a six-year period, as selling the coins became more and more difficult.

 Finally, with his belongings packed in a brand-new bag, he made his way to the bunker. He shook the hand of the guard stationed outside the single entrance point, walked into the concrete structure, and put himself under for approximately fifty years.

17

Mike and Becky's ceremony was beautiful. They married in Maryland, in Mike's hometown. The wedding did not set any attendance records, but their families were there. Becky's parents had traveled down from upstate New York, and some of the most important players in their lives had traveled from Washington. All but one. Garrett was absent and would be so for around fifty more years. Becky could not imagine seeing Garrett again when she was seventy-five years old, but she knew it was possible.

 The reception was in the same facility as the ceremony, and when it was coming to a close, Jim Lambert approached the couple and offered his hand to Mike, who shook it.

 "What a beautiful wedding, guys. Congratulations. I'm afraid I have to get home to my children, but I have something for you." He removed a tiny, gift-wrapped box from the pocket of his jacket, about the size of two match boxes stacked upon one another. "My gift to you both is on the table with the others, and don't worry, it's just a check." He held the tiny box up so they could examine it. "This is Garrett's wedding gift to the two of you. He asked me to deliver it to you personally." Becky took the small box from Jim and smiled. "Good night, kids." Jim nodded and headed for the exit.

Becky looked at Mike, "Oh my God, Mike! I want to open it right now!"

Mike winced. "I think that might be a little tacky. You don't typically open wedding gifts in front of the guests, right?" He took the tiny box from her and put it in the deep interior pocket of his jacket.

"Then we open that one first. As soon as this is over. Okay?" she asked. He smiled, nodded, and kissed her.

An hour later, after countless hugs, handshakes, and well-wishes, they finally arrived at their room. To Mike's surprise, Becky seemed to have forgotten about Garrett's gift. She had made no more mention of it, until she pulled him in for a kiss and the box, still in Mike's pocket, was momentarily pinched between them.

"Oh!" she said. "Let's open Garrett's gift!" Her excitement returned. He withdrew the box from his pocket and placed it in her hand. She popped the gift-wrap apart quickly and opened the box to reveal a key and a tiny, folded piece of paper. She unfolded the paper and read: *1427 Lafayette* in Garrett's script.

"Are you serious? It's a riddle?" she asked Mike sincerely. She frowned, but there was still good humor in her voice.

Mike took his phone out of his pocket and shook his head. "I don't think he meant it to be a riddle. 1427 Lafayette Street is where Garrett's bank is," Mike said. He plucked the key out of the box and held it up to her eyes. "This is a safe deposit box key. Whatever his gift is, it's in that box."

She looked disappointed, but he shook his head. "It's a benefit of getting married on a Sunday. We can go to the bank together in the morning and find out what it is!" She smiled and hugged him.

As a couple, they decided that although they wanted to go on a honeymoon, it would wait until after the baby was born and they had a better handle on their finances. Becky had suggested it, announcing that she didn't want to vomit every morning of her honeymoon, as the morning sickness had already begun before they tied the knot.

On the morning of their first official full day as husband and wife, the couple loaded up Mike's car with the gifts they had opened and catalogued the night before and drove back to the apartment they shared. Becky's last day at the Denali State Radio Telescope Array had been the previous Wednesday.

Just after lunch, they walked into the bank on Lafayette Street and asked for the bank manager. A tall woman of sixty with silver hair and a bright smile asked how she could help them. Mike handed her the key and explained the situation. He expected confusion on the woman's part, but she only nodded. "Mr. Rhodes explained everything to me. You take this back and I'll get our key and we can go into the secure area," the woman said, handing the key back to Mike and disappearing through a door. When she came back, she motioned for the newlyweds to follow her, and she walked into the room with the large safe and the rows and rows of safe deposit boxes. Although there were many small-faced drawers, she inserted her key into one of the larger drawers and unlocked it. "Just let me know when you're done." She left the room, pulling the door closed behind her. Mike unlocked the other side of the box and pulled the drawer out of the wall. He almost dropped it. It was so much heavier than he expected, it took him by surprise. He lifted the box, careful to use his legs and not his back, onto the closest table in the center of the room.

"What on Earth can be in there that's so heavy?" Becky asked. Mike shook his head. He grasped the edge of the lid and looked at her. She nodded. He lifted the lid to see a sheet of paper with Garrett's handwriting on it laying atop banded blocks of cash, each band reading $10,000. Mike lifted the paper out of the box to read it.

"It's like we're in a gangster movie," Becky said. She removed one stack, gasping when it revealed another just beneath it. Mike read the contents of Garrett's note aloud:

"Congratulations Mr. and Mrs. Potaglia. Please first remove all the cash from the box and set it aside so I can explain the gift more completely." Mike picked up the bundles of $100 bills and stacked them on the table. After only a moment, Becky helped him, as there were so many it would take some work to move it. After they had removed most of the cash, Becky let out a loud, high-pitched chirp, slapping both of her hands over her mouth. Mike stared at her, and she pointed down at the box where she had removed one of the bottom stacks of bills to reveal four gold bars. Mike shook his head, placed both hands on the table, and leaned heavily onto it. With all the cash on the table, they could see the bottom of the box was lined with a layer of the gold bars.

"Now we know why it was so heavy," Becky said. "What does the rest of the note say?"

Mike stood back up and lifted the note to his eyes again. "You can now see that my gift is two-fold. There is exactly one million dollars in cash here, and the gold was worth about 1.3 million when I put it in the box a few weeks ago. This money is all yours to spend as you wish, but I recommend getting yourself an accountant." Mike paused and looked up at Becky.

"Is that it?" she asked.

"No, he says, 'Don't worry about me, that's not all the money I have, but I won't need much when I come back. I'll only be on Earth for a few months, and then I won't have a need for any of it. I love you both and hope to see you again, Garrett.'"

"Mike, I don't even know how to react to this, I'm just… shocked!"

Mike nodded. "Me too." He took a deep breath. "But look, for now, it's safest right here where it is. Let's put it all back." They both stacked the cash back into the box. When they finished, Becky snatched two of the bundles out and put them in her bag. He looked at her suspiciously.

"Never in my life have I had twenty thousand dollars in my bag. Today is the day. We can have a really nice dinner on Garrett tonight," she said.

Mike laughed loud. "A twenty-thousand-dollar dinner?" She smiled and helped him with the box, sliding it back into its place in the wall and locking it. Mike then put the key on the ring with his car and apartment keys.

18

The Potaglias, although having made poor decisions in the past, did not do so with the money Garrett had gifted them. They got an accountant and a tax attorney and went through the steps to ensure the transfer of wealth was legal with all taxes paid. They bought a modest house in the Virginian suburbs of D.C. and invested the greater balance of the cash he had left for them. As they had promised themselves, they did not touch the gold and would not unless there was an emergency so dire that there was no other option.

Three months after their first child was born, Becky was pregnant again, and they made the final decision that she would be a full-time mother. Three more children rounded out the Potaglia clan before Mike finally got a vasectomy.

Although they had stuck to the promise of leaving the gold to their children, their investments had paid well enough that they could put the three of their children who wanted to go to college through on a full ride. They helped the other two start off their lives with every opportunity.

Mike had risen through the ranks at NASA and retired when he was only sixty-three. Becky had spent her life raising the children early on and embarking on several projects after the children were older. She wrote a book about the early years of the Lance project, which was successful, as the subject was the talk of the world. She started a consulting business for small telecommunications companies, which was short-lived but enjoyed immensely while it lasted. Many small internet channels interviewed her, and she even appeared on the Today Show in the later years, once the Lance was nearing completion. She recapped for all of America how the amazing story started and was peppered with questions about Garrett. He was the mystery man, apparently buried under twelve-thousand tons of concrete, expected to return in only ten years.

"Do you think he'll really be back? And not only come back, but as he said, not having aged? I mean, honestly, it's been forty years since we saw him. Do you believe it?" the host had asked her.

"Yes," she said. "Everything he told us was true, and he told us a lot. Why wouldn't this also be true?" A dumbfounded look crept over the skeptical interviewer's face, which Becky smiled at politely.

Chapter 14

Distria

1

Garrett awoke, experiencing a Sterilex awakening for the first time, still strapped into the seat of his transport. When he finally regained his vision, he could see a beautiful curve of green and blue in his sightline. Distria.

He felt sick to his stomach and desperately thirsty at the same time. Shortly after the launch, he had taken his gloves off to administer the Sterilex, and they were still off. As the fog in his mind cleared, he recounted the last memory he had of Osa approaching, before the whole of his field of vision had blurred.

Garrett leaned forward only to stretch his back muscles, forgetting the limitations of his restraints. He took a deep breath. A moment after he exhaled, a red light started blinking on the panel, just above the primary display directly in front of him. The text printed above the light read "O_2:CO_2."

He was not experiencing the effects of oxygen deprivation at that point, but he remembered when the alarm sounded that the air recyclers had switched off when he engaged the flex drive. The massive, interactive operator panel was dark, and Garrett hoped it had not stopped functioning. When the tip of his index finger touched the screen, it went from a rich black to a dark gray. Slowly, the image faded back to life for the first time in a hundred and fifty years. With the screen fully illuminated, Garrett swiped over to the life support control screen and touched the "Air Recycler" switch. Immediately, he could hear and feel a light breeze as the ship scrubbed the carbon dioxide out and added fresh oxygen. After only ten seconds, the red warning light blinked out. He sat still, breathing for a few minutes, and then his thirst commanded him to move.

The latch on the panel covering the enclosure beneath his seat was simple. The tech had opened and closed it easily, but he could not reach it. He rocked forward again and could again feel the restraints pressing against his suit. The moment he acknowledged the restraints, he remembered being shown how to release them, noting the lever to his left. Garrett pulled up on the lever and heard a multitude of clicks. He was free, but without gravity.

Throughout the transport were handholds. He grasped one of them with his left hand, pinned both of his feet against the floor of the operator's compartment, and rotated the panel latch with his right. The bag floated within the compartment and was harder to grip than one might expect, but he finally pinched one of the straps and brought it up to the level of his knees. He re-secured his lap restraint to help him function in the weightless environment.

Once comfortable, he opened his bag enough to reach in and pull out a bottle of water. He cinched the bag closed again, took the cap off the bottle, and enjoyed squeezing out a blob of water only to swallow it up. He repeated this process until the bottle was empty. With the water consumed and the empty bottle stowed back in the bag, he relaxed all his muscles and closed his eyes, waiting to feel normal again.

He woke up when the newly freed bag bumped into his face. Annoyed, he grabbed it and shoved it back into its place under the seat and re-fixed the latch. He took inventory of his physical state and was happy to find himself in good condition. The only issue he could sense was the earliest stages of a desire to urinate. He did not want to relieve himself in zero gravity if he could help it and decided to get down to the ground, starting his interplanetary adventure.

Garrett went through his checklist rapidly, scanning the atmosphere for pressure, oxygen, any potential poisonous gases, radiation, temperature, and a variety of other measurements. He looked at his current velocity and verified it was within the acceptable range for his stopping power and descent strategies. He pulled up a scan of Distria that also had a small semi-transparent gray block superimposed over it. The block represented the entry window so that he would land on the ground where the people of the planet would expect him.

He spent about fifteen minutes analyzing his situation before deciding to use the urine recycler. He went through the unpleasantness of that task, used a paper tissue from his bag to clean up after the awful process, and refocused his efforts on entering Distria's atmosphere.

He keyed the data into the transport's navigation screen. After the information processed, it gave him a countdown timer for the deceleration burn. Ninety minutes and eleven seconds. He used the time to scan everything he could on the surface of the planet, to familiarize himself as much as possible with his new, temporary home.

2

As the timer closed in on zero, he fixed the shoulder restraints in place and put his helmet back on. The timer counted down and Garrett braced himself. *4... 3... 2... 1...* First a hissing, and then *BOOM*. Garrett slammed against his harness. His craft was decelerating. It was moving toward a ground speed of zero, so that he could gently drift into the presence of air resistance without need of a sophisticated heat shield. There were six deceleration rockets fixed evenly around the transport, and they fired in three unique stages. The first stage involved the rockets fixed to the upper right and lower left, from his perspective. Garrett did not remember the firing order from his training, but he could see with his own eyes the luminous exhaust gas out the front window. There was a quiet moment as the fuel depleted and then the second stage, the upper left and lower right rockets, lit and slammed Garrett forward into his restraints again. He remembered the last stage; the two center rockets were not only thicker and more violent but lasted the longest. They were the monsters that actually stopped the craft. The second stage was what they called the "metering stage." They were only used to achieve an exact velocity, so that the third stage could begin its work. There was no delay between the moment the craft ejected the four used-up top and bottom rockets, two of them still burning, and when it lit the central ones. The forces went from being uncomfortable to a feeling of being crushed. He was being pressed into his restraints so hard that he could not get in a breath. With every fiber of his being, he focused only on inhaling, but still only managed half a breath at a time.

When the third stage rocket's deafening sound faded, Garrett could see vapor rising rapidly and vertically in front of his eyes. The blackness of space brightened into a light and simple blue. Above him and behind his head he heard a bang, and the words "Crush Chute Deployed" lit up on the operator panel. The craft jerked hard three times as each of the crush chutes released, and then the four small velocity suppression rockets fired. The rockets lasted only ten seconds. As they fizzled out, another loud bang and "Drag Chute Deployed" illuminated the operator panel. It was more effective, and he could feel his body being compressed into the operator's seat once again. Garrett heard the whine of a motor and a metallic *tink* sound, and the drag chute released, unspooling its tether. For a moment, he was in freefall, and when he looked at the monitor, it relieved him to see that the drag chute had greatly reduced his velocity. After another loud bang when the tether became taught, the operator panel notified him that it had deployed the final descent chutes, which were more dynamic than the first two. He could hear the hydraulics tugging and letting out the different para-cords depending on the navigation system's commands. The transport could steer and influence the rate of descent based on the target landing site. He looked at the panel to find the ground was 125 feet away. He took a deep breath, and the hydraulics screeched, whined and hissed, doing their best to offer the softest impact possible.

Garrett would have compared the actual touchdown to falling off a chair. He could not believe how impressively the system worked. "Thank you, Jack! Amazing!" Garrett said. He pulled the restraint release lever and twisted his helmet off. The thought of grabbing his bag crossed his mind, but he did not bother. He just wanted to be out of the vehicle. Close to the floor, by his right ankle, was a long black lever. Pulling on it without simultaneously releasing its lock would be futile, so with his left hand he grabbed the red handle between his feet and pulled it out about six inches. With his right hand, he pulled hard on the black lever by his right foot.

The air pressure in the craft must have been higher than atmospheric pressure at his location on the hilltop. Air rushed out, and his ears popped as the door lurched open. The aroma that filled the cabin was so floral, so clean and natural, that it struck Garrett emotionally. He had not expected scents that reminded him of the women in his life he had loved and left. Wasting no time, he gripped the side of the craft and launched himself out of it. After only three steps, he sat and laid back in the fresh and soft green vegetation of a hilltop field on the planet Distria.

3

Garrett laid on the grass for fifteen minutes before sitting up and removing his flight suit. His anxiety levels were high, but he reminded himself that at least on Distria, the inhabitants knew he was coming, knew about when and where he would land, and knew why he was there. The next four planets would be different. He did not know how long it would take the authorities from Distria to reach him, but he guessed it would be hours, if not a day or two.

The automatic orbital insertion and the final descent went perfectly, so he had no reason to use the thermo-gel evaporate pressure system, which meant that both of his reactors should be safe. He dismantled them anyway. The cells were always dangerous while the plates remained in them. He walked to the rear of the transport and pulled open a large aluminum door, located the control signal leads, and disconnected them from the two reactors. After removing a hand bolt, he drew out and unfolded a small rack fixed next to the reactors and set it up behind the craft. He loosened the fasteners on the heavy gray access covers of both reactors and waited for the gel to drain into the lower collection pan of the rear compartment. When they were both just dripping, he removed all the fasteners and then the two covers. One at a time, and with the heavy radiation resistant glove on his hand, he removed the twenty-four radioactive plates and set them in an appropriate place on the rack.

With the threat of a reaction mitigated, he gathered his flight suit off the ground and dumped it into the back of the transport next to the empty reactors. He retrieved his bag and the Sterilex satchel, which he hung around his neck, drank another bottle of water, and took a walk to stretch his legs. The exercise felt good, stretching his long dormant muscles that were still stiff. He ended up doing an enormous figure eight around the craft, never wanting to get too far from it. The hill was high, and he could see for miles around his location in every direction but the wooded north. After his third bottle of water, he urinated and prepared to take a nap. He planned to lay out his suit on the ground and sleep on top of it. As he walked to the back of the craft, he heard a familiar sound, buffeting. It only lasted an instant, but he stood still and listened. A breeze picked up, and he heard it again. It was not mistakable; it was a helicopter, or whatever the Distrian equivalent was.

After two minutes, he did not need the wind to hear the machine, and another two minutes after that, he could see it approaching from the southwest. He inventoried his belongings and then slung his bag strap over his head for easy carrying. His right hand rose to the Sterilex pouch on his sternum, an unconscious practice that would stay with him for the next twenty years of his conscious life.

4

The glossy black helicopter approached and set down in the soft grass about thirty yards from where he stood. Garrett noted the similarities between it and those that existed on Osa. Eight uniformed and heavily armed men jumped down from the open-air cabin, and seven jogged to within ten yards of his location. The eighth stayed back. He slung his high-powered firearm over his shoulder, and to Garrett's jaw-dropping surprise, helped two little girls down out of the flying machine. The first little girl walked toward Garrett. The second pointed at the helicopter and shouted something at the soldier that had helped her down. She then also turned and walked toward him. The soldier with the fresh instructions signaled the pilot, and the buffeting slowed as he shut down the engines.

The first young girl, not ten years old, stood only four feet in front of Garrett and stared at him with a disapproving look. Dressed in light blue coveralls, she had a deep bronze complexion with long brown hair, loosely braided and hanging down behind her back. As the second girl, a mirror image of the first, arrived, they immediately held hands and looked at each other. Identical twins.

"Uko tayari kuzungumza bado?" the first said to the second. The second rocked her head to the side and said,

"Hepana, bado ni kubwa sana." They then both turned to fix their gazes on Garrett and said no more. *This is so weird,* Garrett thought, standing there, waiting.

Three minutes of the awkwardness passed before the helicopter was almost silent, and twin number two spoke to him. "Hello, can you understand me?" Shocked that she was speaking to him in Osan, he only looked back and forth between the two small girls. "You cannot understand me?" the same girl asked.

"Yes! Yes, I can understand you perfectly," Garrett finally said.

"Excellent," twin-two said. "I am Lina Glenn, and this is my sister, Lana Glenn. We are your translators, Envoy."

"How do you know my language?" Garrett asked, perplexed.

"Osa has sent us much information. We know everything. There are six of us total who have learned Osan. My sister and I are two of them," Lana said, smiling. Garrett noticed that Lina was the better speaker. He had much more difficulty understanding Lana.

"What is that?" Lina said, pointing at the rack with the nuclear fuel plates.

"They are radioactive. Do you know that word?" he asked. The girls whispered to each other in their native language. Lina said something to one of the men behind her, and he nodded. "Danger?" Lana asked.

"Yes, very dangerous," Garrett answered. The whispering continued. Finally, Lina reached for Garrett's hand.

"We will have people come to take care of the danger. You must come with us now." Garrett allowed the little girl to lead him back to the helicopter. One soldier made a hand signal to the pilot, and Garrett could hear the engines winding up again.

5

Garrett quite enjoyed the view as the helicopter flashed at low altitude over the Distrian landscape. Rolling hills, amber fields, and dark green forest unbroken by civilization. Ten minutes of the scenery passed before he saw his first structure. A squat white building with a small, groomed yard. They passed more and more structures before they, and all apparent vegetation, ended abruptly. Garrett could not see out of the front of the helicopter; his view was from the side, and his view suggested they were entering a desert.

They were in the air for another thirty minutes before he felt the craft rock back and could hear the engines edging off their speed. They descended, and just before they touched down, Garrett saw the edge of a building's roof come into view outside the craft.

They deboarded, and with all the passengers out of the helicopter, Lina once again took his hand and led him toward the rooftop door. There were four of the military unit in front of them and four behind walking two abreast. *This is like a prisoner escort,* Garrett thought. An additional soldier, one who had not made the trip, opened the door as the group approached. The leading soldiers broke into single file, and they all streamed into the stairwell.

Three dark staircases and two brightly lit corridors later, they were walking into a large room with high ceilings and an exterior wall made of glass. Bright daylight flooded the room, and Garrett found the setting inviting. After a quick observation, he could see it was a small auditorium, but all the tiered seats were empty. At the opposite end of the room was a large square table, with three chairs on each of three sides and one large chair on the fourth.

Lina led him to the table and touched the center chair, the one facing the lone large chair on the opposite side. He sat down. Lina and Lana flanked him. They all sat in silence for only a minute before five men and two women entered and took seats around the table. An older woman in a blue robe with short white hair and round spectacles took the large single chair facing Garrett, smiled, and spoke to the young twins who Garrett was with. The faces of the children stretched into enormous smiles, and after a minute Garrett realized that the woman was just speaking to them, expecting no translations. After the brief pleasantry was over, Lina leaned into him and said, "We will start now."

Garrett nodded and waited for the questioning. The woman spoke several words before stopping. Lina turned to Garrett and said, "You have traveled a great distance." Garrett looked from Lina to the woman in the great chair.

"Yes, I have. Thirty-nine parsecs." Garrett waited for Lina to translate, but Lana spoke up from his left.

"I do not know the word 'parsecs.'"

"Do you know light-years?" he asked.

"Yes."

"128 light-years."

Instead of translating back to the old woman, Lana wrote on her notepad. Lina whispered to a confused Garrett that Distrian light-years differed from Osan light-years, and Lana was converting the number to be accurate. Lana spoke the sentiment back to the woman in the blue robe in their native tongue with the freshly calculated distance. The woman then spoke for a much longer time, and Lina wrote notes on a pad of paper that each of the girls had in front of them. When the old woman finally stopped talking, Lina began.

"We appreciate your dedication to the task, Envoy, and thank you and your people on Osa for choosing our world to be included in the Orris Project. We started receiving the signals twenty-seven years ago, but it took us the first ten to figure out how to interpret them. Since then, we have made use of the information and could finally have some children learn your language, as you can see. The children, most notably Breck and Jaemis Glenn, have translated everything your people have sent to us."

"Glenn? Are they related to you two girls?" Garrett asked.

"Yes," Lina said. "They are our brothers." Lina shot a glance at the old woman and then back to her notepad. "My name is Cora Sellig. I am the leader of this part of Distria. Welcome, Envoy, to Distria." At that moment, the group surprised him. They all stood and applauded, and in terrible Osan, they all attempted to say "Welcome, Envoy, to Distria." None of them sat, but Cora continued speaking, and when she finished, the gathering began exiting the room. Garrett looked at Lina.

"We know you are tired, Envoy. We will now end our greeting. The twins will show you to your quarters." Lina said, then stood. "Follow us." She took his hand again and led him back out through the door.

6

They walked back up the corridor the way they had come, but veered right, down an unfamiliar hallway. Toward the end, and before the two glass double doors that led outside, Lina stopped. Lana continued another few steps and entered a room through a white paneled door to the left. Lina, gesturing to the door across from it with one hand, said, "This is your room. Lana and I are in that one." She pointed to the door Lana had just escaped through. "Breck and Jaemis are in the next two, and the Florence kids are in the last one on the left. They will answer if you call in the middle of the night. Let us go into your room. I need to familiarize you with our living." Garrett expected her to finish the sentence, but apparently "our living" was appropriate on Distria. He did not think too much of it. He understood. At that point, he would not know how to make a cup of tea or even how to go to the bathroom using the technology of the planet. Lina placed the pad of her thumb on the face of the doorknob, and they both heard a click. She pushed the door open, and they walked in. Garrett could see a kitchen immediately on his right and what he guessed was an entertainment area on his left. Once the door swung shut behind them, she took Garrett's right hand in both of her tiny ones and manipulated it so the pad of his own thumb faced away from him. She placed it on the face of the interior knob and held it there until they heard three high-pitched beeps in rapid succession. "Now you can open this door, too." She dropped his hand and walked deeper into the apartment. Garrett dropped his bag and satchel and followed her.

Over the next thirty minutes, a girl that Garrett thought might be nine years old showed him where the cold storage in the kitchen was, how to use the cooking surfaces, the exotic cutlery and stoneware, and the method they used to wash up everything after cooking. She brought him to the back of the apartment where his bedroom was and showed him where he would sleep, where they had stored clothing for him, and the variety of sizes they had prepared. In the bathroom, the little girl showed him how to urinate and defecate with their technology, rather embarrassing, but he was glad to know, and the shower, which operated similarly to the way they worked on Osa. They walked back up to the front, and she showed him the entertainment system and explained how to use it. Finally, she showed him the phone. When she picked it up, he noticed there was nothing at all interactive about it, yet he could faintly hear it beeping.

"Depending on what time of day you pick this up, it will ring in one of our apartments." Garrett heard a young girl's voice answer "hello?" on the phone. "Thank you, Lana," Lina said into the phone, and hung it up. "If you call in the morning or early afternoon, you will get me or Lana. If you call in the evening, you will get Breck or Jaemis. Late at night is the only time you would talk to one of the Florence kids." She turned toward the door and walked the few paces it took to get there. Before she opened it, she turned and smiled, "Welcome to Distria, Envoy."

7

Over the next four months, Garrett established an excellent relationship with all four of the Glenn children, and the two Florence children as well, the latter being a boy and girl of nine and twelve years, respectively. Breck was the oldest, a seventeen-year-old man who looked exactly like the twin girls except older, male, and with his hair cut short, as his younger brother Jaemis wore it. He was several years younger than Garrett himself and was brilliant. Breck and Garrett spent many evenings talking about the stars, distant galaxies, the not-so-distant ones, the eflix ring, and all the potential outcomes of the greater Orris Project.

The children would often go to Garrett's apartment, where they would play games, eat meals, and practice their language skills. Lina and Lana, especially, had a lot of fun teaching Garrett Destrian, their native language. The children would spend any waking time off that they had with Garrett by one group or another, and rarely the entire group would assemble, usually in the evenings, when they were all awake to play games. They spent the rest of their time assisting Garrett. They translated as he attended thousands of hours of meetings, sat on committees, attended live tests of the various subcomponents of the Lance, counseled designers, and dozens of times gave presentations to massive audiences. Breck always translated them, as they were technically advanced and Breck had the best knowledge not only of the technology but of the Osan language. Breck impressed Garrett for a lot of reasons, not the least how well he spoke Osan. It was as though he was a native speaker. He had no accent at all, unlike his brother and sisters.

Garrett learned that the location where they lived and worked was a military installation. The place had existed before Distria first received the signal from Osa but was then much smaller. Once the government had embraced the project, they chose the site and broadly expanded it. They had already broken ground on a launch track using the

Osan designs and were currently excavating the land where they would build and test the enormous flex drive engines for the Lance.

He was reaching the end of his time with the first group of people, as they needed his council less and less. As a result, he took Breck as a translator to meet with Cora Sellig. At the meeting, he announced he would go under the influence of Sterilex for fifty years. When he woke up, he would see the Lance off, and help with anything else they may need before he himself left for his next mission planet.

"I understand. We cannot thank you enough for your help, Envoy, and although I will surely be gone from this place when you come back, please know that preparations will be made to receive you." Garrett mostly understood what she was saying, as he had gotten comfortable with Destrian, but Breck translated for him, anyway.

"Thank you," Garrett said. "In my absence, if there should be any desire to question me, the best person to stand in for me would be this man, my translator. Breck has displayed himself to me as an authority on all that we are trying to accomplish here, and there is no other man on Distria who knows my mind better than he." The reply took Breck by surprise, and he hesitated, staring at Garrett. "Translate, please," Garrett said. Cora was looking at Breck, waiting for the translation. Breck gave it, and Garrett paid close attention to make sure he left nothing out.

8

Garrett came out of his second Sterilex stint forty-nine years and three months after going under. He had only been awake for six more hours after the meeting with Breck Glenn and Cora Sellig before taking the dose. Once he could walk, he left his sleeping quarters and entered the kitchen. There were several bottles of water in the cold box, but nothing else. They must have come in to clean periodically, and removing the food completely made sense. He drank a bottle of water and sat in a chair, waiting to feel normal again. Halfway through his second bottle, the feeling returned to his left hand, which had been the single holdout during the awakening process. Happy with his current state, he picked up the phone and listened. Nothing. No familiar beep to alert someone that he needed assistance. He replaced the phone in its cradle and decided he did not need help right away, as his head swam. Sitting down on the small couch they had furnished the apartment with, he decided that lying down might be his best option at that point and closed his eyes.

9

The Envoy woke up to the sound of his door opening. When he opened his eyes, it surprised him to find it was dark except for the light pouring in from the hallway as his door stood partly open. It had been broad daylight when he laid down. A familiar voice called into the darkness.

"Garrett? It's Breck. We were notified that you woke up. Are you here?" Breck said. Garrett was astonished. How could Breck still be there fifty years later?

"Yes," Garrett answered into the dark. "Sorry, I fell asleep on the couch. You can turn on the lights, please." The view of the room bounced in and out as the lights at first flickered, but then settled into a bright glow. *Haven't been on in a while,* Garrett thought. He took a deep breath and stood up, turning to the man that had addressed him. Surprised, not because Breck was approaching seventy and sported a head of hair that had gone completely white with a complement of deep-set wrinkles in his face, but because he wore the same uniform that Cora Sellig had worn fifty years prior.

"Breck, are you…?" Garrett said.

Breck nodded. "For the last eighteen years." He reached out to shake Garrett's hand and, as he took it, pulled Garrett in to hug him with his free arm. "Thanks to you, Envoy." Garrett's look of confusion as they released from each other must have taken Breck by surprise, because he laughed hard. "You don't understand? Well, it's simple. You named me your ambassador. There were hundreds of questions, maybe thousands. I was an instant celebrity among all of those working on the Lance." Breck walked into the kitchen and sat on a stool. "When you went to sleep, they released my brother and sisters and the Florence kids, but they asked me to stay, and they even gave me a title and let me keep my apartment."

"You must have been successful," Garrett said, gesturing to the man's robe.

"Yes, mostly. Although I made some mistakes, nothing that ended in disaster. The important part is that as more time went on, I was relied on more heavily, not less. I had wanted to go back to school, but every time I brought it up, they would give me a new title and a large pay increase. Eventually, I was making three times more than I ever thought possible, and I dropped the idea of further schooling."

"How are you still speaking Osan so well after all these years?" Garrett asked, only then realizing how flawlessly the man could communicate.

Breck laughed again. "Garrett, half the planet speaks Osan now. It is not as uncommon as it was. We can thank my sister, Lina, for that. She pushed hard for Osan to be taught to every child in grade school. Now there are universities where it is the primary language, they consider it a more sophisticated tongue."

"That's amazing." Garrett said, and walked to the counter for a fresh bottle of water.

"Are you hungry?" Breck asked. Garrett shook his head.

"No, my stomach still doesn't feel right since waking up." He took a sip of water and replaced the cap.

"Understood. Well, why don't you relax. I'll be back in the morning and we can get started."

Garrett smiled and nodded.

10

Garrett remained on Distria for another eight weeks. He met with engineers and astrophysicists, planners, and on-ship legal teams. During his off time, he selected his next planet, also in the Andromeda galaxy, and named it Planet 2, as he had no way of knowing that the inhabitants called it Rhett. He spent two days reviewing the ship they had built for him, making sure everything was exactly as the plans had specified.

Two weeks before he left, and one day before they did, he met with an auditorium filled with the lottery winners who would board Lance 1, which was orbiting Distria. He spoke to them for three hours, passionately recounting their discoveries on Osa and their ultimate plan to beat the impending doom of the universe. He described Orris and counted them all as heroes for sacrificing themselves for the continuation of their people beyond the collapse. He spelled out the Orris mission plan enthusiastically. He talked of the stall and how the billions of years of preparation would give them the upper hand. He talked of the ultimate reversal and the impending collapse and how Orris would manage the threat. Finally, he shouted that they would be victorious, and that it would not be possible without the group of fearless and dedicated men and woman about to board the Lance. He finished with "Long live Distria!" The crowd leaped to their feet, screaming with delight. Garrett had given the entire speech in Osan. Everyone in attendance understood him.

Chapter 15

End of the Fifth

1

PFC Edward Carter was bitterly celebrating his eighteen-month anniversary guarding the "mausoleum," which was the nickname the guards gave the twelve-thousand-ton concrete bunker that contained the dead alien. For the eight months leading up to that day, he had door-duty, meaning he was the guard stationed right in front of the heavy steel door that served as the only entrance into the bunker. His duty included using lethal force against all who might attempt to enter. He was the last line of defense to protect what all the guards considered a rotting corpse, as it had been in there for forty-eight years without ever emerging. There were thousands of conspiracy theories. The news occasionally played footage of the alien walking into the bunker and locking the door, which was apparent with a loud shudder as the bolt slid into place.

He was anxiously awaiting the relieving guard to make his next round, as Eddie desperately needed to urinate. He could see the sun setting in the west and was at least appreciative of the fact that the heat was dissipating. It was a few minutes after eight o'clock, and that August day had been torture. He felt bad for the day shift guys, the ones who stood in that heat throughout the afternoon.

Eddie's gaze was more and more often bending down toward the flagpole, which was the general area he would first see the bobbing head of Gonzalez, the relieving guard. Nothing. He gritted his teeth together, knowing he could do nothing about the sharp pain in his abdomen.

A loud crash behind him, accompanied by a vibration in the floor, startled him so badly that he spun around with his gun pointed at the very object he was there to protect. Every muscle in his body had tensed so tightly that he thought it would be impossible to urinate, even if he had the opportunity.

The door pushed toward him, and he stepped back, thinking it was a trick by the other guards to make him look stupid. But then a middle-aged man stepped out from behind the heavy door, still with sleep in his eyes and looking unwell.

"Hey," the man said. He stretched and looked Eddie over. "What's wrong with you? You look like you're ready to shoot me?" Garrett said but did not look genuinely concerned.

"No, man! I'm not gonna to shoot you. You just surprised me! And I gotta piss so bad my teeth are floating," Eddie explained.

Garrett laughed. He had never heard the expression. "Has anyone else seen me come out?" Garrett asked. The two men looked around and noted zero reaction or activity. Eddie shook his head. "Okay, follow me." Garrett disappeared back into the mausoleum, and Eddie followed.

Once in the dimly lit concrete room that looked like the largest prison cell ever constructed, Eddie saw Garrett pointing to the front right corner. When he followed his reference, he saw the most beautiful image he could have at that moment. A toilet.

"Knock yourself out," Garrett said, imitating Mike Potaglia. "I'll guard the entrance for you." Eddie appreciated the joke but ran for the toilet. He glanced over his shoulder but Garrett had disappeared. Eddie felt like it took ten minutes to empty his bladder, but it had only been thirty-five seconds. When he had put himself back in order, he walked out to find Garrett jokingly holding an invisible weapon and guarding the entrance.

"Hey, man. Thank you. That was really cool of you to help me out that way," Eddie said. Garrett smiled and shook his head.

"You've been doing the most boring job on the planet for how long?"

"Eighteen months, sir."

"A year and a half!" Garrett shook his head. "I think I owe you a lot more than a bathroom break for protecting me for that long. What is your name?"

"Private First-Class Edward Carter, sir." Eddie had remembered his military training and was trying to make up for his casual first encounter with the national asset.

"Okay, excellent. Can I call you Edward?" Garrett asked.

"Yes, sir."

"Thank you, Edward. Now, is there someone you should notify about my arrival?" Eddie shook his head at first, but then nodded.

"Yes sir, thank you sir." Eddie pulled the radio off his belt and made the call.

Garrett's resurrection consumed the news cycle for a week.

2

Four days after waking, Garrett looked out of the car window as neighborhood after neighborhood in Arlington, Virginia passed. Finally, the driver pulled over to the curb as Garrett had asked. He rose from his seat and stepped out onto the concrete sidewalk at the address he had been seeking. He walked toward the driveway of the house where a much older version of Mike and Becky lived.

Summer was waning, but flower beds were still flush and full. Pollen and salt were the strongest odors, although a heavier, earthier scent he could not identify also made its presence known. The neighborhood smacked of wealth, not only in the perfectly manicured lawns and gardens but also in the obvious tax base. The paved road was pristine, as were the sidewalks that lined both sides of the street. Hedges were trimmed razor straight and the interfaces between lawn and durable structures were edged cleanly. Wealth and care bred perfection.

When he reached the driveway, he turned his head to find a beautiful, dark blue, two-story colonial. The property was neatly groomed, as they all were, and rows of brightly colored flowers lined the edges of the house and hedge lines. He walked up the driveway with his newly assigned agents giving him little space and turned onto the concrete path that led to the front door when he heard a loud voice behind him.

"Well, I'll be damned!" the voice said. Garrett turned around to find an aging couple sitting on a bench swing that bushes had obscured up to that point. Garrett dipped his head and smiled, knowing it was what he should have expected. He approached the two with a smile on his face. "You *really are* going to live through all of it, aren't you, Garrett?" A balding, gray-haired Mike said.

"It never ceases to amaze me. I feel like I left you two a few days ago," Garrett said. Mike laughed hard, and Becky, who had cut her gray hair above her shoulders, slapped him lightly on the chest.

"I feel like you left us about, oh, fifty years ago," Mike said. They all chuckled as the couple stood up.

"I hate to drop in on you like this. Can I schedule a time that we can all have dinner?" Garrett asked. Mike walked up to him and put a hand on his shoulder.

"Stop being dumb, Garrett. I hate dumb," Mike said. With that, he dropped his hand and walked into the house. Becky approached the baffled Garrett and took his right hand in both of hers.

"What he thinks is humor is dumb. What he is saying is that you are a part of our family, Garrett. Come in, we've missed you."

Garrett followed Becky into the substantial house, through the foyer, and into the kitchen. There was a circular wooden table with four chairs placed in front of two large glass doors that opened to the backyard. Mike opened two bottles of beer and dropped a Clotz Ale on the table near where Garrett was standing.

"You converted me; I've been drinking this crap for fifty years," Mike said.

Becky laughed. "It's way better than that rotgut you drank when I met you," she said. "God knows you'd be ten years in the grave if you had kept that up." Becky sat at the table and Mike went to the coffee machine. "Please, Garrett, sit." Garrett sat in the seat where Mike had placed the bottle.

Mike brought the coffee to Becky and sat. For the next twenty minutes, the couple updated Garrett on what had happened after he went under. Just as Becky had finished a thought, Mike stood up. "Wait a minute!" he said. "Beck, Matty should talk to Garrett. Don't you think? Don't you think that would open his eyes to all of this nonsense?" Becky leaned back in her chair and frowned.

"Why? He's already decided, and you know it, Mike," she said. Mike pulled his phone from his pocket and walked deeper into the kitchen. Garrett looked at Becky, who was shaking her head.

"Matt, it's Grandpa. What are you doing now?" Mike said. "Come over… yes, now. There is someone here that you have to talk to," he paused, "Yes… of course it's really him! Don't you think I would know?" Mike ended the call.

3

Ten minutes later, a young man of eighteen came into the house, hesitating at the entrance to the kitchen. Mike looked up and stood.

"Come on in, Matty, and meet Garrett, an old friend of ours," Mike said. Garrett stood and turned toward the young man, whose resemblance to Mike in his younger days was uncanny. He offered his hand. Matt shook it, never taking his eyes off Garrett's face.

"How did you get that scar?" Matt asked, and touched his own forehead as though it were a mirror image of Garrett's face.

Garrett laughed. Since he had arrived at the human era of Earth's existence, no one had yet asked him about the straight, inch-long scar above his right eyebrow. "A meteor," Garrett said. "Shortly after I arrived here, I found a cavern. I climbed down to use it as cover from the elements, but the day after I made it to the bottom, a meteor hit the surface and sent rocks and sand crashing into it. One of the rocks hit me when I was diving for cover," Garrett spoke calmly, and Matt's jaw hung slack.

"That's amazing," Matt said.

Garrett shrugged. "Not really. Meteor impacts were common back then. The real surprise was when I woke up four hundred million years later and saw the moon. The moon got beat up. When I first arrived, it barely had a mark on it."

"Where? I mean, I know it was a really long time ago, but about where was it you landed? From today's perspective." Matt looked genuinely interested in Garrett's adventures.

"Ah, well, I figured it out once, but you'll be disappointed to find out it was just about in the middle of the Atlantic Ocean. There was no water there, yet, of course. There was barely any water anywhere yet. But that could all be wrong.

The tectonic nature of the Earth may have moved me so much that I'm completely wrong. I guess the most honest answer is that I don't know," Garrett said. Mike was smiling and shaking his head.

"How about we all have a seat?" Mike said. "Do you want coffee, Matt?" Matt nodded and sat. Mike went off to fetch the coffee for his grandson.

"Your grandfather wants you to talk to Garrett about your decision, Matthew," Becky said. Matt stirred and looked around.

"You want to get on the Lance, don't you, Matt?" Garrett said for him.

Matt nodded. "I do. I'm so amazed by all of this. Not only because of the stories my grandparents have told me, but by how huge it is."

Garrett nodded. Mike set the coffee in front of his grandson who, like his grandfather, drank it black. Mike sat back down and sipped his beer. "Matthew," Garrett said. "When your grandfather was five years older than you are now, he asked me what to tell his grandson if that grandson wanted to get on the Lance."

Mike snorted. "I did?" he looked surprised. Garrett smiled.

"He did. What did I tell him, Matt?" Garrett asked.

Matt continued looking around, then covered his face with his hands and rubbed it. He relaxed and looked at Garrett. "You told him to stop me from going, didn't you?" Matt asked.

Garrett nodded slowly. "It will be miserable, Matt, not fun. It won't be an adventure. It will be a long, boring life in close quarters and then you'll die. No oceans, no mountains, no bright blue skies, no rain, no sunlight for the rest of your life. Your grandchildren might have a chance of seeing Orris, they might not. Orris might not be there when they arrive. I strongly suggest you withdraw your name." Garrett finished speaking and sat back in his chair.

Matt stared into his cup of coffee. Without looking up, he said to Garrett, "But you did it."

"I did, and I have regretted it since before I even left my home," Garrett said. "My family has been dead for eight billion years, including my daughter, who I never met, and I am forty-something years old, Matt. I have a few months of work left to do and then I will have thirty or forty years left, with nothing to do except wait."

"Wait for what?" Matt asked.

"Death," Garrett said. "Except for your grandparents, everyone I have ever loved or ever called a friend is dead. With my job done, I will retire with nothing to do, no one to see, and nowhere to go. But that will be much more exciting than what you plan to do. At least I'll be able to stand in the sunlight, swim in the ocean, smell the air after it rains. I won't be locked in a metal can until I'm dead." Lies, but neither Mike nor Becky said a word.

Matt looked down at his coffee and then glanced at each grandparent. They were silent, letting Garrett's words sink in. Matt nodded, and then addressed them as a group, looking from person to person as he spoke. "That gives me a lot to think about. Thank you for taking the time to talk to me about it." Garrett nodded and clinked his beer bottle into the young man's coffee cup.

4

After leaving Mike and Becky's house, Garrett went back to D.C. and the apartment that NASA had arranged for him to have during his last months on Earth. Once back at his building, he ducked into a deli and bought a sandwich instead of a proper dinner. He needed to go to sleep early, as he had to catch an early flight the next morning. He was flying to Texas to spend two weeks doing inspections and taking endless meetings.

Finally, back in his apartment, he opened a beer and ate his sandwich. He sat on the couch with his laptop and opened the folder that contained his comms. After scanning through the ones that he had already watched, he saw one from his aged sister without her children and watched it. When it finished, he glanced at the next thumbnail over and saw that it was his daughter by herself, without Lauren. A bolt of concern shivered through him, but he played the video to find out it was her seventeenth birthday. She wanted to know if he got her a gift and laughed. She did not inherit the rich auburn hair of her mother but had the light brown hair of her father, which she allowed to spill down over her shoulders. Garrett could see Lauren in her eyes and facial expressions, and it always moved him when she spoke to him. She updated him on her school life and her personal life. It was a strange situation. Hope told him exactly what she had been up to. She told him things most seventeen-year-old kids would never dream of telling their parents. She said that she knew she would never meet him, and since there was no way he could communicate with her mother, she thought it was important that she tell him the whole truth of her life. When he woke up, she wanted him to know her completely.

In a rare and unfamiliar pang of parental emotion, Garrett wished she would reveal all the secrets to Lauren. Lauren could help her with any problems she was having. Although the things Hope had revealed to him were all fairly tame, he knew his wife could help.

He closed his laptop and went to bed, smiling as he closed his eyes. Hearing and seeing Hope had filled him with joy. Any problems she had aside, she was happy, and Garrett fell asleep with the same smile on his face.

5

The Envoy's plane landed in Houston a little after 10:00 a.m. He had no agenda that first day other than getting to his hotel and having dinner with Hank Forsyth, the current Administrator of NASA, and Pamela Tracy, the CEO of EMX, the private company that NASA had contracted to oversee the construction of Lance 5.

NASA had gone overboard when booking his hotel. It was on the top floor of the building, one of only two on the floor. He could not call it a "room," because it was five rooms. It had a lavish bathroom with a separate shower and tub, and there was a hot tub on the balcony. It had a full kitchen, which Garrett thought was funny, since he did not cook, and an entertainment room with a full wall television, surround sound audio, and the option for a full virtual experience via a light headset.

He enjoyed dinner, and Hank and Pamela impressed him, both of whom he had never met until then. Hank was bald and heavyset, and Pamela was rail-thin and kept her black hair pulled back in a clip. Except for pleasantries when they first met, the dinner consisted almost completely of the two hosts updating Garrett on their progress.

The Lance was complete. It was orbiting Earth, and the on-boarding crew was setting up the living quarters in preparation for the population bound for Orris. They had launched and loaded all the liquid fuel into the tanks, and the nuclear fuel panels were enriched, sintered, and loaded into cold storage in a massive warehouse freezer in League City. They would launch and install them as the last step before Lance 5 de-orbited Earth and departed for Orris.

The transport they built for him, a machine they proudly called T5, was complete and in a hangar at the Houston Launch Rail Facility in Liberty, a suburb of Houston. *It should be T6*, he thought, but did not correct them. He planned to travel to Liberty after the first few days of meetings to inspect the craft.

Four hundred and ninety-six passengers, which included the operations crew, would be in Texas in the next two weeks, when the launches would start. Garrett's last task on his visit would be to meet with them all. He had done it on every planet but Katya. He never made it that far on Katya.

"Garrett, I know you're looking forward to seeing the Lance off. We're excited about it too," Hank said. "But I understand that after it leaves, you will also leave Earth?"

"Yes," Garrett said. "There were twenty-seven of us, and we were each given the assignment to visit five planets and attempt to get a sampling of their populations to Orris. Earth was my fifth planet. As soon as the Lance leaves, I will be officially retired."

"But you're going to leave Earth?" Pamela asked.

"Yes."

"Garrett," Hank said, "I want you to know, if you were to decide to live out the rest of your life here on Earth, you will always have a good job working for NASA."

Garrett smiled at the thought of working for a simple space agency for the rest of his life, and never even trying to reach the object of his entire adult life's ambition. He inhaled to answer, but before he could Pamela spoke.

"Forget NASA, come work for EMX, and I'll pay you your weight in gold."

"I appreciate both of your offers. But I've lived the first half of my life rallying support for Orris. I will spend the second half *on* Orris."

"You will really travel all the way there?" Pamela asked.

Garrett nodded. "When you built my transport, I trust you equipped it with the six reactors that I asked for? Each with twelve plates?" Garrett asked. Pamela nodded. "That's two more than I'll need. By design, of course." Pamela nodded again and sipped her coffee.

"Well, Garrett, if you change your mind, please let me know," Hank said.

"I will," Garrett lied. He would sooner die than remain on Earth.

6

Back in his hotel suite after dinner, he had only one thing he was looking forward to: Hope. Before he had left D.C., he saw that there were more thumbnails of her face by herself, and he wanted to immerse himself in her life. Two desks resided against a wall in a room that he dubbed "the sitting room" and were the only feature other than two sofas and two leather chairs, all facing an oval coffee table.

The first two videos he watched featured Hope by herself. She was happy and excited to tell him about the events of her life and how she was trying to decide what she wanted to do for a living. The time to pick an educational path was looming. After watching both videos, Garrett smiled, thrilled to see his sweet daughter so happy. Other than her hair color, she looked so much like her mother that no one could ever suspect she was anyone else's child. The following thumbnail was different. Hope was there, but so was another woman who Garrett did not recognize. He checked the date of the video, and it was eight months after the one that preceded it.

"Hi, Daddy," Hope said. Garrett thought the woman with her looked familiar, and after watching her for a moment, he realized that it was Olive. She had cut her long dark brown hair short, and it had turned gray. By the look of her, she had lost an enormous amount of weight and was wearing glasses that she never had before. Garrett could hardly believe it was the same woman. "Olive is with me because we have to talk to you about Mom." Tears welled in Hope's eyes, and Garrett thought the look of sadness on her face might kill him.

"Lauren hasn't been doing well over the last few months, Garrett," Olive said. If he had heard her voice before seeing her, he would have known her instantly. "She's been withdrawn. She quit her job three months ago, and she spends days at a time locked in her room. She won't talk to anyone except Hope."

Hope had been trying to collect herself while Olive was talking and then spoke. "Anytime she's like that, I'll knock on her door and she lets me in, but when I ask her what's wrong, she tells me everything is fine, that she just needs to be alone." Olive rubbed her back.

"Anyway," Olive said, "I'm going to talk to Christine tomorrow about her. She's approaching eighty years old, and I didn't want to bother her, but she called me this morning to check in on me and I told her about your wife. I promise we'll get her help if she needs it. I'm not sure if anyone told you about the money, but you don't have to worry about that. Your mother took care of that a long time ago." Hope laughed through her tears. "We'll bring you more news as we have it. We miss you Gar, a lot of people here miss you." Olive stood up.

"Bye, Daddy! I love you!" Hope said, and blew a kiss into the camera lens, where the image froze.

Garrett looked at the clock. It was already 11 p.m., and his first meeting in the morning was at 7:00. He wanted to watch more, to get updates on what had happened, but he knew that there was nothing he could do about any of it. It would all still be there waiting for him when he got back from his meetings.

7

At 1:00 p.m. the following day, Garrett met with Jackie Herrera, captain of Lance 5. Instead of one of the meeting rooms at NASA, Jackie had requested they meet more informally and suggested a café near the Mission Control facility in Houston.

When Garrett arrived at the coffee shop, he looked around while waiting for his order. It was a bright and inviting space; two top tables dotted the floor and there was a bar bolted to the support beams of the clear glass exterior wall, accompanied by stools.

The two had never met, but they had video conferenced, so he knew what she looked like. He heard his name called out to his right and found her standing next to a corner table. She had tied her long black hair into a ponytail and was wearing a light gray tee shirt that said "ORRIS" on it, with a line-art rendition of the monster craft. The one feature that surprised Garrett was her height. She was at least six-foot-three or more.

"Hi, Jackie," Garrett said, and shook her hand. "I love the shirt!"

She laughed and nodded. "I was going to wear my uniform for the meeting, but when you agreed to meet here, I changed my mind. A few of the senior staff had them made up. I thought you might like it."

Garrett heard his name called from behind him, retrieved his order, and sat down with Captain Herrera. It would be the only time the two met in a one-on-one setting, and it was only to give her direct access to Garrett before they left.

He picked up his coffee but spoke before taking a sip. "So! What can I do for you?"

"Most of my questions have been answered already. The manuals are very thorough, but I have a few," she said. "What does it feel like once the flex drives are engaged? I feel like it should crush us to death, even though I understand the physics, mostly."

Garrett smiled and nodded. "It's so boring you might not even believe me. You don't feel anything. The ship isn't pressing itself through the fabric as traditional rocket-driven ships do, it bends the fabric around itself. Since you're not traveling through space, there's no sensation of acceleration. Visually, if you were to look out one of the windows on the bridge, space changes from a crisp, sharp black with stars and features, to a slightly less crisp black with no features at all. Boring." Garrett sipped his coffee and waited for the next question.

"I understand that I won't ever see Orris. Do you have any idea how long it will take the Lance to get there?"

"I have an idea, yes. You know that I'm originally from the Andromeda galaxy, right?" Jackie nodded. "Well, so is Orris. It has been, for the last eight billion years or so, kind of meandering through Andromeda. Don't ask me why. I have no more knowledge than you do on that topic. If I had to guess, it would be that they are in a holding pattern waiting for more people like you and probably gathering resources."

"Do you know how long, though?" she asked.

Garrett laughed, realizing he had not answered her original question. "Sorry, yes, I have an idea. When I first came to the Milky Way galaxy, I calculated a speed of 1,000c. That was Class 4 technology. When I left Telraed for Earth, I was using a Class 6 flex drive and that was about 21,000c. Your Lance is a Class 7. You can expect a touch over 32,000c. It will take about eighty years for you to reach Andromeda. Once you're there, it could take anywhere from one day to eight more years depending on where Orris is, if it's still there at all."

Jackie nodded and looked up at him for a moment before speaking. "Do you think Lance 5 will get there? With all of that distance and all the potential problems? Do you believe we can actually get our grandkids to Orris?"

Garrett thought it sounded funny, a young lady of twenty-seven talking about her grandchildren, but nodded. "Yes. That's why your manuals are so thorough. That's why you and everyone else on board can speak Osan. English will be phased out over the course of forty years, and then it will be Osan only. That's why you'll be forced to retire at the same time. Lance 5 will need a young captain capable of seeing the craft to its destination. After you're gone, and Lance 5 gets closer to Orris, they will establish communication and relinquish control. Orris will take over from there, and they will be home."

8

When Garrett arrived back at his suite, he ordered room service and took a shower. It was only 3:30 in the afternoon, so he had plenty of time to get caught up on the history of his family. Once his room service was there, he sat in front of the television and ate while watching the news of Earth. He paid little attention to the actual content, as the thoughts of his family and the videos were the only thing on his mind.

He choked down the rest of his early dinner and turned the television off. It was too early for beer, so he made a cup of coffee and walked to the desk with his laptop.

Once he located the last file he had watched with Hope and Olive, he opened the next one in line, which was his father, ominously, by himself.

"Hey Gar, I know I usually do these things with your mom, but she had a little accident, and she's in Dinesta General now, recovering. It's nothing serious, but she asked me to come here and make this video just so you would know what was going…" The video image froze, with four minutes left to play. Garrett replayed it, but it was the same. The next video in line was of Brenia by herself. He thought she might give him more of the story, but when he opened the file, it displayed only the frozen image of her face. The next seven videos in order all returned the same result. He skipped videos to get through them quicker, frozen image after frozen image. He created a new folder and then processed his entire channel again with the updated signal he received after waking up. It was only a few months old, and he had high hopes that it came through uncorrupted. It was midnight before the processing finished, and he had fallen asleep on one of the two couches in the sitting room.

9

When Garrett woke up, he jumped to his laptop. He navigated to the new files, freshly deposited in the new folder he had created the night before, and had his heart broken. The new files were just as the old ones were. It was not something that he could correct on Earth. The files were coming corrupted from Orris.

He did the only thing he could, which was to tell himself as much of the story as possible with the only thing available to him: the thumbnails. As he looked from picture to picture, he became sick to his stomach. There was not a single image with his mother, nor Lauren. There were many from his father and Brenia together, and then Brenia by herself. Hope was in only six more videos before her presence completely disappeared, too. Mixed into the others were images of Olive, by herself and several of her with people he did not recognize at all. His father's face grew old and then fell out of the lineup. After his father's last appearance, there were sixty-one consecutive videos from Brenia. As Garrett looked at the tiny pictures, he watched her age, until she was a barely recognizable old woman. The last file in his folder was of a man in his late sixties or early seventies who Garrett did not recognize at all. He had to assume it was Rodney Jr. telling him his sister was dead.

Garrett had so many questions swimming through his head he thought it would drive him insane. What happened to his mother? What happened to Lauren? And why in the world did Hope stop making videos when she was barely twenty years old?

He had to get to Orris. All of his answers would be in the archives on Orris. He thought about the fact that he had two weeks left in Texas, then a few days in D.C. to finalize his earthly affairs. After, he would travel right back to Liberty to launch himself off of Earth and get some answers.

He needed a distraction, desperately. His first meeting was not until 11:00 a.m. and it was only 7:30. He called for his car.

10

"Mr. Rhodes?"

As Garrett walked toward the car, he heard the man's voice behind him. He turned, shaken by what he saw. The man noticed and smiled.

"Jim?" Garrett asked. It was a spitting image of the man, maybe having aged only five or ten years, while fifty had passed.

"Yes, but you think I'm my father, Jim Lambert Sr." The two men shook hands. "My dad died ten years ago. He asked me to look you up when you came back to us. I think he wanted me to know you were real."

"Your father was a great man. I'm sure I don't have to tell you that. But what you might not know was that he was also a great friend of mine. I'm very happy to have known him." Garrett did not realize he was smiling as he talked.

"I got the feeling, by the way he talked about you. I have a favor to ask of you, and this is not something that Dad asked me to do, but I think it would be really cool." Jim Jr. took a piece of folded cloth out of his breast pocket and unfolded it. "This is a gift I got for my dad when he was first appointed NASA Administrator, before my mother died. She took me to the store, and I picked it out." In the unfolded cloth was a silver pin in the shape of a cartoon rocket ship. Garrett recognized it at once. Every day Jim had worn a suit jacket, he had fixed the pin to his lapel just below the American flag pin that he also wore without fail.

"I remember this," Garrett said.

"Like I said, Mr. Rhodes, he didn't ask me to do this. It's just an idea I had and thought would be cool. Would you take it? I think knowing that this pin will end up with you, and on Orris as its final destination, would have made him happy. It would definitely make me happy." Jim Jr. offered a small smile.

"I'd be happy to, Jim. But how did you know I was going to Orris?"

"Where else would you go?" Jim handed the pin to Garrett, who took it. He nodded and smiled, then walked back into the Houston foot traffic.

11

"Liberty Rail," Garrett told the driver when he got into the armored black sedan.

"Liberty doesn't have a rail station," the driver said.

"The launch rail," Garrett said. The driver smiled and nodded and pulled out into traffic. Garrett called Pamela and told her he was going to inspect his transport. Surprised, as she had not expected him for another day or two, she said she would meet him there.

"That's not necessary, Pamela. I had no intention of interrupting your schedule. I just need to know where to go when I get there," Garrett said.

"There's no chance you are going to lay eyes on that beauty without me being there to see your reaction," she answered. "I'll be there in ten minutes. Have your driver pull into Gate C and then just pull over and wait for me. I won't be a minute or two behind you." Garrett thanked her, ended the call, and told his driver the plan.

Fifteen minutes later, Garrett and Pamela were standing outside a hangar. "Are you ready?" she asked. Garrett smiled and nodded. Pamela pushed the door open and walked in. Garrett followed. When he set his eyes on the misnamed T5, he was astonished. It was a lot bigger than the plans had called for.

"This will be a problem, six reactors won't…"

"There are thirty-six," Pamela said. "The plans for a class-7 transport that we received from Orris were not compatible with the modifications you asked for. We puzzled over it for months. Finally, we went back to NASA to tell them we couldn't do it. They told us to make it happen, whatever it took. One of my design engineers said, 'Why don't we just make it big enough to fit everything,' and that is what you're now looking at." She walked around the machine. "Thirty-six reactors, each with twelve plates. 384 solid rocket boosters, twice what you asked for. 835 solid fuel pressure slugs for navigation, six hundred more than you asked for, and the cherry on top?" She walked up to the craft and pointed to four large cylinders welded to the underside of the frame. "Four thousand pounds of liquid O_2 and another four thousand of liquid H_2, connected to twenty-eight micro engines, giving you full control of the craft if you need it using *none* of your planned resources. The extra O_2 is for life support."

Garrett stared, temporarily distracted from his family crisis, which was exactly what he had wanted. He could not believe they could build such a craft for one man. It was thirty feet tall, and at least a hundred feet long, five times the size of his previous transports. He could go to Orris and back twice in the machine.

12

He finished his two weeks with a speech to the Lance 5 passengers so passionate that he surprised himself. He reflected later that his enthusiasm was a product of his unconscious knowledge that it would be the last speech like it that he ever gave. Although there were only five hundred people in the room, it ended with a roaring standing ovation. Garrett did not notice Matt Potaglia in the seventh row back, clapping and cheering.

He flew back to D.C. two days later. His apartment was already empty. He closed his bank accounts, packed his belongings into two bags, and went to sleep on the floor. The next day, he dropped one of the two bags at the Salvation Army and took the last one to Mike and Becky's house. He promised them he would watch the Lance de-orbit and depart with them.

The three of them stood in the living room, watching the large television. Garrett warned them there would not be much to see, and there was not. The Lance moved across the screen and then seemed to blink out of existence. Garrett hugged Mike as he said his goodbyes. Becky kissed him on the lips and even cried.

"The bag in the kitchen is yours. I don't need it anymore. I love you both," Garrett said and walked to the car parked in front of their house, waiting to take him to the airport. They waved and shouted their own sentiments. Five minutes later they would open the bag Garrett left for them to find it was full of cash. They did not even bother to count it.

13

Finally.

Finally, in the transport, moving down the track. Finally, watching Earth fall away from him as he pitched up toward the sky over Trinity Bay. Finally, pushed into his seat as the launch rockets fired. Finally, in orbit, fixing the beacon from Orris into the navigation system. Finally, starting the parabolic burn and administering the Sterilex. Finally, preparing for…

He spilled the last of his Sterilex all over his lap. While the parabolic burn allowed for a rough sense of gravity, the craft not only vibrated, but shook. With the dose administered, he replaced the glass rod in its pouch and pulled the Sterilex bottle cap from between his knuckles. While orienting the bottle to receive the cap, the craft shook hard, and he lost it. He could hear Mission Control yelling at him to start the reactors. When he did not comply, they started them remotely, still within the safety window. Garrett stared at his lap. He was not in a vacuum-ready pressure suit; he had opted for the comfort of jeans and a t-shirt. The measured dose of Sterilex was already in his blood and he had saturated his lap with enough of the stuff to put him under for ten billion years. How much would stay in the material? How much would reach his skin? How much would reach his blood?

He moved to secure the bottle and scrape the liquid off his pants but stopped. His hands were bare skin, not gloved. His head dipped, and his field of view went to pink before he snapped his eyes back open. He was losing consciousness. His chest heaved up and down as he descended into a full panic. He smashed the large blue button to engage the flex drive, clenched his fists, and screamed.

Afterward

My apologies for the way this first book ended. I assure you we will discover Garrett's fate in the second book of the series, *Renegades*, which is already written. I expect it to be available by the summer of 2022. The second book is a wildly different story. It is darker, and introduces a whole new cast of characters, some of which will continue to other books in the series.

I started writing this tale as a short story, never dreaming it would become a novel. The more I wrote, the more detailed the world Garrett was living in became, and the more the whole story fleshed out. When I was at about the halfway point writing Origin & Earth, I had concluded that it would have to be a trilogy, three books to tell the whole story. It remained that way until I was finishing the first draft of this book, when so many new elements of the story came to me that I reoutlined the project, and three books became six. Months later when thinking about how to tie the last two books together, I discovered another part of the story that I had previously not planned for, and thus the last book got pushed and I added a seventh. I'm done. It will be seven.

While the series will jump back and forth in time, I'm going to eliminate each chapter doing so. Renegades goes back and forth between character sets, but not timelines. The series will sample other times; the third book, which I have recently started writing, will be the telling of Garrett's third planet, Katya. This is the one he calls the disaster planet, and we will all learn why. At the end of the second book, *Renegades*, I will tease the fourth, *Last Days*.

Dave Salisbury, December 22, 2021